Praise for *The Broken Places*

'Sunlit and dark, painful and joyous . . . Russell Franklin has crafted a myth-busting novel of rare skill and integrity. Its echoes persist and evolve long after the final pages'
David Mitchell, author of *Cloud Atlas*

'A humane and compassionate look at a fascinating life, the complexity of gender, and the destructive legacy of being the child of the world's most famous alpha male'
Patrick Ness, author of *A Monster Calls*

'I was completely caught up by *The Broken Places* and found it intensely moving . . . The central character is imagined so fully that their fractured memories now feel like my own and I left the book sad to be leaving a person I had grown to care about greatly'
Elizabeth Cook, author of *Achilles*

'This is an extraordinary life lived in extraordinary times . . . I inhaled it'
Sam Baker, *The Shift*

'An enrapturing story about family and expectation' *i Paper*

'Beautiful and sorrowful . . . Franklin's prose is contained and concise: no rambling sentences, no streams of consciousness. This was a favourite trick of Ernest Hemingway's, too: deceptively simple writing that turns assumptions on their heads, and provokes questions about the fixity of selfhood'
Telegraph

Russell Franklin was born in Solihull, and now lives and works in London. He was selected for the prestigious London Library Emerging Writers Programme 2020-2021. This is his first novel.

The Broken Places

Russell Franklin

PHOENIX

First published in Great Britain in 2023 by Phoenix Books
This paperback edition published in 2024 by Phoenix Books,
an imprint of The Orion Publishing Group Ltd
Carmelite House, 50 Victoria Embankment
London EC4Y 0DZ

An Hachette UK Company

1 3 5 7 9 10 8 6 4 2

Copyright © Russell Franklin 2023

A CIP catalogue record for this book is
available from the British Library.

ISBN (Mass Market Paperback) 978 1 3996 0231 0
ISBN (eBook) 978 1 3996 0232 7
ISBN (Audio) 978 1 3996 0233 4

Typeset by Input Data Services Ltd, Bridgwater, Somerset

Printed in Great Britain by Clays Ltd, Elcograf S.p.A.

MIX
Paper | Supporting
responsible forestry
FSC® C104740

www.orionbooks.co.uk
www.phoenix-books.co.uk

'The world breaks everyone and afterward many are strong at the broken places.'

Ernest Hemingway

Author's Note

This is unequivocally a work of fiction, but it was inspired by the very real life of Ernest Hemingway's youngest child Gregory, who in later life was often known as Gloria.

Greg's life was complex. As far as I could discover, there was no clear and decisive moment of self-discovery or transition, and Greg continued to move between presenting as a man and a woman until the end. I therefore personally use "they" when referring to their life in general, but in this book the use of "he" or "she" in any given scene will depend on the pronouns they would have used themselves at the time, in order to reflect their lived experience.

I've used the name "Greg" here, as opposed to "Gloria," because Greg continued to use this name throughout their life. Gloria was only one of the female names they used (though, from what I can tell, their favorite), the rest of which I've omitted for clarity. I therefore use "Greg" when discussing their life in general, and "Greg" or "Gloria" in individual scenes in the book, according to the name they would have chosen at the time.

I make no claims that my approach is definitive, but I hope the reader will appreciate that it arises from a place of love and respect.

RF

Observe this boy.

The way he plants his feet in his oversized boots, weight eased onto his front leg. His body tilted just a little, the gun loose in his hands. All as he was taught.

He keeps his eyes on the wicker basket in front of him. He knows the bird inside will be nervous. It will have heard the muttering of the crowd through the day. It will have heard the guns.

The boy breathes. In through the nose. Out through the mouth.

Beyond the chaos of the crowd, the bay sweeps out in a heat-haze shimmer. But for the boy there is no crowd, no bay, no wider world. There is only his body and the gun; the bird and the waiting sky.

The moment stretches. One last heartbeat for both of them.

When the basket opens, the bird does not hesitate. It leaps with a sound like shattering, and in a few staggered beats of snowy wings it is rising, gathering speed, free.

The boy twists, following its arc. His form is perfect, as unconscious as grace. He waits with agonizing patience for the bird to settle its rhythm, then he sweeps the gun onward, leading the way. One more breath out, and he squeezes the trigger.

The gun jumps with a crack, polished wood slamming into the slender harp-curve of his collarbone, and a swarm of lead snarls into the air as the bird surges upwards, its own desire for life throwing it into the path of the death rushing to meet it.

The boy relaxes, and the gun and the bird fall together. For the first time he feels the sweat running down his narrow back, the rough burn of thirst in his throat.

The world breaks in. The roar of voices, the tumble of limbs rip-curling in to surround him, lifting him into the air as fists smash the sky and a thrown bottle of beer arcs a sepia-toned rainbow over the crowd.

The boy twists again, but awkwardly this time, suddenly devoid of all that loose poise, trying to find the one face that matters in this great sea of faces. For a moment he can only make out a human foam, flashing eyes and gaping mouths and hands stretching out as if for some blessing. Then he sees him, bull-shoulders forging through the chaos with ease.

His father reaches out and plucks him from the crowd, eyes shining as he holds him overhead, like a victory made flesh.

PART I

Key West

1939

"Not now, Gregory."

His mother didn't even turn to look at him as Greg came into the room. She just kept staring down into the front yard, a martini in one hand that she hadn't even sipped.

She seemed calm, but he could see a vein pulsing below the dark bob of her hair. The hint of a pounding heart, and that made sense; it was the stillness that didn't. Why wasn't she *doing* anything?

"Mom . . ."

She ignored him until he reached out and tugged on her sleeve. Then she flinched and checked where he'd touched her like she was worried he might have left a mark on the cashmere.

"Mom," he tried again, desperate, but knowing she wouldn't listen to him if he whined. "Can't you talk to him? Make him—"

"—For God's sake, Greg!" she snapped, her voice shrill and sharp. "Enough! Will you please leave me alone?"

He retreated, stung, and she returned to staring stiffly out the window.

Everything was breaking, and he had no idea how to fix it.

He bolted out of the bedroom, taking the stairs two at a time so fast it felt like falling, and rushed into the front yard right as his father was swinging another heavy suitcase into the back of his car.

"Papa . . ." he said, but it was barely a whisper.

His big brother Patrick was already outside, but he wasn't doing anything either, just leaning on the porch railing with a funny look on his face, like he was waiting for someone to jump out and shout *surprise!*

Papa turned and saw the two of them staring back at him. He looked away, cleared his throat, then seemed to rally.

"What's with the sour faces on you two? Come down here where I can see you properly."

They obeyed, Greg still trying to think of what he needed to say. What perfect words would bring his father to his senses to realize that this was all wrong.

"Now, chins up, both of you. You'll come visit me in Cuba next summer. That's not too far away. Martha can't wait to see you—you'll love her. And we're going to put your room up in a high tower like something out of a story book. It'll be like living at the top of the lighthouse. That sound fun?"

Greg and Patrick nodded dutifully. Patrick had grabbed Greg's hand at some point, and now he was squeezing so tight it hurt, but Greg didn't mind.

"You keep up your baseball, Gig. I'll have something special planned when you come over. And, Patrick, you keep an eye on your little brother for me, you understand?"

"Yes, sir."

"Good. All right, well . . ." Papa leaned forward like he was about to hug them, then straightened and tousled their hair. "All right." He glanced up at the house, maybe hoping to see their mother.

Greg had nothing left. He let go of Patrick's hand and ran.

A part of him thought Papa would call after him, ask him what was wrong, but he made it all the way to the end of the street with no sound but the wind in the orange trees. He hadn't realized where he was running to, but now his feet took him over the grass and through the open door of the Key West Lighthouse.

He climbed quickly—it wasn't very tall, as far as lighthouses went—and stepped out onto the familiar viewing balcony. He'd spent a lot of quiet hours up here, watching the boats trace their way over the shimmering sea, or the birds twist and tumble in the thermals, or his mother swimming steady laps in the pool. Now he cared only about the clear view of their front yard, where he could see Papa slamming the car's trunk closed before taking one last look at the house.

If Greg wasn't there he couldn't leave. He couldn't go without saying goodbye.

But he did. He climbed into the driver's seat and the car backed slowly out into the empty road. Papa waved to Patrick sitting on the grass, then leaned out of the window and looked right up at Greg at the top of the lighthouse. Like he'd known exactly where Greg would run to. Like he understood Greg completely.

He lifted one hand, and despite everything Greg waved back as his father drove away.

7

Havana

1940

Greg's shoes bounced on their laces, weighing down on his belt. Each step sent water sluicing from his shins. The little river wound lazily ahead, stretching out like an old cat in the midday sun, both sides lined with thick rushes that blocked out the fields beyond.

Patrick was treading carefully beside him, probing with his toes for anything that might pinch or bite. With his Yankees cap pulled low and his backpack bulging he looked like he was setting out for the Rocky Mountains rather than killing time until dinner. They'd only been in Cuba for a few days, and he was still getting used to the sheer amount of what he called *wilderness*, even though it was mostly farmland.

Greg ignored him, focusing on the water ahead, alert to every shift of light and shade. On the flight over he'd read in *Hero Stories* magazine about a marooned sailor who'd survived by catching fish with his bare hands. He imagined Papa's face if he came home holding a fish for dinner, caught without even needing a rod.

"Keep splashing about like that and you'll scare off every

8

fish for miles," Patrick muttered, shifting his backpack a little higher.

Greg didn't bother to look round. "Well, if I walked as slow as you, we wouldn't have left the house yet."

"I'm two steps behind you! I'm not slower, just quieter. You don't know anything about hunting."

"We'll see . . ." Greg eyed a shadow beside an old half-submerged tree branch up ahead, almost invisible beneath the bright surface.

He did start walking quietly then, hoping Patrick wouldn't notice as he lifted each foot well clear of the water before moving it forward. He could already see Papa's admiring look, already taste the meat fresh from the bones.

He came the long way around the log, slowly, cautiously, knowing that as soon as he could see the fish it would be able to see him. Then in one smooth motion he leaned over and plunged his hands into the water. Out, gleaming and flapping, came a sodden copy of this morning's newspaper, a smeared picture of President Machado glowering from the front page like Greg had woken him up from a nap.

Greg stared at it a moment, then furiously screwed it up into a ball. Patrick was already laughing behind him.

"Great work. Now we'll have something to wrap your fish in."

Greg hurled the sodden lump in his direction. His throwing arm was legendary among the boys in his little league back in Key West, and sure enough he got Patrick in the face with a satisfying slap.

His brother staggered a little, wiped a weak smear of ink from his cheek, and shrugged. "All right, I guess I kinda deserved that."

As they made their way around the bend, a tall bandy-legged bird cocked an eye toward them and leaped into the air, rising in a few powerful beats and soaring off in jerks. Greg shaded his eyes and watched it go.

"Wow." Patrick clambered onto the bank to get a few more seconds before it slipped from view. "Good thing Papa's not here." He cocked an imaginary gun in his arms and mimed firing.

Greg wasn't sure that was fair. He didn't like to think of Papa shooting something as strange and silly as that vanished bird. But he supposed he had seen Papa shoot an awful lot of different things.

He clambered up onto the bank beside his brother, pulling his shoes from his belt and stretching his legs out in the sun. "Feels like I'm being spit-roasted."

"You look like it too." Patrick started rummaging through his backpack.

"Do you have to bring that *everywhere*?"

"It's called being prepared, dummy." And to prove his point he pulled two bottles of Coke and a Swiss army knife from the bag's depths. "But if you don't want one . . ."

"Okay, I take it back."

Patrick sniggered and flicked off both caps.

It was only when Greg held the still slightly cool bottle in his hand that he realized how thirsty he was. He drank half of it in one go, then burped up the fizz.

"Gross," muttered Patrick, taking a sip.

Greg burped again, then reached into his shorts pocket and pulled out a crumpled pack of cigarettes. "I came prepared too."

"You steal those from Martha?"

"Nope. Papa left them by the pool. You want one or not?"

"Yeah. Did you bring matches?"

"Knew you'd have some."

Patrick sighed, his small victory stolen, and dutifully pulled out a box of matches. He lit them both up. "Choke on it, smart aleck."

"I thought I was a dummy."

"You're both. And a thief."

"A master thief." Greg took a long pull, letting the warmth fill his lungs. His head spun a little. He supposed it had been a while since he'd last smoked. Since Papa left to come and live with Martha at the finca, there had been no half packs of unfiltered cigarettes left about the house in Key West begging to be pilfered, and stealing one of his mother's slender Silk Cuts from her purse would have been a capital offense.

Everything felt good. The cool clear water running over his toes. The perfect blue sky overhead like a fresh coat of paint. The taste of sugar and smoke on his tongue.

"Here." Patrick took off his baseball cap and offered it out. "Put this on."

"I'm okay."

Patrick jammed it backward onto Greg's head. "Your neck's burning, Gig. You look like a lobster."

"I'm fine!" said Greg indignantly, pulling it off and shoving it back.

Patrick only leaned away, open palms refusing. "I know you are. Humor me."

Greg flattened his hair and grudgingly put the cap back on, pulling the bridge so low it almost touched the collar of his shirt. He hated to admit it, but the shadow did feel cool against his skin.

He took another sip of Coke. "Thanks, Pat."

His brother said nothing, just kicked his feet in the water, humming happily.

Greg rested back on his elbows, looking at Patrick out of the corner of his eye and trying not to make it obvious. He was pretty sure his shoulders were as broad as his brother's now. He was two years younger, and a lot shorter, but where Patrick looked like he was built out of coat hangers and old bicycle parts, Greg had what his father called *a boxer's build*. Even so, everyone who saw them could tell they were brothers. They had the same shock of dark hair and eyes to match, the same strong jaw, though Patrick took more after their mother, and Greg their father.

Overhead, a flock of birds swept past, black as coal against the bright sky. A moment later, a cloud of minnows darted by in the martini-clear water at their feet.

"This place is crazy," Greg said.

"Yeah," said Patrick, watching the fish lose themselves in the shining rush of the river's surface. "I guess it's okay. Mom would hate it though."

"Because of the bugs? Or because Martha's—"

"—DON'T ruin this, Gig."

There was a long pause, and Patrick sighed. "Sorry."

"It's okay. She's okay, Pat. Kinda."

"I know . . . but I don't want to think about it right now . . . Can I have another smoke?"

"Sure."

Patrick lit up and was taking a slow pull when there was a rustle behind them, the crack of a thick stem breaking.

12

They both froze, Greg splashing soda down his chin. A few seconds passed before he dared whisper, "What was that?"

"I don't know," Patrick whispered back. "Some animal."

"Duh. What sort of animal?"

"I don't know. What lives in Cuba?"

"A lion?"

"There's no lions in Cuba, dummy."

"A cheetah then."

Patrick just snorted and, as if in response, another heavy rustle came from the undergrowth.

"You sure there's no lions?"

"Yes . . ." said Patrick, sounding a little uncertain this time. "It's probably a monkey or something."

"Want to try and sneak up on it?"

"What?"

"Let's see what it is. Come on."

"Gig, wait!"

But Greg was already pulling on his shoes and scrambling into the undergrowth. He crawled forward on his belly—he'd seen soldiers doing it in the movies when they were sneaking up on some enemy camp—forcing aside grass and plants he had no name for with his bare arms.

He paused, listening for more rustles to guide him.

"What's the hold-up?" Patrick whispered from behind, almost comically loud.

"Just listening for snakes."

A moment's heavy silence. "You don't actually think there's snakes, do you?"

"Probably. That's why Papa told us to stay out of the fields: full of snakes and spiders."

13

Patrick wriggled forward, looking like a giant snail with his backpack on. He paused only to whisper in Greg's ear as he passed. "You're full of shit, Gig."

Greg smiled to himself as he followed his brother. After a few body lengths he found a suitably long stem of grass, yanked it free of the soft earth, and leaned forward to slide it along the back of Patrick's neck as he gave a soft but clear *hiss*.

Patrick yelped, twisted, and grabbed the stem with both hands, as though to strangle his fanged attacker. It took him a few seconds to realize what he was holding, and to spot his little brother rolling on the crumpled grass behind him, helpless with laughter.

"Greg." He spat, pushing himself up. "You're dead."

Still laughing, Greg set off running, crashing through the undergrowth, hearing his brother charging after a few steps behind. A monster of an iguana burst from the grass in front of them, its legs pumping akimbo like train pistons as it hurried off for safer cover.

Greg ran like his life depended on it. His brother was older, taller with longer legs, but Greg was lighter on his feet and wasn't carrying a big stupid backpack, so every time he heard Patrick gaining on him or felt his fingertips brushing the back of his T-shirt he changed direction sharply, turning on a dime and leaving his brother scrabbling in his dust.

He made for the barrio—the little town of San Francisco de Paula that clustered around their father's house—hoping to lose Patrick in the narrow streets and alleys. Within minutes he was pushing through some trees and jumping down into a dusty road on the outskirts, his brother still right behind him. He darted around a car and almost made it to the mouth of a nearby alley when his foot slipped on some loose stones. It was only a slip—he was too sure-footed to fall—but it gave Patrick enough time to catch his hand as he raised it for balance and pull him into a headlock.

"Looks like a snake's got you, Gigi," Patrick crowed, spinning round and round so Greg couldn't find his feet, "watch out, I think it bites." He rubbed his knuckles into Greg's scalp.

It would have been the easiest thing in the world to reach around and punch Patrick in the liver—his father had shown him how—but Greg only pulled at the arm squeezing his throat. He was shorter, but stronger, and he could feel his brother's grip slowly begin to weaken even as he continued knuckling Greg's skull.

Too slowly. His head was starting to feel like a punctured football. "All right. I give, I give."

Patrick finally let him go and leaned against a wall to catch his breath. Greg sat in the dust and rubbed his throat. "Jeez, Patrick, are you trying to kill me?"

"You started it!"

"Why would you beat up your poor little brother?"

Patrick blew a raspberry and scooped the fallen hat from the ground. "Here, wouldn't want your *poor little neck* taking any more damage."

Greg jammed the hat back on and let his brother pull him up, and it was only then that he noticed the group of boys sitting in the shade of a gnarled tree on the other side of the street. He must have nearly jumped over them when he came leaping through the bushes.

There were six of them, watching still as cats, faces unreadable in their private patch of gloom. Greg could feel his sunburn spreading up onto his cheeks and knew he must be blushing. *Why would you beat up your poor little brother?* He hoped they didn't speak English.

Patrick seemed embarrassed too. He coughed into his hand, glanced at Greg, and kicked a nearby pebble aimlessly.

The silence seemed set to last forever, but then one of the boys pushed himself to his feet like a weary old man.

"Eres de la casa grande?" he asked. *Are you from the big house?*

He clearly meant the Finca La Vigía, the farmhouse Papa lived in with Martha. It wasn't huge by Key West standards but compared to the higgledy-piggledy houses of the barrio it was a mansion.

Greg nodded. "Si. Acabamos de llegar." *We just got here.*

The boy nodded. Then, "English?"

"American."

"But speak Ingles?"

"Si. Yeah."

"You are Papa's sons?"

"You know our father?" Patrick asked.

"Si. He plays . . . ah, the baseball with us. He buys us balls." He turned and muttered to the other boys. They murmured back, all nodding except for one boy who spoke sharply, too fast for Greg to follow with his clumsy Spanish.

The standing boy looked at him a moment, then shook his head before turning back and stepping out into the sun. He sauntered over and offered Patrick his hand.

"I am Finco Ramos. Ramos."

"Patrick." The two shook like diplomats. "And this is Gigi. Greg."

Ramos looked Greg over approvingly. "You are look-ing like him . . . Giggly?"

"Greg." Gigi was a family name, the hard double g a childish slurring of Greggy. Hearing a stranger say it made him feel embarrassed.

By then the other boys had ambled over with careful indifference, introducing themselves with shrugs or half-hearted handshakes. Only one boy held back, the one who had spoken to Ramos before.

Greg ignored him, focusing instead on trying to read the mood of the group. Most looked his age, and a few looked as old as twelve or thirteen, the same as Patrick, but they all acted like they were much older and found speaking to American children faintly boring.

All except Ramos. He stood nodding as the introduc-tions were made, then stepped forward and clapped both boys on the back. "You come with us. We show you de Paula."

Patrick and Greg glanced at each other. Maybe they couldn't trust these boys, but on the other hand it would be a bad idea to offend them. And Papa *had* mentioned that he had a group of local boys lined up ready for them to play a proper game of ball with. It would be awkward to skirt out of their company now only to meet them outside the house this evening.

Patrick nodded, and the group moved as one down the twisting lane. The Cuban boys took them to the town square, a small space overflowing with men jostling and shoving, gathered around what sounded like a cockfight. They led them through the market where old men with dusty skin sat dozing beside stalls overflowing with bright fruit. They showed them the church at the heart of the town, a magnificent living ruin that towered over the nearby houses, throwing its shadow over the righteous old ladies who passed back and forth through its doors.

Greg's misgivings soon faded. Once their natural reserve began to fade, the boys seemed enthusiastic guides. San Francisco de Paula was a small town, with little to its name besides its closeness to Havana, and they all seemed to take it as a point of personal pride that a famous man had decided to settle among them.

The reluctant boy still hung back, refusing to speak to them or even catch their eyes. His name was Cordaro, and he took no pains to hide that he resented these pale, half-mute interlopers with their fine-cut clothes and their rich father.

A fight was brewing up. Greg could feel it, and knew it was inevitable, but still he tried to keep his distance. There was enough Key West lingering in his blood to hold him back, enough of his mother's starched shirts and elegant furniture. That would change in the months and years to come, as his father took him to the Cuban boxing rings and taught him that what mattered was punching first and punching hardest and that a man should do both.

When the fight came they were playing at matadors on the dirt road where the fine houses of the town's center gave way to shacks clustering its western flank. They had no capes, so were using their shirts, kicking up the soft dust as they charged and leaped.

It was a game without rules, or without rules that any of them could have put into words. They only knew that one of them was the bull, one the matador, and the rest picadors helping the matador get away or the bull corner the matador on their whim, and watching out for the infrequent cars.

Greg was the bull, Cordaro the matador, and as the rest of the boys danced around them, their imaginary steeds fierce and their stick-lances sharp, the two had eyes only for each other. Cordaro was taller than Greg, longer-limbed and hard to catch, always letting Greg's finger-horns snag the fabric of his shirt as he slipped aside at the last moment. But Greg was tireless, and soon he could hear Cordaro's panting as he passed by, feel his shoulder grazing the other boy's belly. As they wheeled to face each other again in a whirl of dust, Greg knew that this time he would have him.

He could see Cordaro knew it too. So perhaps it was fear as much as spite that made him kick out as Greg came at him again, catching his leading foot and sending him sprawling into the rocky ground. The shouts and laughter died as Greg pushed himself up, spitting dust and inspecting a thin gash along his forearm that was already dripping blood.

The play fight was over; there could be no more delaying. His father's stories swirled in the back of his head, tales of whiskey and insults righted by a swift and final punch. Lesser men crumpling like sheets unpegged from the line and true great men standing undefeatable. Yet still, something held him back.

One of the boys, Rodolfo, came round to hand him his shirt. He had told Greg that he worked in the house sometimes, making good money by opening doors and serving drinks when guests were expected, and perhaps it was some sort of loyalty to his employer that made him gaze at Cordaro with such thick contempt. Either way, Greg was grateful.

Cordaro smiled. "Un accidente. Giggly."

The group of boys gathered round, expectant like sailors waiting for thunderclouds to split open.

Greg could feel them watching him, but still he hesitated. He could almost feel his father's gaze. He didn't feel afraid, but he didn't want to fight. Was that cowardice?

He knew Papa would say yes.

As the pause stretched to an unbearable length, Patrick finally stepped forward and put himself between them. He said something to the older boy, his Spanish too quick for Greg to follow. Cordaro shook his head dismissively, and when Patrick spat on the ground and turned away, Cordaro gave him a parting shove. It wasn't too hard, barely enough to stagger him, but for Greg it was like a key in a lock. He leaped forward.

The fight was brief but vicious, a flurry of punches, knees, and elbows before a grapple where Greg's brute strength won out. He managed to twist Cordaro off balance and work a fist free to strike him hard in the gut, then the middle of his face. He felt the taller boy's nose burst like a ripe plum.

Cordaro's legs went from under him, and Greg let him fall awkwardly into the dust. The older boy lay still a moment, stunned, then pushed himself up to sit swaying like a drunk, his nose bleeding heavily, the left side of his face already starting to swell. For a second, even through the adrenaline and the sweet ache in his knuckles, Greg was worried he'd really hurt him.

Then Cordaro shook his head in a spray of crimson, and when his eyes met Greg's they were clear. It was a relief, though Greg was careful not to let it show on his face.

Cordaro wiped the blood from his lips, pinched the

bridge of his nose almost daintily, and tilted back his head. "You fight like a brute," he muttered in English, his voice a nasal whine.

"You fight like a girl," Greg sniffed back, adrenaline still pulsing through his veins, fists clenched and ready at his side. "Peleas como una niña."

"All strength, no style."

"You've got neither. I'll beat you again if you want me to prove it."

Cordaro loosened his fingers experimentally from his nose and, when a fresh spurt of blood did not emerge, shrugged.

Ramos laughed. "Cobarde. He fears you, Gigi."

Cordaro snarled. "I fear no one. I fight you here. Same tomorrow."

"We can fight now," said Greg, stepping forward, "Lucke . . . luchemos ahora. Ahora!" In that moment he would have fought anyone and anything. He could almost see himself, strong and fearless in the midday sun like a hero from his father's stories. Even the caution in Patrick's eyes couldn't dampen his spirits. He forgot that the fight had been for his brother in the first place. He'd fought because he wasn't a coward, and he'd won.

Cordaro only muttered, not meeting his eyes.

Satisfied, Greg and the rest of the barrio boys left him to gather himself in the dust. There would be no fight tomorrow.

All drunk on his victory, they ran breakneck for no reason at all, swarming through the narrow alleys and out along the boulevards, past the cockfighting ring stained black with the blood of tiny martyrs, around cars and horses, old men made of leather and young ladies cut from

21

silk, fruit sellers in aprons and police officers in full uniform with crisp white gloves despite the suffocating heat. Even Patrick got caught up in it, laughing and whooping with the rest.

They moved like a shoal, thinning to a line as the suburbs contracted and they flowed through the heart of the town. Brightly painted doors flashed past, small tumbledown porches scrubbed raw, houses crushed tight together, the world cut from deep shadow and burning light. Then the town breathed out and they drew themselves together once more, pouring over walls and into yards where bleached washing wilted over lines, dodging half-asleep guard dogs and sharp-eyed housewives alike.

Finally, even the barrio stuttered and gave way to fields. They ceased being bodies and became only ripples in a sea of green, heedless for a few minutes of the snakes and the spiders and the angry harvesters, just running.

They found themselves breathless and sweating at the edge of the field. Ramos came over to Greg, pushing thick black hair from his brow. "It is past the time. Papa will be waiting for the game."

Greg hid a frown at how easily that name fell from their lips. *Papa.* Like they had some claim on him.

The group drifted out of the fields toward the finca, thirsty and tired. Up the curving street to the house, passing a dog pooled beneath a wall like something tipped from a ladle, a black cat promenading on bone china feet along the bricks above, an old man in a broad hat trimming the bushes with precise, regular clips of his secateurs.

They trooped through the wide iron gates to where the house sat low and long among the trees. The only thing that broke its squat profile was the square tower where

22

Greg and Patrick slept, the lookout that gave the house its name, Finca La Vigía.

The barrio boys didn't bother knocking at the door. They headed straight down the path between the side of the house and the tower. Lush plants overflowed their borders on both sides, pulling at their legs, and cicadas screamed from the undergrowth and from high up on the walls.

They stepped into the yard to find Papa already waiting, sprawled out on the steps of the back porch, one hand swirling a heavy glass to the faint clink of ice, the other loose about a baseball.

He stood as he saw them, leaving the drink behind but flipping the ball into the air with a flick of his wrist. He caught it deftly, then without warning sent it spinning into the midst of them. They all reacted too late, and it caught Rodolfo on the shoulder and skittered out of Ramos's grasping hands.

Greg saw Rodolfo flinch and take a half step back, but the boy resisted rubbing at his shoulder. He'd learned that much already. Weakness was not acceptable, not in the barrio and certainly not in the finca.

Papa laughed, his voice deep and booming, his cheerful mood evident. That was a good sign, a sign that his writing was going well, and that no jealous journalists had said anything bad about him in the papers that morning.

"You boys need to work on your fielding. You don't always get a warning. Baseball's not all about the bat, you know."

"Yes, Caballero." Rodolfo scrabbled in the scraggy grass, gathered up the ball and threw it back underhand.

Papa grinned at them all, and his eyes met Greg's. The

next second the ball came whip-cracking toward him, faster than before, and at an angle, so Greg had to throw himself sideways just to brush the leather with his finger-tips. His body moved before his mind knew what was going on and it was almost a surprise to find himself lying with a mouthful of dry grass and the grubby ball clutched in his stinging hand.

His father watched him push himself up, his face un-readable, then without changing expression bawled out "PATRICK!" in a voice that could have killed a cat at ten paces.

Patrick forced his way to the front of the group. "What?"

Papa blinked in surprise. "I thought you were still inside."

"I've been out all day."

"I see that. Well, too bad. Go grab the bats and gloves for me, son. I'll be at the plate."

Patrick sighed and trudged inside as the rest of the boys followed Papa. Greg hesitated a moment, watching his brother's receding back, then hurried after the group.

Papa had laid out countless small bribes to try to make the finca—this house where he lived with a woman who was not their mother—feel like home to his two visiting sons. Their room at the top of the tower with its view over the whole town. The absence of a curfew or a time to get up. Letting them drink whatever booze took their fancy. And now, apparently, a baseball field.

It was really no more than a few old cushions laid out in a diamond, lines wilted into the grass with salt, but crowded with bodies as it was now, Greg felt almost like he was back at little league in Key West, which he sup-posed was Papa's plan.

24

After the boys had slaked their thirst from a garden hose and Patrick had joined them with a bat and a few gloves, Papa warmed each of them up in turn with some gentle underarm throws, only turning overarm once they were reliably cracking the ball the length of the field.

Then they began in earnest. Like the matador game, they didn't keep score, but relied on a general sense of who had hit the furthest, who had made the most spectacular catches.

Papa pitched throughout, occasionally advising them on their form, what they were doing wrong or right. The rest of the boys laughed and chattered, but Greg kept mostly silent, focused on where the ball would go and where he would need to put himself to catch it, or—if he was batting—on his father's pitching hand, trying to keep his whole body tensed and ready.

The game simmered along nicely for an hour or so before Greg hit a real cracker. His father had to duck to avoid having his eyes knocked out and the ball sailed like a dream over the pool and into the bushes at the far corner of the garden. There was an appreciative murmur from the boys, but Greg looked only to Papa.

His father met his gaze and nodded with a smile, and Greg felt a rush of pleasure, of relief.

From the porch came applause, and they all turned to see Martha leaning in the doorway, a newspaper rolled under one arm to free her hands. When she saw them looking at her, she gave a wink. "Gigi, sweetheart, you're a natural."

Despite himself, Greg felt a blush creeping up his neck, then a sudden flare of breeze as a new baseball ripped past his cheek like a miniature cannonball.

"Eyes on the game, Gig," his father said, rolling shoulders thick as market hams. "We're not done yet."

It should have been Rodolfo's turn to bat next, but neither he nor any of the other boys moved to take Greg's place. There was silence as Gigi readied the bat for a second time.

His father's next pitch was the fastest so far, and Gigi couldn't get his bat around fast enough even to clip it. The next was barely a second later, a vicious foul ball he had to lurch backward to avoid, leaving him on his ass in the dust.

"Come on, Gigi," said his father mildly, as Finco threw the balls back into his waiting hands, "I thought you were a natural."

Greg, his breathing ragged, forced himself back up and into position. He didn't complain. He knew better than that. He only tightened his grip, hardened his jaw, and watched as his father wound up for another huge—

"—Ernest."

Again they all looked to the porch, but Martha had moved to the bench beneath the trees, a fresh tumbler of whiskey balanced on one knee.

Though two people had never looked less alike, in that moment she reminded Greg powerfully of his father. Something in the way she held herself: the teetering poise of a high-wire artist with no safety net.

"If you're done impressing children, I'd like to see you sometime today."

His father lowered the ball and stared at her over the heads of the boys who, unaware of the difference an absent *the* could convey, were waiting expectantly.

Greg kept his hand tight around the bat at his side, feeling the sweat grow cold over his back. He had to be ready. He would get it this time.

As the sun settled weightless onto the distant rooftops of the barrio, Papa dropped the balls into the dust with a shrug. "Well, you heard the lady, boys, no more fun. Get home before your mothers start to worry." He walked into the shade of the trees and pulled the smiling Martha to her feet, letting her place her hand on the small of his back as they went inside together. She glanced back at Greg as they climbed the steps, expressionless.

Like filings freed from the grip of a magnet, the group found itself suddenly disbanded. The barrio boys flowed out into the jaws of the evening on fleet yet silent feet. Greg and Patrick watched them go, feeling the ache of their quieting bodies in the evening light. A gunshot cracked somewhere out in the twilight, not close enough for anyone to react.

Only when the last of the boys was gone and the groundsman had locked the tall gates behind them did Patrick say, "For a second I thought she'd messed up."

Greg just shook his head, remembering all the hours back in Key West when he and Patrick had hunkered down in their rooms like soldiers in foxholes, listening to the screams and shouts and smashing of china below. "They don't fight."

"Yet," said Patrick heavily. "Are you okay?"

Greg felt his shoulder throb dully. He felt his hands tremble, though he kept them squeezed at his sides. "Yes."

Havana

1942

"He's not growing out of it. I thought he was, but he's only gotten better at hiding it."

Greg paused on the stairs, the condensation from his glass of water cold on his fingers. His father's voice was loud with drink, but not slurred.

"Are you sure?" Martha's voice this time.

Greg knew he shouldn't be hearing this. Eavesdropping was for sneaks. But he couldn't make himself move.

"Yes, I'm damn sure. All scrunched up and secreted away in an old pencil case. If I hadn't run out myself I'd never have found it. Wanted to throw up. That childish cheerful little pencil case, with *that* inside it. Like a metaphor for the whole thing . . ."

The underwear he'd hidden in his pencil case. They'd found it. The hair on the back of his neck prickled with guilt and dread.

"Maybe it's time to get him some help."

"Absolutely not."

"But if he—"

"—You have a rotten apple on the branch, and you look at the tree. No."

"It doesn't have to be public, we can find someone discreet, but this thing is clearly festering in the dark. Greg is a great kid, but there's something very wrong with him and it isn't getting better."

"You know what they'll say, Martha."

"About you?"

"Of course! Are you listening to me? It's Pauline he gets it from—her family's full of sickness—but no one will care about that."

"Are you sure you should have another?"

"You're really asking that now? I don't deserve a little comfort? She's polluted my son!"

"All right. Well, if he's not going to see someone about it, maybe you should talk to him. Get it out—"

"—Fuck you, Martha. What the hell do you know about what it's like to have children? To watch it all come to nothing . . ."

"Well, fuck you too, dear heart."

Greg felt cold water pattering on his toes, soaking into the runner on the stairs. He steadied his grip on his glass of water and made himself take one step up, then another, and then somehow he was back in the room he shared with Patrick, leaning against the door.

Havana

1940

Life at the finca soon settled into a routine.

Most mornings, Greg ran wild with the local boys over the island. Sometimes Patrick joined him, sometimes all his brother wanted to do was sulk in his room for no reason.

He fell in love with Cuba quickly. With the dry fields coated with crops mineral-bright in the sun, and the deep woods where animals could be heard but never seen. And with the people, who were proud and fierce and generous.

Sometimes he would go out alone at night, climbing over the finca's walls and out into the sleeping island blanketed with stars and murmuring through its dreams with the lazy putter of generators and the distant crooning of gramophones.

He felt that Cuba would never change, and that nor would he so long as he stayed. The same day would pass by again and again, sometimes hot, sometimes bustling with storms, but always the same friend in different clothes.

Two weeks into their stay, Greg and Patrick were spending the morning lounging by the pool, both drinking their father's rum crudely cut with limes they squeezed in their hands.

Greg swam and splashed in the sunlight while Patrick sat in cross-legged silence beneath a parasol, lost in the gloomy mood that had gripped him since Papa's roaring phone call with their mother before breakfast.

Greg didn't mind. Sometimes you didn't have to talk to be better off together, and the rum would work its magic in time. They were both experienced drinkers already. Back in Key West, Papa had let them sneak drinks whenever their mother was out for the evening, claiming they were better off getting used to it in moderation now than passing out in a gutter somewhere when they turned twenty-one. And here in Cuba, with their mother an ocean away, he'd thrown his drinks cabinet open and said he knew they wouldn't embarrass themselves. So far they'd never drunk more than they could handle, terrified of breaking that sacred trust.

Sure enough, after an hour or so Patrick did emerge, though not to come cannonballing into the pool as Greg had hoped. He sat at the edge, dipping his feet in the cool water.

"Papa really seems to like Martha," he said, as Greg paddled over.

"I guess so."

"Don't you think she's kind of young for him?"

"Um, maybe?"

"She'll probably get bored eventually."

"How much rum have you had, Patrick?"

"Not a lot. I won't be drunk for the game."

"You sure?"

"Are you listening?"

31

"I'm listening. I just don't know why you're talking about this."

"All I'm saying is, she seems all pretty and young and smart, but she won't stick around."

"Why not? Papa's not *old*, and he's fun . . ."

"Papa could take a shit in a bun and you'd call it a hotdog."

Greg leaned back, stung. "That's not true."

It was a lame comeback, but Patrick nodded. "Sorry, Gig, I don't know what's wrong with me today."

Greg, still surly, sank into the water up to his eyes until he was peering at his brother like a crocodile.

"I said I was sorry. Maybe I HAVE had too much to drink . . ."

Greg stood. "I'll sober you up then."

"What—"

——Greg's splash caught Patrick full in his open mouth and filled his half-finished glass.

Calmly, like a bank manager setting his desk in order, Patrick placed down his glass, wiped his sopping hair from his eyes, and stood up. "You know, Gig, you look a little drunk yourself."

By the time it was over, they'd both burned most of the booze from their blood, and Greg was pretty sure he'd swallowed half the pool in the process.

They dried out and passed the midday heat hiding beneath parasols reading books borrowed from Papa's library. Most were as perfect as if they'd just arrived from the bookshop, so they had to be careful not to let so much as a single drop of sweat or water stain their pages.

They were restless by the time they heard the gates open

32

and the chatter of the barrio boys crowding up the drive, both scrabbling to pull on their clothes and go meet them.

Gigi could already feel the easy relaxation of the day fall away from him. He had come to dread and anticipate the daily games in equal measure, and that didn't feel strange to him.

The boys were clustered at the front door, unsure if they were early and fearful of disturbing the great man in his work. Ramos saw them coming and raised a hand in greeting. "Is he ready?"

"He will be now," said Patrick. "We heard you coming from the back of the house."

Ramos winced. "And . . . feliz?"

Greg nodded. There had been music spilling from Papa's office window since lunch, and that was always a good sign that the morning had gone well.

Ramos grinned, and Greg smiled back, but it was forced. He was already thinking of the game to come.

"Boys!" Papa's voice boomed from the open door, and a moment later he came striding down the steps. "Good to see you're all on time for once. Cordaro, the Sourpuss, your black eye's finally clearing up. Must have been a nasty tumble you took . . ."

Cordaro, who had eventually given in and joined the rest each evening, mumbled something in Spanish, scuffing the grass with his bare foot.

"Yes," Papa glanced at Rodolfo, "I've heard all about it." And then at Greg, giving him a secret, just-between-us smile that almost made him forget about the coming game.

"Anyway, I've got a treat for you all. This is a proper team we have here. And a proper team should be kitted out appropriately." He paused, as though one of the boys

33

might raise some argument, then plunged on. "So. You boys head inside. Martha has your uniforms ready. You can store them here when you're not wearing them, easier to keep them in good condition that way."

There was a moment of continued staring.

"Well? Get in there!"

And they went, leaping up the steps and into the wide dark hall like sparks up a chimney. Sure enough, the double doors at the end stood open into the sunny dining room where Martha was waiting in a long cream dress, the uniforms laid out carefully beside her on the glossy table, so white they had to spit into their hands and wipe them on their shirts before daring to touch them.

"There's a name on each of them," Martha said with her velvety chuckle, as if she and these boys from the township had been friends for years. "If any of you can't read you can tell me your name and I'll show you which one is yours. We had to guess the sizes of course . . ."

All the boys shouted out at once, each desperate to be first. Only Greg and Patrick lingered at the back, strangers neither to bright new clothes, nor Martha's charms. They watched the others change into their spotless new uniforms, watched Martha smile and laugh even as her eyes never lost the sharp and shifting gaze that always reminded Greg of the lens of a camera. And so it was Ramos, strutting and posing like a young rooster, who came over to point out the logo over his own heart.

"Look, Gigi. Look."

Picked out in gold stitching was a shooting star and the words: *Estrella De Gigi*—The Gigi Stars.

The brothers read together for a moment, then Patrick walked forward without a word. He stripped down and

34

pulled on his own uniform, crisp lettering shouting from his chest, and walked outside.

Greg watched him go. He wanted to call him back, but didn't know what to say, so moved to the table as the other boys crowded around. He reached out and touched the shirt, the golden lettering.

"Your father was insistent," said Martha.

"Estrella De Gigi!" one boy shouted, and all the rest took up the cry, howling and jumping.

Greg took his hand away and saw that his fingers had left a long smear of dirt upon the white.

When they all flooded out into the yard, he found his father and brother sitting on the steps waiting, their heads crooked together like conspirators. His brother said something and his father laughed. Even with his own name blazing over the chest of every boy there, the sight made Greg's stomach twist.

Patrick was playing well, cracking ball after ball to the very edge of the finca's grounds, battering the succulents and laying waste to the planted borders. A few of the boys had already murmured that today might be the day he finally beat Gigi.

Greg pretended he didn't hear them, pretended not to notice his father whooping every time Patrick sent another slugger soaring.

The game ran into the evening, no one wanting to be the boy who mentioned that his mother would be expecting him, especially not when Greg was still losing. The laughs and jokes began to fade as the day died and the sky turned to glowing amber above them, humming with light. Greg could feel them casting glances at him. He didn't glance back, didn't do anything but stare at whoever was standing at the plate.

It was Patrick—it felt like it was always Patrick—one eye half closed as he tried to guide the sweat away from his eyes. Their father pitched a ball fast and low, and Greg watched his brother's body tilt perfectly as he cracked the ball with the very tip of his bat, the sound as sweet as the stroke. The ball flew into the gathering gloom and struck the far wall at the edge of the yard.

It was easily the furthest a ball had gone that day, maybe the furthest one had gone in all their games so far. Papa lifted a hand against the setting sun as Patrick took a slow victory lap around the crudely drawn diamond. "Pretty damn good, Patrick, that's about as far as I used to hit a ball at your age."

Patrick shrugged as he came back to hand over the bat, but couldn't stop the corners of his mouth creeping up.

"I guess I'll have to get the uniforms changed already. How does Estrella de Patrick sound, boys?"

Greg felt like he'd been slapped.

"Now, it's getting a little late, and much as I dread the thought of angering your mothers, what do you say we let Gig have one last shot at getting his title back?"

The boys might not have understood every word of English, but they got the gist. They looked to each other, torn, not wanting to stop playing but wanting to anger their mothers even less.

It was Greg who stepped forward. "Let's keep playing. It's not that long till my turn."

His father only smiled, looking around for protest from the other boys. They all remained silent.

"I thought you might say that, Greg."

The night had almost entirely swallowed the town by the time Greg picked up the bat, the wood dark with sweat and burst blisters. His own hands were already rubbed raw, but he ignored the pain, twisting his fingers against the grain and feeling every dimple and divot through his tissue paper skin.

Papa was watching him. One of the boys threw him a fetched ball, and he caught it without taking his eyes off his son.

"You ready, Gig-man?"

Greg said nothing, only brought the bat up above his shoulder, widened his stance, breathed and—

—a flash of grubby white skimmed the corner of his vision. Now his father was standing one arm outstretched, and Greg didn't need the sun to see the little smile on his face.

"I thought you were ready. That's strike one."

Greg still said nothing. He thought he would be sick if he opened his mouth. He squeezed the bat tighter, until he felt his skin begin to tear.

The ball was returned, and this time, when his father went from casual stance to a whip-slash throw, Greg was ready. Or, if Greg wasn't—if Greg didn't even see the ball come at him—his body was, and the next thing he knew he had already swung, already felt the kiss of contact fuzz up through his arms.

In the last dregs of the evening the ball arced skywards. Over the grass and the low bushes and the far wall into the streets of San Francisco de Paula, into the night.

Some of the boys cheered. Papa put his hands on his knees and laughed. "Damn, this boy! I'll call the Red Sox first thing in the morning."

37

The relief that ran through him was so strong Greg felt sick all over again. He took one deep steadying breath, and looked for his brother, half proud, half ashamed, not sure what he wanted to see. For a moment Patrick's face was knotted like he was trying to swallow something too large for his throat. And then—just like that—he stopped trying, shrugged his shoulders, and started cheering with the rest. His body was loose with the ease of it, his smile genuine as he gave a thumbs up.

Greg could never have explained the envy that ached in his chest.

No one needed to say the game was finally over. The boys all ran into the house and changed in a hurry. Greg sat on the steps and watched them rush out in ones and twos, their bare feet flashing as they jogged home, their minds no doubt already turning to the beatings they might receive for their lateness. He felt guilt, but no regret.

Overhead, the giant ceiba tree that shaded the front of the house swayed softly to a breeze too high for him to feel. Patrick was a ghost out on the lawn, gathering up the balls and abandoned gloves.

Their father passed up into the house, humming to himself, then stopped at the door. "We're going to have to find something you're no good at, Gig-man. Builds character."

Greg looked up, trying to guess what would please him. "Maybe. But who wants a loser's character?"

His father laughed. Not at him, but with him.

A few more boys slipped past, shouting goodbyes, but Papa ignored them. He bent down and ruffled his son's hair. "True. Know what makes a good loser, Gig? Practice. Don't you change." He grinned and rested his hand on the back of Greg's head. That was all, but it was enough.

He went into the house, and Greg turned back to the yard to see Patrick coming toward him. He didn't need to ask to know his brother had heard Papa's words. Maybe he'd been meant to.

Patrick sat beside him, the bat clasped between his knees. "Good hit."

"You too."

"Thanks. I doubt I'll match that any time soon. I've never played so well in my life. You think you could hit one over the wall again?"

A shrug. "Maybe. I want to try."

"I guess the key's to drink the morning before a game. We should make that a habit."

Greg grinned. "Deal."

He hesitated a moment, then leaned against his older brother.

"You okay?" Patrick shifted, put an arm around his shoulders.

"Yeah."

"You always say that."

"I'm always okay."

Inside, the telephone rang. Martha's voice murmured, then she was at the door.

"Patrick, are you out here? Oh, there you boys are. How sweet . . . Patrick, your mother wants to speak to you."

He stood up. "Coming."

When he was at the door, Greg said, "Patrick?"

He stopped, half in the light and half in the dark. "Hm?"

"Why don't you care?"

His brother tipped his head to one side, then grinned.

"Because baseball's dumb. I know that because I'm no good at it."

"No. Really."

"Really? Because it doesn't matter, Greg. It really doesn't matter."

He disappeared, the door swinging shut behind him, and Greg could hear him on the hall phone. "Hello? Hello, Mama. Yes, I'm fine . . . Playing baseball . . . Yeah. Yeah, I did okay, you know . . ."

The doorway blazed again as Rodolfo, last as usual, came charging out and jumped feet first over the equipment still piled on the steps. He twisted as he ran down the drive, light on his feet, and called back, "Hasta luego, Gigi la estrella!"

Greg only raised a hand, watching his friend disappear.

Inside, Patrick's voice was soft. "Yeah, I miss you too. Do you want to talk to Gregory? OKAY. All right. I'll tell him."

Greg didn't turn as his brother leaned out. "Mama sends her love. She had people coming for dinner, or she would have . . ." He trailed off.

"Sure. I know."

There was the screech of car wheels in the middle distance. The wild barking of a dog. The usual sounds of the barrio.

Greg stood, gathered up the bat and gloves, and went inside.

It wasn't until the next evening that he linked the distant screech of car tires with the death of Rodolfo. The car had hit him barely twenty feet from the gates of the finca, down a narrow side street the boys sometimes used as a

40

shortcut. It had been moving slowly, but without head-lights, and both wheels had gone over the boy's abdomen before the driver even realized what had happened.

Rodolfo had managed to crawl a short way—not toward home, but in the direction of the finca with its tall bright windows, with its cold sodas and clean white baseball shirts—before the pain overpowered him.

He'd been found half an hour later by his father who'd come out to look for him. He hadn't been dead then, but it hadn't taken much longer. Where the taut stretch of his little-boy stomach should have been, there was only a dimpled cavity. Blood was dripping from the corner of his mouth and staining the back of his shorts.

It wouldn't have occurred to his father to seek help at the big house, to ask the famous man to drive him and his dying son to the hospital where the techniques that might have saved Rodolfo would certainly not have been wasted on another penniless boy from the barrios.

Rodolfo's father had understood everything the instant he saw the small heap in the middle of the road, almost invisible in the starlight. In the days to come he would tell Greg that he had lost three brothers and a sister growing up, and that his own father had died from stepping on a nail that poisoned his blood. He understood the world.

He took his son home, so that he could die in his own bed.

It took a while before news of the death reached the finca.

No one appeared at the gates the next afternoon. Not knowing that each had been kept home by families already moving to make their condolences, Greg assumed there was some festival in town that the Americanos weren't invited to. Patrick—nose-deep in some Russian masterpiece—was having one of his down days, so Greg adventured by himself down at the creek, finding it strangely freeing to be alone.

He imagined he was his older half-brother John—Papa called him Bumby, but he didn't like it if Greg and Patrick did. He'd only met John a few times, but that made it easier to imagine he was him, exploring Cuba years before when Papa had first come to visit. That distant time when the island was no doubt barely tamed.

He returned at the first hint of evening, looking for a whiskey and soda and maybe Patrick's company, but found his father standing beneath the ceiba tree, his normally tanned and ruddy face pale and grim as he looked down at Rodolfo's older brother Rene at the bottom of the steps.

And so the next day Greg found himself standing with Patrick in the cool darkness of what had been Rodolfo's home. Neither of them had ever been there before, or to the homes of any of the boys. It had never even occurred to him to be curious about where his friends lived.

There was no glass in the windows, only shutters, so they could hear Papa murmuring soft condolences to Rodolfo's mother and father. Greg couldn't help but imagine the scene: the body laid out pale and wretched, waxy in the candlelight, his father's broad shoulders bent inwards as he took the grieving mother's delicate hand.

It was a scene from a movie. There was nothing of real life in it. He could not imagine Rodolfo really dead. He had seen him just the day before yesterday.

Gigi la estrella!

He wanted very much to go in and see the body. Then it might become real. But his father had forbidden it, so he stood watching lizards scuttle back and forth over the shutters on stiff legs, and the dust settling on the windshield of his father's huge Chrysler.

Greg found he couldn't take his eyes from its thick tires, couldn't stop hearing the sound of distant brakes cutting through the night, and before that, himself: *Let's keep playing*.

A week later, it was Rene who was opening doors and fetching ice while Papa and Martha sat by the pool, his courtesy so exaggerated it would have seemed sarcastic if not for the great look of concentration that permanently creased his brow.

Rene, it soon became apparent, considered the master of the finca a borderline deity, not so much for the enormity of his reputation, but because the great man had deigned to visit his family's humble dirt-floored home in their hour of darkness. It had, he declared more than once, been an honor to bring his parents to tears.

Papa clearly found this new arrangement entirely satisfactory, and, after a few more days of appropriate mourning, the baseball resumed with Rene filling Rodolfo's position.

Even weeks later, their father still called Rene Rodolfo as often as not, and most of the time didn't even realize his mistake, as though Rodolfo had merely aged a few years.

Greg didn't have that problem. He never spoke to Rene. He couldn't even look him in the eye.

Los Angeles

1951

It was late, a fat moon waltzing overhead, and Greg was sitting on the library steps with the building's Gothic face all lit up behind him.

He wasn't sure why he was there except that it was quiet, a good place to settle his nerves, smoke a joint, and avoid going home. In the last hour only a few people had wandered by, passing from amber pool to amber pool beneath streetlights hazy with moths. If he looked hard enough, Greg could barely make out the dust of their wings drifting down as they beat themselves to death against the scalding glass.

Two months in, and he was already regretting having left the garage, already feeling like he didn't have what it took to be a college man. College had been a mistake, he could see that now, but it was a mistake he couldn't get out of— not without humiliation and disappointment back home.

The problem wasn't the work, or the distant threat of exams. Everyone had told him that college would be a big step up, the end of his long career of academic coasting, but in truth it was all easier than he'd expected. Maybe too easy.

The problem was something else. An ache he couldn't quite place.

A group of young men went stumbling by, already drunk and their night barely begun. They spotted Greg alone on the steps and called for him to come with them, but he waved them on, the sweet smoke from his joint stinging his eyes.

They passed on good-naturedly, making sure he knew they'd be at the Cabana. That they'd buy his whiskey all night if he changed his mind.

They didn't know him, of course, but they knew of him. To them he was only a name, a campus curiosity worth taking along for the novelty.

Greg missed the garage more than ever. He hadn't exactly been close with the guys there either, but at least when they'd invited him out they'd expected him to pay his way like everyone else. If he pissed them off they'd been ready to settle it with a clean fight and no hard feelings afterwards, even once it had become clear Greg punched like a draft horse kicked.

He'd liked the work too. Everything in a machine has a purpose. With enough knowledge and patience, you can fix anything.

The only thing he hadn't liked about the job had been the money, and Shirley had downright hated it. Then again, his wife hated pretty much everything about Greg being an oil-stained mechanic. The grime, the long hours, the working-class stink of it. And that was probably fair. He hadn't exactly lived up to her expectations.

Greg drew deeply on the joint, until his head spun and the embers singed his fingers. He didn't let himself flinch, only flicked the butt to die in the shadows and held his breath for as long as he could. The grass quieted the dull thud of his thoughts. Just a little, but he'd take what he could get.

He knew what would really ease his mind, of course, but that was forbidden. This was a new stage in his life. He was going to be a father. He could not fuck up.

The truth was, it didn't matter how much he hated college. There was no backing out now. Shirley, his family, everyone thought he was finally making something of himself. Even his mother had flown out from Key West when she'd heard he'd enrolled. She was the only person who could come from the airport looking like she'd stepped out of a French boutique, her white Dior dress without a crease.

"Well," she'd said, perched neatly on the sofa in their dank little apartment, Shirley's passable Tom Collins held between the tips of two slender fingers. "Isn't this . . . nice."

"It's good to see you, Mom. Shirley . . ." and he'd patted Shirley's hand like they were an old married couple. "She's been looking forward to meeting you."

"Well, I hope I haven't disappointed . . ." She'd smiled at his wife in a way Greg hadn't recognized, though he'd felt Shirley twitch beside him. "And I trust my boy's been behaving himself?"

"Of course, Mrs. Pfeiffer. Greg's—"

"—Hemingway, dear. Mrs. Hemingway."

"Mrs. Hemingway, then." Greg could feel Shirley losing her temper. He squeezed her hand. "Greg's been—"

"—is that right, Greg? Have you been good?"

46

"Yes."

"Yes?" Her look laden with meaning.

"*Yes.*" He pushed the words out. Anyone, but especially his parents, brushing however lightly on the subject of what was really wrong with him was intolerable. It was like a bad tooth. Every inadvertent touch an agony, yet he couldn't stop tonguing away at it.

"Don't lose your temper with me, Gregory, I believe you. Coming out here was exactly what you needed: a reset." Her smile had been genuine, and maybe there had even been some pride there. "Look at you. My college man."

One brief smile, but it had been enough. As a kid he'd learned to survive on just a handful of those in a month.

"Did you see the way she looked at me, like I was shit she'd found on her shoe?" Shirley said fifteen minutes later, once his mother had announced she had friends in LA to visit, finished her still-icy drink in one gulp, and swept herself away, her goodbye kiss not quite touching Greg's cheek. "And she talked to you like you were still a kid. How did you ever live with that bitch?"

Shirley didn't understand, of course. The worst she'd ever seen was when Greg hadn't managed to clean his nails before she'd gotten home, and he hadn't let himself slip once since he'd started college. He had it under control.

"Don't talk about my mother like that."

She'd laughed, but stopped when she saw his face. That had probably been when things had started cooling between them.

Greg rolled and lit another joint, but only stared at it. Maybe he could give Patrick a call. It would be good to hear his brother's voice.

But no, Patrick didn't want to hear from him. He was busy at Harvard, busy setting up his own life as far away from all of them as he could manage. Greg couldn't resent him that.

"Hemingway."

A shadowy figure was standing at the foot of the steps with his own joint glowing between cupped fingers. Greg had to squint to make out his features: thin hair slicked back in what he probably thought, combined with his hooked nose, was a hawk-like profile. He looked like a greased-up vulture.

Greg's memory—the sort of hoarder that would have filled a house with old cereal boxes just in case—threw out a name. Richard Shipman, another trust-fund kid he barely knew.

Shipman shifted a little, thrown by Greg's silence. "Hemingway, that you?"

"It's Greg."

"Greg. Great." Shipman straightened. "A few of us are going over to Blondie's. There's a show on and my father gave me his invite. Loose women, free champagne. You should come."

Greg stood. It was time to head home. Shirley would be wondering where he was, and he didn't really like the way Shipman was looking at him. Like a rare coin he'd found on the pavement. A lot of them looked at him like that.

In spite of himself, he nodded. "Sure. Let's go."

He barely lasted an hour at Shipman's party. There was only so much small talk he could take with people over-bred as racehorses before he wanted to gouge his own eyes out with a champagne flute. He'd tried to drink his way through it, but that had only made things worse.

Shipman had tried to catch him at the door, but Greg had shouldered him aside like he was made of straw. He heard him fall but didn't look back.

No one followed after that, but pretty soon he started running anyway, trying to use up some of the surging adrenaline from his blood. Couples and groups flashed by on all sides, ignoring tarmac and sidewalk, ignoring the chill in the night air and the clouds drifting thuggish over the face of the moon. Even in glimpses, they seemed so at home in their skins, so comfortable in each other's company.

Greg wanted more than anything to slip among them, to discard himself in the gutter like a mask, but he knew there was no escape. He kept running.

Havana

1942

"Steady now, Greg. It's patience you need to be a really good shot. Patience."

Greg felt one of Papa's blunt fingers thud into the soft flesh of his temple. He didn't flinch. Every atom of his being was focused on the yawning stretch of blue between the trees.

"Don't expect to get it first time, or the second. No one's born with it in them. It's something you have to get a feel for."

A line of sweat worked its way down his spine. The chill of the gun's stock stung his hot cheek. For a moment, he wondered how the gun could be so cold when the air was so warm, but he pushed the thought away.

Focus.

"You can't shoot at where it is; you've got to shoot at where it's going to be. And take into account bullet drop and wind of course. The further the distance the greater the drop, and the bigger the influence of the wind depending on its strength."

Greg let his father's voice fade into the background.

None of what he was saying made much sense. He just wanted to shoot the gun, hear the bang.

"All right. Ready?"

"Ready." No hesitation. Never let him see you hesitate.

There was a metallic click, and a dark disk—the clay, Papa called it a clay—was whipping through the air. Despite his confident words, after so long a build-up the suddenness of its arrival took Greg by surprise. He swung the gun wildly, and though he didn't mean to pull the trigger there was a huge crack and the gun punched him so hard in the shoulder he tumbled to the ground in a cloud of pearly gray smoke.

His father grunted, sounding satisfied. "You didn't plant your feet like I told you. And you should have kept the butt of the gun tight. Essential with the twenty gauge. Thing kicks like a mule."

Greg clambered back to his feet. His shoulder was smarting and his head ringing, but worst of all was the disappointment. He'd wanted to hit his first ever shot so badly. Wanted to show Papa he was still the same Greg.

Gingerly, he pressed the hard wood back against his collarbone.

"Sore?"

Greg looked up into Papa's small perceptive eyes. So much about his father seemed too large, too rough, to belong to a man who made his living behind a desk, but when you looked at his eyes it made sense.

"No."

"Don't lie to me, Greg."

". . . A little."

"Best not overdo it, then. If you end up scared of the gun, it'll ruin you for good. We'll ease you in gently."

Greg hesitated, saw Papa still watching him, and pressed the wood harder to his shoulder, ignoring the ache.

"One more."

Papa grunted again, but Greg couldn't tell what he meant by it. "You sure? It's no good pretending to be tough."

He never would have said that before. A lot had changed since the scene in the bedroom last year—it'd been weeks before Papa had even looked him in the eye—but maybe they could still get back to how things were. The fact that he'd even taken Greg out to shoot had to be a sign it was possible.

He ground the stock against his collarbone, pushing himself into the pain.

"Well all right . . . Don't close your left eye. You need that for depth perception. Ready?"

Greg dutifully opened both eyes wide. The gun felt heavy in his arms, heavier than wood and metal had any right to be. "Ready."

The cicadas roared with one voice, unseen but all around.

A click, a whir, and the clay was flying.

Greg's finger tightened around the trigger, but he forced himself to relax. *Patience.* He followed its rocket-arc, his body loosening, his breath slowing. And right as the clay was about to slip behind the trees, just as he could feel another grunt mounting behind him, he exhaled, and gently squeezed.

The gun kicked again, but this time it was tight to his shoulder, and his body moved with it. He stood firm, and now he could actually see the little cloud of lead-shot burst from the muzzle, cross the naked air in half a second and crack through the heart of the distant clay in a bloom of dust.

Smoke dripped lazily from the gun's twin muzzles. It smelled wonderful, like a hundred struck matches.

"Not bad," Papa said coolly. "That was a pretty good shot."

Greg's elation deflated, but he didn't let it show as he swung the gun onto his shoulder. He knew better than that. "It's pretty easy, to be honest. I don't see what the big deal's about."

At last, Papa smiled, and the weight that had been gathering in Greg's chest faded faster than the gun smoke. If there was one thing Papa admired, it was a winner. And if there was one thing he loved, it was an arrogant winner.

So long as that winner was him, or his own.

Papa took the gun and put it over his own shoulder. It seemed much smaller in his hands. "That's enough for now. You've got to let your body adjust. Tomorrow we'll come back and you can really cement it in. Then we'll move on to actual birds. There's a hell of a difference between a clay and a bird . . . It speeds up, for a start."

He started back toward the clubhouse, probably thinking of the ice-cold daiquiri waiting for him.

Greg followed after, rubbing his sore shoulder now his father's back was turned. The loam was soft beneath their feet, the woods cool and quiet to either side. Overhead, the sky slowly shuffled through an endless deck of clouds.

The clubhouse wasn't far away, but out here among the trees it felt like they were in the middle of the wilderness. The two of them sole survivors of some terrible plane crash, making their way back to civilization with only their wits and courage to count on.

"There's going to be a big competition here at the Cerro next month," Papa said, not looking back. "You should come along with Patrick and me, get a sense of it. Watch how the pros shoot."

"Okay." Greg tried not to sound too excited. It was happening. He'd known if he could just shoot well Papa would see it was all a big mistake. That he'd simply caught Greg in a game. A horrible, stupid game they could all look back on and laugh.

A bird broke cover and swept trilling over their heads. Both watched it pass, not breaking stride.

"Gun isn't loaded," his father said, as if by way of explanation.

"If Patrick's shooting," Greg asked after a minute, watching the edge of the treeline approach ragged and bright ahead of them, "will Mama come and watch?"

His father only sighed. "This isn't a woman's thing, Greg." Even the mention of Greg's mother was enough to put him in a bad mood these days, as though it was she who'd left him.

Still, it wasn't a no.

"Maybe I could shoot. If it's still months away . . . if I practice."

"It's an international shooting competition, son."
"So?"

His father turned then, at the edge of the treeline, everything behind him vague in the midday glare, the thick green leaves hanging low around his head. "So . . . so what?" He laughed. "You are a damn natural, Gigi—no surprise." It was the first time he'd used that nickname for months. "All right. We'll see. But you've got to practice. I don't want you showing me up. You'll have to earn a spot like everyone else."

"I won't. I will."

"Okay then. Swell."

His father looked at him another moment, head cocked, a small smile on his face.

The Shooting Club was about half an hour's drive from the house, near Rancho Boyeros where the houses were big and the fences high. After a brief squabble over the passenger seat, Greg and Patrick had both been banished to the back, and now they leaned against each other in truce, occasionally shifting to keep their legs from sticking to the baking-hot leather.

Their father had both windows open, one arm trailing in the sun. The only sound was the buffeting air and the regular clicks of Patrick biting his nails until Papa told him to cut it out, and then only the wind battling with the chassis. Greg wished he'd put on the radio, something to distract them, but kept quiet.

They slipped from the low-slung houses of their neighborhood and into the open countryside. Fields of sugar cane ready to be burned pulsed in the breeze on both sides, thick and glossy, impossibly green.

Another, almost identical town seemed to jump up from nowhere, and there were other heavy, glaring cars crowding the road as they edged and nudged their way past finer and finer houses, doorways giving way to towering gates, fences to walls.

They heard the club before they saw it. Music and loud voices blurring into one unbreaking wave, the usual crack of guns eerily absent. Greg watched the back of his father's neck twitch as he cleared his throat.

Then the car was swinging up the long gravel drive, the low roof of the club leering up from behind well-tended trees. The long shady porch and front lawn, normally populated by the occasional crusty old ex-hunter or bored-looking local in a waiter's jacket, was swarming with people. Men in suits despite the heat, women in cheerful cocktail dresses just short enough to avoid the dust, countless staff carrying drinks on trays, and—very occasionally—someone who looked like they were actually there to shoot.

Papa hooked one hand over the curve of the steering wheel and sat there for a moment, blowing out his breath in one long huff. If it was anyone else, Greg would have said he was nervous, but this was Papa. Sure enough, when he spoke his voice was a confident boom. "Ready, boys?"

"Ready, Papa."

All three stepped out into the glare of the day.

It was only when the reporters gathered round that Papa finally seemed to relax. He knew most of them by name, and had no doubt written for all their magazines. *Field and Stream*, *Sports Illustrated*, and every Cuban paper was there to cover the shoot.

It was the Cuban championship, and top shooters had flown in from all over the world, but it was only Papa the press seemed to care about. They jostled around him like puppies.

"Mr. Hemingway, sir, are you here to compete?"

"If the best hunters in the world are coming together, seems like it's my duty to put my name in."

"You think you'll take the cup?"

"Well, we'll see. I haven't picked up a gun in half a year; too busy with my marlin—that's the real sport of men— but we'll see how far instinct can take me. My boys'll be taking part as well." Papa gestured over his shoulder to Patrick and Greg standing like props in the wings. "They haven't been shooting long, but they should give more than a few of the pros here a run for their money."

The reporters looked over, but, seeing two skinny boys each barely taller than the guns slung over their shoulders, they took only a few polite snaps before sending another round of questions Papa's way.

Greg and Patrick were both used to this. They passed the time watching the well-dressed gentlemen and ladies stuff canapés into their mouths like they hadn't eaten in weeks.

The competitors were easy to spot among the crowd. A few stood out in leather vests with every spare inch covered with patches, insignias, and awards, and they seemed more than happy to explain where they'd gotten each one to any passerby who so much as glanced at them. The rest you could pick out by their stillness, the way they didn't talk or laugh or even eat, only stood drinking whiskey or gin with small infrequent sips in the shade of the clubhouse, waiting for the competition to begin.

Gigi didn't need to ask which group were the ones to watch.

He looked at his father, halfway through a choice story, every movement of his body sharp with satisfaction as the reporters fell about with laughter.

The buzz from the whiskey had started to fade, and Greg could feel himself getting more and more nervous.

"I'll be right back," said Patrick, before slipping away in the direction of the clubhouse, a sheen of sweat coating his brow. Greg felt his stomach twist in sympathy. He'd managed to hold onto his breakfast so far, but he wasn't sure how much longer that would last.

He'd been disappointed their mother hadn't come, but now he was almost relieved. Anyway, he'd known she wouldn't really. She and Papa never spoke except on the phone these days, and she usually cried afterwards. Some of that was his fault, he knew. He remembered a night not long after he'd come back from Cuba last year, when he'd walked into the living room to see his mother slam the receiver down. She'd turned to him with her bottom lip trembling and said, "Well done, Greg, this is a fine rage you've gotten him into."

The memory made him want to put his hands over his face and hide.

"Ernest's boy, I heard. Correct?"

Greg jumped. He hadn't noticed anyone come near, but now a tall, thin stranger loomed over him, dark glasses peering down over a brimming champagne coupe. Gigi watched the bright bubbles slip helpless into the small black hole between the man's lips before they smacked in appreciation. "Lost your tongue?"

"No sir. I mean, yes, I'm Greg Hemingway."

"Gregory. A pleasure." The man's bony hand enveloped Greg's like a spider wrapping its legs around a fly. "I've seen your name in the listings. You're entering the competition? Well. Celebrity does demand its little indulgences. And the son of the Great Writer . . . How could we turn you away? I'm sure everyone will be watching most closely to see if you live up to your father's name and its many . . . opportunities."

Greg felt another strange twisting in his gut, but something about the man's tight smile forced open his mouth. "Good. I always shoot better with a crowd. I'll even buy you a drink from my winnings."

For a moment, the man's pencil-line eyebrows rose from behind the obscurity of his sunglasses, then a thick, hairy arm emerged from over his shoulder and wrapped itself around his neck.

"Esteban Ventura, you bastard. Where have you been hiding?"

The man's rod-straight spine refused to bend, but his knees finally buckled as Papa pulled him round. "In plain sight, Ernest, as always."

"Exactly the sort of riddle answer I'd expect from you. Well done."

"I do my best." Ventura tried to keep his icy composure, but it seemed to be proving difficult in the face of Papa's enthusiasm, his good mood probably fueled by the daiquiris he'd consumed while entertaining the journalists.

That was the thing about Papa. He was like the sea. However he felt—happy, angry, bitter, sad—you couldn't help but be swept along.

"And what have you two been talking about?" Papa asked. "Giving my boy a few words of advice no doubt."

"Of course."

"And what pearls did he offer you, son?"

Greg hesitated for a second, his eyes seeking out some human spark behind the smoky lenses. No small part of him was tempted to stir up trouble, but something about the man's unwavering gaze checked him. "He said I should

59

shoot to show everyone I deserve to be here, that I'm a worthy Hemingway."

Papa liked that. He clapped Ventura on the shoulder. "You watch, the boy's my son all right. He won't let me down, will you, Greg?"

Greg swallowed. "No, sir."

"Damn right. Now come on. We need to find Patrick and steady our nerves. See you out there, Ventura."

"A pleasure, as always, Ernest." Ventura gave a slight bow. "And, Gregory, I'll look forward to your perform-ance . . ."

They found Patrick in the clubhouse, kneeling on a barstool and politely trying to convince the ancient local tending the bar that a white rum on the rocks was a com-pletely reasonable order for a twelve-year-old.

"Tell him, Papa!" he pleaded as he saw their father shouldering his way through the crowd, Greg following in his wake.

Papa frowned at Patrick but leaned over the polished oak. "If my son orders a drink," he said in a voice both very low and very loud, "you fucking well get him a drink, amigo. Hop to it."

The bartender, seemingly unfazed, nodded and turned to the long line of bottles gleaming on the back wall.

"Drinking before the shoot?" Papa asked, finally round-ing on his son. "What are you thinking, Pat? Are you taking this seriously? Did I waste my time bringing you out here?"

"No, I . . . I want to steady my nerves." Patrick's voice faded away as their father glared.

"Bullshit." The rum arrived and their father drank it in

one gulp before adding, "two Cokes," without so much as glancing at the bartender.

The old man nodded obediently and shuffled off. As Papa returned to questioning Patrick's weakness of character, Greg watched him go over to the fridge and pull out two bottles. His crisp white shirt crumpled as he stooped, and he took a moment to pull it flat. On his unhurried way back the man saw Greg staring and gave the slightest wink as he set the drinks down, as if to show he didn't have a care in the world.

"Thank you," Greg said.

"You're very welcome, young man."

Then another customer was leaning over the bar, clicking her fingers in his face for attention. The bartender didn't flinch. He nodded to Greg once, then turned and silently took the woman's order.

Greg could only marvel at his self-control. When something rubbed Papa the wrong way it could ruin the whole family's day—when they'd still been a family—but here was this man letting it all roll off his shoulders like rain from a mountainside.

Greg was wondering if that was something he'd been born with, or something you could learn, when his father's hand fell onto his shoulder.

"You paying attention, Gig-man?"

"Hm? Oh yeah."

"Good. Drink your Coke. The sugar will do you good. The listings have been posted and you're first up. I know, it's not ideal, but it's a random draw so you'll just have to be a man about it. And hey, starting off the whole competition is pretty swell, don't you think?"

★

61

It felt like only a few minutes later that Greg was stepping out into the furious sun, his lips still sweet and cold.

The crowd had formed a rough horseshoe around the shooter's stand and the first few feet of the open field. Beyond them, men in white uniforms were readying the launching baskets, the faint fluttering of unseen wings rippling over the grass. Beyond that spread the suburbs of Havana, grand and squalid. Then, only the sea.

A sharp-eyed local with a clipboard was waiting by the shooter's point, undaunted by the blistering midday heat.

Greg stepped up with his gun broken over his arm. Loaded two cartridges with numb fingers.

The chatter began to hush. His own heartbeat boomed in his ears.

He snapped the gun straight. Cocked it. In an instant it went from a lump of cold metal to a living thing in his hands.

The crowd had gone silent now, but the air was still tangled with shifting bodies, clearing throats, ice on glass.

Sweat was stinging his eyes, running down his sides. He lifted the gun.

The attendant leaned forward. "You are ready, señor?"

Greg took a deep breath.

"I'm ready."

Havana

1941

Greg tiptoed softly up the stairs.

Martha was out in Havana proper, but he didn't know why, or for how long. Papa was in his study, scribbling away with his stubby pencil, sometimes muttering under his breath.

Once, Greg wouldn't have dared to slip into their room unless he knew they were both out of the house and exactly when they were due back. Even then, he would have left hours on either side, enough time for them to come back if they'd forgotten anything or decided to head home early.

Now, he paused outside his father's office door, peering through the crack to make sure his back was still stooped over the desk.

He didn't really understand what it was Papa did when he was sitting there all morning, but he understood how important it was to him, and so he felt confident as he tiptoed down the hall and into the bedroom.

The floorboards were cool beneath his feet, the long stretch of them running all the way from the front of the house to the back, lit by wide windows on both ends. He made sure to leave the door gently ajar behind him so that he would hear his father coming, just in case there was any break from routine.

His mother's clothes would have been best, but Martha's would do. Her mink scarf was thrown casually over the back of the chair at her beauty station. It was probably worth a fortune—certainly Greg had never seen any of the boys' mothers from the barrio wearing anything like it—but he only ran his fingers through its ghost-soft fur as he passed.

The dresser stood tall, all glossy oak, its twin doors like the entrance to some medieval castle. Reverently, Greg pulled the doors apart, letting their momentum carry them open as he stood back.

He pulled off his old polo shirt, his stained navy shorts, his boxers, and dropped them in a neat pile. He drew out a yellow dress at random and slipped it over his head. It didn't fall so much as flow over him, the fabric so thin he could see the wardrobe and the window and the chair that had been his mother's all recast in gold.

He stood still then, just being. Feeling the limits of his body and the dress against it, the weight of the glass beads at the hem warming in the sun. He imagined his mother wearing this dress, the way her shoulders would dip first one and then the other as she walked beneath its delicate straps, how her body and the dress would move separately, but together.

It didn't feel like getting dressed, but it never did. It felt like a slaking off, a snake scraping away its dull skin and laying bare the tender jewel-bright flesh beneath.

He lifted the hem in small fists—carefully, with reverence—and moved over to the full-length mirror in the corner. The boy with the broad shoulders and the quick fists was gone. Probably he was outside somewhere, running the fastest or climbing the highest or whatever else he had to do to feel real.

This girl didn't have to worry about any of that, here in the quiet room. No one to beat, nothing to prove. Content to be.

She was still Greg, of course, but a different Greg.

She stepped back, looking at herself, and started to spin, felt the dress lift, swirling around her. The smile became real then. She laughed.

The door opened, and Papa took half a step in before freezing.

They stared at each other, and the only thought that went through Greg's head was, *I forgot how quiet he is. How can he be so big and so quiet?*

Emotions crawled over Papa's face. Disbelief writhed into something Greg could not understand—the look of a man who has spotted an old and hated foe—and on into naked disgust. He looked at Greg like he had found something squirming under a stone.

The girl vanished like smoke and the boy found himself stranded, wanting to hide, to disappear, to be anywhere except here in this dress with his father looking at him like *that*. "Papa, I—"

—But his father turned away, and closed the door softly behind him.

Havana

1942

"Have another, Gig. It's a celebration, after all."

"Okay, Papa."

"You'll be sick if you're not careful."

Papa frowned at Patrick. "Are you his brother or his mother?" A few people at other tables in the little restaurant glanced over, but he didn't notice. His voice only seemed to be getting louder as the night went on. "If he can handle a gun he can handle a few glasses of wine. Let the boy drink."

Patrick leaned back in his seat, red-faced and bleary-eyed. He'd spent most of the day sitting in the shade after crashing out halfway through the competition, growing tired and restless and probably drinking too much himself.

Their father poured a healthy measure of white wine into Greg's already half-full glass. "This is the good stuff. I used to drink this in Paris back in the day. A hell of a lot cheaper over there, you can imagine."

Greg nodded as though he understood. "Thanks, Papa." He took another mouthful. According to his father, the wine had a bouquet of honeysuckle and melon, a body of apple, oak, and elderflower, and a long dry finish. All he could taste was a vague citrusy vinegar. He pretended to savor it.

He hadn't been sure how Papa would react to having his son place so much higher than him in the competition. So when he'd picked him up—when he'd beamed as people had come over to shake their hands, to compliment him on his gunslinger of a son—Greg didn't think he'd ever been so happy.

In that moment there had been no shadow between them. No wrongness. No disappointment.

It had felt better than all the wine in the world.

He sipped again.

"That's the stuff, son."

Patrick kept his eyes down and focused on eating the last of his lobster. Papa didn't so much as look at him. "Goddamn, Gig. After that sixth bird I knew you were hot. Like you had a built-in radar."

"I didn't even have to think about it," Greg admitted. "I just kept firing, and they kept falling out of the sky."

"That's what being hot is, son. You were working on instinct alone."

"He only got fourth place . . ." Patrick grumbled to his plate. "That's not even podium."

"And you're lucky you didn't come last after you fell apart like that." Papa gave Patrick a reproachful look. "Your brother outshot some of the best in the world today. He'll be in the papers. You think you could show a little fraternal spirit."

Patrick winced. "I am happy for him. I'm not saying he didn't shoot great. You were great, Gig. I . . ." Whatever Patrick mumbled after that, it was inaudible, and their father decided to let it go.

"Well, Gig, you'll have a fine story to tell your mother now, at least." He took a long drink from his own glass, bright beads of condensation dripping onto the tablecloth. "Quite a contrast to life in Key West, huh?"

"I wish she could've been there," Greg sighed, imagining her standing on the grass in an elegant dress, her neat features lit up in admiration for her extraordinary son.

"You think she would have come?" Papa gave a sharp laugh. "She'd have stayed home with a gin and tonic and you know it. She was never exactly the smothering type."

"She might have," he lied.

"Afraid not, kiddo. I've seen reef sharks with more maternal instinct. Did she ever come to see you play ball back in Miami? No, that was always your papa cheering from the sidelines."

You came once, Greg thought, but didn't say. It felt traitorous.

"I gave you your own team, for Pete's sake," Papa said, like he could read thoughts.

"I know. I'm grateful."

"Good." He refilled his glass and smiled. "Don't pout. Today you're a winner."

"I'm not. Patrick's right, it was only fourth place."

"Bullshit. You're a damn champion. You shot against men, and you beat them like a man. Ha, look at that grin, Patrick! He knows it. So, are you going to give up baseball, now you know where your true talent lies?"

"No way. I'm better at baseball anyway."

"Bullshit again."

"Sure I am. And it's more fun. Shooting's too easy, all you have to do is follow the bird and then sort of . . . relax. Easy. I don't know how people miss."

"Steady, Gig." Papa leaned forward, suddenly serious. "Nothing kills a gift like bragging about it. You've got to keep it inside you. You talk about it too much, think about it too much, and it vanishes . . . trust me on that one."

Greg looked at him, then at Patrick, staring glumly at the remains of his lobster, his face half hidden by his worn old cap. "Okay. I guess I just mean . . ." He nudged Patrick's leg with his knee, and when his brother looked up, he smiled at him. "Shooting's fun, but it doesn't really matter."

Patrick hesitated a second, then gave a weary smile back.

The stars and the streetlights blurred as Papa drove them home. Patrick lay slumped over the back seat, his mouth open as he snored, a small frown on his face. Greg had the window down, the cool air flowing over his hot cheeks, the low drowsy hum of Havana washing over him: the murmur of generators, the drone of flickering filament bulbs, the soft rum-slurred voices mingling on porches and terraces, the ever-distant whispering of the sea. He held his hand out, felt the drag of the air—the whole world pushing against him and losing.

The finca was all lit up, every window blazing like the end of the world and the distant lighthouse trailing spears of gold overhead, illuminating his father's face as they pulled in. Greg could see every detail of his hands on the steering wheel like a woodcut. It struck him for the first time that his own hands could have been his father's in miniature.

Patrick barely murmured as Papa picked him up and carried him into the house. He smiled at his middle child, finally relenting now the boy couldn't see it. "Poor fella. No boy worth his salt can stand being outdone by his brother." Then a conspiratorial wink to Greg. "And he has to put up with it a lot."

While he carried Patrick up to their shared room in the tower, Greg stood on the drive and watched the lighthouse turn. He couldn't have said how he felt. Somehow sad and tired and heavy all at the same time, but not quite any of that. They'd mixed like colors into a feeling he had no name for.

It didn't make any sense. The shoot had gone better than he could have hoped. Papa was proud. It felt like the last year hadn't happened. Like things were back to normal.

The lighthouse turned and turned. Spears of light, searching in the dark, finding nothing.

Maybe he'd had too much to drink . . .

He went in to splash cold water on his face, trying to dispel the feeling that he was falling. He heard his father come in from the tower and pour himself another glass of whiskey, Patrick safely tucked up in bed. Greg felt suddenly exhausted, and he retraced Papa's steps up the twisting staircase to their bedroom.

Patrick was lying on his side. In that moment he seemed younger than normal, more vulnerable.

Greg sat on the edge of the bed, and Patrick stirred, opening bloodshot eyes.

He tried to think of something to say, but nothing came besides, "Pat . . ."

They looked at each other, then his brother smiled and said, "You were great today, Gig."

"I'll never shoot that well again."

70

"Who cares? You did once . . . That's something."

The light from the doorway darkened, and their father rolled onto the bed between them.

"Hell, this was a good day." He reached out and pulled them in, one on each side. "I can't think of the last time I had such a good time on land."

Greg squirmed into a more comfortable position. "Is fishing that much better?"

"Incomparable. A bird is nothing but a moving target. A six-hundred-pound marlin is an opponent. And the sea. Damn, Gig, the sea . . . You loved it, didn't you, Pat?"

There was no answer from the other side of his father's slow beating heart.

"Sleeping off the booze, I guess. He didn't have much to do but drink once he crashed out. Tried to keep him on the Coke, but I was still shooting myself." Normally, he might have sounded annoyed, betrayed even, at the thought of his son not being able to handle his rum, but now he was indulgent, almost fond. "He did okay. He did his best. Always does, Patrick, you've got to give him that. Heart of a lion."

They lay in silence a while, staring up at the ceiling, listening to sounds of the old house creaking on its foundations.

Greg had begun to doze off when his father laughed. "You should have seen their faces today, Gig. All those patch-sewing peacocks. Their mouths puckered up like a dog's asshole when you got that last bird. Most of them've been passionate shooters their whole life, and along you come . . ."

"I thought I'd missed it at first, let it go too far," Greg

admitted. "I only knew I'd hit it when everyone started cheering."

"Plenty of room to spare. Christ, what a shot." He yawned, and his arm curled tighter, pulled Greg a little closer. "You see, Gig-man? You see? Whatever this poison is that's got you, this sickness, you can beat it."

Greg didn't say anything. He knew what Papa was talking about, of course. The girl in the room. It was the first time he'd spoken about it. The first time he'd so much as hinted about it without that sneer. "Listen, Mr. Gig," he sighed. "I get it. I remember a girl in Paris and wanting to go over and kiss her just because she had so much damn red lipstick caked on. I wanted to get that lipstick smeared all over my lips. So I get it, but you have to fight it."

Greg didn't see how that was the same thing at all. Kissing a girl and being a girl, or dressing like one at least . . .

Soon Papa was snoring, but Greg lay wide awake, staring up at the ceiling.

I get it, but you have to fight it.

And he would. He rolled over and pressed his face to his papa's side.

Los Angeles

1951

Greg spent the night bouncing from bar to bar, often not even finishing his drink before he had to move on. It was like there was a pressed spring in his head, one wound so tight it was quivering. Only moving eased it, loosened the tension a fraction, enough to let him breathe.

He knew this feeling. In a way he'd known it all his life, but in childhood it had been subtle, days of melancholic lethargy or restlessness that came and went without reason. The older he'd gotten the worse it had become—lethargy had become despair, and restlessness became a mania that erased all his hard-won self-control—and the last time it had been this bad he'd nearly killed his brother.

He'd since been diagnosed with a condition that went by the charming name of *manic-depressive insanity*. There was no cure, no way even to manage it besides drug cocktails or electroshock therapy, all closer to torture than medicine.

He simply had to control himself. This didn't feel like a bad one. He could ride it out.

Eventually he gave up on the bars and just walked, losing track of where he was as he passed restaurants and low apartment blocks and the gated entrances to golf courses and all the other squat ugly buildings that made up some of the most desirable real estate on Earth.

Hours passed before the runaway train in his head finally began to wind down, dawn hinting in the east. He started to feel in control again, and found he could even sit still as his taxi took him home, his head leaning against the window. Not thinking anything, counting breath after breath.

Soon he was trying to ease open the door to his apartment. The top hinge was squeaky, but if you gripped the handle and lifted while you pushed . . . there, quiet as a shadow.

He was barely two feet inside when he caught his foot on one of Shirley's exquisite shoes they couldn't afford. Normally, he would have righted himself without breaking stride, even in the dark, but now there was too much whiskey soaked into the aching meat of his brain. He fell hard, cracking his head against the coffee table.

"Fuck." He tried to push himself up, his arms shaking, but it was no good. The world was spinning too fast.

"Greg?"

"Fuck."

The lights clicked on, shockingly bright. "What the hell are you doing, Greg?" Shirley's face swung into his vision, a lovely pissed-off moon hovering over him. "Do you have any fucking idea what time it is?"

"Had a bad night. Not feeling good."

He tried to push himself up again, but the floor bucked beneath his hands.

"I don't give a shit, Greg. Jesus. I've got an audition before work tomorrow. Get fucked up if you want, but sleep on the grass if you're going to wake me up."

"I know. M'sorry. I didn't do anything. No trouble. Just too much whiskey."

She looked at him for a moment, flipping a mental coin, its edge thin as a blade.

For a moment he was brought back forcefully to the first night she'd looked at him like that. The night he'd first seen her, walking into a party arm in arm with her boyfriend. Long black hair and espresso eyes.

Later that night she'd cornered him by the drinks table, gotten in close to whisper in his ear over the music. He'd asked her where her boyfriend was, and she'd given him that same look, then said she didn't care. She'd leaned up against him, and his body had read every swell and curve of hers like braille. And when she'd kissed him, he'd thought: *This is everything I want.*

Eventually, she sighed. "Greg . . . You're useless, you know that?"

"Yes."

He closed his eyes, hearing her move to the sink and run him a glass of water.

Yes.

She placed it beside him, then dropped what felt like a damp washcloth over his face before padding back to the bedroom door.

The lights went out.

Greg woke to the door slamming.

He could hear the morning traffic rumble outside. The hurried footsteps of the agency assistant with the shiny suit who lived above. His own heart beating, slow and steady.

He took careful stock of himself, stretching his extremities, running his fingertips over his face. A bruise on his

75

shoulder, probably from the fall. A dull ache in his shin he couldn't explain. His bottom lip a little swollen. A gobstopper-sized lump above his left eyebrow that was tender to the touch.

Nothing too bad, considering how much he'd drunk. He didn't even have much of a hangover. He'd inherited his father's monstrous constitution, and his body at least seemed almost indestructible.

In fact, he felt good. Last night had been bad, yes, but it could have been so much worse. And now it was done. He had a whole new day ahead of him.

The thought was energizing, rejuvenating. A brand-new day—infinite possibilities.

He listened to the footsteps of the man above, the bang of a door below. He was perfectly sealed away in here. He could do whatever he wanted. There was nothing to be scared of.

Somewhere, way back in his mind, the last scrap of his judgment whispered that this wasn't right. That this was how it felt when the mania was burning white-hot: like there was nothing wrong with him.

He lay a little longer, held by one last shred of hesitation, but the energy in his body was surging, drowning out that last quiet voice until he was sure it had never been there at all.

Shirley would be out all day. He'd have the clothes back in her wardrobe hours before she got home. She'd never noticed before. Never suspected a thing.

He stood and went to get dressed.

Havana

1942

"Patrick? Patrick, are you asleep?"

". . . I was. Why are you up?"

"I wanted a glass of water."

"Okay, but why are you on my bed?"

"Nothing. I was just—"

"—ow, don't sit on my leg, you idiot. You're dripping water!"

"Sorry . . . I guess I wanted . . ."

"Spit it out, Gig, or I'm going back to sleep."

"Okay. I heard Papa and Martha were talking, and . . . You know that . . . thing I do sometimes?"

"Thing? Oh . . ."

"Yeah. I was thinking—"

"—I don't really want to talk about it, Greg. Go back to bed."

"I know. No one does, but . . . I mean—I know I shouldn't, but . . . do you think it's bad?"

"Dammit, Greg. Why are you asking me this?"

"No reason."

"Look. It doesn't make you bad. It's a nasty habit, like

picking your nose. You're not hurting anyone, it's just . . . disgusting is all."

"Right."

"Okay?"

"Yeah. Disgusting."

"Greg, I didn't—"

"—No. You're right. I know you're right. I need to . . . Well, goodnight."

". . . Night, Gig."

Los Angeles

1951

Greg chose Shirley's ugliest dress—the sort of too-blue normally exclusive to candy and mouthwash. She'd never miss it if he stuffed it at the bottom of the trash can, and Greg wouldn't have cared if it was made of sackcloth. He didn't need to look good, he was just getting a fix, so his brain would keep quiet for another few months.

Still, as the cheap shiny fabric settled around him it did feel . . . electric. Like it was a different set of nerves that was—

—*No.* He shut the thought down like a man stamping on an extremely venomous spider. He walked into the bathroom and stared at himself in the mirror, made himself look long and hard. Thick muscled shoulders, stubble on his jaw, chest hair peeking over the neckline of the dress.

He made himself say the truth out loud. "Disgusting."

That did the trick. He was a man with an illness, an imbalance in his brain that made him dress in women's clothes. That was all.

And one day he would beat it. One day he would be cured.

But not today.

Their apartment was in the top corner of a horseshoe-shaped apartment complex, and so long as he kept to the far left, Greg could stand in the sun without anyone spotting him as they left for work. He knew he shouldn't be out here, that this was a mistake—the rushing energy he felt in every limb let him know he was in the grip of a mania, but it also didn't let him care.

The concrete of the shared walkway was dusty under his feet, still cool from the night. The sunlight was warm on his bare skin. He breathed deep, and the exhaust-choked, double-fried city air was sweeter than a Cuban spring morning. It seemed new and strange to look down into the familiar sun-smashed courtyard as people emerged one by one from their nests and let the great big city sweep them away.

A bird was singing brash and fearless from somewhere up on the roof. Greg listened as heels clattered down the stairs, as mothers called out after kids who studiously ignored them, as the ever-present hum of traffic swelled into a roar he knew would last half the morning. The bird sang through it all. No doubt it was a plain little bird—it sounded like a house sparrow; Greg remembered them pecking around in the dust at the finca—and there wasn't much music in that staccato chirrup, but somehow there was a glory to it.

Greg wished he'd learned to play an instrument. Maybe it wasn't too late. He could head down to a pawnshop right now and probably find half a dozen violins and guitars going cheap. He could teach himself. Practice every day. It would be easy.

But he wasn't supposed to go anywhere. That's what he'd told himself when he opened the front door.

Why? What was he so worried about? LA was such a big city, would anyone recognize him if he took a walk around the block?

There was a soft pat of wing striking ether, and he looked up in time to see the sparrow pass by as it zipped over the courtyard and out of the complex, small and dull and reckless as a god.

Greg watched it go, feeling the sun begin to slide down his shoulders.

Who was he to deny a sign?

Why the cinema, he didn't know. The cinema was Shirley's domain, where she worked collecting stubs and scraping gum off seats until her modeling career took off—due any day now as it had been since he'd met her. On balance, this was probably the worst place in the world Greg could be, apart from maybe his father's study. He had no explanation for why his feet had brought him here, but found he didn't need one. It would be fine.

Things didn't go too badly at first. He bought his ticket for *An American in Paris* without a hitch. It didn't even bother him that the booth-boy with the dropped-pizza face kept his eyes firmly on a spot somewhere over Greg's shoulder through the whole transaction.

His good mood faltered by the time he was two steps into the auditorium. He realized suddenly and powerfully that he didn't want to be trapped in the dark for two hours when there was a bright world waiting outside. A few seated people turned to look at him as he stood there hesitating, and a scrawny-looking guy Greg was sure he could have turned inside out with one hand actually pointed and laughed.

Coming inside had been a mistake, he could see that now. He needed to be out in the sun, in the open air.

He felt a little better once he was back in the atrium. If he'd gone straight outside he might have spent the rest of the day wandering through Los Angeles until the rushing in his head ran itself out. Instead, he headed for the bathroom.

He'd finished up and started washing his hands when there was a loud rapping on the door. He ignored it, using extra soap and cleaning under his fingernails. He'd painted them blue to match the dress before he left.

Next came banging, the sound of a meaty fist striking cheap plywood again and again. Greg took his time drying off.

When he came out there was a cop waiting. He was almost as wide as he was tall, which was very, and his off-the-peg uniform looked about two sizes too small. Somehow that only made him seem bigger as he frowned down at Greg through thick, bushy eyebrows, opening the conversation with a serious, "Son."

"Sir."

"I think you went into the wrong bathroom there, son."

Greg glanced at the silhouette of a stick figure in a dress etched onto the door. Maybe this had been a step too far, but he didn't like the way the cop's lips were twitching, like he was trying not to smile while he lined up the story he'd tell about Greg at the bar tonight. "No, looks right to me."

"Have you been drinking, son?"

He felt a moment of satisfaction as the cop's mouth

narrowed into a chiseled line. It was actually impressive when he managed to speak without ruining the effect.

"No." Greg spotted a crowd of ushers lingering by the popcorn stand, watching with bulging eyes. "Fuck no, it's not even twelve o'clock."

"There's no need for vulgarity."

"Well, we'll have to respectfully disagree on that. So, if there isn't anything else . . ."

"Just don't let me catch you going in there again. That shit ain't right, you understand me, son?"

"I'm not your son." Greg's voice was calm, even though the cop was really starting to tick him off. "Now, if you'll excuse me, I think I need to take another piss."

The cop took a half step forward. "Don't do it." He seemed to be genuinely pleading for Greg to reconsider, but Greg didn't need to. His judgment was fine. Perfect. He'd never felt more sure of himself. Dressing up had always helped him relax, vented pressure, but doing it out here, in the world, was something else altogether. He felt like a rocket.

"Look . . . buddy," the cop tried again, sounding like he was using the last shreds of his patience. "You can wear what you want, wear a fish on your dick for all I care, but you're not going in the women's bathroom. Go piss in the rough with the rest of us."

Greg placed a hand on the door. "Officer, there's no need for vulgarity."

"You go in there and I'll put you in cuffs. That's a promise."

Greg hesitated for a second, but only a second. "I'd like to see you try, you fucking pig." He pushed into the bathroom and the cop came tumbling after, grabbing a handful of dress to try and pull him back. There was the sound of tearing fabric, and Greg had enough time to shout, "This is my wife's, you mother—" before two beefy arms wrapped around him, trapping his arms and forcing all the air from his lungs in a huff.

The cop was huge, and clearly well used to crushing the life out of undesirables, so Greg went for surprise, throwing all his weight forward and pushing up with his legs until he felt the cop lose his balance.

In the few seconds of strange calm that followed, Greg caught sight of himself in the long mirror above the sinks: the tatters of the dress's bodice hanging around his waist, bent double with the huge cop stretched out on his back, both legs waggling but refusing to loosen his grip.

He had a sudden memory of one of his mother's photographs from the long trip to Africa—the one where they left him behind with a nanny—of a woman carrying her precious baby swaddled on her back. He'd just started to laugh when the cop's struggles finally overbalanced him, and they both toppled head first into a closed bathroom stall.

There was a scream, but Greg couldn't see what was going on. There was too much blood in his eyes.

He writhed around, trying to pull himself up, but caught only a smooth leg. He let go sharply, "Sorry, miss," and a pointed heel cracked him square in the forehead and knocked him back onto the tiles before the full weight of the cop slammed onto him.

A few minutes later he was sitting peacefully in the corner, his hands cuffed behind him as the cop washed the blood from his eyes with surprising tenderness. As the man's face bloomed out of the darkness, Greg felt a little relief to see he didn't have a scratch on him. He supposed his own head must have taken the brunt of the door. "You okay?" he asked.

The cop lowered his handful of wet toilet paper and sat back on his haunches. "Fine. Day's work. You?"

"Still pretty good, actually . . . Sorry about calling you a pig."

"Hmm." He resumed easing blood from Greg's eyelashes. "CR's on its way. Me and you are gonna wait here."

"That seems fair."

"Are you sure you haven't been drinking?"

"I have a condition. It's . . . it doesn't matter."

"A condition. Sure."

And then from behind: "*Greg?*"

They both turned. Shirley was standing in the bathroom door, outlined against a gawping crowd. She looked particularly lovely, her stupid little cinema-issued hat struggling to contain the swirling ocean of her black hair.

Greg smiled, taking her in. "Hello, darling. Sorry about the dress."

Greg went to sleep still smiling on a thin prison mattress and woke up feeling as if he'd been mugged by himself.

The mania that had been running hot yesterday had died down now, leaving him to sift through the ashes. He spent the morning lying there in his over-lit cell, trying to figure out how things had spiraled out of control so quickly, and failing. None of it made any sense, but he was stuck with the consequences anyway.

Oh God, the consequences. Shirley knew. He fought down nausea, trying to piece through his memories of her coming into the bathroom. How had she looked at him?

There had been confusion, anger, embarrassment, but that was all. It could have been worse.

Maybe anger was an understatement. She'd squatted down close to Greg so she could scream-whisper while they waited for the squad car.

"Greg . . . What the *fuck* are you doing?"

"I . . ."

"Is that *my dress*?"

"It's not a very nice dress. We can just throw it away." Now, in the prison cell, Greg could look back on how little sense he'd been making. At the time it had seemed like an entirely logical thing to say.

"*What?*"

"We can throw it away and forget about this. I . . . I have a sickness, Shirl, but it's not a problem."

"A sickness?"

"Like the mood swings, you know. That sort of thing. But it's okay. I have it under control."

She took a few long seconds to process this. "Under control? How long have you— no, I don't care. Greg, have you lost your fucking *mind*? I work here. My friends are here. I can never, ever show my face here again. Why the fuck have you . . ." She seemed to choke on her words, but Greg had nothing to offer. At the time, he hadn't understood the question, but now that word loomed as large for him as it had for her. Why? Why walk down the street in front of everyone? Why go to the one place his own wife might see him? Why use the fucking women's bathroom?

He groaned and put one arm over his eyes.

News would get out. What if his friends heard? What if someone told Papa?

He pulled the dirty pillow over his mouth and screamed.

He was doubly cursed. The mood swings: fine, he could just about live with them. The urge to dress up he could control when he was sane. But together they were ruining his life.

The cell door swung open, and a beady-eyed cop called in. "Hey, look who's up. One phone call, should have got it yesterday but you were high as shit so we're doing it now, get a move on."

"I wasn't high." Greg swung his feet off the bed.

"Fuck you weren't. Get your ass up you—"

—Greg stood. The cop took a half step back, but he was still too close. One good punch and Greg could . . . No, even he wasn't stupid enough to hit a cop.

He trudged obediently along to the phone bank. The station seemed sketched entirely from charcoal. Black and white tiles on the floor. Gleaming ebony doors dividing stained ivory walls. Black uniforms on white skin passing by as Greg clutched the greasy plastic receiver to his ear.

One call.

Shirley? She was probably hoping they'd throw the book at him. Any phone call with Shirley would be short and sharp and mostly comprised of four-letter words.

Papa? He'd rather die.

His mother? She'd pay his bail, sure, but she'd also give a soft huff of disappointment. Maybe there'd be a touch of irritation in there too. She'd done her best to ignore Greg's problems, as though they wouldn't exist if she didn't notice them. But here he was, shoving them back in her line of sight again.

The only other person Greg could think of within

striking distance was his aunt Virginia, a kind woman with the patience of a saint, which probably explained why she'd always had so much time for him.

The operator patched him through, and after only two rings he heard the click followed by her familiar greeting, "You've got me."

He smiled. He'd forgotten how much he liked her. "Hello, Jinny, it's Greg. I'm not sure how to ease into this, but I've been arrested. I'm actually in jail right now. This is my one phone call, just like the movies."

"Arrested? Greg, what?"

"I got a bit drunk and caused some trouble. Nothing serious, but the cops wanted to make an example out of me."

"Hold on one second, Gigi."

"Greg." But he realized he was talking to no one. "Jinny? Are you there?" A moment's silence, then the sound of the receiver being picked up.

"Gregory."

He felt a moment's shock at the sound of her voice. "Mother. Hi— Hello. I didn't know you were in LA."

"I came to see Jinny. Tell me."

"Didn't she tell you?"

Silence. His mother was never given to repeating herself.

"I've been arrested, Mom. In LA."

"For what?"

"Talking back to the police. Fighting."

"And that's all?"

"That's most of it."

"Gregory . . ."

"Yes. *Yes*, okay?"

A pause. "Have you told your father?"

88

"No . . . it might be simpler if we kept Papa out of this."

"A lot of things would be simpler if you only had one parent, but he deserves to know." Any chance to hear his voice.

"Mom, please."

"I'm coming down now. You're at Central?"

"Yeah. You're coming? I mean, you don't have to. All I need is someone to post bail."

"You're not going to need bail, Gregory. I'm on my way."

Within an hour she was standing in his cell, dressed in immaculate cream and amber, some invisible force repelling all the grime and filth of the place away from her.

Dressed in the ill-fitting prison-issue uniform they'd forced him into upon his arrival, Greg sat on a low lumpy bed in the corner, looking at his hands, his feet, anywhere but her. He wanted to worm his way down the drain in the corner, the one meant for piss and vomit and blood.

It wasn't the beautiful clothes, he realized, or the stylish sweep of her fringe. It was how she held herself. Hermetically sealed and completely in control.

"How could you be so stupid?"

"I don't know. I . . ."

"What?"

"I don't know."

"Nor do I. I don't have time for this. Jinny's sick, actually sick, not just trying to get attention."

Still Greg stared down at his hands pooled loose in his lap. "How bad?"

"We don't know. She'll be all right, hopefully, but she

89

needs some looking after right now. That's where I should be."

"I'm sorry."

She let out her breath. "All right. Let's collect your things."

"What things?"

"How would I know?"

He couldn't remember bringing anything with him, but his memories of the previous day seemed like a series of over-exposed photos. Everything too bright and nothing in focus.

"Okay . . . Thanks for coming, Mom."

"Well. This is supposed to be what mothers are for, isn't it?"

"Breaking you out of prison?"

"Coming when you call. Though I notice you didn't actually call me."

"I didn't think you were in LA."

"I thought you only wanted bail?"

He tried to think of a clever response, but he had nothing.

"I'm good for that at least, aren't I? I haven't . . . smothered you and fussed over you as you'd like—"

"—I never wanted—"

"—but whenever you've needed me, I was always there."

A bare-faced lie.

Greg let it go, stood. "I should have called. I guess I was just too . . . embarrassed." Embarrassed wasn't what he meant, but it would do.

"Well, it's done now. Come on."

★

90

She had brought him a damp flannel wrapped in wax paper, a comb and razor, and a change of tasteful and expensive clothes with the price tags still clipped neatly to their labels.

In a few minutes they transformed him from an untrustworthy future con into a young gentleman of means. The sort of guy you might ask to keep an eye on your bike while you dashed into the store.

The stony-faced officer at the custody desk didn't look fooled as he slid a thin metal tray over the counter. Greg peered down and saw the shredded remains of a bright blue dress lying like a songbird hit by a truck.

"Oh for God's sake . . ." said his mother. "Spiteful bastards. Take it, Greg. We'll throw it in the first trash can outside."

He reached out almost hesitantly, pinched each delicate strap between thumb and forefinger, and lifted the dress from the grubby tray. In the space beneath, one flip-flop and a pair of frilly black panties were obscenely entwined.

He could feel the officer staring at him, and even though his soul felt like a salted slug, he made himself lift his eyes. After a long moment the guard looked away. "You taking this shit, or what?"

"Watch your mouth you . . . civil servant." His mother snatched up the remaining articles and stuffed them into her dainty handbag, then took the dress from Greg and stuffed it in after. He was surprised she managed to make it all fit. "And you can tell your boss that I meant every word. I have dinner with the commissioner next month, and I can't wait to tell him how you assaulted my son who had committed no crime."

The custody officer muttered something inaudible, but

kept looking away. After that there were just a few forms to sign, then the twin doors of the police station were opening into a cauterizing Los Angeles morning.

Greg closed his eyes and took a long, deep breath— ignoring the car fumes and the thick tang of piss— letting the sun fall on his face. "Thanks, Mom."

He felt his mother move past him and opened his eyes to see her shoving her whole handbag unopened into the nearest trash can.

"Don't you need any—"

"—NOTHING I can't replace. I don't want to look at that . . . filth." She stood there a moment, the fierce light sinking into her jet-black hair without a trace, her body rigid.

Greg could only stand there, like a child, waiting.

"Phone me first next time," she said at last. "Please."

"Does Pa— does Dad know?"

"Yes. I sent him a telegram, and I phoned him right before I set out. It seemed unfair to keep him in the dark."

A bitter divorce, years of one-sided hate, countless petty cruelties, and still . . .

"How'd he take it?"

She turned, her face expressionless. "Not well. But you know how your father feels about all this. He was hoping you were getting back on track. You're due to be a father yourself."

"You think I don't know that?"

"Do *not* speak to me that way, Gregory. Honestly, you're giving me a headache."

". . . Sorry."

Greg looked away sulkily. A pretty blonde in high heels was clicking past. He put back his shoulders without thinking and was rewarded with an appreciative glance as she passed. One thing he had to be grateful to his father for was these shoulders. Sometimes at least.

"I saw that," said his mother, dryly.

"What?"

She shook her head. "You are your father's son, I suppose." But Greg knew that from her that could only be a compliment. "Now, I'll give him another call tonight. He'll have had a chance to think it over and calm down. We'll smooth it over. You were always his favorite."

But not yours. "Were."

"I should get back to Jinny."

"Let me buy you lunch, Mom."

She looked up the street as if expecting someone, then checked the delicate silver watch on her delicate white wrist. "I really shouldn't . . ."

"An hour. I haven't seen you in six months."

"Oh, the guilt game. Don't be so tiresome, Gigi—"

"—Greg—"

"—*Greg* then. Fine. An hour, but then I've got to get back."

"An hour's fine. Especially now I know all I have to do is get arrested for you to visit."

"Don't turn that charm on me, young man, I invented it." But she was smiling. He offered her his arm, and she took it.

When the phone call came the next morning, Greg was within arm's reach of the receiver.

He'd been sleeping on the couch. Shirley was in the bedroom, maybe packing, maybe just making noise so

93

he'd think she was. It didn't really matter either way. He was already thinking of the marriage in the past tense. Maybe it would end tomorrow, maybe next year, but it wouldn't last.

He couldn't blame Shirley. She'd done her best, and if he could have divorced the man who had gone out wearing that dress—the memory of it still made him want to curl up into a ball—he would have done it without hesitation. He envied her.

She'd probably come back. She'd always come back before, but for the first time he wasn't sure if that was a good thing.

The phone started ringing, but Greg ignored it for a while, watching the first of the dawn's rays slip through the blinds, thinking about the future.

After half a minute the unseen caller still hadn't given up. He sighed, reached over and groped for the receiver. "Hello?"

"Greg?" It was Jinny's voice, but without its usual confidence, the hidden smile that said life was a joke only she was getting.

"Jinny? What's wrong? Is everything okay?"

"Greg."

Something about the way she had said his name sent a prickle of dread down his spine.

"Greg. Gigi. It's your mother. I— I'm so sorry."

Jinny told him the story.

After finishing her evening phone call with the man she would always consider the one love of her life, Pauline Pfeiffer had dried her eyes and drunk a strong martini to settle her nerves before returning to bed.

Later, Jinny would remember that she had been complaining about stomach aches for days, had barely eaten. It hadn't seemed significant at the time. She'd thought her high-strung sister had an ulcer.

Hours slipped by. Coyotes came down from the hills and loped across the yard, silver-brushed in the moonlight. The only sound was the distant roar of the streets, and sometimes the wind moving listlessly through the leaves of the two palms in the front yard.

Then came the screams.

Laura, Jinny's partner, got there first. She found Pauline hunched over in bed, eyes closed, screaming and screaming with her hands over her belly as though something terrible was trying to claw its way out.

Jinny and Laura had carried her thrashing and howling to their little hatchback and set off down the twisty mountain roads like a one-boulder landslide—skipping red lights, skimming pedestrians, possibly killing a possum.

After only the most cursory of examinations, the doctors wasted no time bumping Pauline to the top of their priority list. Her screams were putting the other patients on edge, and doing nothing for their own hangovers. And in any case, her health insurance was deluxe premium.

Any hope the surgeon had of finding the problem vanished as soon as he pressed his scalpel into the pale skin of Pauline's swollen abdomen. It was like lancing a blister. A wellspring of blood rushed up and spattered onto the freshly scrubbed tiles of the surgery floor.

He did his best, desperately groping inside her for the rupture. He was not hungover. He was finely trained and exquisitely skilled and hopelessly outmatched.

Pauline died on a stainless steel operating table fifteen

minutes after she'd been admitted. She had no final words. No final thoughts beyond wanting the pain to end— wanting nothingness to take her—and relief when at last it did.

Greg and his mother had never been close, despite his best efforts. He had heard her say on more than one occasion that she could not begin to tolerate children until they were at least six or seven and capable of a little rationalism.

It hadn't been one of her party quips designed to shock. No, they'd never been close, yet the memories he did have were so strong . . .

Those few times she had reached out and placed her small hand on the nape of his neck. When he'd been able to bring his father out of one of his foul moods, and she'd kissed him on his forehead. When he'd been sick with measles and she spent half an hour reading to him at his bedside, the lamplight soft upon her skin.

And the memory, too, not of being with her, but of always wanting to be.

He had not been able to pair that cool, elegantly dressed deity with the slab of white meat laid out in the hospital morgue.

He had asked to see her, even though Jinny had already identified the body. He knew he would not be able to accept it as true if he didn't. Perhaps that had been a mistake. It still didn't feel real, but now every time he closed his eyes he saw that grimace: pain's signature indelible on his mother's face. He was afraid that one day it would be all he would remember of her.

Since then, Greg had been careful. He hadn't gone out, hadn't touched a drop of drink. He'd just sat on the couch, the TV turned way up. He could almost feel the tightrope beneath his feet, feel himself swaying.

Shirley had tried to talk to him, and he had seen her mouth moving, but she'd made no more sense than the TV, and after a while she'd shouted something and gone away. He supposed that was what she had been saying, that she was going away.

The sun was low, the windows recast into sheets of bronze and the shadows slabs of annihilation, when the phone on the side table rang.

Greg looked at the receiver rattling in its cradle, confused. Finally he blinked and picked it up.

"What?"

"That's some way to say hello."

Something in him twisted, and he fought back tears. "Papa."

"Gig."

"You've heard."

"Yes. It was no way for her to go."

"I'm sorry. I should have called. I couldn't think how to say it. I couldn't—"

A pause. His father could use pauses the way other men used fists. "You should have. But I can understand it, I guess."

"Are you okay?"

"Me? What are you talking about?"

"I don't know. It's a bit of a . . . a shock."

"Hm. Yes, I'm all right. Working like hell. Keeps the black ass at bay. You?"

"I don't know. I don't think it's sunk in yet."

"It was no way for her to go, a woman like her. We didn't . . . but that doesn't mean I . . ."

"No."

"I want you to come home. Get out of LA. Come visit. Patrick's coming. The three of us, we could go out on *Pilar* like old times. You might not get seasick this time. Water's been pretty swell, the last few days. Soft as a lamb and clear as gin."

Greg was almost leaning against the phone. The Cuban sun, soaking through skin and flesh and right into your bones, like you'd never be cold again. Bright green fields running on forever. The cool water lapping against the hull. "That sounds pretty good actually."

"Or shooting. You're still the best natural shot I've ever seen, Greg. If you'd only kept at it . . ."

"I know."

"You never could keep at any— I mean, we could all go shoot some birds again. You could show me up like you used to."

"Okay."

"You'll come?"

"I'll get on a plane tomorrow. It'd be good to see Patrick."

"Terrific. I'll have Maria do up the spare room. Can't have you bunking together any more."

On the other side of the phone someone said something. Mary, or some newer mistress? A cat mewed loudly, probably sitting on Papa's lap.

"She was fine yesterday," he said into the silence, not sure what it was he wanted. Perhaps just to talk about her. "She had the cops jumping to attention." Perhaps to talk it through, to make the death real and stop this limbo. "She had on that little white dress you bought her the year before you . . . separated. She'd looked after it. It looked brand new. She looked brand new." Or maybe to make her feel alive again. To share the memories only a family can hold.

Before the end, his father had treated his mother with a derision most men could not have mustered for their worst enemies—but surely he must have still had some feeling for her deep down.

It didn't occur to him that he had no idea where Shirley, now heavily pregnant, was.

"Well." His father gave a long sigh, like a burst of static from a radio tuned low. "She was under a lot of stress. A lot. She phoned me last night to talk about your . . . It wasn't an easy conversation."

"Oh, yeah."

"Gigi . . ."

"It wasn't . . ." Words failed him. He tilted his head back and looked up at the bloom of mottled mold on the ceiling. The apartment smelled of sweat and shame. "I'm sorry that happened."

"Sorry?"

Fuck his reticence. His famous fucking reticence. "Yes. I'm sorry. I fucked up, but it's done. Please let's not—"

"—You could at least sound ashamed." His father's voice had hardened.

"Aren't you always the one saying some things don't have to be said?"

"Don't get smart with me, Greg. Not after this."

"I'm not being smart, I'm just trying to—"

"—In fucking public, Greg! As if I'm not hounded by the papers enough."

"This isn't about you, Papa!"

"No, you shit. It's about you. What you're doing. What you're falling into. I thought you were getting clear of it. Getting a hold of it."

"I am!" Greg found himself standing, his knuckles white around the handpiece. "This was one slip. One fucking slip to stop me ripping my own fucking eyes out."

"Don't you dare feel sorry for yourself."

"Why not? Someone has to."

He waited for his father's sarcastic retort, but there was only silence.

"I'm dealing with it, Papa."

"I still don't understand how this happened." He only sounded tired now. "You were . . ."

"I'm dealing with it. I am."

"You call this dealing with it?"

"They took me in for starting a fight, that's all. It wasn't that big a deal."

"Not that big a deal?"

"No."

"Well, it killed your mother."

Greg paused. Licked his lips. Swallowed. "What?"

"It's poisoned you, every bit of you, and it just killed your mother. You can't pretend you don't see it."

And for a second Greg did see it. The way she had held her stomach as they left the cell. The weight she seemed to be carrying as she had looked at him on the street.

"I didn't— I don't—"

"—Heart attacks don't fall out of the fucking sky, Greg. Christ, are you incapable of thinking of anyone else? Can't you understand what your . . ." He took a deep steadying breath that said more than all his words together. "The stress. The shame. Do you have any idea what that does to a parent? The rot. Have you given a thought as to what it's done to us? Goddammit, Gigi, what else do you think killed her? At least be a man about it. Have some damn guts."

Greg said nothing, listening to his father's ragged breaths, then let the phone fall.

PART II

PART II

Havana

1947

"So, do you think you'll go down to the harbor with Papa today, Gigi?"

"Greg. You know I hate that stupid nickname. No, I don't think so."

"I always forget you don't care for the sea. Such a shame . . ."

"Yeah, I guess it is . . ."

Greg leaned back and felt the wicker chair creak beneath him. A sulky cat darted out from its shade, so fast he only saw its broken tail flick angrily before it had disappeared into the bushes. He felt a surge of jealousy. The days when he could just run away into the fields were long gone.

Mary straightened, her secateurs glinting as they caught the sun, only the inner blades dark with the bruised pulp of the flowers she was deadheading. She loved deadheading, cutting off the old growth.

"Well, probably best you give him a bit of space right now, after your little . . . well."

"Yeah."

She smiled her strange, meaningless smile, and bent

back to the bushes beneath the porch railing. The clean sound of steel on steel filled the air.

Greg didn't smile back. Again the question rose to his lips, and again did not pass them: *What does he see in you?*

He still wasn't quite sure where he stood with his father's newest wife. In a strange way he resented Mary as he never had Martha, even though Martha was the one who'd actually forced his mother out.

Against every expectation, he had always felt something like satisfaction whenever he saw Martha kiss his father's whiskery cheek, or found her sunbathing by the pool, or heard her typing noisily away in her own study.

It made no sense, but he had felt it most after one of his mother's long calls with his brother, or when he recalled her at some drunken party telling everyone again *how much* she had wanted to give Ernest a daughter, how disappointed they had both been at two boys.

He'd been able to talk to Martha about anything: whatever book he happened to be reading, geopolitics, the intricacies of baseball. She'd seemed to know everything about everything. Even now he had fond memories of the two of them eating pineapple and drinking martinis by the pool, of mock-sparring with her raptor-like intellect that had proven more than a match for his mother's.

And, perhaps most surprisingly of all, she had enjoyed his company. He'd never doubted that. Sometimes, after a big fight with Papa, she had sought him out too, and he'd listened patiently as she'd eviscerated his father with words, fileted him with a fury Greg couldn't understand—how could you love someone and hate them at the same time?

Mary was more rabbit than raptor. Perfectly nice as long as everything was to her liking, but that was all. Every year, when school broke for the summer and Greg and Patrick were packed off to Cuba to their mother's quiet relief, the three of them resumed the same old game of polite nothings as though they had never met. Greg was certain Mary would really have rather they spent the summer with their mother—not that she'd ever tell Papa that.

Plus there'd been the small matter of the theft of her underwear . . . That probably hadn't helped.

Papa had taken it very badly.

Normally, Greg might have tried to make some excruciating small talk, but right now he felt too restless, too unfocused. It wasn't a bad feeling—he felt good, like he had a full tank of gas and wanted to use it.

So, when Patrick came slamming through the door and twirling Papa's car keys on one finger, Greg jumped up without a clue where he was going.

"Pass me the keys, Patrick. I'm driving."

Patrick didn't even glance at him. "Maybe when you've passed your test."

"This isn't Miami. Give me the keys or I'll lie in front of the car."

"I'll drive over you."

"No you won't. Papa would kill you. He loves that car and it'd take ages to get all my guts out of the undercarriage." The ghost of Rodolfo flashed in his mind, but he ignored it.

"Fine," Patrick scratched at a fresh pimple on his chin, "but when you get pulled over I'm not saying I was driving."

"Fat chance. You know I drive better than you." It was the sort of thing he'd tried to stop saying, the sort of thing a shitty little brother would say. He wanted Patrick to snap something ratty back at him, to make them equal, but he only frowned and threw Greg the keys.

Greg caught them and slid over the hood of the car, trying to look stupid and hoping his brother would say something.

Sure enough: "How hot is that metal?"

"Hot enough I think I just cooked my ass medium rare. I never learn."

Patrick laughed, and it was okay again.

Greg dropped in behind the wheel. He loved everything about this car. The smell of it, the smooth feel of the leather, even now when the air was stuffy and the seats roasting. Normally, the interior was cool and dark from sleeping in the garage, but Papa had driven home from a bar last night and left it sprawled over the drive like a murder victim.

"Where are we going?" he asked as Patrick plopped into the seat beside him.

"Post office. Papa's ordered me a new Scott and I want to see if it's shown up. I'll use it after lunch if I can."

"Right."

A new twelve gauge. And a sickeningly expensive one. Unlike Greg, who had lost interest in shooting as he did most things once he'd gotten good at them, Patrick still went up to the Cazador at least twice a week to keep his aim in. How much of that was to please their father, Greg chose not to guess.

The engine purred into life at the first turn of the key, precision engineering at its finest, and Greg swung out through the gates. As soon as they were on clear road he let his foot ease down and felt the car leap forward, eager. Something in him buzzed in response, heady with the power of it: a thousand pounds of honed steel attuned to his slightest command.

"Easy, Gig," Patrick said, his voice soft but his hand clenched on his knee.

For a second, Greg was tempted to slam on the gas, let the beast run and turn the world into a blur. But Patrick's knuckles were white. He made himself ease off.

"What's with you today?"

"Nothing. Relax, Patrick, we're the only car on the road."

"It's not just that. You've been . . . weird the last few days."

"Weird?"

"Jumpy." A one-shouldered shrug. Patrick wasn't looking at him, choosing instead to stare out over the heaving carpet of sugar cane still cat's-eye bright from last night's rain. Greg stared at the back of his brother's head a moment, then shrugged in turn.

He wasn't going to let Patrick get him down. He didn't feel weird. He felt good. And okay, maybe him feeling good was pretty weird these days, but who cared?

Greg put the window down and rested his elbow in the wind, then flinched when the chrome trimming singed the thin skin of his underarm.

Patrick shook his head, still not looking. "It's true. You never learn."

"Shut up."

"Don't worry. It's one of your charms."

"Pretty fucked-up charm."

"Those are the best sort."

Some kids were playing in the dusty road. One had his shirt over his arm, the other held his fingers pointed at his temples. Matadors. Greg smiled, and slowed to a crawl as they parted for him.

"I can't believe their parents let them play out on the roads alone," Patrick said softly. "Anything could happen to them."

"We used to."

"And look what happened."

Greg felt that like a blow. There was a long pause. He pressed his foot on the accelerator once the kids were well clear.

"So, what are your fucked-up charms?" he asked as they got back underway.

"What?"

"Fucked-up charms. If not learning is one of mine, what are yours?"

"Me? I don't have any. Plodding reliability, that's me through and through. The bell curve of my life is a straight line."

"It's served you pretty well."

"What?"

Greg eased his arm back out the window. It still hurt, but this time he didn't let himself pull away. "I'm just saying, you played the long game, and it worked out. There's only one person here Papa can't look at without flinching."

He glanced from the road to find Patrick staring at him. "Where's this coming from, Gig?"

Greg didn't know. His mouth didn't seem fully his own. This was Patrick, the only one who'd ever really stuck with him.

"I'm just saying. Mediocrity worked out for you."

Patrick was silent, and Greg couldn't look at him. Nothing felt real.

They came up behind a cart piled mountainous with pineapples, and the car felt like an extension of his body as he shifted up a gear and swung out to overtake. Green and orange flashed by the window, and for a second he was tempted to reach out and grab one as he passed.

Fields gave way to suburbs. He glanced into the rear-view mirror and saw a plume of dust roaring in his wake, like the tail of a comet, like he was falling from heaven but would never hit the ground.

Finally, Patrick spoke. "You're going too fast, Gig."

"No I'm not."

"Gig."

"Why are you always such a damn sissy, Patrick?"

"Gigi!"

A shape swift and slender as a bird darted out of a drive-way and into the street. Greg had only an instant's glimpse of a dark, serious face—a scar tracing from a bottom lip to the crook of a chin—before he was yanking the wheel so hard to the right the whole world twisted over and his only thought as the first crunch of the impact shook through him was: *not again.*

He woke to pain. The last thing he could remember was the car spinning like a girl turning cartwheels. It felt like he'd ended the right way up. There was that at least.

He opened his eyes, but there was only a blur, like those paintings his father had shown him in books, sworn to take him to see when they went on that long-promised trip to France and Spain. Swirling beauty, a hint of a smudge enough to convey some peasant boy lean and full of life.

Some boy . . .

And suddenly all he could see was Rodolfo, seven years

dead, as he had only ever seen him in his imagination: his stomach purpled and so deeply crushed his spine was jutting up like a ruined train track beneath the skin.

A horror tore through him then. And it was deeper even than that one awful death. It was deeper than anything he had a name for. It was everything.

Then, as quick as it came, it was gone, leaving him with only normal human panic, normal fear.

His vision began to clear. He forced himself to sit up, wincing as his neck gave a little throb, and took in the ruined front of the car, the pulped trunk of the tree they had come to rest against.

"Shit."

Rodolfo leaped again into his mind, the real memory this time: the dark stain he had found on the dusty road the next morning, the smear where his friend had dragged his ruined body.

The door opened with a groan and he fell out into the dust, ignoring all his aches and pains as he stared into the shadowy space beneath the car, jagged with bits of chassis and an axle as thick as his arm that had snapped like a match. And nothing else.

He looked back down the road: no huddled form. He pressed his brow to the ground and sobbed with relief.

A moment later a groan brought him back to himself, one word electric in his brain.

Patrick.

He threw himself round to the door. His brother was slumped against the dashboard, and Greg couldn't figure out how he'd made a sound because he was out stone-cold. Or . . .

"Patrick." He pushed his way into the car. "Patrick. No

no no, Patrick." Greg eased his brother back into his seat and saw that blood was gushing from his nose.

"Patrick."

A lump the size of a fist was beginning to rise on his brother's temple, a darkening bruise mantled over it.

"Patrick."

It suddenly occurred to Greg that he shouldn't be moving him. What if he'd broken his back or his neck? What if even now the delicate nerves inside his spine were fraying against some shattered jut of bone? Should he hold him still? Should he ease him back down? He could feel himself panicking, losing his head.

"Patrick."

I've killed my brother. The thought was a death sentence. Immediate and certain. There are some things you can't live through.

He laid Patrick down as gently as he could and slipped back out into the hot sunlight.

Sure enough, a small crowd of locals had gathered round at a cautious distance. Every house had someone standing in the shade of its porch as if expecting a parade. He scanned the street. This was not the barrio; there were a few cars here and there, old but meticulously maintained. He looked up. No telephone wires.

"Shit."

One of the watching men was standing beside a grand old Packard Runabout, its fading canvas roof the only sign it was almost as old as Greg.

"Hey." Greg waved his arms, wincing as something grated in his collar, but ignoring the pain. "Hey. Señor! Señor, por favor, ayudame. Mi padre. Mi Padre Hemingway. El gran escritor de la Finca La Vigía! Dile qué pasó.

113

Por favor." The rough Spanish stumbled from his lips, and the man watched impassive, his arms crossed, his eyes sunk deep in his weathered face. Then, with a soft huff, he turned and opened the door to his car.

"Gracias! Gracias, señor!" Greg yelled after him as the car pulled out of its covered alcove on what was all of the man's property and turned back the way they had come, tootling off up the road at a breakneck twenty.

"Gracias," Greg whispered again.

Then he was back in the car. Checking that his brother was still breathing, trying to judge if any of his limbs were broken.

"It's okay, Patrick. You're going to be okay, I promise. Can you hear me? Patrick!"

His brother had opened his eyes. Both were blood-shot, the tender edges of the lids a deep scarlet. Patrick said nothing, only frowned at Greg as though he was the strangest thing he'd ever seen.

"I'm sorry, Pat. I'm sorry."

In the hospital, the silence was suffocating. The only sound was the steady ticking of the old clock on the wall.

Greg sat on the wooden bench that lined one side of the corridor, his shoulders bent, both arms on his knees and his hands clasped in front of him.

Further down, his father was crouched in an almost identical pose. Greg didn't look at him, but he could feel him there. His silence oozed from his every pore, filled the air like smoke.

Greg wished he would say something. Anything. Swear at him, blame him, curse him. Maybe even comfort him.

But there was only silence.

At the end of the corridor, a doctor emerged through a set of swinging doors. Boy and man lifted their heads like gun dogs, but the doctor did not so much as glance at them as he strode by, his heels cracking against the tiles.

For an instant, before he lowered his head, Greg saw the ugly yellow bruise developing along the side of his father's jaw, and his stomach snarled in on itself. It couldn't be true that Patrick had done that. Not Patrick.

The delayed scent of iodine wafted over them in the doctor's wake.

His father cleared his throat, but said nothing.

They had tried keeping Patrick at home at first. The ancient local doctor who had driven out to the finca recommended bed rest, ice packs always against his temples. Rest and darkness and peace.

Greg had haunted the house like a mangy cat. Unable to sit still or focus on anything, half eaten alive by guilt, but aware wherever he ended up of how unwelcome he was, how judged. Aware that he deserved it.

Papa had seemed possessed. He had spent every night on the floor beside Patrick's bed, spent every waking minute sitting in the little chair at his side just watching him sleep, his bullet-hole eyes unwavering as though his will alone was all that was holding his child in the world.

He barely slept. Didn't eat at all that Greg saw. By the evening of the second day he was cracking under the pressure. He cut his hair short and tried to dye it red with a bottle of Mary's formula, only to come to his senses halfway through and end up with cotton candy fuzz. It would have been funny, any other time. Instead, it seemed somehow obscene.

For all that the old man had never been much good at showing it, Greg had never doubted that his father loved his middle son. But he had never felt it so powerfully, never seen it so naked and unashamed.

Greg had to wonder if he'd have been quite so broken if it was his youngest son lying there, then felt ashamed. Papa was right. He was rotten.

Through the entire ordeal he had barely glanced at Greg. Not since he had first looked through the open door of the smashed car and seen Greg cradling his brother against his chest, his shirt soaked with blood. There had been one look of absolute contempt, and that was all.

It was a look Greg had become familiar with over the last few years. Things like the shooting competition had pushed it down into deeper waters for a while, but it was always there, waiting for an excuse to surface. Now it was jumping clear, dancing on its fin like one of the great black marlins his father loved.

At first, Patrick had seemed to get better. The swelling had slowly but surely gone down. His sleep had seemed less absolute. He tossed and turned, murmured as if caught in a vivid dream.

Greg had watched it all from the doorway. He hadn't been able to make himself enter the room and face his father's silence, his brother's suffering. He was a coward. This whole thing had finally shown him that. All he wanted to do was run away, and—if his brother died—blow his brains out.

His grandfather had shot himself before Greg was born. Papa had always despised him for the weakness of it, claimed to have none of that craven instinct himself, but now Greg knew it slept in his father's blood, waiting for the chance to emerge in the next, weaker generation.

Then, just like that, Patrick had woken up.

Greg had been sitting in the hall. His legs were outstretched before him as he softly rapped the back of his head against the wall, feeling the ache in the back of his skull grow, wondering how it would feel a thousand times worse.

In the main house, Mary started playing music, then thought better of it. The dull rip of the needle leaving the record had seemed to blur into his father's cry of joy, and then into a jagged shout.

Greg had been on his feet in seconds, and even so he was only through the door in time to see his father and brother spilling from the bed together. Papa still had his arms half around Patrick as if caught mid-embrace, but Patrick was thrashing his way free, trying to bite and kick and punch his father any way he could. Trying to kill him—his face said it clearly—trying to tear him apart.

There had been no trace of Patrick in that face. His brother had trickled out with all the darkness and blood and he had left this animal behind. His brother was smeared over the car's ruined dashboard, drying in the Cuban sun.

Greg threw himself forward. His brother was still taller, but Greg had been stronger for years now, and fueled by terror he lifted Patrick like a doll.

"Don't hurt him!" his father bellowed, as if Patrick wasn't that very moment trying to twist his head around and sink his teeth into Greg's face. When he couldn't reach he began to buck, thrashing and writhing until the back of his head cracked into the bridge of Greg's nose.

Greg saw white, and for a moment his grip must have slackened, because Patrick was crawling around in his arms, his wide eyes blazing.

Then Papa was there, calmly bundling Patrick up in his blankets and grappling him with one arm.

"You okay?" He lifted his free hand to Greg's chin, turned his head.

For that moment there was nothing between them, only his father's clear attention examining him like an arrowhead plucked from a stream. Greg felt suddenly aware of the smoothness of his own chin, and the roughness of Papa's fingertips. He wanted to lean against him, to press his brow into the hollow of his shoulder. Instead he said: "Yes, sir."

"Good. Call a taxi."

So they sat. Waiting. Longing for news, and dreading it.

Greg played the moments before the crash over and over in his head. His brother begging him to slow down, knuckles white. The world a bright rush. His own chest a firework ready to burst. Everything had felt so right in that moment. Now it seemed like madness. He could not begin to fathom what instinct had pushed that accelerator down.

I'm just saying. Mediocrity worked out for you.

They both jumped up as the doors banged open again, and this time a different doctor came clipping toward them. He whispered to Papa in soft and lilting Spanish. Greg could barely hear him, but he knew all he needed from the man's face.

His father hesitated a moment, then nodded, his expression that of a man forced to chew glass.

When the doctor returned to his unknown world behind the door and Papa had sunk back into his former pose, Greg remained standing, waiting until suddenly all his guilt and shame thorned into anger. "What? What the fuck did he say, Papa?"

His father regarded him coldly. "Electroshock," he said at last. "They're blasting his brain. Trying to reset it, or something."

Greg slumped as the anger ran out of him.

Then they heard it. A sound that Greg would never forget.

From behind the closed doors came a boom. A low, bone-aching grunt of power. Then another. And another. Like huge, storm-tossed waves throwing themselves against the cliffs again and again and again.

It was all Greg could hear. The booming of the waves running through his brother's head.

Tanzania

1954

The fire was burning low.

A hyena gibbered somewhere nearby, the sound bubbling with insanity. Greg didn't bother looking up as the laughter grew closer, closer, then gradually drifted away. The Serengeti was saturated with moonlight, silver-etched all the way to the horizon, but he knew he wouldn't have seen a thing.

Patrick was out there somewhere, moving through the bush as silently as any predator, trying to use this bright night to finally see a hunt in action.

Greg shifted his daughter in his arms. Lorian was in a deep sleep, untroubled by the sounds of the night, her normally surly face relaxed and open as she dreamed.

He and Shirley had done the right thing, coming out here. They'd been rough years since his mother had died, and he couldn't remember when he'd last felt at peace like this.

"What was *that*?" Shirley asked from their tent, poking her head from the safety of the mosquito net.

"Just a hyena," Greg said, trying to give her a reassuring

smile. "They talk big, but they're scavengers, they won't come near the fire."

"It sounded awful."

"Nothing to worry about."

She hesitated a moment, then slapped her cheek and made a small sound of revulsion as she examined the palm of her hand. "Are you coming to bed?"

"In a minute. It's peaceful out here."

"Horrific, you mean."

He tensed, waiting for the inevitable.

"How much longer, Greg?"

He sighed. There it was.

"Don't sigh at me. It's been a month. A month of bugs and dirty clothes and sunburn. I'm not being unreasonable."

"I know you're not."

"So?"

He rolled his shoulders, trying not to jostle Lorian as he did so. "I don't know."

"Days? Weeks? I need to—"

"—I said I don't know!" Lorian immediately started awake with a little gulp. He tried rocking her, hushing her, but she was having none of it, and her mewling quickly turned into an open-mouthed wail.

"For God's sake . . ." Shirley squirmed out of the tent, her pale bare arms luminous in the moonlight. "Give her here."

"It's fine. I've got her." He tried changing how he was holding her, but it made no difference.

"Greg. Just give her to me."

He handed the girl over, trying not to feel resentful when she fell to snuffling as soon as her mother's arms wrapped around her. As though it wasn't Shirley that had wanted to leave the girl back in America with some nanny. He was the one who put his foot down, who insisted they all had to stay together, and now here she was, squalling every time he picked her up.

He clenched his hands into fists, fighting down the poison. He knew he was circling a bout of depression like a fleck of scum circling a drain, but it was hard to resist the negativity it cast over everything. He needed to relax, let all this flow over him. Find that calm place and—"

"—so, you never said. How long?"

He snapped. "As long as I say, Shirley!"

She bridled, rocking Lorian against her chest. "I am not—"

"—then go, if you hate it so much!" He pressed his fists to his temples. "You think I want to listen to you complaining every second of the damn day? That I want to hear what a mistake this all was? Run back to America with your tail between your legs, just like always."

She took a step forward. If she hadn't been holding Lorian, Greg thought she might have taken a swing at him. "*Me* run away? Why do you think we're here in the middle of fucking nowhere, you self-righteous prick? But you're right. I don't know what I'm staying for. This is crazy. You're crazy."

"I am *not* crazy."

She gave him a long look that worked its way into him like a barbed hook. He'd told her that the clothes had been a passing compulsion, a random by-product of the mania, and she'd believed him, but that couldn't undo what she'd seen in that cinema bathroom. She'd watched him at his most manic, peered down at him in his darkest pit of despair, and somehow she'd still stuck with him.

But he could see it in her eyes now. She was done.

"Lorian and I are going home tomorrow." She turned and carried the girl back to their tent. "You stay here. Keep shooting your little gun and see if it fixes anything. Waste your life if you want, but you're not wasting ours."

Greg took a breath to say something cutting, and then let it out in a long sigh. "Okay."

She looked surprised for a second. He could only see half her face by the firelight, and what came next was too subtle for him to catch. "All right. Good."

She ducked into the dark mouth of the tent, and pulled it closed behind her.

They'd come out here to get away from things, to leave their problems behind. What had they been thinking? Greg was holding all their problems in his hands, and there was no running from them.

Patrick stole back into the camp an hour later, materializing from the moon-soaked dark without a sound, light-footed and loosely jacketed against the cold. Greg had only been in Tanzania for a month, while Patrick was nearly a year in and most of that working as a guide, but it still surprised Greg how at home his bookish brother seemed in the savanna.

"Any luck with the lions?" Greg asked.

"Not tonight." Patrick dropped down on the other side of the fire, his gun over his knees. "They started moving over toward the flats, and the wind would have been behind me if I'd followed them."

Greg tossed him his hip flask and watched him take a long pull of brandy.

"Thanks, I needed that. Anyway, I only need to get lucky once and—" Patrick paused, frowning. "What's up, Gig?"

Greg thought he'd been doing a great job of acting happy and relaxed. He could fool most people easily enough, but somehow Patrick always saw through the bullshit.

"I might need to sleep in your tent tonight, Pat."

"Oh . . . bad?"

"She's heading home tomorrow. Taking Lorian."

"Right . . ." Patrick eyed the sealed face of Greg's tent, but asked no questions. He'd always been good at minding his own business and had ignored Greg and Shirley's endless fights as though they were a feature of the weather. It was one of many things Greg admired about his brother. "All right, but you're out in the bush if you snore."

Greg leaned into the joke gratefully. "There's lions roaring half the night, but you're worried I'll keep you up?"

"The lions aren't sleeping next to me."

"You're going to get yourself killed one of these nights, you know."

"You're the voice of caution now? That's got to be a first."

"I didn't say you shouldn't do it. So long as you're aware it's slow-motion suicide."

"I hate to break it to you, Greg, but that's life."

The first rule of bushcraft was that you didn't stray from the fire after sunset. Night was when the sleepy sunbathing predators unsheathed their claws and went prowling, and they could see a hell of a lot better in the dark than any intrepid hunter.

Patrick knew that, of course, but he still went out on these bright nights. Now he took out a cloth and started to carefully clean his gun, though he hadn't fired it. "I want to see a pride hunting, Greg. Just once. I don't know how much longer I'll be here."

"You planning on packing up?"

"Maybe, I don't know. I can't spend my life in the bush."

"Why not? This is the classic career path for Harvard graduates."

"You're hilarious, Greg."

"Honestly, I still don't understand why you came out here in the first place."

"I like nature, I like the big sky."

"I like Scotch, I'm not moving to Scotland."

"Hilarious."

The jokes felt hollow in his mouth. His wife was leaving him. He had no plans for tomorrow, let alone the rest of his life. No amount of pretending was going to save him from the trough he could feel coming.

Greg had started to think of the slow cycles of depression and mania as peaks and troughs, waves that lifted and dropped him and were outside his control. He'd felt this one coming before the argument with Shirley—maybe it had caused the argument with Shirley—but now it was really settling in. Tomorrow was going to be a hard day.

Patrick was still looking at him. Had he missed some step in the conversation? He shrugged, tried to pick up where he'd left off. "I just don't get it. I always assumed you'd end up in a law firm or a college or something."

Patrick frowned. "So did I, but . . . I don't know, I won't do this forever. I guess I didn't want to be a sissy." He shook his head and laughed. "Jesus Christ."

Greg said nothing. He understood. Of course he did. In a way they were both here for the same reason: to feel like a hero from one of Papa's books, the sort of man he'd approve of.

Patrick returned to polishing his gun. "I was never like you, Greg. I was never good at the things he loved, but I could stick at things. That was one thing you could never do."

Greg felt the truth of it like a slap.

"You know, I used to wish you'd let me win sometimes, so maybe he'd look at me like he looked at you, but"—he lifted his head with a smile, his voice abruptly switching from melancholy to cheerful—"instead I ended up in the asshole of Africa nannying morons who don't know which end of the gun goes bang."

"Well," Greg said slowly, still a little thrown. "I guess we had a weird childhood, being raised by an icewoman and Hercules. It knocked a few screws loose in both of us."

"Oh, come on. Mom wasn't that bad."

"For you maybe."

"You—" Patrick bit back whatever harsh words he'd been forming, but Greg didn't need to hear them to know what he was going to say.

"You can say it, Pat. You should be pissed off, after what I did . . ."

"Don't start this again."

"Why not? It's true. I—"

                              "—No it's not! You fucked up, that's all. You didn't kill her."

Greg knew that wasn't right, but just hearing his brother say it . . . He felt a burn behind his eyes and had to lean his head back, squeeze his eyes shut. This was the trough, not him—tears were constantly waiting for the slightest excuse to fall. "That's the problem. I just keep fucking up . . ."

Patrick gave him some time then tentatively tried, "You know, you could . . ." Greg shook his head, but he plowed on. "I know you don't want to hear it, but—"

"—I'm not having shocks, Pat. I keep telling Papa that, and he keeps going on about it."

"You're talking again?"

"Only letters. Not many, but . . . I've tried to patch things up a bit. Apologized." It had been hard work. They were both stubborn, bruised, but maybe there had been a few hints at parental tenderness amidst the sideways insults and barbed questions.

Patrick finally finished cleaning his already spotless gun and resorted to staring into the fire. "I bet he'd like to see you. You know, in the flesh."

"I'd take that bet."

"He loves you, Greg. You only argue because you're so similar. I sometimes think that's why he . . . you know." He shook his head. "He just worries. I know the shocks seem . . . drastic, but they work. He saw them save my life."

"I know . . . I was there too." Greg remembered sitting in that hospital corridor, listening to the pounding. A shiver ran through him.

"A reset," Patrick said, as gentle as someone easing a worm onto a hook. "That's what the doctors always called it. A way of getting your brain back on an even keel. You're like a lighthouse these days, and if something messed you up, maybe a reset's exactly what you need."

Greg stalled, trying to think of some excuse. Patrick was

right, he didn't have anything to lose, so why was he so hesitant?

"I'll think about it."

"That's fine. It's an option is all."

"All right." Greg shook his head, trying to clear his thoughts and failing. "I'm going to sleep."

"There's a spare roll under my camp bed. Make sure you shake the spiders out."

"Sounds cozy."

"If that's not good enough I've got a patch of scrub with your name on it. Good luck shaking the spiders out of that."

Dawn was barely beginning as Greg stepped out from beneath the canvas.

He didn't bother to light a fire or cook breakfast. There was a constant twisting in his gut like a hand was in there, dirty fingers winding through his intestines.

Twilight. Alone. No supplies. No means of getting help. Nothing but his rifle. Every rule of hunting broken, and Greg was no Patrick—he was still a clumsy interloper here. This was insane.

He walked out into the bush.

This was what a Hemingway hero would do. Leave his troubles behind to hunt and commune with brutal nature. Find himself, cure himself by willpower alone.

It was all such bullshit, but here he was.

The sun seemed to jump up all at once, bloody and dripping, and the blue sky unrolled over the huge sweep of the Serengeti. Greg had thought he'd seen big skies back in America, or on the sea, but the curve of the world fell away faster here, heaven just an arm's reach away.

It was too much. He had to look down.

When had it gotten this bad? It felt like his mind had been flayed, everything was so raw.

To his left, his own distorted shadow stretched off into infinity. To his right, a vague cluster of silhouettes moved cautiously in the morning haze. Gazelle probably, or impala.

Further on, the silhouettes of a small herd of giraffes moved with awkward grace. Greg looked at them critically, feeling the weight of his gun on his shoulder, but made no move toward them.

He knew what he was after today. Only one thing could fill this emptiness.

He carried on, pushing through a thick clump of low scrub that all the guides had told him was to be avoided— the perfect place for a lion to ambush an unwary hunter. He moved recklessly, forcing the brittle branches aside, not caring as they scratched his legs. The dust puffed from beneath his heavy boots.

It reminded him of being a boy in Cuba, when his father had taken Greg and Patrick to the boxing rings that were really no more than bare patches cleared in the forest.

The dirt there had looked perpetually soaked, darkened by the spilled sweat of a thousand fighters, but when the first pair took to the ring it had always bruised up just like this beneath their feet, spooling through the lights of torches hung low in the crooked trees as though cringing away from such violence.

Greg had been a good fighter. He had beaten every boy his own age, and the locals had cheered that the son of the great man should have the same greatness in him—perhaps even more, who knew? Then his father had put him up against bigger and bigger boys until he had come back with his face so bloodied and swollen that at last even Martha had said enough.

At first Greg had thought his Papa was putting him against those bigger boys because he was sure he could beat them, because he believed in his son. But as the fights went on and Greg kept winning his father only seemed to get angrier and angrier. Then the boys had gotten too big, and Greg had started losing fast and hard, and that hadn't made Papa happy either.

At the time it had made no sense, but looking back it seemed obvious. Despite all the myth-building, all the half-truths, all the dirty sucker punches . . . Papa couldn't fight for shit. Not really. Sure, he could knock around thin-armed poets in Paris and untrained locals in Cuba, but when it came to *real* boxing he was all strength and fury. No great skill.

He pressed forward with his feet even as his thoughts looped and tangled.

It killed your mother—

       —Patrick's vague, cotton wool gaze after the shocks. No more his brother than if they had wheeled out a doll from the theater—

       —The whole golden bloom of his childhood growing steadily darker, breaking apart around him. And trying to stop it even as he knew that it was *him*. He was breaking it. He was ruining everything—

       —His mother on the sidewalk outside the prison, just looking at him. Saying nothing and everything. Gone now, because—

       —Little Lorian's face over Shirley's

shoulder, unreadable like some Attic mask. Him feeling only relief—

—*It killed your mother.*

—*It killed your mother.*

—*It killed your mother.*

He squeezed his eyes shut, and then he heard it: a low rumble, summer thunder with no clouds in the sky.

Greg stopped, listening, and for a blessed moment his mind was empty.

It came again. Faint but powerful. It reminded him of swimming as a boy, diving in the bay and hearing the thrumming engine of a cargo ship a horizon away.

He dropped down to the ground. Pressed his still-damp cheek to that soft, barren earth, and listened.

For a long time there was nothing. Only the steady beating of his heart, the buzz of a mosquito, the hushed whisper of the dry grass.

Then . . . There. Closer. Greg could feel it lingering in his gut.

He looked about. He needed to do this now. His thoughts were circling wider and wider, with no center to hold them. He needed to act.

The land was flat here besides a few low clumps of scrub that could never have covered the bulk of a herd. But there was no sign of them.

The gun was still cold in his hands, though the sun beat down on it, though it was slippery with his sweat. He tried to focus.

The night Rodolfo had died, Greg had not let him get even to first base. So desperate to impress his father, that looming monolith in the gloom, so goddamn desperate. Every nerve and sinew stretched to the limit, ready to snap like guitar strings. Never once had it occurred to him that Rodolfo or Patrick or anyone else might want to win as much as he did, might want to feel good.

He checked the chamber again. The round sat there, seemingly inert, but Greg wasn't fooled. He could feel it waiting.

Again came the rumble, and then a real trumpet, a circus toot. Greg turned a hard right and followed the sound, snapping twigs and scattering stones with every step, all caution cast aside.

His mother gave a soft little huff as they walked out onto the streets of LA. So tired. Trying to speak to him. Trying to say, *Please, Greg, I can't take it any more.*

He was almost jogging, squeezing the gun in both hands, squeezing it so tight the glass might crack as he stood silent on the stairs, listening to his father rage.

To watch it all come to nothing.

I don't want to look at that . . . filth.

You see, Gig? I knew there was nothing wrong with you.

It killed your mother.

The ground dipped, and there they were.

In the cupped hands of the savanna was a pool of Serengeti sky. The elephants strode through it, vast and serene like Zeppelins.

There were more young than Greg remembered, lingering by the edge. An old matriarch lifted her trunk and let cooling water flood along the back of another, tracing over every detail.

Greg had never seen this family before. He stood, breathing so heavily it sounded like sobbing, watching them.

132

The matriarch spotted him standing on the rise of the land. She eyed him, her ears flapping uncertainly, then began wading toward the shore.

The others followed, a great troop of them lumbering toward him, dripping as they emerged, their feet sinking deep into the soft mud then collecting powdered earth as they came up the bank. It looked like they were wearing socks.

Greg almost laughed. Instead, something finally broke inside him, and he closed his eyes, let the gun fall as he dropped to his knees.

The soft boom of feet came closer, and a rough snort, like his father blowing pencil shavings from his desk. Greg opened his eyes, his fractured mind almost expecting to see his Papa sitting there.

Instead, a brown eye surveyed him, lined in soft lashes that flickered as it blinked, dark and vast and intelligent, looking down at him with a mild curiosity. Its gaze swallowed him.

A rumble that made his bones ache. She was huge. Each tusk weighed more than Greg's whole body. He could feel death closing in.

He closed his eyes again. Waited. Then felt something brush against him.

He tensed, hoping it would be quick.

Footsteps.

Light and shadow sluiced over him. Bright to dark. Bright to dark. To bright.

Greg knelt alone at the lake's edge, his gun shining beside him, his shoulder damp where she had touched him.

★

Patrick was cooking breakfast at the fire. He looked up startled as Greg stumbled into the camp. "Heya, Greg, early hunt? Where's your gun— Greg?"

"I'll do it."

"Do what?"

"The shocks. I'll do it.'

Rochester, Minnesota

1954

The booming was everywhere.

It did not seem to come from outside him but from within. Steady, rhythmic, like huge waves breaking against jagged cliffs. Nothing could resist such a force forever. Whole continents slipped away until the ocean was seamless.

And still it did not cease, did not relent. There was only the pounding, breaking down his fears and his terrors and his thoughts into fragments, into shards he could not hold onto, and still the booming went on and on and on, until the shards were dust, a sand that could not abide but only flow, slipping away through a hole that was once a man.

It was bliss.

Greg woke up clean, like a spring lamb, or a new sheet of writing paper before you've sullied it with ink.

They left him propped up in a corner chair with padded arms, and he was quite content. He'd only just woken up, but still he felt exhausted, as though he'd gone ten rounds with a giant.

He knew that was due to the shocks, because they'd

told him so, but he didn't know how they knew, nor how he had come to be here, nor what he'd been doing before. But that made perfect sense. New things did not have a past, and he was freshly minted.

When the memories did begin to return, they came back slowly. Cautious as field mice. He let them come at their own pace, feeling nothing but a mild curiosity as he remembered who he was.

Gregory. Greg. Gigi.

He'd come back from Africa recently, though he wasn't quite sure why he'd been there.

He could remember very strongly now how scared he had been when they'd fitted the electrodes to his temples, terrified, but less scared of the shocks than of walking back out into the world as he was. He supposed it should have upset him, remembering something like that, but it didn't. What he had done to his mother, his breakdown, the no doubt dramatic changes they had now forced upon his brain, the soulless room he sat in, the bright breezy world beyond the window—it all seemed very distant. Or, not distant, but hollow somehow. Thought without feeling. Action without intention. His life was just a sequence of events. No more, no less.

Occasionally, a nurse would come by and wipe his chin.

Once, a doctor came, and said how pleased he was with the treatment. They had *run him hard*—the epileptic fits the shocks induced lasting 90 seconds at a time—but Greg's body had held up like a champion's. Greg must have his father's stamina. The doctor was a great admirer of Greg's father and seemed keen to know whether Mr. Hemingway would be visiting.

Greg smiled back, and said he had no idea when his father might visit. He didn't know whether his father knew he was here.

The doctor had nodded, opened his mouth, and then it was night. Greg realized he was back in bed. It was very comfy, even though he could feel plastic under his sheets. Even the darkness was comforting, enclosing, maternal. Which made sense. Nowhere was darker than the womb. In the beginning, there was always darkness. The beginning and the end. He fell asleep smiling.

When he woke, his father was seated in the corner chair. Greg could tell from his scraggly beard and creased shirt that he'd not been traveling for comfort. Still, judging by the way his father was looking at him, he probably looked better than Greg did.

"Hi, Papa."

"Hello, Gig-man. How are you?"

"I don't know. Better, I think."

This probably wasn't real. He hadn't seen Papa in years. Not since . . . since what? Greg looked out the window. For the first time he noticed he could see the sea. It seemed impossibly vivid. Brighter somehow than the sky.

"Your doctor's a damn sycophant, Gigi." His father was crouched beside him now. "But he did say they had to use so much juice on you it would have killed most people. Doesn't surprise me at all. You always were indestructible. You take after me in that. In a lot of ways."

Greg dragged his eyes back to his father's face. Up close his face was like dry cracked earth, yet there was still a youth about him, if only in the eyes. "I don't feel indestructible."

137

"No . . . Well, you must be. They've said I can take you home. They're very impressed with you, Greg."

"That never lasts."

His father swallowed. "Now, come on. You're doing swell. No one outside the family even knows you're here—this is strictly between us."

"Okay, Papa."

"And I'll do my bit to grease the wheels. That doctor's a brown-noser, let me tell you, but if he says I can get you out of here I'll sign the damn Bible for him. You good to go, Gig-man?"

"I should pack . . ."

". . . THAT'S all taken care of, remember?"

"Sort of."

"Well. They said that's to be expected. Nothing to worry about. We'll get you out of here."

"Okay, Papa."

"Okay. Can you get up?"

"They fried my brain, not my legs."

Papa laughed, though he didn't sound amused.

Greg took small careful steps out of the room. It turned out moving a body was more like driving a car than riding a bike. You could lose your touch. He had a strange feeling that if he fell he would shatter like porcelain, smash open over the white floor and the nice nurse would have to come and sweep up the pieces of him and—

—His father's hand closed firm but gentle around his arm. Greg felt a swell of gratitude. He would not fall.

They walked out together. One small step at a time.

His father had rented a beautiful open-top sports car, the kind Greg loved. It looked even better than the sea had.

He helped Greg lower himself carefully into the passenger seat, his hands cupping each shoulder.

Greg had liked that. It reminded him of being very small.

Papa sat down beside him and turned on the engine. He let it purr for a bit. He knew Greg liked the sound.

Then they were running. The road blurring beneath them and rising, lifting them as it climbed the headlands and ran along the coast.

The wind was in Greg's hair, and it felt good. The sun was warm on his skin, and that felt good too. So did the rumble of the engine beneath him. And then Papa pulled out a half bottle of whiskey from beneath his seat. He tugged out the cork with his teeth and passed it to Greg without a word.

Greg took a mouthful. It burned and sang and glowed down his throat, and that felt best of all. Even if all this went wrong, at least it'd let him taste whiskey for the first time again.

And still his father said nothing but reached over and placed his hand on Greg's knee and squeezed.

Greg beamed back, a smile of such childish gratitude his father would come back to it again and again in the years that followed. A treasured relic like the rabbit's foot he kept in his pocket and had turned over in his fingers so many times all the hair had rubbed away and the skin turned shiny.

"It's okay, Papa." Greg said, loud above the whipping wind and the engine of the gorgeous car. "I think I'm going to be okay now. I think they fixed me."

Miami

1960

"I couldn't imagine you as a doctor."

"Well, thanks for the vote of confidence."

"I don't mean you couldn't be one. Sure you could. You just don't seem the type."

The cafe was crowded, but Greg caught the eye of the stressed-looking waiter. Always managing to get served was one of his most underrated yet valuable abilities. "Well, my grandfather was a doctor."

"My grandfather built railroads. You don't see me blowing up Chinamen in tunnels."

"Didn't you go to some snooty boarding school? Your grandfather must have been pretty damn good at laying tracks."

"Don't you chip in. All right. So he invested in railroads. Same thing, isn't it?"

"Come on, Tommy, you know Pete doesn't like it when you rattle the scenery in his salt-of-the-earth-working-class-origin story." Greg smiled as a fresh Americano was placed in front of him, black as tar. He dropped in a sugar cube but didn't stir. He loved getting to the bottom of a cup and taking that last mouthful of pure sweet after all the bitterness.

"Hey, can I get one as well? Hey! Fuck, is that guy deaf?"

Tommy looked back and forth between them, as if waiting for a fencing match to resume.

Greg peered at him, trying to get the measure of the guy. In these first few weeks of college everyone was sussing everyone else out. A year from now, the three of them might be best friends. Or they might never remember that they had sat here together in the Miami sun, sharing lunch and coffee and gossip.

They were sitting on the deck of the Lighthouse cafe, a crappy place on the Cape that got by on decent prices and the best sea view in Miami.

Greg was here for the view just like everyone else, but not of the ocean. He always took the same chair if he could, because he knew that if he leaned back and looked to the left he'd be able to see the Cape Florida Lighthouse a little further down the coast, pushing up defiantly above the trees. Lighthouses always made him feel nostalgic.

Peter eventually managed to wave over the waiter, and another round of coffees was doled out.

"I could get used to college life," said Tommy as he loaded up his cup with cream and sugar. "It's only a shame that classes have to get in the way."

"Enjoy it while it lasts," Greg said. "No one expects any work out of us for the first term."

"And how do you know that?"

"I was here last year."

"So you . . . ?"

"Dropped out? Yeah. I have delicate health, ironically.

This is going to be my year though. Top of the class. Second time's a charm."

"You have delicate health? Fuck, Greg, I don't believe you've ever so much as followed through on a fart."

"Okay, you've caught me. I'm a serial dropout. It's a hobby, and I've been coming back every year since Miller's opened."

"Ha ha, so fucking droll. All right, so what's wrong with you?"

Greg looked at him through the smoke of his cigarette. "Peter, that is not a question a good middle-class boy asks."

Tommy grinned. "I'll ask then. You get the VD?"

"Unfortunately, faithfulness to the wrong women is one of my many faults. No, if you have to be boors about it, I— I have bad nerves." Greg took a long drag of his cigarette, hoping it helped him seem casual when he felt like he might snap at any moment.

Peter scoffed. "I'll believe that after I believe the clap."

"If you don't want to say you can just tell us to fuck off."

They didn't believe him. It was both a disappointment and a relief.

Peter rolled his eyes. "Well, I'm bored. You guys know any good bars in this city?"

"Is any bar good at midday?" Tommy asked.

"Sure. The best bars exist outside of time."

"Well, Mackay's downtown pretty much never closes."

"Sounds pretty much good enough."

"Not for me, thanks." Greg stood, stretched, and took the steps down onto the little path that ran from the deck to the road. "Think you can drop me on the other side of the bridge? I can walk from there."

"Walk where?" Tommy asked as he stepped out himself. "What have you got planned?"

"Thought I might see what's in one of those textbooks everyone keeps going on about."

"Studying?" Tommy sounded like Greg had announced he was off to have his teeth pulled for recreation.

"Isn't that what students do, for etymology's sake at least?"

"Relax, Greg. We only just got here,"

"You did. This is my second year, remember?" He flicked his cigarette away, and they both watched Peter finish his coffee and stand in time for the suddenly attentive waiter to swoop down with the bill. "Top of the class and all that. In fact, I'll walk from here. I need the exercise."

"You sure? The professors'll be giving us more than enough work down the track. You might as well enjoy yourself while you can."

Greg shrugged, waited for some clever response to occur to him and, when nothing did, said: "I don't want to fuck this up."

He and Tommy eyed each other a moment, then Tommy shrugged back and they both started heading to his car. "Fair enough. I guess if I was you, I'd do the same."

"What does that mean?" Peter asked as he caught up with them. It was odd, seeing them lined up: Tommy big and hulking and thoughtful, Peter skinny and well tailored and thick as pig shit.

Tommy nodded farewell to Greg and pulled open the heavy car door. "He doesn't want to get by on his family name. You should try it, you stupid fuck."

Peter went to follow, then hesitated and gave Greg a

look from the corner of his eye. "You see much of him? The old man?"

"No. Just letters."

"Right. Okay."

Tommy had started the car, and Peter had to run to get in before he pulled out with a screech. Then the two of them were gone, only a blare of horns and a plume of snail-brown smoke to tell of their passing.

Greg let out a small sigh as he relaxed. It felt good to be alone.

That was partly why he'd let them head on without him, but it was also true that he needed to study. Before the shocks, his brain had eaten everything that got too close, like a whirlpool. There'd been no effort to it, no work. But these days, committing anything to memory was like trying to stuff more clothes into an already bursting suitcase. You had to sit on the bastard for half an hour just to force one sock in.

He'd underestimated that on his first attempt—had thought he could cruise by as effortlessly as he had at school. By the time he'd realized he actually needed to take notes in class—hell, that he needed to write the names of his new friends on the palm of his hand—it was too late. He'd cracked under the pressure. The breakdown had been nowhere near as bad as the one after his mother, but it had been more than enough to end his academic career.

He wasn't going to make that mistake twice.

He wasn't going to fuck up again.

The fact that it was so hard now—and what that implied had been done to his brain—didn't actually bother him. After all, he doubted he would have been here at all without the shocks.

Sure, maybe he'd lost a bit of himself, but he'd gained everything else. He only had to be careful. Take it one step at a time.

He'd meant to walk home straight away, but instead found himself heading back down the shady track by the side of the cafe that led to the beach.

After the darkness of the path, the sea was blinding, seeming to burst its bounds and drown the world in light. The sand shifted uncertainly beneath his loafers as he took a few uncertain steps forward, letting his eyes slowly adjust.

People popped into existence in groups: families, dog walkers, children running wild in the shallows. Greg tried to imagine how the beach must have looked before it was so crowded with people and junk, when those first pioneers came over the rocky plains and mountains to see this glorious sliver of heaven. But it was impossible. There was too much human flotsam in front of him.

Imagination had never been his strength. His mother had told him so often enough when he was a boy, trying to ape his father by scribbling down his own silly stories.

He had been thinking about his mother a lot lately. He wasn't sure why. Maybe just because he could.

For years it had been too dangerous to let his thoughts even begin to stray toward her. It was far too likely to set him back a leap in his journey of small steps. But now, for the first time in years, he felt stable. He could remember how she'd looked on the last day, aging with the grace of a woman who wasn't trying to impress anyone, as confident in that piss-soaked jail cell as an admiral at the helm of his battleship.

And there was pain, of course, but not the weight of a falling sky, that soul-annihilating shame that had pressed down on him for years. He had killed his mother, and there was nothing to do but keep on living.

A group of children ran by, their red-faced heavy-set mother chasing after them with a bag full of towels and windbreakers beating against her side. Greg watched them recede into the heat haze swelling over the sands, their bodies appearing and vanishing like desert wanderers.

He looked away before they disappeared for good. He wasn't here for the people, or the beach, or the sea. On the headland to his right, looming over everything, the familiar shape of the Cape Florida Lighthouse rose up from beyond the horizon.

As far as lighthouses went it was fairly squat and unimpressive, but now distance and his low position made it seem a slender needle, fragile and unblemished in the midday shimmer.

He took half a step forward, as though some invisible thread running between his breast and the glittering eye of that needle had tightened. The urge to go climb it was almost overwhelming.

He shook his head and turned away, beginning the long slog back up to the road.

He had work to do.

There was a certain karmic justice in it. The boy who had come top of so many classes without opening a textbook hunched over his desk for hour after hour, laboring to drill even the basics of modern medicine into his flash-fried brain.

It was okay, though. The day flowing through the

window was fine, the coffee steaming at his elbow was hot and strong, and the packet of cigarettes in his breast pocket was more than half-full.

He was going to come top of the class again, and this time he was going to earn it.

He turned a page of *A Study of the Human Circulatory System*, which he'd been poring over for the last few hours, and found, laid out like a star chart, a map of all the key veins and arteries in the human body. Beautifully simple. Stunningly complex. He had told Peter that doctoring was in his blood, and maybe there was some truth in that, but the thing that truly kept him coming back to the profession was the sense of peace it brought him, the sense of order. It was the same comfort he had found in his work as a mechanic, what felt like a lifetime ago.

Everything had a cause, an origin. There was no randomness. No right and wrong. Only a system working precisely to its mechanisms. Everything, no matter how complicated—no matter how seemingly random—could be understood, could be fixed.

Looking at that chart comforted him. He traced its whorls and eddies with his fingertips.

But a moment later he frowned, thinking, and withdrew his hands from the yellowing paper. A stray breeze flipped the pages to a chart of minute text and Latin names, but Greg didn't react. Still frowning, he lit a cigarette and leaned back in his chair.

Finally, as the embers were burning his fingertips, he flicked the dying butt out the window and turned the pages back to that beautiful image of human order. He studied it a moment longer, then nodded, pulled a sheet of paper toward him, and began to write a letter to the Los

Angeles Coroner's Office, explaining and proving who he was, and making his request.

A little over two months later—when Greg was decidedly not the top of his class, but doing okay—a nondescript brown envelope arrived in the mail.

That morning he skipped class for the first time. He took the envelope to his desk, read the contents, smoked three cigarettes in quick succession, and phoned Jinny.

They spoke a while, then Greg sat on his bed and smoked another cigarette, his free hand coiled into a fist so tight he could feel his own pulse. He wanted a whiskey more than anything, but he would not let himself have one.

When he felt calm, he went to his desk and wrote a letter to his father saying exactly what he thought of him. He poured everything into it, every bit of rage and doubt and guilt and hate that had soured in his guts all these years. Then he sealed and sent it before he could think twice. Fuck it, let the die fall.

He never heard back. Six months later, Papa was dead.

Ketchum, Idaho

1961

Greg sat in his rental car looking up at the house. An ugly bunker of a building, all concrete and sharp angles like some little piece of Soviet Russia plunked into tedious Middle America.

Maybe his father hadn't been crazy after all. Maybe he'd done the only sane thing.

He laughed out loud at this, then took one long breath, his hands tight on the steering wheel.

Any minute now he would get out of this car and walk up the path through the parched square of grass pretending to be a yard and join the family. His family. He leaned his head against the wheel.

A curtain-twitch at one of the tall windows caught the corner of his eye. No doubt Mary was watching, wondering if he'd cracked again. It probably ran in the family.

He took one more steadying breath and forced himself out of the car. When he straightened he could see the tips of mountains rising up behind all this suburban drudgery, pine-swept and snow-capped.

Perhaps there was snowmelt running down through those thick dark forests, streams so cold and pure they seemed clearer than the sky above. Dappled trout, clean and muscular, might move through their waters, their wimpled fins trembling in the swift current.

So, not all bad. Not all bad.

Despite his trepidation, or because of it, he strode up the drive, took the front steps in a leap, and banged his fist against the door.

It opened almost immediately, and he found himself eye to eye with Mary, last wife standing, wearing a rigor mortis smile.

"Greg . . . What happened to your face?"

"What? Oh." He touched his cheek and winced. He'd almost forgotten last night's fight. "Nothing. Friendly disagreement with a few guys at a bar."

The disagreement had been about whether Greg deserved to keep his teeth after they'd spotted the bright red lacquer on his nails, and for this asshole-of-nowhere part of America it had been a pretty civil discussion—no bottles or anything. Then again, if they'd known what he'd been wearing under his deck shorts half the bar probably would have ended up stamping on his head.

Instead, Greg hadn't had to spill his drink to handle three boondocks dipshits who thought wrestling with their brothers had taught them how to fight. He probably should have left before it all went down—he'd felt their eyes on him, known it was coming—but that would have been too much like running away, and that was forbidden. Anyway, after the lanky one had surprised him with that first sucker punch he'd gone pretty easy on them, all things considered. Just a few carefully placed taps to put them down, no broken jaws or blood under the skull. The shocks had played a number on his brain, but his body remembered everything. Every lesson. Every touch. It all left an indelible mark.

"Greg?"

"Sorry. What did you say?"

She crossed her arms. "You never change, Gigi."

"Greg. Change is for the weak, Mary. I am a bulwark against the tide."

"Greg, of course. I'm sorry. I forget. Sometimes the years slip away and I . . ." She looked somewhere over his shoulder, then shook her head.

"Don't worry about it."

She seemed to realize how long he had been standing on his father's porch, and moved aside with a gesture of welcome. In the midday light the doorway was a slab of pure ebony behind her, but he gathered himself and stepped in.

He swam in nothingness, unhooked from the world, before his eyes adjusted and a room of familiar objects leaped from obscurity, dragging their half-buried memories with them. The long table where they'd had lunch every day they weren't on the *Pilar*. The little porcelain figures Greg had always hated. The threadbare rug, worn at the corner where his father had passed from the drinks cabinet to the finca's back door, faded along one edge where the Cuban sun had fallen through the window in the afternoons. The paintings on the wall, tributes of his father's time in Paris, most of them picked up as gifts or as thanks for a meal or a shared bottle of wine, and most of them now priceless.

Mary appeared beside him. "How are you, Greg?"

Normally it would have been an innocuous question,

especially at a time like this, but not to Greg. He swallowed. "I'm . . . doing okay. Thank you."

"The medical degree's going well?"

"No . . . No, I dropped out."

"Oh, Greg. Again?"

"It just . . . stopped making sense, I guess."

"You'll find something that sticks eventually, I'm sure of it."

"Right. Is anyone else here?"

"Not yet," said Mary, sounding as uncomfortable as he to find them alone together, "but . . . Valerie's in the far room. You two should meet! Your father was very fond of her."

Greg knew the name. His father's long-term private secretary and number one fan, long-term confidante of Mary. Another in a long line of worms to force their way into the apple. Though he supposed he didn't have much high ground there, considering his mother had been the first.

"That's all right. I think I need to use the bathroom."

"You'll like her, Greg. Everyone does."

People used to say that about me. "I look forward to joining the legion, but right now, I need to piss."

Mary waved him away. "Use the spare bathroom. It's up the hall."

The bathroom for guests. That figured.

Greg didn't need to piss. He needed to get away. Being in this house was like being in a mausoleum. A royal tomb with all the familiar little sainted objects laid out.

He placed his hands against the sink and leaned forward. One deep breath in, one deep breath out. He was shaking, but he was okay. The treatments had cleared him out. No way he could have handled this before, but now he could keep a hold of himself, keep himself steady.

He lifted his head and found himself staring down his own reflection. He looked like one of those black-and-white oval photographs of men newly back from the front. Not a pretty sight, but he made himself stare a while, taking stock.

How had he gotten here? He'd been handed everything—good looks, good brains, athletic talent, his mother's wealth, his father's name—and now here he was in this dingy guest bathroom, too scared to go downstairs, to leave this safe place and go back into the world.

He tried to trace the path of it, to find the wrong turn somewhere between those white beaches and mothwing-dusty boxing rings and his father lifting him up after that last perfect shot—between all of it—and here.

He could find none. It seemed to him a straight path. There had been no turning, no other trails he might have taken.

And if so, hadn't those golden years been just an illusion? This was who he was, who he had always been. This bruised and swollen face in the mirror.

He had a stick of bright cherry-red lipstick in the car, and he had to fight an urge to go get it, to stand in front of this mirror and slowly paint a gaudy flower in the middle of all that carnage. He gripped the edge of the sink.

Why did it always come on so strong in times like this? It was like some part of him was always busy keeping these urges in check, and the moment he let himself be distracted they rushed forward and tried to eat him alive.

It didn't even make any sense. They were only clothes. Here he was, feeling like he was suffocating in himself, trapped in his life, wanting more than anything else to rip himself open and just *get out*. They were only clothes, they couldn't change anything. But the messed-up connection in his head didn't care. It insisted everything would be okay if he would—

—A knock on the door. Greg flinched like he'd been struck.

"Greg? You missed Valerie. She's gone for a walk."

"Boo fucking hoo," he muttered.

"What was that?"

"I said be right out."

Mary was waiting for him outside the bathroom, and she followed only a step behind him on the stairs, as though afraid that if left alone he'd grab some priceless heirloom and jump screaming out the window. As if anything in that house really belonged to her.

"You can stay here if you need, Gigi," she said without enthusiasm.

"Greg. No, I'm fine. I've already rented a hotel room. You're going to need every bed you can spare."

"I'm sorry. I always forget. Yes, there's going to be a crowd all right. I doubt there's a man in the world who could claim more admirers than your father. There are presidents whose names mean less."

Greg could think of nothing to say to that. He walked over to the hunting trophies lining the wall, glassy-eyed and open-mouthed, horns and tusks splayed. Even with the damage to his memory he could still remember standing in the dining room in Key West as his parents shouted and screamed upstairs in those last apocalyptic days of their marriage, looking up at these long somber faces. He'd tried so hard to lose himself in imagining what it must be like to slay such monsters. To be that powerful. To fear nothing.

"Magnificent, aren't they? Brought back over the course of three trips."

"I know, Mary. I was there when they were unpacked." He knew that was true, though he couldn't quite remember being there.

"Oh, of course. I'm sorry, Greg. I'm all a bit muddled today. I . . ."

"Don't worry. I'm being a pedant." He reached out and touched the swirling horn of a kudu. Still sharp after all these years. "And they *are* magnificent."

"Yes. Did you bring back any of your own, from that trip you took?"

"No," said Greg softly. "No I didn't."

"I see, well, the rest are still at the finca, of course. There just wasn't enough wall for all of them. The way things are going over there I dare say we'll struggle to get them out."

"The Generalissimo isn't generally a big respecter of private property."

"No, but we'll manage it. He thought the world of your father. I can't even tell you how many papers we had to leave behind there when we moved. We'll manage all right, Val and me. She's unstoppable. Can I get you a drink?"

Greg hesitated. He'd expected her to want him out as soon as possible. Why should his father's death have changed their mutual discomfort? "Er, sure. Rum, if you have it."

"Gregory Hemingway. This is still your father's house. Of course we have rum."

Despite everything, Greg smiled.

The ice clinked in the glass, then cracked as the rum

flowed over it. "You know," Mary said, as she sliced into a lime, "they still serve Hemingway Daiquiris back in Havana. They use grapefruit juice. Can you believe that?"

"They were serving that when I was a kid, minus the name, but they'll slap his name on anything, won't they? There's a Hemingway everything now. You can order his favorite cocktail in half the bars in Miami, and it's different in each place."

"They should try one of Papa's actual cocktails."

Greg had never liked it when Mary called his father that. Knowing that it had been at his father's insistence somehow only made it worse. He let it go. "I think glancing in the direction of the fruit bowl was as close as he got to a proper daiquiri. If he could have figured out how to freeze booze and cut out the ice altogether, I think he'd finally have been happy."

"Well," Mary handed him a heavy cut-glass tumbler filled with a generous jigger of rum, a wheel of lime entombed in ice like some lost arctic vessel, "he deserved his comforts. And he was never a man to take life diluted. Come on. Let's drink these out on the deck. It's the glory of the house."

"By all means, lead on to glory."

She pushed through the double doors at the back and they stepped out onto a wide sweep of wooden boards. Beyond it, the valley fell away cloaked in the dark woods Gigi had spotted earlier like something from a European fairy tale.

"Not bad. I guess this is why you bought the house."

"Partly. It was a bit of a rush job. We had to get out of Cuba in a hurry."

"Of course." Greg took a drink. The rum was good,

and Mary hadn't messed it up with any sugar. Cocktails were for inferior spirits. He could taste the sun beating down, the dry ache of the earth, and the sharp lime cutting through all of it. He could taste the green.

"Good, isn't it?"

"Cuban?"

"Of course."

"It tastes Cuban."

"And what does Cuba taste like?"

". . . a lot of things."

"Don't ever be a writer, Greg."

That stung, but he let it pass over him. He sensed he was going to have to let a lot of things pass over him for the next few days.

"Well, you did well for a rush job. It's beautiful."

"Yes. We spent a lot of time out here, before the accident."

Greg hesitated, took another drink. The word *accident* hung between them like gun smoke.

"I suppose we should go inside," said Mary at last. "I want to be able to hear the door."

Back in the house, Greg eyed the hunting trophies again. Dead eyes gleamed, opalescent in the gloom. He followed their gaze over to the far side of the room, where two double doors stood firmly closed.

He knew with sudden absolute certainty where it had happened. Probably the old man had looked out the back window over all that rough free space before he'd done it. Watched the river singing.

No doubt the doors would be locked, and Greg made no attempt to breach the boundary. It would have been a messy affair.

"I hope you didn't have to see . . . anything," he said to Mary, stumbling over his words.

"Ah." Mary closed her eyes a moment, all the answer he needed.

"I'm sorry."

"I told him to be careful with those damn guns," she said, and finished her rum. The bright, brittle sound of the ice filled the air long after she had returned the glass to her side, her hand shaking heavily. She seemed not to notice. "He always thought he was indestructible. He'd survived enough to kill ten men, but I told him . . . Such a stupid accident." Her voice broke.

Greg opened his mouth, then closed it again. A few weeks ago, another Greg would have told her how unlikely it was that his father, however stupid, however drunk, would polish a loaded shotgun pointed at his own forehead. He'd have said that, and a lot of other things besides. But that Greg had faded away like a summer storm. Same sky, different weather.

Whatever her faults, Mary had loved his father. She had never tried to hurt him. It was more than Greg could say. It occurred to him that he'd always thought of Mary as merely the latest model, the newest indulgence, eventually to be replaced. But what had it been now, fifteen years? She'd been married to him longer than anyone.

He kept his silence.

"It was the shocks," she said quietly. "They muddled his brain. He couldn't write, couldn't think straight. They . . ." she paused and looked directly at him. "How do you do it, Greg? How?"

Greg had nothing that would comfort her. "I should

go," he said, and finished his drink. "I need to check into my room."

"Of course." She blinked and dropped her gaze like someone who'd realized they had committed a faux pas at a party. "Let me show you out."

At the doorway she paused, fingertips on the brass handle. "I'm glad you're here. I know it hurt him, the things that passed between you two. He'd have been happy to know you came."

Unseen behind her, Greg closed his eyes.

"Well, see you tomorrow. Take care, Gigi."

Out on the front porch the world seemed more vibrant than he remembered. As though everything outside was celebrating that it was not that gloomy house, not that dark sealed room.

Greg covered his face with his hands for a moment, fighting for control. He found it, barely, and walked to his car.

Shotgun to the forehead. Showier than Greg's grandfather, but in essence the same. It made perfect sense. He'd been trying to destroy the one true enemy.

He'd rented an open-top car, and the sky stretched vast and immovable overhead as he sped down the featureless roads. It made him feel like he wasn't moving, like it was the world rushing by beneath his wheels. If he slammed on the brake the rubber would burn and the world slow not at all, just keep running like some projector's wheel spinning out of control, the film an unknowable blur.

He kept his mind carefully blank, focusing on each turn, each gear change. All he had to do was keep going. No thinking about why he was here in Idaho, or what they were going to do tomorrow. He knew the pit of despair he was circling very well. The downward slope started gently, so that moving a little closer to peek over the edge didn't seem like such a big risk, but by God it steepened quickly, and before you knew it you were sliding headlong, scrabbling desperately for any handhold as you plummeted into darkness.

He took a corner hard and braked harder when he saw a figure ambling along the side of the road. The runaway world reluctantly gave way to reality, and he jerked the wheel to keep the car well clear as it screeched to a halt.

He pulled himself up by the windshield, visions of a child's tire-print belly pulsing in his head. "What the fuck do you think you're doing? Haven't you ever heard of walking against traffic?"

The woman stared him down coolly, unimpressed and completely unintimidated. "Haven't you ever heard of a speed limit? And I crossed because it seemed like a good idea to be on the outside of a tight curve. If I hadn't, I'd probably be folded into your grill right now."

Greg hesitated, a scathing retort dying in his throat. Now that he'd had a chance to look at her properly he realized he knew her, though he'd never seen her before in his life.

It was his father's secretary, she who'd slipped out while he'd been staring down his own reflection. Valerie. He recognized her from his father's letters. The old man's powers of description had never faltered.

She tilted her head, cocky. "What? I thought you were supposed to always have a comeback, Greg."

"We haven't met, have we?"

She snorted. "You look just like him."

160

There was an Irish lilt to her voice. He'd known that, but it still surprised him, sweetly musical for all her spite. Like birdsong. He let himself drop back into the driver's seat.

"Can I give you a ride?"

"Depends where you're going, I'd think."

"I was planning on driving up to the mountains and right into a gorge."

"Oh, well." She came over and vaulted easily into the passenger seat, not a second's hesitation. "In that case, I'll buckle my seat belt."

He forced a smile. They were skirting so close to it, this awful thing that had happened, but not quite touching it. "I thought you were a Catholic."

"And I thought you were the wild child of the family. Corrupting the soul of a young Catholic girl should be a perfect pre-funeral jaunt for you."

"The wild child?"

"Mm-hm. Which for your family," she drew a cigarette from the pack in his shirt pocket, "is quite an achievement."

Greg fished his lighter from his pocket and offered her a flame. "I think I'm starting to see why my father was so keen on keeping you as his assistant. He loved a good fight."

"His reasons were threefold." She breathed in, the tip of the cigarette glaring. "My excellent shorthand, my absolute discretion, and my ability to drink him under the table." She let smoke cascade from her nose. "Weren't you going to give me a ride? So far, this is only a seat."

Greg opened the choke, shifted the car back into drive, and they set off.

She finished her cigarette silently, the bruised smoke

coiling gently up before vanishing into their slipstream, then pushed herself up so her hair caught in the wind. She might have looked glamorous if she hadn't been squinting and baring her teeth like a dog on a family road trip, but glamour didn't seem to be a big concern of hers.

"An open-top car really is the last word on civilization," she said when she settled back down into the seat, her hair a wild tangle.

"Not modern medicine?" Greg asked, watching her out of the corner of his eye. "Inoculations, c-sections, electroshocks?"

"Compared to this? All savagery."

"You're probably right."

"You don't have your own choice?"

"Me?" He didn't let himself think. "Ice. Jesus, can you imagine a world without ice? No whiskey on the rocks."

"But you can't feel ice in your hair."

"Cocktails like cat piss. Champagne going tepid in the sun."

"Okay. I concede. Ice."

She was pretty, but not beautiful the way his father's letters had led Greg to expect. He'd raved about his new assistant every chance he got, not even trying to hide that he was in love with her. Greg had no idea if the feeling had gone both ways. He didn't know how many mistresses had never become wives over the years, and he didn't much care. It had ceased to be his business after his own mother had been shunted into the wilderness.

"Shouldn't you ask me where I'm going?" she asked.

"Why would I do that?"

"To drop me off." The slightest uncertainty in her

voice. Wrong-footed. Clearly not something she was familiar with. He felt pleased.

There was a long clear stretch of road ahead. "I thought we'd already agreed on our destination . . ." He looked her full in the face, no attempt to keep his eyes on the road, and slammed his foot down.

It was just for a second, but long enough to make the car leap beneath them. Her eyes widened, then she laughed, "You shit!" and he couldn't help but join in as he slowed the car to a leisurely cruise.

It felt good to laugh despite the ball of black swelling a little bigger inside him every day. And it felt even better to laugh with her, because he could sense that for all her quips and her iron-clad indifference, she felt the same.

He couldn't have said how he knew it, but he would have bet his life on it. They were two soldiers crouched in the same foxhole.

"It's good to know Papa had someone who could keep up with him," he said, more relaxed now the laughter had broken the last lingering awkwardness between them. "Not like he could get that from Mary . . ."

"Mary's a good woman," she said, loyally and without hesitation. Greg couldn't decide if it made him like her more or less. "And besides, I was never a match for your father. He taught me a lot. A hell of a lot." She looked away.

"I don't believe you. If you couldn't keep up with him, he wouldn't have liked you so much."

"In the bar maybe. Being his secretary didn't take much. Typing out his letters. Buying plane tickets. Making sure he got home at night."

"Right . . ." Greg found himself wondering again whether they'd been lovers, but now hoping not. "I imagine the last one alone was more than enough to earn your pay though."

She smiled. "He could be such a damn ass when he'd had too much, which was half the time. What am I talking about? You knew him better than me."

"I don't know about that."

"I guess he hid more from you than anyone else. Probably because you're so similar."

They were silent for a few moments. The trees swept by, the sun fizzing between their boughs. A chipmunk darted into the road, and Greg slowed as it panicked, giving it time to flee back into the undergrowth.

"You probably think I'm just another empty-headed hero-worshipper . . ." she said at last. "Maybe I am, I don't know. But I knew he wasn't perfect. I could see his flaws, but they didn't make him any less . . . incredible."

For a second, Greg really did want to twist the wheel and send the car screaming into a ravine. Then he sighed and let it pass. He was getting good at that.

"Take his letters. He could write the meanest shittiest things you've ever read in your life. And the very next sheet of paper he could write the sweetest most thoughtful . . . and beautiful. There was this one sick kid and . . . oh, I guess it doesn't matter now."

"I guess not . . . So, did you ever write his letters to me?"

"No," she said, immediately.

"Did you read my letters out for him?"

"Maybe." Perhaps she heard the tension in his voice, or maybe she just knew enough. "Some."

164

"Which ones?"

"All the ones that he asked me to read for him. Didn't you hear me? One of my key qualities, discretion. I know you and your father could trade blows sometimes, but that was none of my business. Still isn't."

And maybe that really was all she knew. He hoped so. The idea of this woman knowing . . . It was unbearable.

The trees dropped away, and the town jumped up around them.

"All right. Where are you going?"

"Nowhere really. I needed to get out of that house."

"Same here."

"Drop me at the post office, if you can. I need to send a letter home. This all happened pretty fast."

"Sure. Where's that?"

"No idea. Let's ask someone."

"No, I mean home."

"Oh, Ireland. We can ask this guy."

"You're really going to let someone else *tell you* where to go? We can find it ourselves."

She rolled her eyes but smiled as a blur of a pedestrian passed them by.

"What's the rush? You sure you don't have somewhere to be?"

She looked at him straight on, then, and it was like a punch in the chest. "Nowhere in the world."

He wanted to reach out and touch her. He wanted to lean away.

They found the post office after nearly twenty minutes of cruising around town, trading occasional observations, but mostly at peace in each other's silence.

She didn't open the door when Greg pulled to a stop, just stepped up and vaulted onto the sidewalk.

"I guess I'll see you tomorrow," she said, looking down at him.

The funeral. The thought filled him with dread. "Yeah. I'll be there. I might not be so . . . talkative, though."

She winced, seemed about to say something, then shook her head and turned away.

She called over one shoulder as she left: "It was good to finally meet you, Greg."

He watched her go. "It was good to meet you too, Valerie."

Then he went home to dream about his father.

Bimini

1938

"Keep close to the boat," his father grunted.

He'd been short with everyone all day. Some letter from a critic he'd not taken kindly to. Once, he would have laughed that sort of thing off, but now they rankled with him for days.

Greg's mother was sitting on the top deck in a cream all-in-one bathing suit, her broad hat pulled low over her sunglasses, reading herself away from the smell of fish.

Patrick had already escaped into the water. Greg could hear the spit and gurgle of his snorkel as he circled the *Pilar*. No one ever told him not to stray too far.

"You hear me, Gig?"

Greg kept his eyes on the deck. "Yes, Papa."

"All right. Go on, get us some lunch."

At last. Greg grabbed a snorkel, mask, and a speargun and—shirking the ladder altogether—threw himself overboard in a graceless heap. The water slapped up around him, cool and bubbly in his wake, and then he was kicking at the surface, spitting in the mask to stop it steaming up before strapping it on tight.

He didn't have to waste time looking for fish. Papa had

anchored the boat on a reef more than a mile offshore—a fragile upthrust of coral and clear water in the endless dark push of the Gulf Stream—and the fish were everywhere, fearless, flaunting their fresh-coat-of-paint colors, their picture book shapes. Greg could easily imagine he was the first hunter that had ever swum here, and it might well have been true.

He kicked off, eager to be free of the boat whose hull he could hear sounding like a drum with each lick of the water. Beneath him, barracudas hung like daggers, perfectly still in the current. A shoal of bright blue fish he had no name for rippled past, silken electrics dancing from nook to cranny. A little to his left, a large stately jewfish tempted him, but he was wise enough now not to waste his spears on something he couldn't bring down.

He turned in the water, scanning this way and that. A few streaks of silver flicked across the edge of his vision, and he twisted, raised the speargun, and fired—all instinct. A second later he had a fat grunt wiggling on the end of his line, writhing and contorting as it died, leaking a line of thin purple blood that spiraled up toward the surface like cigarette smoke.

He hauled it in, pleased with himself. The grunt was a big one. Even his father might be impressed. He looked around for more, but there was only cloud after cloud of tiny bonito and other fast swimmers he had no chance of spearing. He fastened the grunt to his belt and started to swim, trying to let his senses relax into the same state he managed to find when he was batting well, every sense as open and unassuming as a blank notebook.

But he couldn't find it, that empty place. Something kept drawing his attention. Again, he turned. In the distance, he could see the end of the reef, all its tangled chaos stopping as straight and sudden as the edge of a table. Beyond that, inky darkness yawned. Open blue.

Even with the heat of the sun filtering through all around him, Greg shivered. To think that so much of their time in the boat they were mere meters from that void, held up by a thin sheet of bright surface over miles of empty darkness. To think that the big fish his father hunted lived their whole lives in such a place . . .

There was nothing human there. Nothing warm, or soft, or kind.

And yet he drifted closer, wanting perhaps to take a peek at that distant ocean floor, to see inky sands littered with wrecks and treasure chests and the wandering ghosts of mariners drowned when men still sailed by the stars.

The fish spooled and drifted around him, like thoughts after whiskey.

He kicked harder.

A turtle drifted past, going in the opposite direction. Its hard shell was tufted with weeds and barnacles, a piece of the seabed come alive.

The edge approached, and the swelling darkness behind it seemed to swing down and backward at the same time, expanding, trying to suck him up like a pair of monstrous lungs.

Greg hung there, still a little way from the edge, fighting the insistent current that wanted to pull him out. He could feel the small waves of the surface ruffling his hair again and again as he hesitated.

He couldn't do it. He knew now what he would see if he strayed over that edge: the end of everything. And in an instant the magic that held him up would be broken, and he would fall like a stone into a blackness vaster than the sky.

He turned and swam toward the *Pilar*. Calm, steady strokes, not letting himself panic.

When he got back he was going to see if he could steal Patrick's shorts. Sneak up on him and tug them free all at once. He'd pin them under a rock so his brother would have to dive down—which he hated—to get them, or else climb naked into the boat and head back to shore in a towel.

Well, not really. Greg would get the shorts back for him if he had to, but maybe, just maybe Patrick would dive and get them himself, and maybe his brother would get over his stupid fear and the two of them would go hunt out an underwater grotto together, find the ruins of some lost pirate ship and become richer than their father in one fell swoop.

That would make Papa happy. His sons famous, but not for writing or boxing or anything like that. Maybe he'd be so proud he'd stop giving a damn about the critics, who were two-bit puffed-up know-nothings anyway, as everyone knew.

Greg was in the middle of this pleasant daydream when he realized that all the fish had disappeared though he wasn't even halfway back to the boat. There was no flick of fins, no flash of silver. It was almost hard to believe so much life could have packed itself away so neatly, like a conjuring trick.

But there was something—movement over to his left, not bright, but—

—The shark seemed to slip out of empty water, one enormous ripple of muscle powering toward him. And then another, and another. Three of them, tails twitching back and forth, blunt noses forcing the water aside, black eyes staring.

His speargun slipped through his fingers and spiraled down as he rushed to the surface, screaming, calling out for his father in wild panic.

"Papa. Papa, sharks! They're after me, Papa!"

Shirtless on the deck, his father did not hesitate—did not try and maneuver the boat or ask questions or stop to get a harpoon gun of his own—before Greg had finished speaking he had leaped headlong over the side, a half-finished glass of iced rum still clutched in his hand.

Greg started swimming toward him, his usually elegant front crawl reduced to a wild thrashing of limbs, expecting every moment to be seized by teeth long as fingers.

When Papa's arms finally closed around him the relief was so great it was like they were already back on the boat, towels wrapped around their shoulders, laughing over the whole thing and picking the sweet white flesh of the grunt from its sweet white bones.

With a calm Greg would always remember, his father pulled the still bleeding grunt from his belt—the blood, he realized, *the blood*—and threw it overarm in the direction of the sharks as hard as he could. Then he was pulling Greg up onto his back, letting him wrap his arms around his neck and saying, "If anything happens, just start swimming."

His strokes were strong and steady like always. Every second Greg expected to feel two tons of cartilage and teeth smashing into them, tearing them apart to leave bright bloody swirls in the water.

Then he was on the deck, shivering, his father crouched

over him, his white-faced mother wrapping a towel around his shoulders. He had time to see a swirl of foam out over the reef, where the sharks were squabbling over the remains of the grunt, before his father picked him up, towel and all.

In the years to come, whenever Greg remembered the worst of his father, this memory would always swing up like a counterweight: the feeling of Papa pushing him up and out of danger with his own body, putting himself between Greg's skinny frame and the thing of muscle and teeth below. His father holding him tight as the boat rocked the both of them, not wanting to let go.

No matter how messed up it all got, no matter how many memories were burned away, that remained.

Ketchum, Idaho

1961

Greg stopped by the house to pick up Valerie and Mary before the funeral. He leaned on the horn for a second rather than go get them. It probably wasn't the gentlemanly thing to do, but he felt safer tucked away in the car. He'd braved his father's house once, and that was enough.

Mary emerged first, her eyes red and puffy. Greg felt a rare surge of affection for her. Valerie trailed after with a small brown package in her arms, probably his father's Bible—he wasn't one for piety, but he knew a good book when he saw one. She was pale but dry-eyed and straight-backed. Greg felt a surge of affection for her too, for completely opposite reasons.

"Thank you for the lift, Gregory," Mary said thickly, patting his arm once she'd lowered herself into the passenger seat. "You're very kind."

She was making the effort. He knew he should say something gracious back, but he just nodded. He didn't quite trust himself to speak yet. He felt completely numb, and that was good. He wasn't sure how much longer the numbness would last, but he had a feeling it would be like a dam breaking when it went.

Valerie slipped into the back seat. Her eyes met Greg's for a moment in the rearview mirror then slipped away.

Greg switched on the radio, then switched it back off. The bright cheerful pop made him want to smash his head into the steering wheel.

The only sound was Mary's muffled sniffles as they made their way to the cemetery. Greg drove on autopilot, and the journey seemed to pass in a haze that lasted all the way through the ceremony. He remembered watching the priest's mouth move, remembered Patrick hugging him and his half-brother John taking him by the arm.

Then they were at the graveside, watching the coffin fall away from them, out of the sweet July sun and into the darkness. It seemed so wrong. Papa had loved the sea and the sky and the mountains, and here they were sealing him away from all of it beneath this bland sweep of suburban graveyard, this unremarkable land bloated with the dead.

But it didn't matter. They weren't sealing anyone anywhere.

Papa was gone.

It hit him then, and he carried on standing at the graveside even as he broke beneath the surface.

He already knew he was heading for another round of major destruction. Depression or mania, he didn't know. He'd done well—it had been nearly two years since a total collapse—but he knew the symptoms by now. The nausea in his gut, the ache behind his eyes, the crushing heaviness pressing down on him. Oh yes, he could almost feel them placing the electrodes on his temples.

A reset. God, he needed a reset.

But there was nothing to be done, he could no more have stepped from this path than he could jump into the grave and pull his father from the earth. He was a broken machine running out his own destruction. There could be no deviating.

He held onto himself until he'd dropped Valerie and Mary back at the house, then he drove to the nearest gas station and bought a quart of the cheapest whiskey they had.

He was getting out of the car at the motel when he noticed the package sitting on the back seat. He assumed Valerie must have forgotten it, and he almost left it, but then he thought of her realizing she'd lost something so precious. He scooped it up, and only then saw there was a note pinned to one corner.

Greg,
We were going through Papa's papers, and wanted you to have these. They're yours, after all.
Val x

He set the whiskey down inside and used his rental car keys to prize up the tape and open the package. A neat stack of papers fell out, all different colors and sizes bound neatly together with string.

Letters. All of them. Every letter he'd ever sent his father. Papa had kept them all.

He reached out with a trembling hand and picked up the stack, and there at the top, creased with repeated readings, was his last letter. He remembered writing it very clearly.

In a shaky scrawl, he'd respectfully made the case that people do not die of shame.

If they did, Greg would have been six feet under years ago.

People do not die because their children are a disappointment.

If they did, his father would not have outlived Greg's tenth birthday.

People die for concrete and explicable reasons. They die because their cells betray them. Because time has worn out parts of their bodies that cannot be renewed. Because they didn't check the safety on their gun.

Greg politely explained that the publicly available autopsy report (copy enclosed) clearly and explicitly showed that his mother, his father's wife, had died of a tumor in her adrenal gland causing a huge discharge of adrenaline, resulting in an immediate spike in blood pressure so intense her arteries had burst inside her, and furthermore that she had most likely been suffering from this condition undiagnosed for many years. It was a stretch to attribute this to Greg's arrest, the time difference being too vast and disappointment not leading to spikes of adrenaline.

Furthermore, if anything was to blame it was a certain phone call she had taken with her husband before retiring. A phone call where, as one of her own sisters had attested, the gruff male voice on the line had been so loud it had carried through the whole room as it spat out words like *poison, pollution, ruin*. Words like *corrupted him*. Words that had left her sobbing. Words no man should ever say to a woman, let alone to his wife, let alone to the mother of his children who he'd driven out of the house to replace with a woman who would drop him after half a decade of dealing with his self-serving overbearing psychotic shit.

Papa could say and think whatever he liked about Greg,

because his opinion was worth less than nothing. He was a used-up old husk putting out nothing but self-parodying drivel that the critics laughed at over their martinis, who had driven away three wives and all his children.

Was it worth it? That ten years when the critics gave a damn? The handful of real stories and the two decent novels and the little line of prizes on the mantelpiece? Was it worth destroying all the living, breathing people who loved you? I hope so, because you don't have anything else. Nothing.

You made me think it was my fault, you shit. Just to soothe your own guilt, or just to fuck me up more than I already was. You did that to your own son. Didn't you feel anything? Watching me fall apart? Picking me up at the clinic? Not the smallest glimmer of shame? Of course not. What's the point of the bit actors but to break apart as the hero rises? Well, fuck you, Papa. You're no hero. You're just an old man with a poisoned family and a fading legacy.

And it was you who killed her, not me.

It was you.

Greg took a shuddering breath, his eyes skimming over the words again and again. His last words to his father. Then he picked up the bottle of whiskey and drank it dry.

PART III

PART III

New York

1967

The leaves were starting to fall. They gathered in the
gutters like secondhand fire, flowing in tatters over the
sidewalk with every stray gust of breeze, and thickest in
the park where they covered the grass almost completely.

Greg sat on the bench and watched the kids pile them
up and take turns jumping, disappearing one by one as
they threw themselves recklessly into the flames.

Such a simple thing, but they seemed never to tire of
it, and he thought he would never tire of watching them.
Only one, Brendan, was his—the rest were newly made
best friends that Brendan would forget the second they
were out of sight—but it didn't matter. They were all
perfect.

He supposed he shouldn't think of Brendan as his, but
it was hard not to. In truth, he was the child of an Irish
writer Valerie had fallen in love with in the years Greg
was busy trying to drink himself to death. The relationship hadn't lasted long from what Valerie said, and the
poet had succeeded where Greg had failed not long after
Brendan was born. A boy needed a father, for better or
worse.

His mind strayed to his own children, Maria, Patrick, and John, the only good things to come from that disastrous second marriage. Greg felt a familiar stab of guilt. He didn't have much clue about where they were or what they were doing, save that they'd stayed with his uncle Les for a bit while their mother was having her own struggles. He'd lost most of those years to the booze and the shocks—so desperate for those brief windows of calm after the treatments that he'd gone back again and again, swapping doctors and taking assumed names when they'd inevitably started to blanch at the sheer amount of voltage passing through his skull.

He'd reset himself a hundred times. He still believed it had saved his life, stopped him from running completely off the rails, but the cost had been high. For everyone.

That wasn't much of an excuse, of course. Back then he'd been more focused on fixing himself than being a father, but what good was that to them?

He tried to focus on the few memories he did have. Patrick, a tiny ball of joy, artless and incapable of malice. Maria, just a smile half hidden behind a fringe in his fragmented recollection. John, a sensitive hellion, capable of anything. It was always the thought of the boys that made his mind recoil, want to flit away to any other subject as if merely thinking of them was a sort of contact, a laying on of hands by which a curse could be passed down yet again. Father to son, father to son.

Maybe the best thing for all three of them was to grow up unsullied by their father, loose links free of the family chain. That was the beauty of Brendan, he could be Greg's son and free of him at the same time. Or maybe these were lies Greg told himself to ease his conscience.

It didn't make much difference, in the end. Deeds are text, intent only ever subtext.

Brendan had found something—some hideous bug, knowing him—and was holding it out for the rest to see. Greg couldn't see the thing take flight, but he saw the children's faces all lift together, open and guileless with wonder.

So much of the world was like that, he thought, the thing itself invisible but for its effects. He had read in the papers the other day about a new sort of star they had discovered over in England—the scientists, not the star—one that pulled in light instead of putting it out. You could see it only in the telltale flickering of ordinary stars if it happened to pass between them and Earth. How much was out there, he wondered, that simply left no trace?

"Dad!" Brendan was running up, his chubby arms pumping like a sprinter's, his face scrunched up in determined focus.

Greg was ready for him, and when Brendan jumped he caught the boy neatly round the waist and hoisted him up, letting the boy wrap his arms around his neck.

"Dad." He put his mouth to Greg's ear and dropped his voice to a conspiratorial whisper. "Charlie keeps being silly and getting ants in his hair."

"Does he now?" Greg looked and saw a boy who must be Charlie stalking back to his mother beneath the line of yews, kicking sulkily at offending twigs. "And I don't suppose you had anything to do with that?"

Brendan shook his head in a corona of silky hair, and for a moment Greg could smell his shampoo. The fragility of his little body was terrifying.

"Hmm. Okay." He shifted his weight to one arm and

checked his watch. "You're going to be late for school."
The real world beckoned.

Once he'd dropped Brendan off, he took the subway
uptown. He'd made a reservation for one night at a small
but well-run hotel that he used semi-regularly. He had
a few on rotation, but he liked this place because they
let him check in early and knew how to mind their own
business.

He checked his watch again. Nine thirty. That gave
him half an hour. Perfect. He slipped into a big faceless
department store and bought a dress, makeup, and underwear. It was all perfectly respectable: he was a man buying
gifts for his wife, with a wedding ring to prove it. A good
husband. He didn't have to pretend to be relaxed—he'd
done this enough times.

Valerie knew nothing about any of this, of course.
There were a lot of things she was better off not knowing—primarily that Greg had spent years cursing her for
giving him his father's letters right when he was at his
most vulnerable. It had felt like an attempted murder that
had very nearly succeeded, but which had still managed to
destroy years of his life, and his second marriage . . . until
he'd actually tried to confront her about it.

The manipulative, cruel Valerie of his mind hadn't been
able to last five minutes in the company of the real thing.
There was no malice in her, then or now. On their drive
to the post office he'd met her at her lowest, but when
they saw each other again she'd been in high spirits, and
Greg hadn't stood a chance. Witty without being cutting;
smart, but never condescending; beautiful without a hint
of vanity. She'd dazzled him as no one else ever had, and

against all sanity she'd seen something in Greg that made her want to keep him around.

There was a new kid on the front desk of the hotel—that was another thing he liked about this place, the staff got swapped as often as the sheets—who set aside a heavy-looking textbook to check him in.

He glanced down as she scrawled *Nick Adams* in the guest ledger and saw a page dense with equations. "Heavy reading for a Monday morning."

She followed his gaze and blushed. "It's not for pleasure, promise. I have a test tomorrow and if I don't pass my dad'll skin me alive."

"Physics?"

"Pure mathematics."

He whistled. Her blush deepened, but she smiled. She knew she was clever, and she loved it. Greg found himself smiling back. *Good for her.*

"Well then, I won't keep you. I've failed a few exams in my time. Not fun."

"Physics?"

"Medicine. I'm giving it another shot, though. You know what they say, if at first . . ."

"My dad says you only lose when you give up."

"Boy, I hope so. Just make sure you have some fun when you've passed, okay?"

Her smile became a grin, surprising in its wickedness. "Will do."

For a second Greg envied her. She'd be getting dressed up, going out with her friends, young and pretty and . . .

He nodded to her and turned on his heel. Enough of that. It was that sort of thinking he was here to get rid of for another few weeks.

He locked the door behind him and laid the clothes out on the bed, savoring this moment, drawing out the antici- pation. He felt safe here, able to take his time. It was one of the rooms he always took, on the corner with a balcony. A little worn down, but clean and cared for.

He showered, then sat naked at the vanity table to paint his fingernails, then his toenails. He'd chosen a lemon yellow. Not his usual taste, but sometimes you had to be daring. Next he made up his eyes, applied lipstick, added a touch of blusher.

When he was done he took his jacket and slung it over the mirror. He'd already checked the lock twice, but he did it once more to be safe. Sometimes he still had night- mares about that time his father had walked in on him. The hinge on which their whole relationship had turned. Nothing had been the same after that, no matter how hard he'd tried to be the perfect son.

No need to think of that now. This room was sealed off from that world.

Finally, he slipped on the dress. He'd ordered their biggest size, but he still had to stretch it to get it over his shoulders, being careful all the time not to get any makeup on the neckline. He really should have applied the makeup last, but he couldn't help himself. He'd come to love this moment of transformation. With the mirror covered up he could imagine the dress falling over his hips, slipping halfway down long silky legs.

Thinking like that was forbidden, normally, but here it didn't matter. What happened in here had nothing to do with the Greg out there. And the world out there had nothing to do with the person in here. There was no such thing as the past. No parents. No failed marriages and distant children. Only this moment.

This was his safety valve, the system that gave him control. A change in modern medical advice had been the key to changing his thinking, to stop thinking of this as a disease and start thinking of it as an addiction, or more accurately a dependency. Where going cold turkey wasn't an option, the current best advice was to manage the dependency. Instead of trying to fight a battle that couldn't be won until the need became explosive, you had to set regular releases of pressure. A safety valve.

And it worked. Between this and Valerie, he was pretty much living a normal life. And in the rare moments when he felt himself slipping anyway, he had the shocks to reset him. He was using them properly now, a targeted strike against his wayward brain, rather than a carpet bombing.

He took a turn around the room, smoked one of the cigarettes he was always assuring Valerie he'd quit and enjoyed the pink imprint his lips left on the stark white paper, then called room service and ordered brunch.

He had his routine perfected. He unlocked the front door, then slipped into the bathroom and locked that behind him, waiting for the knock.

When it came he called through. "I'll be a minute, can you set it down on the bed?"

He waited for the door to click open, then close again, and even then he unlocked the bathroom door slowly and peeked out. When he was sure the room was deserted he rushed out and locked the main door. Safe.

Then he could really relax. He sat on the bed and ate slowly. He pretended he was out with Valerie, at some nice but simple restaurant in Miami with the windows

187

open and a sea breeze coming through. A pretty young waitress showed them to the best table in the corner and said, "What can I get you, girls?" and they gave each other a devilish look and said, "Let's start with cocktails, shall we?"

They laughed at each other's jokes and shared secrets and she lent Valerie her lipstick and of course Val looked beautiful in it. Then Val said, "You know, that dress really does bring out your eyes," and she blushed and put her hand over Val's and they—

"—Mr. Adams?"

He jumped up so fast he nearly knocked the tray off the bed. A voice at the door. Was it locked? He knew it was locked. It was definitely locked, but what if it wasn't?"

"Mr. Adams. Nick?"

"Yes?" Christ, why was he making his voice deeper than normal?

"I'm so sorry, I gave you the wrong key. You're supposed to be in the other corner room."

He hesitated. "Does it matter?"

"It wouldn't but we have a guest checking in later who specifically requested a room that gets the sun in the morning. I'm so sorry, could you swap?"

"Not a problem," he called, psychotically cheerful. And it was true. He'd gotten what he needed. The safety valve had done its job. "I'll just get packed up. Can you give me half an hour?"

"Of course. Thank you so much."

"Don't worry. Easily done."

He didn't have to be careful getting undressed. There was a part of him that enjoyed stretching the dress out of shape, smearing lipstick all over the fabric. It felt cathartic.

Like he was hurting whatever it was he had to indulge in here.

He shoved the clothes and the makeup into the plastic bag from the department store, then meticulously cleaned the nail varnish from his fingers and toes and shoved the bottle of remover in the bag after everything else. Only then did he take a scalding-hot shower, scrubbing his face raw to get off every trace of makeup, before dressing, un-hooking his jacket from the mirror, and heading back out into the world.

"I'm so sorry, Mr. Adams," the girl said as he passed by reception, "I can give you a reduced rate if you—"

"—Not a problem." He kept on walking, flashing her a grin before the doors swung shut behind him. Back on the street, he shoved the bag elbow-deep into the first trash can he came across, making sure it was good and buried. He wished he could burn it, but that would attract too much attention.

He still had a bit of time before he had to pick Brendan up, so he stopped by the grocery store to pick up some essentials—Valerie was working long hours these days, and he liked to make himself useful.

He paused when he saw the *New York Post* piled up next to the oranges, the byline boasting a reveal-all-secrets interview with Christine Jorgensen for the publication of her autobiography. Greg knew the name, of course—he'd been outraged when he'd first heard about her, a GI who claimed to have become a woman. Outraged that such a thing was even possible—it hadn't been in any of his medical textbooks—and horrified that someone could be so far gone as to do it. And she'd been so . . . public about everything. The whole thing had made Greg's skin crawl.

Now though, Greg felt no anger, just a vague sense of pity. A dedicated drinker shaking his head at an alcoholic.

He tossed the newspaper back on the pile and picked up a shooting magazine instead.

Valerie was already home when Greg let them through the door, seated on the couch with a book, her shoes beside her and her feet tucked up neatly like a cat. She didn't lift her eyes as Brendan stormed through to the kitchen, but she tilted her head, as if unconsciously, for Greg to kiss her cheek, which he did.

"Hello love you're back early."

"Mm-hm." She held out a hand, her slender fingers light on his forearm, but holding him there more effectively than shackles as she finished her paragraph, folded over the page, and closed the book. "I'm sorry, what did you say?"

"I said, tough day?"

"Oh, no. I left early. Had a bath. After the weekend everyone was taking it easy today." Her fingertips ran over his skin and she slipped her hand into his.

"I don't think I'd be relaxed if they'd had me working on a weekend."

"Yes well, launching our biggest book of the year with a six-month turnaround was a stupid decision, but it is a damn good book. I want to do it justice . . ."

"You will."

She squeezed his hand. Her fingers were slender, but strong.

"Oh, and before I forget, there's a permission slip on the table by the door, could you take it with you when you drop Brendan off tomorrow?"

"Sure. What's it for?"

"Oh, just sports. Boxing classes after school. Saying we won't hold them responsible if he gets hurt. Everyone in this city's so damn litigious, even the schools."

Greg thought about that for a moment. "Are you sure that's a good idea?"

She shrugged loosely. "What's the worst that can happen? They're kids, and they'll be wrapped up in so much padding they'll bounce if they knock each other over."

Greg remembered boxing in the dust. The sweat stinging his eyes. His lip swollen and bloody. Desperately keeping his guard up against the blows of a boy nearly half as tall again as he was, trying to focus but all the while feeling Papa's eye on him from the corner, not sure if he'd be angrier if Greg won or lost.

He thought of Brendan's thin arms around his neck.

"Valerie," he said, keeping his voice very level and calm. "No."

She stiffened, and he thought she might argue, remind him that he was only the boy's stepfather and *she* was the one who'd decide what her son did and did not do, thank you very much. Instead she stared at him perceptively for a moment, then said, "OKAY." And that was that.

Greg coughed, suddenly embarrassed. He wondered if she'd noticed that he'd started to sweat. "Maybe he could try tennis?"

"Hard to find courts in New York."

"What are we paying them for? Do you—"

                                                —There was a
shout, and the sound of something falling over in the kitchen. Greg sighed and turned, but Valerie pulled him back as she stood.

"Don't worry, I haven't seen him all day. Make yourself a drink and hit the books. You've got to study if you're going to be *Doctor* Hemingway next month." She paused in the doorway. "Besides, he needs a firm hand."

"Don't we all."

When she was gone he moved to the drinks cabinet and poured himself a finger of bourbon. He surveyed the room: one wall a monolith of well-worn books and knickknacks, the tasteful modern sofa that contrasted artfully with the Persian rug, his desk tucked into a corner and surrounded by a jungle of potted plants. It was all Valerie: friendly clutter, gentle order. None of his fragmenting chaos. That was what he liked best about this apartment, their tumbledown New York hidey-hole. That it was hers. That, more than anything else, made it feel like home for him.

Valerie, the safety valve, and the occasional round of shocks, that was all he needed. Unfortunately, Valerie didn't approve of electroshock therapy, thought it barbaric—probably because it had done so badly for his father in the end—but he wouldn't give them up. She didn't know what it was like to be hurtling along in a car with no steering wheel.

He sat down on the couch, stretched out his legs, and let himself relax for a few blessed minutes, watching the motes of dust tumble through the evening light. He moved only to fish Valerie's discarded book from under himself.

Islands in the Stream, Ernest Hemingway.

He tossed it to the floor and sipped his whiskey, tried to go back to watching the world unfold. But the light had changed, or he had, and he couldn't reach the Zen-like state he had found so easily before.

He leaned over and pulled the book back toward him. He didn't need to go to the cover page to know that it would be inscribed: *To Valerie, with love, Papa.*

The book fell open to a well-worn crease.

The smallest boy was fair and was built like a pocket battleship. He was a copy of Thomas Hudson, physically, reduced in scale and widened and shortened. His skin freckled when it tanned and he had a humorous face and was born being very old. He was a devil too, and deviled both his older brothers, and he had a dark side to him that nobody except Thomas Hudson could ever understand. Neither of them thought about this except that they recognized it in each other and knew it was bad and the man respected it and understood the boy's having it. They were very close to each other although Thomas Hudson had never been as much with this boy as with the others. This youngest boy, Andrew, was a precocious excellent athlete and he had been marvelous with horses since he had first ridden. The other boys were very proud of him but they did not want any nonsense from him, either. He was a little unbelievable and anyone could well have doubted his feats except that many people had seen him ride and watched him jump and seen his cold, professional modesty. He was a boy born to be quite wicked who was being very good and he carried his wickedness around with him transmuted into a sort of teasing gaiety. But he was a bad boy and the others knew it and he knew it. He was just being good while his badness grew inside him.

Greg stood, crossed to the bookshelf, and stuffed the book spine inwards on a high shelf. His hands were shaking, so he poured himself another drink.

Childish laughter spilled out of the kitchen, drowning out the sound of the whiskey sloshing into the glass. Greg paused, listening. Valerie said something inaudible, her voice low and musical, and Brendan squealed like a ghoul. She started laughing too.

Greg tipped the whiskey back into the bottle and sat down at his desk. He pulled his textbooks toward him with weary determination and started going over the same material he'd gone over that morning, and the day before that. He hoped that this time it would stick.

New York

1968

"I suppose it's more of a tingling, really. Maybe a . . . sensation. Is that the medical term?"

There were 163 ceiling tiles in Greg's office. Most were the color of an overcast sky, but those directly overhead had a sickly yellow-brown tinge. His predecessor must have been a dedicated smoker.

The General Motors New York offices were almost aggressively drab. When Greg had taken the job he'd felt excited. The third try at medical college really had been the charm—it had been his first attempt with Valerie for a wife, which he doubted was a coincidence—and now he was going to be putting all those years of hard study to use, setting limbs shattered in the machines of industry, rebuilding bodies chewed up by the march of progress. Instead, on his first day he had been shown up to his grubby office on the fifth floor, and the endless troops of stressed middle-managers, weary pen-pushers, and drug-hungry execs had begun filing in.

He supposed he should have read the job description.

"But it's not all the time. Mostly it starts at the end of

the day. By the next morning I'm fine, but it just starts all over again."

Four o'clock. One hour to go. He had never been so aware of the second hand ticking away. A sequence of eternities seemed to yawn between each neat mechanical movement.

"Like I said, it's a sort of a . . . tingling. Almost an ache, really."

Greg adjusted his position, and the cheap leather chair he'd been meaning to swap out gave an awkwardly loud belch. At least it surprised his "patient" into silence.

"Lenny," Greg tried, "I don't know what to tell you. Nothing's changed since last week."

"I understand that, but—"

"—it would be frankly unethical for me to prescribe you medication when we both know damn well your jaw wouldn't ache so much if you didn't get through three packs of bubblegum by lunchtime."

"Ah, but it's not possible for me to stop. It's an addiction. I feel weird if I don't have some bubblegum, I grind my teeth."

"Have you considered chewing one piece at a time?"

Lenny looked at him as though he had suggested cutting off his own nose and chewing on that, and even through his shock his teeth worked away, masticating wetly. Greg felt like he was staring into the open mouth of a loaded cement mixer.

"You need a good wedge, Doc, and I can't chew gum with no flavor. Adding to the wedge is part of the pleasure."

"The wedge . . . right." Greg glanced at the clock. He

could have sworn it had gone backward. "Look, Lenny. I'm not giving you painkillers unless you actually catch your hand in the presser— don't even think about it, I can see your mind working. You'll regret it and I might still not give you anything out of spite. Think about that."

Lenny looked up at him sulkily. "I don't know why you're being so unreasonable."

Greg resisted the urge to rub his temples. "I'm an unreasonable man. Monstrous, really. So it would be pointless for you to show up again next week."

"Well . . ." Lenny sighed. "I'll see if it clears up, Dr. H, but it can get so distracting . . . it's hard to work."

Greg sighed. At least Dr. H was better than Gigi. "See you next week, Lenny."

"See you, Doc."

When Lenny had gone and the sound of his relentless chomping had receded down the hall, Greg leaned back in his shitty chair and stared up at his stained ceiling. He glanced at the clock. Five minutes past four.

He sighed.

At half past, with no more appointments for the day, Greg was stalking the halls. Another half hour in that office and he'd pull open the window and take a swan dive onto the Manhattan sidewalk. New Yorkers didn't have time for that. Imagine the damage to all those freshly shined brogues.

He found a water cooler on the eleventh floor, drank a cup, then filled another, watching the thick opalescent bubbles chuckle upwards like jellyfish. He emptied the second cup in the pot of a wilted-looking office plant nearby and went to fill up another.

"Hey there. You all right?"

Greg realized his cup was running over, cool clear water tracing the tips of his fingers and pattering on the beige carpet.

"Shit." He tipped a little into the overflow—which was already full and just sent another splat of water to the floor—then drank the rest in two gulps.

Beside him was a man he half recognized. A patient, maybe, though that didn't mean much. Greg had prescribed something for "nerves" to half the men in the building by this point.

"You don't remember me, Doc?"

Greg shook the man's soft hand, and his run-down brain had a sudden flash of inspiration. "Sampson, right? Richard Sampson. You had the . . . rash."

Sampson coughed softly. "Yeah, that's me all right. The cream did wonders, by the way. So, what brings you up to high altitude, Greg?"

"Oh, nothing much . . . Paying an office call."

"An office call? I didn't realize that was an option!"

Greg cursed himself silently. "Only in . . . extreme circumstances."

Sampson's eyebrows rose. They were thin, freshly plucked. Greg thought it made him look faintly effeminate, but guessed he wasn't in much of a position to judge. "Is someone in a bad way?"

"Ah, not life-threatening. I can't say any more. Confidentiality, you understand."

"Right, right." Sampson looked disappointed, but he took it on the chin. "Can I?"

Greg realized he was still blocking the water cooler. He stepped back, ignoring the squelch beneath his shoes. "Be my guest." Christ, he sounded like an idiot. It must be a symptom of office life. "Well, I should probably get back. Gotta get my stuff packed up. If I'm not home at half five on the dot the nanny'll start charging overtime."

"Sure. Family responsibility. Hell of a drag, but it keeps us out of trouble, right, Greggy?"

Sampson gave a conspiratorial wink that made Greg want to punch him. He wondered if that would be breaking his Hippocratic oath. "It's just Greg."

Sampson didn't seem to hear. He laughed to himself, leaning against the water cooler like a man settling in for the long haul. It tilted alarmingly, and Greg willed it to pitch over with every fiber of his being. "Ah, I was a hell of a wild buck until my kids came along. They give you a sense of perspective, you know what I mean?"

"Sure." Greg crumpled up his paper cup. There was a bin next to the water cooler, but that would involve getting closer to Sampson, so he threw it overarm into the wastepaper basket on the far side of the room.

"Nice shot. Yeah. I mean, one minute you're seeing more girls than you can count, drinking late every night, not giving a damn about anything. And then BAM," he crumpled his own cup, "suddenly it's all about getting a stable job, bringing home the bread, and you spend all your time worrying where the good schools are and where the colored neighborhoods aren't. Not that that's a problem after a certain pay bracket, am I right, Greggy?"

Greg had a vivid memory of the sun on his back, down at the harbor fishing with Rodolfo, Ramos, and all the rest. Greg had sliced his hand open trying to gut their first catch, and Rodolfo had ripped a long strip out of his shirt to bandage his bloody palm even though he must have known his mother would beat him ragged for it. He'd only had two shirts.

Greg opened his mouth, then closed it again. There was no point.

Sampson nodded, and threw his own cup toward the far bin. It made it about three-quarters of the way rolling, but Sampson acted like nothing had happened, adjusted his heavy cufflinks, and resumed his lean. "So. How many?"

"What?"

"How many kids have you got?"

"Oh." Greg hesitated a moment. "Four."

Sampson blinked. "Not bad for a young fella, Greg."

Greg sighed, accepting he wasn't going to escape easily. "It didn't seem so hard."

"No. Hey, that's great. Best thing you can do is start your family young. I wish more guys had the sense to settle down early. How old's your oldest?"

Greg had to pause a moment. How old *was* Lorian now?

The pause lengthened painfully. "Er, fifteen."

"Right. Well . . . Good age. Mine's ten. He's a bit too young to actually . . . do anything with, you know? I'm thinking I'll wait until he's about twelve before I take over from the missus."

"How do you know?" Greg asked idly.

"What?"

"If your son's ten, how do you know fifteen is a good age? It could be terrible."

Sampson stared at him. From deeper in the maze of corridors behind him, a bell gave a long weary groan. "Well . . ." He straightened up, the water cooler rocking back and forth noisily. "Clocking off time. I'll see you around, Greggy."

"Sure," said Greg, watching the water slop back and forth, back and forth toward a slow equilibrium. "See you around."

Back in his office, packing up, Greg found himself staring idly out the window. Below, New Yorkers were flooding out of work, a human deluge of hopefuls and malcontents, few of them born here, almost none of them ever planning to go home. Men in crisply pressed suits rubbed shoulders with flat-capped shoe-shiners. Young women in black office skirts slipped into the bathrooms of diners and emerged in frocks and petticoats on their way to basement jazz clubs and juke joints. Trust-fund prep-schoolers wound their Bentleys through the juddering flow of dented taxis looking for pickups. It swallowed you up, this city. You forgot the rest of the world existed. But it did.

Somewhere out there that solemn girl he had last seen in Tanzania was becoming a young woman. He wondered what she looked like. Lorian. Did she have any of him in her? He hoped not, for her sake. But what if she did? What if she too, in her teenage years, was discovering that her mind was a lighthouse?

For most of her life Greg had been a human disaster zone. Shirley had taken their daughter and left him in Africa for precisely that reason and he'd never blamed her for it, at least not when he was in his right mind. They'd both been better off without him.

In the years that followed, he'd made a lot of mistakes, hurt himself and others. He'd been a bad husband, a worse father. She'd been better off having him just be a name in her birthday cards. A name on a check.

That had been true, but he was better now, wasn't he? He still had his ups and downs but . . .

Maybe it wasn't too late.

He had a vague memory of being told the girl liked to fish despite neither her mother nor stepfather showing anything but contempt for the sport. Perhaps some things really could travel through the blood, even skipping whole generations.

Greg himself had hated fishing—probably because he'd had no talent for it the way he'd had no talent for anything that required patience—but even he had some treasured memories of being out on the boat with Papa. More and more of them the longer these calm years stretched.

He looked up at the clock. It was half five.

He picked up the phone.

Key West

1939

"Swell."

"What is?"

"Just this."

Greg watched Uncle Les look around his brother's boat as though seeing it for the first time, then out at the heaving sea all around, an expression of sudden shock on his broad face. "By God . . . you're right, Captain! Once again your writerly powers of description have let me see the world afresh."

Greg hesitated. It was dangerous, making fun of his father. But then Papa threw back his head and let out his rumble of a laugh. Safe, Greg smiled in turn, looking over to Patrick and John, who grinned back from their seats, fishing rods in their hands and matching daubs of zinc over their noses.

"Screw you, Baron. I'm off duty."

"Clearly."

"You couldn't write a note to the mailman, and you're mocking me?" Papa shook his head and wound in his own line just a little—the new Penn reel humming sweetly, the line shining and dripping like a squeezed lemon as it rose from the water. "Grab me a beer, would you, Gig? Or better yet, a rum if your mother remembered to pack the limes."

Greg jumped up from his perch beside the two men, eager to be useful. He'd felt pretty sick when they were motoring out—though he'd been careful to hide it from his father—but once they'd killed the engine and let the boat settle to a gentle roll his energy had come back with interest.

Inside the main cabin of the *Pilar* the air was cool and damp, smelling faintly of salt and a lot of the bottle of brandy that had fallen out of Papa's bag while they were turning out of the harbor. He rummaged quickly through the lunch hamper, a jumbled hoard of heavy sandwiches double-wrapped in creamy wax paper, hard-boiled eggs, avocados, oranges, but no limes.

"Gig-man? You brewing it yourself in there?"

He dove his fist into the icy slush in the cooler, yanked out the first beer he could find, and ran to the door, then after a moment's reflection ran back and grabbed another for Uncle Les.

Both men grinned gratefully when he emerged, a can in each fist. Les finished the last of his own beer with a slurp and tossed his empty into the boundless gulf.

"You've raised a good boy, Ernest."

"I know that." Papa smiled at Greg as he took his own beer, then reached out with one arm and scooped him onto his knee. "Get a feel for it, Gig-man," he whispered, leaning forward. "Fuck horse racing, this is the sport of kings. You versus the sea."

Greg placed one hand on the reel and looked down the

slender length of rod glowing in the midday sun, to the great purple roll of the ocean.

He'd barely begun to get settled before Papa was hoisting him back down. "A few more years yet though. Need to get a bit more muscle on your frame. The only way you'd catch a fish now is as bait."

Too young to fish, too young to shoot. Greg cast an envious glance toward his brothers. One broad, the other lean, both bigger than him, both intent on the water and their dinky rods.

John, somehow sensing Greg's gaze, leaned back and looked over his already pink shoulder. Greg quickly looked away and wandered further up the boat. John seemed incredibly grown up, worldly and well traveled. He hadn't spent his childhood in boring Miami. Paris, Madrid and who-knew-where in Italy had been John's stomping grounds.

He climbed up to the top deck and looked out to Bimini, a dark hump on the horizon where his mother was probably sunning herself by the pool. The sky completely clear except for a few lone gulls that spiraled overhead. Below, the Gulf Stream was a river with no bottom, searching relentlessly for something Greg would never know. It pulled and pushed and fumbled and quested, turning the boat this way and that as though this time, *this time*, it would find what it was looking for. Up top, the rocking felt much worse than it had on the deck, and Greg decided that he wanted to get back down as soon as possible.

John caught two fish, and Papa clapped him on the back and said he was growing up into a hell of a man. Even Patrick caught something, but Papa had to cut the line when they realized it was a mako shark. He still seemed to count it as a catch, though, and he and Les and the two boys all drank a beer together.

Greg watched from his gently swaying perch and tried not to feel jealous.

As soon as Papa let him fish, he'd show them. He'd be the best.

Later, the boat was quiet. The sun, which had been a fierce ball of white beating down on them all day, began to fatten and bleed to red as it approached the horizon.

Les was at the stern, telling Patrick the same old story of his own hunt in Africa that had bored Greg the first time he heard it, but which always seemed to hold Patrick enthralled. John had drunk one too many celebratory beers and was sleeping it off below deck.

Greg drifted away from his uncle and brother and stared over the side, watching the Gulf Stream sluice over the polished black hull of his father's boat. Water that seemed thick as paint, then sometimes great brushstrokes of clear where he could see down and down as if he was looking out an airplane window.

It gave him something like vertigo, and when the stern clipped the first of the swells that would kick up now they were drawing closer to land, he felt a lurch of nausea twist through him.

He stepped away from the edge, shaking his head until the feeling passed.

"You all right, Gig-man?"

He shaded his eyes and saw Papa looking down at him from the wheel.

Greg climbed up to the top deck, and when he came

close his father cupped a gentle hand to the back of his head.

"You beat?"

"No. I was just thinking."

"Ah."

"About how big the sea is."

"Nothing bigger. Not on this earth anyway. And all of it's alive."

"Alive?"

"Yeah. The sea is life, Gig. No doubt. Especially here. Every inch is teeming with it. Plankton in every drop. Tuna and sharks and turtle and sailfish every square mile. You drop a stone over the edge of this boat and it'll hit something on the way down."

Greg imagined that. Dropping some stone and hitting a confused shark on the head. He grinned. It didn't seem quite so scary now.

"That's the beauty of it," Papa continued. "Fecundity, that's the word. Every man in America could take to fishing tomorrow, devote every hour to it, and we still wouldn't even scratch the stocks that are out here. The sea can't be used up. It's a wilderness that can never be tamed."

"Like the wild west?"

"Ha. Yes, something like that. But with dolphins for sheriffs, and sharks for bandits."

"So what are we?"

"Us?" His father looked at him, as though surprised he could ask such a question. "We're the cowboys of course."

Gigi leaned into his father's side, and his father let him.

"John did good today, huh?"

"Yes, he did. Shame it was a shark, but he battled it like

a man. That's all you can do, after all, fight the battles that come to you with everything you have."

"Like cowboys."

"Yes, Gig. Like cowboys."

Bimini

1968

"So, what sort of thing do you fish for back home?"

Lorian lifted her head from scrutinizing the distant blot of Bimini receding in their wake. Her platinum-blond hair fell over one shoulder, and she surveyed him with eyes every bit as dark and unreadable as the little girl's he remembered.

"What was that, Greg?" she asked.

She had been looking at him that same way on the whole flight over, as if he was something she had dredged up from a river. Some bottom feeder she could not identify.

"I said," he took great effort with every word, because right now everything was an effort, "your mother said you fish. What exactly do you fish for?"

She looked up at him silently, just long enough to be insolent, then let out a long Mississippi drawl, "Catfish." Kayetfeesh. A parody of herself. He knew from their stilted small talk on the plane that her accent was mild.

In a better time, Greg might have found some way to break through her scorn and disinterest. Entertained her. Charmed her. At his best it might have been easy, but he was not at his best. Far from it.

He was heading into a depressive trough, was already deeper than he'd been in years. He'd known the darkness would come back eventually—not even Valerie could keep it away forever—but it couldn't have chosen a worse time.

He knew he probably should have checked himself in by now, had everything blasted clean. But Lorian's trip had been planned for months, and by the time this particular bad patch had come along it had been too late. What would she have thought if he'd canceled a few days before she was due to fly out?

So he had two choices: get the shocks anyway and meet her for the first time in years with a head full of cotton wool, or suck it up and be a father.

Perhaps he'd made the wrong call. Every time she stared at him he could feel her looking past his defenses, past his bluster and bravado, and seeing the second-rate second-class shitbag excuse of a man he was. Was he imagining it? He couldn't tell, but it was obvious she wasn't impressed.

She turned away from him now, walking with instinctive sea legs toward the prow, one hand trailing along railings that were blinding silver in the sun, her pretty lilac nails glinting.

She may have found her father underwhelming, but she seemed to like the boat. When they'd come into the harbor and seen captain Bob waving to them from the deck of the long sleek powerboat, her eyes had widened for the first time since stepping into their no doubt shabby-seeming New York apartment. Her room had been smaller than she had expected. Their car was older than the convertible she'd gotten for her sweet sixteenth. New York had been dirty and crowded. The plane they had flown into Bimini on had been "rickety." But the boat? The boat had earned only silence, which Greg was starting to learn was high praise indeed.

Right now, Bob was standing up at the wheel, jewelry flashing on every finger, huge sunglasses turning his eyes into black mirrors reflecting two seas back at the world.

Greg knew he should go after her, but there didn't seem much point. He was fighting a losing battle. With her. With himself. Neither of their hearts were in this.

It seemed that was the only thing he had in common with his daughter. Neither of them liked him very much.

The mineral blue of the Bimini coast began to darken into navy and purple as they passed into the Gulf Stream, exactly as Greg remembered, and the choppy breakers stretched themselves into low powerful swells.

To Greg, sailing into the Gulf Stream always felt like a sacred event. There were few more powerful forces in the world. The gulf moved a billion metric tons of water a second, dictated weather all over the planet, and scattered plankton and krill so that whole oceans' ecosystems could thrive.

It was like sailing on a god.

His father's god. There weren't many places that had a more mythical significance to Papa than this bottomless current just off the American continental shelf.

This was where his father had been his truest self, for better and worse.

Lorian had climbed up onto the captain's deck, a slender waif beside Bob's muscular bulk. She said something to him, and he laughed, a gold tooth winking from the moist darkness of his open mouth.

Something inside Greg twisted.

Bob saw him looking and gave Greg one of his unreadable grins that said nothing but somehow always seemed mocking.

For a moment Greg wondered why he had paid Bob to take them out. All those years ago, on the family trips to Bimini, Bob had always been his father's first choice to pilot his own beautiful boat *Pilar*, but those trips hadn't made many happy memories for Greg. Not once he was old enough to take part in the actual fishing.

"This will do," Bob boomed suddenly, his voice easily overpowering the throb of the engines. "Let's get you set up, Mr. Hemingway."

He killed the engines, and a minute later Greg was strapped into the chair at the back of the boat, the chair in turn bolted solidly to the deck. It occurred to him then that he probably should have worn long sleeves. It was due to be a hot day, and the morning sun was already blazing.

Bob had started threading fat slices of mullet onto hooks big as witches' fingers. There were two outriggers on either side of the chair, each carrying a line down to the very surface of the water to make sure the bait moved naturally in the boat's wake. When the time came and one of those lines had five hundred pounds of pissed-off sea monster on the end, Greg would have to quickly knock the locking pin out before the line snapped, and then the battle would begin.

The thought made his hands tighten into fists. But at least Lorian finally seemed interested. She was circling the chair like a shark, taking in everything—the huge rods, the slender outriggers, the lengths of taut line. It was the first time she seemed like a kid, full of curiosity as she laid her hand against the side of one of the massive reels, the brass shining between her spread fingers, and said, "Greg, how big are these fish?"

"You'll see." He forced out the words, trying for playfully mysterious, but sounding only smug. It was a common thing when he was low—the simplest acts of communication seemed as alien as semaphore. Damn, he was tired, and already starting to feel queasy. If only the timing had been different. If only he could have met Lorian as himself, or even in a peak; anything but this.

Lorian retreated, and Greg silently cursed himself.

After half a minute he heard a laugh, then the sound of Bob mock-retching. A shiver went through him. Betrayal. Shame. He knew without a doubt that they were laughing at him. That Bob was telling her of all the times the boy-Greg had spent whole trips leaning over the rails. He looked straight ahead, pretending not to have heard.

There was a bit more muttering, a bit more laughter, and then Lorian was beside him again, her hands full of coins.

"Bob said I should throw these in. For good luck. Seems dumb, but whatever."

Greg's heart sank even further, down to drag through the silt. Offering up the coins for luck was as old as fishing itself, but he should have been the one to think of it, to give them to her. It was something a father should do.

Too late now. Despite her words, she held them in her cupped hands like another girl might have held rosaries in prayer, then leaned over the rail and threw them in one bright scattering. They turned in the air, all shapes and sizes and denominations, and struck the side of a wave in liquid staccato. For a second, Greg could still glimpse them, glinting like fish as they rippled down into the bruised dark, seeking the miles-distant ocean floor where no more hands would trouble them.

He was half tempted to dive in after.

But the engine was starting up again, a long tail of creamy foam rising up and then stretching behind, slowly disappearing into blue infinity.

Greg sat silent, trying to ignore how much worse the hum of the engine and the slap of the waves felt when you were strapped down. A part of him, and not a small part, hoped that the seas would prove empty. Sometimes it went like that for days at a time. And wasn't nothing better than failure?

But there was Lorian, staring up at him, for the first time not scornful, or reserved. He could still salvage this. There was still hope.

If he could only catch a damn fish, somehow he knew it would define the whole day. The whole trip. Nothing else would matter. Their whole lives together, as father and daughter, might rely on one of those slender lengths of line disappearing into the tumbling gulf.

Catch the fish. Get Lorian on a plane home before he fell apart. Get to the clinic and clean himself up.

He had a plan.

He watched the water churn as minutes slipped into hours, watched a few terns circle high overhead.

He remembered how, after he had lost his first fish to panic and inexperience, his father's anger had been unspeakable. Perhaps it had been because he'd brought a friend out and wanted to show off his youngest son who excelled at everything so easily. Greg's failure, not only in skill but in nerve and courage, had struck his father like a personal affront. So Greg had spent the whole trip strapped in a chair like this one, miserable, seasick, and ashamed, while his father had taken his gun and blasted the ancestors of those terns out of the sky.

Terns mated for life, so once he had killed one— knocked the life out of it in an instant and sent it spiraling limply into the surf—the other had always stayed, circling the boat, calling and calling. His father had let them linger a while, stomping over the deck and making terse remarks, but the next shot always seemed to come from right behind Greg's chair.

He'd spent half a day buckled there, watching the small bedraggled corpses of the terns churn in the boat's wake, diminishing into distance.

The bird overhead called out again, and its mate looped in to join it. Greg looked up at them, the sharp backslash of their wings, the clean lines of black and white, the delicate foolishness of their legs tucked uselessly beneath them. He smiled for the first time in days, then brought his attention back to the water.

They saw the fish long before it took the bait. A sudden plume of spray moving into their wake, a glimpse of a broad back glittering in chain mail. Silver. Sapphire. Chrome. The dorsal fin unfurling as it surged.

There was a moment for Lorian to say: "It's huge . . ."

And it was. A leviathan.

Then it struck the bait with the force of a runaway sedan, and the air was full of the unfurling line's scream.

"The rod, man! The rod!" Bob yelled.

Greg rammed the safety pin down with the heel of his left hand and grabbed the rod with his right. While the line was still running loose he jammed the butt into the cup between his legs and locked his arms.

The fish was bolting back and forth with impossible speed as it tested the limits of its trap, more like a fly dancing through the air than five hundred pounds of armored fish pushing its way through a turbulent ocean. Then without warning it banked hard right, no feint this time, just a headlong dash.

"Let him go, man! Let him go!"

Greg did, and Bob pushed the ship's twin engines into a snarl as they chased the fish out over the heaving face of the sea. They had to. If the marlin turned all its monstrous power against the line it would have snapped like a thread of cotton.

Lorian was pressed up against the railing, knuckles white, her eyes wide and hungry.

Greg took heart and, as if it could feel his resolve, the fish grew weary and began circling back. Bob killed the engines and shouted, "Have at him, have at him, boss," and Greg heaved on the rod. It was like trying to rein in a bull. The fish's hesitation was the only thing that made it possible. In a game of pure strength, it would have ripped his arms out of their sockets.

"He's running. He's running!" Bob shouted as the engines kicked back into life.

Can't he say anything once? Greg thought bitterly, letting the line go with relief.

He was already sweating, the muscles in his shoulders already on fire. How had his father done this all summer? How had he *enjoyed* it?

He heard the engine die again and, before Bob could shout out another echo, he snapped the tension on the line and started hauling. The sun seemed to have doubled in size, smashing down on the back of his neck. His palms were raw.

He was about to ask Lorian to run and fetch a bucket of water to pour over his hands when he heard her gasp. How she knew it was coming he could never guess, but half a second later the fish leaped.

It was magnificent.

Half a ton of gem-cut, gleaming muscle rising from the sea like a dancer, its tail thrashing the water into thunderclouds so that it seemed to hang there, supernatural, king of the sea. Its flanks were sky and storm, its belly pure mercury, its mouth a gaping gash of bloody red. And staring out at them was its huge gray eye, watching them, seeing them.

Greg heard Lorian whisper, "Now that's a fish," before the monster let itself fall back into the surf with a crack. And then the line was running out all over again, somehow faster this time, as if the fish had seen him and found him wanting. As if it knew it could beat him.

Greg's fingers moved toward the reel and, as if he was psychic, Bob called out, "Let him go, man, you gotta let him go."

Greg snatched his hand back. That wound of a mouth flashed through his mind. That Lorian eye.

He did not want to catch this fish. He wanted nothing more than to be off this boat, out of here. Home.

Whatever it was he felt, it must have shown on his face, because suddenly he heard laughter. He looked at Lorian, and yes, she was laughing at him, at his naked fear.

Anger rose up in him. Not at her, or the fish, but at himself.

"Let him go! Let him—"

Greg slammed on the reel, rearing and yanking, hoping he could rip the jaw out of the fish, wishing he had a gun so he could blow its heart out and be done.

The line snapped with a clear ping. The fish was gone. No final confrontation, no mutual destruction. Just a sweet summer day, a tumbling wake of foam, and an empty sea.

"Ah man. Why'd you—goddamn it, man. Goddamn it." Bob's voice was laden with grief, maybe even anger, but it was Lorian's voice that cut the deepest.

"You lost him." She stared out into the blue, then looked up at him, her gaze pure disappointment. "You lost him."

Greg knew that look. He fumbled at the straps binding him in place. The mix of adrenaline and surf and defeat was a tight ball in his stomach, and he barely managed to throw himself over the railing before it rushed out of him. Cornflakes and stomach acid and the liberal dose of whiskey he'd had to steady his nerves that morning.

When it was over, he was left weak and trembling, expecting to hear a gunshot any moment. He wiped his mouth with his sleeve and rested his head against the scorching hot metal of the railing.

"Sorry, Greg." Lorian was still standing there, and he couldn't tell if she was talking about the fish, his sickness, or everything else.

He turned his head, keeping his temple to the metal, and looked up at her. She was staring at his hand as he held himself steady, and he realized there was still a streak of poppy-red varnish clinging to his thumbnail. How had he missed that? He was always so careful.

Some craven part of him wanted to yank his hand back, hide it away, but it was too late.

"Call me, *Father*, will you?" he panted, wanting that at least. That one small scrap to take away.

She lifted her eyes, and they said everything, but all that mattered was that they said no.

Lorian was back on a plane to Mississippi the next day.

Havana

1970

The finca was less a museum, and more a mausoleum. It had reminded Greg of Mary's home in Ketchum once his father had passed; all those carefully preserved relics, offerings in the shrine to the vanished god. He'd never liked Mary's house and he certainly hadn't liked the Hemingway Museum.

Places like that made him feel like he was walking through formaldehyde, that he might head to the door and find it locked, painted on, and him another part of the exhibit.

Observe the son, lesser striking from the same cast. Note the imperfections, the cracks.

The whole time he'd been reminded of his father, how it had ended with so many cruel words passing between them.

Valerie had liked it, though. Maybe she'd been gratified to see that all the work she and Mary had put into preserving these fragments of Papa's life had been put to good use. Or perhaps she was just feeling nostalgic for a past that wasn't hers, turning over the photos to read the inscriptions on the back, climbing the tower to Greg and Patrick's old room, their childhood sheets still laid out on their beds as though, if you waited long enough, you might hear their light steps on the stairs before they rushed in, sunburned and dirty-faced and incandescently alive.

Greg had touched his old pillow with one hand, felt the thin fabric catch on his calluses, then gone to wait for Valerie outside.

They'd come to Cuba to inspect the patch of hillside Mary had given to them as part of her continuous dealing out of his father's estate. Papa had never written a proper will, so it was left to Mary as last wife standing to dole out snippets of his possessions, money, and land with the air of a pope issuing indulgences. Never mind that most of it was from long before she ever shared his bed.

Greg had responded to her offer with his tried and tested method: ignoring her. But after a hard winter in New York, where the endless slush was grayer than the sidewalk and the bitter wind ran like a train through the canyon streets, the idea of having a place in the sun had become strangely irresistible, so he and Valerie had flown out to take a look.

While in Cuba, Valerie had insisted they spend the morning drifting through the dusty rooms of what had been the finca, but which had become—after Mary's generous, perhaps not entirely voluntary, donation—The Cuban People's Hemingway Museum. Or something similar. These things always had *People's* in the name somewhere.

"Do you remember it much?" she asked Greg, as they left the crowded streets where he had played as a boy, the streets where Rodolfo had died, and began climbing the long hillside trail to their plot of land.

"Cuba, or my childhood?"

"Either."

"Bits and bobs."

"Bits and bobs?"

"What do you want from me, woman?"

"Obedience, but that's beside the point. I grew up in Ireland, remember? I can't imagine being here as a kid. It must have seemed like one big theme park."

"I don't— here." He held out his hand and helped her up over a boulder that had come loose and settled on the trail. A twisted ankle would be a bad idea. It was rough terrain, and no one else was taking this path. They were alone but for the roar of a billion insects and the quiet gaze of the jungle. "I don't think kids know the difference. You only know what you know."

"Thank you. Very poetic." She left her hand in his, slightly damp from the exertion of the climb, small and perfectly formed.

"You wanted poetry? Forsooth, what can a child know of this boundless world when his vision is no more than a nutshell? How can he dream of the infinities receding behind every chosen moment when he knows no more than a handful of instants?"

"That wasn't poetry, that was cod-Shakespeare. Bad cod-Shakespeare."

"Why are you so cruel to me, my love?"

"It's my hobby, my love. So?"

He sighed. They walked higher, their hands loosely joined. Valerie pretended to be looking out over the marbled shimmer of the sea that came in jumps and starts through the trees, but Greg knew her well enough to ignore that carefully controlled surface. He chose his words slowly.

"Well. I remember more than you think. Quite a lot. Some bits are a bit vague, but there's still some things so vivid they might have happened yesterday. But it all . . . doesn't really connect together, like a big pile of gems I can pick through."

"Or like someone smashed all your stained-glass windows."

"Val . . ."

"Sorry. I just worry about what they've done to you, those shocks."

"It's the only thing that helps, Val. The only thing that resets me."

"Does it though, really?"

"Yes."

She only sighed.

They walked on. There was a crash in the undergrowth to their left. Valerie pressed closer, but Greg knew it was probably only a clumsy young hutia bashing its way past. There was nothing in these forests to be scared of.

"And anyway," he added, "the longer I'm here, the more pieces keep popping back into my head. Maybe it's all still in me somewhere. But buried. Jumbled up. Maybe if we spend some time out here . . . you know I'm good at jigsaws."

"You hate them."

"They're incredibly tedious, but I'm good at them."

"So are five-year-olds."

"Pah, I'll take any five-year-old in America in a good clean jigsaw competition. Now, a seven-year-old, that might be a challenge . . ."

"You're an idiot."

"You married an idiot."

"Someone has to look after you."

The forest swelled around them as they rose. The light, filtered through a thousand leaves, seemed thicker somehow, like they were laboring underwater.

It felt good to be back. The house had been awful, but these hills and forests and lush fields were different. They were just as he remembered, but not because they'd been preserved or locked in time. They were self-renewing. Always changing, always the same.

Valerie was right: things had been pretty rough the last year or so. It had started shortly before the trip with Lorian, and there had been some pretty deep troughs since, but in this moment? He might have been a kid again, wandering purely for the sake of it, his whole life ahead of him.

Something moved across the trail, a weasel Greg had forgotten the name of. It surveyed them with blackberry eyes before slithering back into the undergrowth.

They didn't talk for a long time. They didn't need to. It was enough to listen to the sound of each other's breathing, ragged at the edges from the climb, and the roar of life swelling on all sides.

Greg knew Valerie would break the silence a second before she did. He heard it in her breath.

"Give me one of them."

"What?"

"One of the gems from your big pile."

"Give you one of my precious treasures?"

"Yes."

"And what would I get in return?"

"Nothing, but give it to me anyway." There was no play in her now.

A hundred moments swirled through Greg's mind, gun smoke on a sea breeze.

Fish in the bay, old dock workers smoking neat cigarillos in the shade, leather-faced and barely born beneath the smooth and ancient stone of the storehouse.

His brother, blood rimming his eyes.

Broken birds falling from cut-glass skies.

His father seated at a cafe table out on the promenade in Havana, an after-dinner whiskey in his hand, gesturing as a man in tight trousers strutted by. "What do you think, Greg, a solid kick between the legs'd straighten his step out? Not like he has much use for it."

Lizards moving staccato through smoldering sunlight.

Cats with crooked tails and paws pink as rose petals.

"When I was young," he said at last, "I found a cocoon on the bush outside our front door. The island's still full of butterflies, but I swear there were twice as many then. Things barely live a day, but they're all rough-and-ready gorgeous little sky pirates. Dodging cats and hurricanes and hornets. All frayed around the edges . . ." The forest started to thin out as they climbed higher. The sea flashed brighter to their right.

"Anyway, I took this one and put it in a shoebox I kept under my bed until it hatched. Checked on it at least twice a day. Until I didn't. I guess it took too long, and I forgot. I didn't find it again until I came back the next summer. I didn't even know what it was until I opened the box up and there it was, this butterfly the size of your hand. Perfectly preserved. And its wings . . . they were blue like a kingfisher all mottled with gold. Not a scratch on them.

"I still remember that moment so clearly. When I

opened the box and saw it. A lot's gone, but that? I'll never forget that. Those wings . . ."

"It happens," said Valerie quietly. "You were a kid. Kids forget. You shouldn't be ashamed."

It took Greg a moment to understand what she meant. "I wasn't ashamed. Well, maybe a bit, but if anything, I was jealous. It was perfect, Val. That one alone, untouched."

He carried on up the rise before realizing he couldn't hear her footsteps. She was looking at him, hands on hips. "Ten thousand years, Gregory Hemingway, would not be enough for me to understand you."

"Well, that makes two of us." He grinned. "And isn't that exciting?"

She didn't smile back, but she didn't frown either. She only said, "I worry about you, Greg."

"I know, but . . . I'm trying, Val. I really am."

"I know."

"I'm better with you than I've ever been."

"I know that too. But I think the balance has shifted. They hurt you more than they help."

The worst part was, she was right. Once, the shocks had jolted him out of whatever mania or depression he'd been spiraling into, stopped him in his tracks like a mental handbrake. Now the numbness lasted maybe a day at best.

"All right."

"All right, just like that?"

"Well, you always win in the end. Thought I'd save us both some time."

They smiled then, both of them. She followed him up, offering her hand again. And taking it he felt like a thief riding out of town on the king's horse.

Greg slowed to a halt as a fence came into view. It was

twice as tall as he was, its gray links crosshatching over the green. "What the hell?"

Valerie walked forward and placed her hands against the wire. "Are you sure you got the right place?'"

"My memory isn't that fucked. We all walked up here together the day after my parents bought it."

"What happened?"

Greg came to stand beside her. He wound his fingers through the cold mesh and shook at it, earning him nothing but an ache in his shoulders. It was well made and unmoving. "Well, shit." He turned and leaned against it, looking out over the gull's-eye view of Cuba that was supposed to be their holiday home outlook.

"Here, Greg." Valerie had walked along the fence's perimeter. She was pointing at a metal sign bolted in place. "Property of the Museum of Natural History. Gift of the Ernest Hemingway Estate."

They stood in silence a second, and some jungle denizen even Greg didn't recognize took the chance to let out a gibbering chuckle.

"I told you we should have written a thank-you letter," Valerie said quietly.

"A thank-you letter for her high-handedly giving us something that was bought with *my mother's* money?" Greg turned and smashed his foot into the fence. "Spiteful. Miserable. Scheming. *Bitch*!" Every word punctuated by the whack of leather on steel.

When he finally stopped, Valerie placed a hand on his heaving back. "Want to go back in the box, little butterfly?"

He looked down at her, and she up at him, not knowing which way he would go, but not afraid. Then they both began laughing, at themselves, at Mary, at the vibrant forest all around. Greg leaned himself against the fence again, rested his head back against it and felt the rough metal dig into his scalp. "Oh, fuck Mary so-proud-to-be-a Hemingway. I never had her down as a communist."

"The workers of the world, united by spite." Valerie didn't sound angry so much as genuinely bemused. She'd never given up her fondness for Mary. "Well, we're still on holiday. And at least we had a nice walk. And the mosquitoes of Cuba got to have a feast." She leaned into him, her head tilted back so the tip of her chin touched his. "And so what? What were we going to do, sink half a fortune into building a place we might use once a year?"

He took a breath to make some cutting remark, and felt her body shaped to his. He put his arms around her. All his rage, burning white-hot only seconds before, was gone. She was right, of course she was right. And what did it matter anyway? What did any of it matter, except this?

New York

1974

Greg sat at the desk with his head in his hands, staring at the snaggle-toothed grin of the typewriter.

Minutes passed in agonizing slowness. No words came.

How had Papa done this? Not once, but day after day . . . No wonder he'd blown his brains out. It was a miracle he'd lasted so long.

Greg was not his father, no matter how hard he tried, no matter how many attempts he made. This was supposed to be his story, his life, but every sentence he wrote felt like someone else's—false, forced. When he layered rich descriptions, he felt like a peacock. When he wrote in the terse, lean style that seemed most natural to him he felt a pretender, a cheap imitation. He already knew what the critics would say.

Why put himself through that?

No one was expecting this. He had nothing to gain and so much to lose.

"Greg?" Valerie knocked on the door, knowing it would be locked.

"I'm OK," he said dully. "Just thinking of putting a hammer to this typewriter."

A pause. "It probably deserves it."

He smiled, despite himself. "Yeah. It had it coming."

"Look, you want to see a film tonight? It's still not too late to get a babysitter?"

God, he loved her. She knew what was happening, had ridden these waves with him often enough to recognize that lurch in the belly when a deep trough was coming. She was throwing him a rope. *Come on. Distract yourself.*

"No. Thanks, love, but I can't just give up."

"Okay." No accusation in her voice, though they both knew what his answer meant.

It was ironic, really. Valerie had been the one to suggest writing it all down. She'd started prodding him after she'd found the rough notes he'd made in those long calm years when they'd first moved to New York, the stablest of his life.

Each page had been a new memory, tender shoots rising from the ashes of a forest fire. She'd thought he had been following some creative need, some inherited talent, and he hadn't had the heart to tell her he'd been trying to preserve those recollections while he could. Some part of him had known it wouldn't last.

He'd had no pretensions of being a writer—he'd seen what a real writer was more closely than almost anyone— but somehow his wife's words had gotten under his skin. He'd found himself idly rearranging his scrapheap of memories as he leafed through them, playing them off against each other for effect, linking them by imagery or tone.

Each time he sat down he would undo the previous session's work, finding new patterns, a new order in the chaos. That had been the problem that had first really gripped him: how do you give a narrative arc to something as messy as a life?

It had been infuriating, but fascinating. He'd found himself enjoying it.

Too bad he had burned every last page a few months after the fishing trip with Lorian. He didn't blame the girl for that, of course. If it hadn't been her it would have been something else. An argument at work. A disappointing burger. None of it had been her fault.

Now he had no material to work with. He'd even called his uncle Les and begged to borrow his memories of Papa. Offered him ten percent of the profits and everything if the thing ever got published, which—with the Hemingway name behind it—really meant finished.

Les had done his best and sent over the result, and Greg had slowly realized what would have been obvious to anyone who wasn't in the middle of a breakdown: that you can't tell your own story with someone else's recollections.

All Greg had were fragments. He could feel the full memories tantalizingly close, hidden below the scar tissue, but there was no way to reach them.

He heard Valerie pad away down the hall, and held his hands ready over the keys. Nothing. He brought his fists down with a crunch. For a second despair almost swallowed him whole, but he forced himself to his feet. Over at the mantelpiece, he took the prescription bottle of pills from behind the clock and tapped one into his hand. A cheerful little chunk of chemistry.

He tipped his hand over, and the pill crunched beneath his shoe. It wasn't working. None of them worked. He had already spent so much time searching through journals and studies for new chemicals he could prescribe himself to police his mind, to shut down these alien longings, to try and keep his mood swings in check.

No such panacea existed. Only the shocks worked, and even before he'd promised Valerie to stop the treatments, the windows of relief had been getting shorter and shorter. If he did go back and they too began to fail him . . . He felt a surge of fear that cut through even the despair.

He moved back behind the desk and stared at the typewriter. One of the keys had come loose. The H.

He tried to press it back into place, but as soon as he let go it tumbled down the face of the keyboard with a brittle arachnid skitter. He paused, then stepped on it too, felt it bend, crack, crunch beneath his weight.

Things that did not work deserved to be broken.

He sat down. He could write without an H. He could pencil them in later. His father had written nearly everything with a set of pencils he sharpened constantly with a pocketknife, the sort a carpenter might have used to note where to saw.

He paused. He could see those stubby pencils, and then his father, a mountain stooped over a desk.

He opened the drawer—the top one—and pulled out Les's notes again. Crumpled and greasy from being endlessly pawed over, he smoothed them out one more time with his hand and started skimming through them, looking for any scrap of detail that would bring it all back, some keyhole he could peek through into how it had been—how it had really been.

None of the biographies had come close—he'd read them all. Monster. Hero. Genius. Hack. All storybook tales chasing the ghost his father had created in the tabloids, the phantasm he had summoned up with his few sweet words. But Papa . . . the man was elsewhere, breathing and living in the moments between publications and awards—accident-prone yet skillful, proud but generous, cruel but capable of such simple kindness. His father had been a real man. A real father. He had lived.

The typewriter clacked as Greg chased him. Reckless, headlong, not letting himself think about the words pouring out, chasing echoes and fragments sifted from the ruins of his memories.

He had called avocados crocodile pears. He had taken off his glasses at the slightest hint of a camera. He had taught Greg to swim in the pool beside their house, holding the boy's thin body with the care of a true believer lifting a sainted relic. He had lied as other men breathed, and believed every lie he spouted the moment it left his lips. He had slowly broken the heart of every woman who'd tried to love him. He had slowly made everyone love him, and then broken them too.

And suddenly Greg's hands were on the side of the typewriter, lifting its heavy black carcass over his head and throwing it headlong into the wall.

He leaned against the desk, veins bulging on his arms, his breath coming fast. He was almost surprised to see a small stack of papers by his hand, each page pocked with spaces where the Hs should have been.

Havana

1946

Papa laid the story on his lap, spread the flat of his hand against it, so the decisive lettering of the typewriter showed through his fingers. Greg's own fingers twitched, as though there was still time to snatch the papers back.

His father squinted out the window. The sky was cloudless, only a few distant and lonely birds circling like God's own afterthoughts.

"You know," he began at last, "the work has been coming hard to me, lately. The craft I mean." He coughed, then gestured to the pile of correspondence waiting patiently beside his chair. "Every day I get letters from young men looking to make a living writing. They send me their work, ask for my advice. There's so many that want to do it, and so few of us that can. I send back words of encouragement to the ones with some talent, which is few, and advise the rest to get a good practical degree. Bullshit never does them any good in the end."

"No, Papa."

"Well . . ." He lifted up the story and glanced at it again, as if it were a painting to be taken in all at once. "Well. No one that has written to me, boy or man, has even half your talent. I'd barely change a word here. Barely a word."

This had gone too far. It was time for the truth. Time to speak.

Greg hesitated. "Thanks."

"The writing really has been getting hard lately, Gig. In fact, it's been wearing me out. That old black ass has been coming round more and more often . . . Maybe I could help you, show you what I've learned. Maybe it's time for you, not me."

Greg understood the enormity of the statement. For his father, writing was like a Japanese sumo ring—the goal being not only to remain inside, but to force others out. This scared him, but he only said: "Thanks, Papa. I don't know if I have anything to write right now though."

Papa gave one of his hard sure nods. "Of course. You don't want to force it. Nothing's more likely to kill the gift while it's still growing in you. Write what you want, and if you feel like it you can bring it to me, and I'll give you some advice, help guide you, the sort of thing I'd have killed to have had starting out."

"Okay, Papa."

There was a moment of silence before his father gave in, finally breaking into a reluctant grin. "Damn it, Gig. This is good stuff. I never would've believed you . . . Here, let me fix us both a drink to celebrate."

One of the house's many cats crept in through the open door, tiptoed over the floorboards on bone china feet, and wound itself back and forth through Papa's ankles as he poured expensive Scotch. A little to the right of this, on the bottom shelf of the corner bookcase, Greg could see the unassuming blue leather of the book of Russian short stories he'd copied from.

The shelf was clean, of course—the staff saw to that—but Greg had found a layer of dust lying over the tightly packed pages of the book itself. Crisp fresh pages he'd almost had to peel apart to leaf through.

Copying—stealing—hadn't been his purpose at first. He'd been looking for inspiration, something to make the words flow after hours of sitting at a typewriter and biting his nails.

But that excuse could only take him so far. At some point he had realized that the book was far too pristine to have ever been read. Had copied down each carefully chosen word one at a time, pressing the keys softly as if Papa might be able to hear the deceit taking place. Had taken the story to his father and handed it over with his name below the title.

Greg could not trace the line from that first moment—entering his father's study and perusing the bookcase—to now, sitting in the wingback chair as Papa handed him a glass half-full of a whiskey older than he was.

They drank together, and still Greg said nothing. How could he? It would break Papa's heart, break the fragile trust that was building back up between them.

No, that was a lie. It wasn't kindness that was holding his tongue. It was fear.

Papa clasped him on the shoulder. A small gesture, but after how things had been between them the last few years it almost made Greg cry.

As he walked out, he couldn't help feeling that he'd failed some sort of test, and for once this wasn't one his father had set.

New York

1976

Greg sat alone in the kitchen. The streetlights glared through the shutters, casting lambent bars over the room that strobed and flared as each lonely taxi swept by. There was a glass of whiskey beside him, but he hadn't touched it. He was past the place where such things could help.

He was dressed in a white polo shirt, khakis, and silk underwear he could feel sliding against his skin whenever he moved. The sensation steadied him and unnerved him at the same time. It didn't belong here, in his own home. The safety valve he'd so carefully built had started venting into his real life. A hint of perfume here. An unexplained absence there.

He could feel the residue of the mania that had been riding him these last few days burning in his blood, even as he slipped straight into a depression. He'd done everything he could to spare Valerie and the kids from the worst of it, which meant he'd barely been in the house.

Greg the babbling tyrant, or the walking corpse, or Greg the ghost. Those were his family's choices. Either way they got hurt.

The gun in his hand was heavy, well oiled. He had bought it only yesterday, from a pawnshop on the Lower East Side. There were six shiny bullets—*rounds*, his father's voice corrected—waiting inside.

Tomorrow he would launch the book he'd written in scraps and shards night after night over these last few tortured years. He'd gotten through eight typewriters in the process.

There would be a grand party, of course. Everyone in New York worth knowing had RSVPed. His publisher was thrilled—normally it was difficult getting a first-time author's mother to show up for a launch, let alone the great and good of the American literati.

Even some of his father's old friends were coming. Gods deigning to step down from Olympus. Right now the thought of seeing them made him feel sick, but tomorrow he might be back on an even keel. A week from now, he certainly would. But it wouldn't last.

He was losing control. The cycles of mania and depression circling faster and faster as he approached the center of the whirlpool. The cross-dressing kept overflowing its limits; Valerie had actually found a bottle of unfamiliar perfume beneath the driver's seat of the car. Of course she assumed he was cheating, but that was better than her knowing the truth.

If she ever found out, there was no way she'd stay. She had too much self-respect.

He lifted the gun, feeling the weight of it. Maybe things would get better, maybe he'd find a way to put all the pieces back in place . . . But what if he didn't?

Upstairs, his children were sleeping. He could feel them, even if he couldn't see them. Especially then. Wouldn't it be better to spare them from all the pain he would bring into their lives?

Outside, some drunk shouted, reckless and bereft.

The barrel felt cold against the soft flesh of his temple, the keyhole into his skull as though God had designed for this when he first made Adam out of dust.

Had his father felt this strange peace before he pulled the trigger? Papa had always scorned Greg's grandfather for killing himself—he'd hated the weakness of it, but in the end he'd understood, as Greg now understood in turn. Sometimes, you just needed to take control.

He breathed slowly.

In through the nose. Out through the mouth.

His fingers tightened around the trigger, but one stray thought made him pause: who was next?

His children were sleeping with no idea that their father was forging another link in a chain that stretched back generations, a link that now connected directly to them.

The drunk started singing as he wandered on. All squalls and sunshine, like a child.

After a while Greg stood, emptied the gun of its rounds and dropped them one by one into the garbage. He held the gun out as well, looking one more time into that black mouth, then wrapped it in newspaper and placed it on top of the kitchen cupboard.

He knew he should go to bed. He had a big day tomorrow.

Instead he lifted his coat from the hook by the door and headed out into the night.

Greg walked quickly, turning up his collar against the wind. He knew some people trapped in a dark patch

239

struggled to get out of bed. For Greg it was the opposite. Rest, darkness, stillness, they were all little deaths. Drinking, hunting, fishing, walking, anything would do as long as it wasn't thinking.

It didn't matter where he walked so long as he kept moving. He'd pound the pavements for a few hours and be back home and in bed before Val woke up. He'd already given her enough to worry about.

He loved New York at night. It was hard to see it when he felt like this, but he could still catch brief glimpses of its grimy beauty. The moon gliding between the concrete canyons. Mirrored skyscraper windows pocked with holes into the lit-up offices of workaholics. Dirty webs of glass tubing flickering into words and dancers and infinitely pouring martinis and a thousand other neon constellations. It was all the ugliness that made the beauty shine. The red-faced drunks. The piss-stained alleys. Dog shit smeared over a curb. You needed both.

Greg kept moving, cutting through alleys or jaywalking rather than stopping at a crosswalk even for a second. Pretty soon he had no idea where he was, one more face in the crowds trickling out from the nightclubs and bars, staggering home before the dawn like vampires.

Greg had never felt so middle-aged. All these slim kids in their tight-fitting clothes, all garish colors and sequined collars, didn't they know how ridiculous they looked? Half of the men had girls on their arms; normal pretty girls walking along with their man in his knee-high boots like all this was perfectly normal.

Never mind middle-aged, he felt like a dinosaur. When Greg was a kid, you'd have gotten yourself arrested at best for dressing like that. Hell, he'd had a cop threaten to put him in the hospital when he'd accidentally gone out wearing eyeshadow in a manic phase.

There was laughter, and his eyes flashed to the side door of a rough-looking club. He stopped in his tracks. The crowd broke and parted around him, a few guys muttering complaints, but he didn't notice.

There was a group of women in a loose circle, all still laughing at some shared joke.

Some people might not even realize what they were, but Greg was like an antique dealer spotting the minute signs of a forgery. Long sleeves to hide the size of the hand offering out a pack of cigarettes. A loose scarf concealing an Adam's apple. The slight rash at one jaw from scraping again and again to remove even the slightest hint of shadow. Greg took it all in in an instant—his gaze honed by a lifetime of self-dissection in front of a mirror.

He couldn't believe it. They were just standing there, out in the open. He felt a sudden pulse of anger. Didn't they have any *shame*?

One of them cast her eyes over the crowd and saw Greg staring. For a second she seemed cautious, even fearful, but then she seemed to see something in his gaze. She half-smiled, and gestured him over.

Greg span away, ramming blindly through the crowd, shouldering people aside left and right. Someone grabbed at his sleeve, "Hey, watch where you're going, you—"

—He turned and put his whole body weight into a punch. It barely skimmed the startled man's jaw but was still enough to put him on his ass. Greg stood over him, breathing through his nose like a bull as everyone turned to look. He waited a moment to see if anyone else had something to say, but no one would even meet his eye. He turned to push his way through the crowd, but there was no need. They parted for him.

He needed to get out of this city. That was obvious now. How was anyone supposed to keep hold of themself in this place? It had gone mad.

He didn't let himself think after that. He'd gotten good at controlling his thoughts, and he made himself only a body moving through the city. He got home a few hours before dawn, and found Valerie gently snoring and none the wiser. Despite feeling caustically awake he made himself lie down beside her and stare up at the black ceiling.

Tomorrow—tonight, by now—his book would be launched. He was going to be a published author like his father. A good chunk of the family was going to be there, and the press, and even some of Papa's old friends and hunting buddies, and when they saw Greg they were going to tell him that it was a hell of a book, that his Papa would have been proud.

"It's a hell of a book, Greg."

"Thanks, Pat."

"And you've got a good turnout."

Greg shrugged. "Free drinks."

"I think I saw John's girl earlier. She's as gorgeous as they say."

"Margot? I'm honored. I think tonight may be our first time meeting."

"John not visit much?"

"No one visits much, Patrick. It's part of the black sheep role."

Patrick took a sip of his drink. The ice cubes slipped up the class and cracked against his teeth.

"Oh, don't be sour. You visit the most."

"Well, you'll know her when you see her."

"She's got the Hemingway look?"

"Some. But really, she's just that beautiful, she couldn't be anything but a supermodel."

"Didn't she change how she spells her name?"

"Yes, It's M-A-R-G-A-U-X now. French. I said she was beautiful, not smart."

"Fame makes people do funny things."

Patrick smiled, their childhood swelling unspoken between them.

"That's one of the many things I like about Montana. You never see famous people there. They all leave as soon as more than ten people know who they are."

"So the opposite of New York."

"Pretty much."

Greg nodded and waved to a passing cousin. "Sounds good, actually."

"I thought you loved it here."

"I do, or maybe I did. I don't know. This city isn't a movie. I mean, it has its good points, don't get me wrong, but there's a lot less romance and speakeasies and martinis at the Ritz than tiny apartments, traffic fumes, and only feeling the sun on your skin for the ten minutes it's directly above you."

"Big cities have never appealed to me."

"Oh sure, a true country boy at heart."

"You know, I really am. I like the same things about Montana that I liked about Africa. With each new day, it all gets wiped clean."

"Well, God knows I could use some of that."

"Well, I could use some more whiskey. Go mingle, Gigi, it's your party."

"Don't let anyone else hear you call me that. It'll be carte blanche."

Patrick squeezed his arm and headed off toward the bar.

Wading through the crowd, it was a constant battle not to be waylaid, and even when Greg did manage to move with momentum he was constantly shaking hands, giving nods of recognition. People who wouldn't have given him the time of day a few months ago were suddenly eager to press the flesh, to touch their cheeks to his.

It occurred to him that his father had been published to acclaim at twenty-one. In a sense, this was all he'd ever known.

He accepted a hug from a woman he assumed he was supposed to recognize, then slipped past her toward a waiter with a tray of champagne. The chandeliers, hung low and turned high, set every glass ablaze. A young woman got there before him, and he knew in a second it was Margot. Margaux.

She was as beautiful as Patrick had said, with the family's broad forehead and strong jaw, but gentled by her mother's petal-soft lips, by bright vixen eyes beneath eyebrows so thick and dark they could have been daubed on with charcoal. As extravagantly, aggressively feminine as a lily gaping open.

What must it be like, to look like that?

The thought, the ache that came with it, and the reflexive twist to crush it down, were all indistinguishable.

She drank deeply, and her eyes met his over the rim of the glass.

Something passed between them in an instant, mutual and strange. It hit Greg like a punch in the gut.

What Margaux saw, looking back, Greg couldn't guess and didn't want to know.

That passage came to him, the lines he'd always loved and hated from his father's *Oceans in the Stream*, about darkness and recognition.

For a long moment they stared at each other, seeing each other, knowing they were seen. Then as one they turned away and moved off through the crowd.

Good luck, Greg found himself thinking. *Good luck*.

"What a magnificent book, Greg."

Greg almost knocked over the man who had stepped into his path, and it took him a few moments to untangle his mind from the strangeness that still felt like it was lingering in his blood. "Erm, thanks."

"I trust you read my review?"

A critic then. Oh no. "Of course. Thank you, very kind write-up."

The critic nodded sagely, a deity accepting praise for his beneficence. Greg was sure he should know him. He almost recognized the face . . .

"Most doctors I know barely have time to cheat on their wives, let alone write a novel. How the hell did you do it, Hemingway?"

"Same as anyone else. One word at a time. Monogamy was probably an unfair advantage, I'll admit."

The critic laughed. "Sure. Sure. Well, it was never going to be a fair comparison, was it? With your blood."

"I only use blood for curses and death threats. Ink is a lot more economical." Greg couldn't remember if this guy was from the *Times* or the *Tribune*, but either way it was probably best not to tell him to go fuck himself, even if the review had already been published. Never trust a critic. One of Papa's many lessons.

The man laughed, but it was like honey over sour milk. "And here's the muse."

Valerie was weaving her way through the party, gorgeous in a long cream dress, a saucer of champagne caught in an endless upwards cascade at her fingertips.

She smiled stiffly at him, last night's despairing quarrel when he'd finally gone up to bed obvious if only to him, and gave a nod to the critic—Tim, Tony, Tom?

Tim/Tony/Tom leaned forward to kiss her cheek, but she dodged him neatly, offering her other cheek to Greg while pretending not to notice.

Greg had a echo of last night's anger in him too, and perhaps an echo of the despair. Even so he couldn't help but admire how deft she always was, how in control.

He touched his lips to the corner of her mouth, and whispered, "I'm sorry, bird."

She said nothing, but he felt her relax.

Tim/Tony/Tom cleared his throat. "Good to see you, Valerie. You look divine. You know, seeing the two of you together, it occurs to me you've been with two Hemingways now."

Greg frowned, not liking the subtle way he'd leaned on *been with*.

"Care to give a fan some small insight into the family's creative process?"

Valerie frowned too, but she somehow made it look playful. "I'm not sure, Andrew—"

—*Andrew*, damn.

"—it's a hell of a question."

She looked at Greg, one of her brief glances where he could sense her mind moving faster than anyone else's in the room. "But I don't think I can give you a meaningful answer. How can you compare two types of genius? How can you explain it to someone who's never experienced it?"

Now Andrew was frowning, but Valerie only smiled at him.

"Oh, you know what I mean, Andrew, we're not the wordsmiths in the room."

"I like to think—"

—"Oh, of course, Andrew. Don't we all? I'm in the same boat as you, dear." She gave him an affectionate pat on the shoulder, then slipped her arm through Greg's. "Can we have a quick word, sweetheart?"

"Of course, my love," said Greg with genuine feeling.

She slipped a fresh glass of champagne from the tray of a passing waiter, and together they pushed into the crowd, leaving Andrew looking like he'd eaten a bad oyster.

"That was probably a bit too much," said Valerie softly. "You should talk to him later, pretend you actually do read his reviews. He'll love you for that. It's the good critics you have to watch out for, the ones who wouldn't change a word of a review if you had their grandmother at gunpoint. Andrew's essentially a Labrador in a tux. All he wants is attention. Praise."

"I'll do that. Have I ever mentioned how glad I am you're on my side?"

"Not often enough."

"What was it you wanted to talk about?"

They came out of the crowd in front of the jazz band his publisher had hired to recreate the feeling of his father's heyday. "Nothing. But I thought one of us was probably going to punch him if we didn't get away."

"Good, enough talk."

He turned her round and kissed her, and as a blaze of saxophone and trumpets washed over them, he felt her mouth smile against his.

At last they broke apart, and he realized a good chunk of the nearby crowd had turned to watch them, smiling and elbowing each other appreciatively.

Valerie rolled her eyes, but didn't stop smiling. "You always did love a crowd."

"No. I *like* crowds. I know what I love." Greg twisted the wedding ring on her finger with his thumb, its curve smooth against his calluses. He tried to find words to tell her what she meant to him, how all this—the book, the crowd, the man who had survived this long—was hers, all something she had built.

The crowd fell silent, and after a second Greg could hear the clinking of a spoon against crystal. At the far end of the room, his new publisher was standing at the foot of the stairs.

Linus, a short and portly man who bestrode the world of publishing like a literary Hercules, pushed his glasses further up his nose.

"Ladies and gentlemen, thank you so much for coming. I have to admit, when my assistant told me someone had gotten in touch with a Hemingway memoir, my first thought was: *Oh Lord, not another one.*" Everyone in the room laughed, except the various Hemingways.

Greg leaned over to Valerie. "Is this my book launch, or a roast?"

"Hush. He's just an old ham playing the crowd."

"But, as we all know, in the world of publishing you simply don't turn down the offer of a Hemingway. So, I dutifully sat down with a blessedly slim manuscript on a Sunday morning to peruse." He gave a dramatic pause, made to sip his champagne and realized his glass was empty. "I think it can't have been later than 10 a.m. when I gave Greg a call to say we wanted to buy the book, that we *had* to. This book," a copy of *Papa* had appeared as if by magic in his hand, "is unlike every book about the great man that has gone before. There's no getting lost in the myth. The reader never wonders what's real and what has been slipped in to appeal to our preconceptions. This book has the authenticity of truth. By God, you think, he wasn't just a colossus from history, he was a man like any other. A living, breathing man! I cannot stress to you what an achievement that is, how many tides and currents Greg must have had to fight against to get to that pure unfiltered truth. I can't stress to you how many other works have failed." There were a few uncomfortable coughs around the room. Greg's eyes flicked to his uncle Les, scowling beside a large arrangement of chrysanthemums. His own books had not been critical successes. "So please, put your hands together for the author: Dr. Gregory Hemingway."

He gestured Greg forward as applause broke out, and Greg found himself standing on the stairs staring out over a small sea of people: Valerie beaming up at him from the back, friends, colleagues, people it had been propitious to invite, celebrities, friends of his father, and scattered among them the strange troop of demi-royals that counted as his family, that handsome and disheveled high-achieving tribe that had risen up like the turbulent wake behind a fast sure ship, milling aimlessly as they dispelled and diminished.

He'd had too much to drink.

But even here, exactly where he'd wanted to be for so long, in the heart of glory, surrounded by the great and the good and basking in their admiration, the same thoughts that had been swirling about in his head for months returned:

Is this it?

Is this all there is?

Is this who I am?

Until now he'd been able to shut them out, but now a new urgency gripped him. He needed to get out of this city, before it got under his skin.

He cleared his throat, made his humble speech thanking everyone once and Valerie twice, and stepped down, knowing one thing above all.

If he was going to survive, something would have to change.

PART IV

Havana

1943

Papa had been having a lot of people to visit lately, mostly younger artists he was interested in, but the man who came in from the twilight was very old, forty at least.

Papa took him by the hand straight away, then pulled him into a rare hug. "Teddy, you bastard, it's been too damn long."

"Hello, Ernie," the man said, patting Papa on the back. He was a tall man, but he spoke with a soft voice, as though there was someone sleeping lightly in the next room.

"Let me introduce you," said Papa, wheeling him round to where the rest of them were lined up. "Martha, my beautiful and devoted wife." Martha didn't normally dress up much, but tonight her hair was styled like someone in a magazine, her dress creaseless and so white it seemed to glow in the soft light of the hallway.

"Enchanted." The man nodded. "I've heard so much about you from Ernest's letters. And to think I assumed he was exaggerating . . ."

Greg almost thought he saw a pink tinge across the bridge of her nose as she politely kissed the man's cheek.

"It's a pleasure to meet you, Theodore. Ernest speaks very highly of you."

"And my boys, Greg and Patrick. Excuse the state of them. They're both little savages."

"I'd expect nothing less." Teddy pointed to Greg with his chin. "My God, doesn't he look like you?"

"Yep. A cutting straight from the tree. Now come on, Marie will sulk if we make her keep the food hot."

Greg felt a bit foolish at the pride that swelled in his chest. He knew he shouldn't care so much, but there had been a few years when Papa never would have agreed to something like that. Since the shooting Greg had accepted it would never be like it was before, but at least it was better than it had been.

His euphoria lasted him all the way to the main course, through Teddy and Papa talking endlessly about people Greg had never heard of, and a lengthy and well-worn sermon by his father about the virtues of bullfighting and the moral weakness of objectors to the sport. Eventually even Greg's attention began to drift.

If Patrick was in a good mood tomorrow maybe they could go fishing. Not sea fishing where you got sunburn and threw up, but down by the river where you could sit in the shade and eat jam sandwiches and smoke—

"—ISN'T that right, Gig?" Papa asked out of the blue.

Greg nodded automatically. "Yes, sir."

"Damn right. You see, Teddy, I raise my kids right." Papa laughed. "Damn, this is good whiskey. Let's both have a top-up. How about you, Marty?"

"I'm sure it's excellent," said Martha with a small smile, the first words she'd spoken in nearly an hour, "but I'll stick to my martinis. Clear spirit, clear head in the morning, and I'm working on a story for—"

"—all right, suit yourself." Papa waved a silencing hand, then bellowed, "Top us up on the Macallan, Maria!" with an explosive volume that made the half-dozing Patrick jump so hard he cracked the back of his skull on his chair.

Greg grinned at him, and Patrick stuck his tongue out in return, then lolled his head in an exaggerated display of boredom.

Greg ignored him. This wasn't boring. Teddy was a friend from when Papa was young. He'd been there for all those times Papa still talked about like they were the biggest adventures of his life.

And, as if Papa could read his mind, he leaned back and pronounced: "Damn, but those were good times in Paris. In a way the city we fell in love with was born right then."

"The war changed everything, I suppose."

"Was that your first time in Paris, Mr. Brumback?" Martha asked, finishing her martini, but not calling for another.

"Teddy, please." He gave a small smile. "No, I was very familiar with Paris. It was heartbreaking, watching the Germans smash her apart."

"You soft-hearted ass," Papa cut in, already near the bottom of his own whiskey, the ice clacking against his teeth as he took another swig. His voice was playful, but very loud. It put Greg instinctively on edge, unsure of what was coming next. "Destruction renews. Paris survived, and we had the time of our lives."

"Yes, Paris survived, but—"

"—Marty, did I ever tell you the story of when I went bomb chasing?"

She smiled, all teeth and no eyes. "Tell me, Ernest." Which even Greg noticed was sidestepping the question— Papa had told the story at least ten times, but that didn't matter. It was a great story.

"Well, we'd got off the boat from Chicago and jumped on a train, and Teddy here was straight into his hotel for a shower and sleep in a proper bed, but I was having none of it. That wasn't what I'd come to Paris for." Papa leaned back in his chair, warming to his story. "So I jumped in the first taxi I saw and said: take me to where the shells are falling. The taxi driver nearly soiled himself, skinny French fella with a pencil mustache. Didn't matter how many francs I pushed at him, the man had no balls—that's why Paris fell right there."

Martha kept smiling. Teddy watched Papa talk and sipped his own drink.

"Anyway. I could see the guy was a lost cause, so I told him what I thought of his manhood and got out. Luckily I managed to talk my way onto an army jeep, told them I was an American reporter here to help and they must have liked the cut of me—recognized a fellow military man. Pretty soon I was riding with them, bouncing over the cobbles straight into the teeth of the falling bombs." He reenacted it, his chair creaking, whiskey splashing onto the table. "We pulled in at Place de la Madeleine just in time to see the church get hit by an absolute monster of a shell. Everyone was panicking, but as a reporter you have to keep your head on, same as in the army, so to me it looked like it was happening in slow motion. There was this sound like an old car door slamming, a shudder, and then the whole roof cracked inwards." He splayed his hands in a mock explosion. "Maybe half a second of silence before the boom and there was dust and glass and chunks of stone the size of your head flying everywhere. Absolute carnage. But the first thing I thought wasn't, *I need to get into cover*, it was, *this is it, this is what I'm here for*." He finished his whiskey, wiped the dregs off the table, and smiled. "I spent the rest of the day like that, chasing bombs through the city, knowing one could fall on my head at any moment and not giving a damn because this was living. This was history, and I was watching it being made."

Still Teddy made no comment. He ate his dessert in small bites, listening to Papa's next story of how he shot a lion straight in the heart right as it was lunging for him in Africa.

Only when Papa had started eating himself did he speak again. "You boys must be very proud of your father."

Greg nodded immediately. "Yes, sir."

"And you, Patrick?"

"Yes, sir. They teach some of his books in school."

"That is impressive."

"They're doing damn fine in school," Papa cut in. "Straight As across the board, which is a miracle as I don't think I've seen Gigi open a textbook in his life."

Teddy watched Patrick carefully scooping up the last smears of his chocolate gateau with his spoon.

"Always out shooting or playing ball, but it's hard for me to tell him to hit the books when he's already top of the class. Did I tell you he won the Cazador's shooting competition last year? I'd barely finished teaching him how to hold a gun, but when it's in your blood. Built-in

257

radar . . . You should have seen the faces on some of those old boys when a kid in shorts shot them into the ground!"

Greg waited for Teddy to ask about it, for Papa to proudly launch into the story, but Teddy's eyes barely flicked to Greg before returning to Patrick.

"Very impressive. And how about you, Patrick, do you study?"

"Yes, sir. I have to." He kept his eyes down but cast a sideways glance at Greg. "I don't mind though. It's kinda fun."

"I understand that. That'll serve you well if you decide to go to college someday. Talent counts for a lot less than hard work there."

Patrick looked pleased at the thought, but also a little uncomfortable, unused to being in the spotlight.

Teddy just smiled. "Do you have any idea what you want to do?"

Patrick opened his mouth, then glanced at Papa, thick arms crossed as he watched his son. Patrick shook his head.

An assistant librarian, Greg wanted to say. *A clerk in a secondhand bookstore.* He bit the spiteful words down and pushed himself back from the table. "Can I be excused?"

Martha looked to Papa, who shrugged, as wrong-footed as Greg by this unexpected focus of their guest's attention. "Sure. But don't wander off."

Greg slipped down from his chair. Patrick and Teddy were talking about something else—even Papa was joining in—but Greg didn't care. He felt rotten, mostly because he knew he didn't have any right to feel angry, and that only made him angrier.

He made his way out onto the porch and sat down

on the love seat, the chains creaking as the bench began gently swinging.

The evening had come and settled down while they'd been trapped inside. The sky was bubblegum pink and ready to pop. A group of boys from the barrio ran past the gates and one waved for Greg to join them, but he only shook his head, arms crossed in an unconscious but perfect imitation of his father.

He tried to let his imagination wander, tried to imagine himself fearlessly driving into a storm of exploding bombs, but somehow it wouldn't stick.

The door swung open, and Greg turned to watch Teddy step out onto the boards with a cigarette between his lips, patting down his pockets for a light.

Greg looked away, determined to ignore him, but Teddy spoke first. "And how about you, Gregory, do you like your Papa's stories?" His waiting cigarette bounced along to each word like a conductor's baton.

"I guess," agreed Greg reluctantly.

"You know it's all bullshit, right?"

He hesitated. "What is?"

"All of it. Except the writing." He finally found a book of matches from some hotel or bar, and for a moment his profile was etched in bronze as he lit up and took a few slow, appreciative puffs, gazing out not at the kids or the street but at the darkening horizon. "He always had a bit of it in him, but now there's nothing else. It's disappointing."

"I don't . . ." Greg had no way to respond, no frame of reference for an adult saying these sorts of things.

"No one knew where the next bomb was going to fall, not even the Germans," Teddy continued easily. "They were shelling from over a hundred miles away. They were aiming for Paris, that's all, and lucky when they hit. Your Papa came back to the hotel with me, had a shower, a spot of lunch and a bottle of wine, then jumped into a taxi while I went to take a look at the hospitals."

"That's not true!" The man sounded so sure, but Greg didn't care. "And anyway, I'd know. Papa's a terrible liar."

"Ah, that's the key, isn't it? He's a terrible liar when he thinks he's lying . . ." He thought a moment then laughed. "Maybe he's spent too much time making things up. Can't tell the difference any more. He's no coward, your father, there's plenty of stories he could have trotted out to show off, but he chose that one, even though he knows I was *there*." For the first time, he looked at Greg. His gaze was searching, piercing, like a scalpel trying to seek out a tumor.

Greg didn't know what he was looking for. The man was jealous of Papa, that much was obvious. Probably because he didn't have his own war stories, because he'd never jumped in a jeep and driven into the jaws of death, and—

—HAD the jeep been in the story last time? The thought struck out of nowhere, unexpected, unwelcome, but irresistible. Greg found himself thinking back to the last time Papa had told the story. Hadn't he had to pay the taxi driver a big fistful of francs to get him going? Hadn't the guy been terrified the whole time while Papa felt no fear?

Through all of this, Teddy watched him. Whether he saw what he hoped for, Greg never knew. He only shrugged, placed his half-smoked cigarette down—not dropped, but placed—and ground it neatly beneath his heel. Then he paused, hand on the door. "Did you really win that shooting competition?"

Greg hesitated, then mumbled, "Fourth place."

"That's still pretty damn impressive. Good for you."

"I don't think I'd be able to do it again."

"So?"

"Did you say all this stuff to Patrick?" Greg asked, not knowing why he wanted to know.

"I didn't."

"How come?"

"Your brother doesn't need to hear it . . . Look after yourself, kid."

He went inside. Papa shouted something, and Teddy laughed in response.

Greg stayed outside for a while, watching the darkness creep forward and the first few stars kindle into life overhead.

Jordan, Montana

1977

Greg wound down the window and let the clean air flow into the car. The sound of the engine grew even louder, the shitty little Subaru caught in a perpetual war cry, a never-ending death charge. Greg leaned his arm against the frame, looking out over an infinity of green fields, and felt content.

It was about as far from New York as you could imagine. Nothing but a sky that seemed too big for the horizon, a few straight-talking people spread out thinner than a miser's butter, and this silence that was everywhere. Montana.

He'd done the right thing coming here, getting back his sense of purpose. He was going to do *real* things here. He was going to fix people. Make them whole. He was going to push back death with his bare hands. There had been a few stumbles along the way to real doctoring, sure, but who cared? He was here now, and now would always be king. Thank God.

It took him nearly half an hour to get to the McKinley Farm, or to the farmhouse at least. It was impossible to know when he'd hit their property—there was barely a fence to be seen, and the land itself was featureless.

McKinley himself met Greg at the door, cap in his hand. And Greg couldn't deny he felt a swell of pride. People knew how to respect a doctor out here, knew it wasn't just another job like being a mailman or a butcher. It was a vocation.

"Dr. Hemingway?" the old man asked.

Greg nodded, seeing no curiosity in the man's desiccated face, no flash of recognition. McKinley had probably read nothing but the Bible in his entire life.

This place was perfect.

"Yes. Is she upstairs?"

"Aye. Thanks for coming."

McKinley led him upstairs to his ailing wife. Their bedroom was dark and old-fashioned, even for Jordan, all heavy wood and pink frilly fabric. Greg struggled to imagine the man beside him, who looked to have been born in his faded shirt and Levi's, settling down to sleep in this shrine to chintz and cotton.

The face that peered up at him from among the laced pillows was as lined as her husband's, but where his eyes had receded into some unknown location in his ancient head, hers had grown vaster, meltwater pools blinking in the twilight.

First Greg crossed to the window, pulled back the curtains with what he felt was one decisive movement, and turned back to examine his patient.

He saw McKinley watching him from the doorway, his expression unreadable.

"I need light to examine her," he explained, suddenly aware that he was standing in their bedroom, their most private space, quite possibly where Mrs. McKinley had given birth to their children.

But McKinley only nodded. "You do whatever you have to, Doctor."

Greg sat himself gently on the bedside, trying to disturb nothing, but unable to stop himself when the bed gave way like a blancmange. For a second he worried the thing would swallow him whole before he wobbled to a slow halt.

He coughed. "Hello, Mrs. McKinley. I'm Dr. Hemingway. You can call me Greg."

"Ah yes." Her voice was like wind through dry grass. "Roger told me. Fresh from New York. My word."

"Well, not quite fresh, I spent some time at Fort Benton, but essentially yes. I wouldn't be too impressed though, I was mostly just a pet practitioner at General Motors."

"Do you hear that, Roger? General Motors!" She sounded like Greg had told her he'd personally performed a tonsillectomy on Jesus Christ.

"Aye," was all Roger responded, still standing sentinel in the doorway.

Greg thought about relieving her of her illusions, but left it. She didn't need to know about the tedium. The hours of nothing punctuated by the occasional case of sniffles or a sprained back. Let her have confidence. That was half the battle.

"So," he began, "I understand your chest has been giving you some trouble."

"Oh, Lord yes. For a few weeks now, I don't like to complain of course, but today . . ."

"Can you describe the sensation for me?"

"It's like someone's been sitting on my ribs. A boy maybe, not a man. If you sat on my chest I'd be dead for sure."

Greg smiled. "All right. Anything else?"

"A bit of a headache."

"And you've been drinking water?"

"Oh yes. Two glasses a day and milk before bed."

"With a good slug of whiskey in the milk," Roger piped up.

"Hush, Roger!"

"Well it's true. Lord, woman, you don't lie to doctors. You want to wake up dead?"

"You mind your own business, Roger McKinley."

"You'd be amazed how many people lie to doctors," Greg said, lifting up the woman's oh so slender wrist with a smile. "We take it into account."

Roger chuckled at that. His wife shot him a belligerent look.

Oh yes, Greg thought, *I bet you were a handful in your day.*

He turned her hand over and felt her pulse. She was so thin her bones were like cuts of tumbleweed winding through her flesh. Greg found himself hoping she had indeed had children in this room, a whole brood of them. He counted along, feeling the faint kick-punch combo that made everything in the whole world work. "Your pulse isn't too fast. One. Two. Three. Four. Five. Do you feel that?"

She nodded. "Just about."

"Where do you feel it?"

She gestured weakly with her free fingertips to her jaw, just below her ear. That settled it.

Greg mentally rechecked the chart he'd glanced at before he set out an hour ago. He still hadn't had any shocks in a long while—he'd gotten through a bad manic phase at Fort Benton on his own, though it had cost him

265

his last job. His memory was working okay. "Margery, may I call you Margery?"

"Of course, Doctor. Better yet, you can call me Marge, everyone else on the Lord's earth does."

"Greg, please. Well, Marge, you've nothing worse than a case of high blood pressure. Unpleasant, but very treatable. I'm going to write you a prescription that will make you feel better, and you'll need to lay off the fatty foods for a while."

"And the whiskey?" Roger asked.

"Oh, Roger, you shut your mouth. I'm sorry, Doctor."

Greg laughed out loud. "It depends on your definition of a slug. Alcohol in moderation is fine. Good for you, in fact."

"You hear that? Good for me."

"Shouldn't have told her that, Doc."

"In moderation," Greg insisted, fishing his prescription pad from his shirt pocket.

He stepped out of the McKinley farmhouse into the crisp Montana air feeling better than he had in years. Almost like a boy again, like the artless cocksure little punk he'd been before he'd gotten so lost.

He pushed the thought away. He'd spent too long chasing the past. Now was the time. Now, and the future.

Soon Valerie and the kids would follow him out here. She hadn't wanted to leave the glory of New York for this empty nothing of a state, but she'd see the beauty eventually. Greg would buy them all a big house with a porch. In winter he'd take them skiing, and in summer he'd take them camping. And they would be happy.

Bozeman, Montana

1978

It was looking to be a cold one. The first flecks of goose-down snow were lazing through the air when Greg came up to Patrick's neat suburban house. When he'd first looked at Montana on a map, he'd thought he and his brother would be living practically next door to each other, but he'd forgotten how huge the state really was. The drive from Jordan had taken him six hours.

Patrick was already waiting for him out front. He had the garage door open and the snowmobile standing by on breezeblocks. That was Patrick for you.

Greg spun the car around and backed up the drive, Patrick guiding him in with hand waves as if he didn't have rearview mirrors. Anyone else and Greg would have found it annoying, but it was good to see his brother standing there in his crisp shirt and his neat slacks, watching out for him.

They hugged when he got out. There had been a time after college when they'd stopped hugging, but since their father died they'd started it up again by an unspoken and instinctual agreement.

"It's good to see you," Greg said, and it was true.

267

Though he saw his brother every few months these days—one of the best things about Montana—it still didn't feel like enough.

"You too, Gig."

"Still with the Gig shit."

"If anyone gets to call you Gigi, it's me."

"If anyone shouldn't call me Gigi, it's you. You're supposed to be in my corner."

"Of course I am. Always safer behind you than in front of you."

"Depends how much I've had to drink. I have hard elbows."

Patrick patted him on the shoulder and looked up at the low and pregnant clouds. "You sure about this? We're in for a blizzard. Don't know if you'll be able to outrun it, especially in that old can."

"It's a good car. It has sentimental value."

"Well, that's the only value it has. And that's more important than working brakes?"

"Sentiment over safety, every time. Hope so anyway, it's all that's stopping the family from leaving in the middle of the night."

Patrick looked up again, frowned. "We'd best get on with it."

"I was hoping for a beer break, but you're right." Greg moved to open the car's trunk.

They folded down the back seats, and despite the car's advanced years they went down smoothly, not so much as a creak. Greg felt strangely proud.

They eyed up the snowmobile, readying themselves for the task. "You look tired," Patrick said, not even glancing over.

"Fine. Just . . . long hours on the job. And I drive to Valerie and the kids most weekends. I'm hoping this thing will tempt them to come out to me for once, but until then . . . six hours each way."

"Well, you're doing it right. You can't go straight from New York to Jordan. Start them off in Bozeman. It's beautiful out by you, Valerie will see that . . . Not much you can do about the long hours though."

"Those I can deal with." Greg sighed and rubbed his face, feeling his thick stubble scratch his palms. "I hope you're right. I don't know how much longer I can do this . . . The kids'd love Jordan. They're pretty outdoorsy for New Yorkers, and I've got an actual pony with their names on it at the nearest stables . . . A pony!"

"Emotional blackmail."

"Nothing's beneath me, you know that."

"Nothing ever was. Nothing ever will be."

"I think it'll do Valerie good. I hope so anyway."

Patrick shrugged and moved to a small fridge in the corner of the garage. "I can't give you the break, but I can give you the beer." He handed Greg a Bud and flicked off the caps with his key, surprisingly practiced.

Greg watched his brother take a drink. His own bottle was cold in his hand, and somehow it felt good despite the frigid weather. He took two long gulps and burped mightily.

Patrick laughed. "You never change."

"No one does. Not really."

"Well . . ."

Patrick sniffed, moved round to the snowmobile like a boxer sizing up a tough opponent, and said lightly, "This is going to be a bitch."

Greg put both hands under the chassis and tried to lift it. "Well, damn . . ."

Patrick took another sip of beer. "Took me and three neighbors to get it on the blocks, and they've all gone mysteriously to ground for round two. Hope you're as strong as you used to be, Greg."

"This had better be worth it."

"It will be. Trust me." He tapped the side of his half-empty bottle against the snowmobile's snub nose. "Closest you'll get to a speedboat in a landlocked state."

"You ever miss it? The sea?"

Patrick thought a moment. Opposite was a row of neat suburban houses, identical to his own, but Greg felt like his brother was looking past them somehow, out over the huge sweep of this vast unwavering state. "No," he said at last. "I thought I would, but I don't. You?"

"Not really. Maybe sometimes, but I like keeping my lunch in my stomach."

"It wasn't all puking and gull shit. There were good times too."

"Yeah."

"Do you still remember it all?"

"No . . . but I've got enough."

Patrick grimaced, but covered it by turning to put his beer up against the wall. "Come on, we've got to get this thing loaded and you on your way, unless you want to spend the night."

"Not an option." Greg finished his own in three long swallows. "I've got work at six."

"Just take it slow. Like I said, it was a four-man job to get it out here."

"I could do this myself."

270

"Sure? You look a little soft around the edges . . ."

"Ouch . . . Well, I've started running. Might try a marathon next year."

"I thought you were tired?"

"I am, but it's relaxing. Hard to explain."

"Sure. Come on. Three. Two. One."

Patrick wasn't kidding. By the time they had the snowmobile loaded, the car was sitting an inch lower on its suspension and there were deep purple grooves in Greg's palms. Even then it wasn't exactly a neat fit—they ended up having to tie the trunk closed with some old decking rope—but it was the best they could do.

The snow fell gently outside, but with gathering pace, the world slowly blurring behind a thickening curtain of white.

They both knew Greg should have got going by now, but both hesitated, and when Greg looked to the corner of the garage, Patrick smiled and fetched them two more beers. They leaned against the side of the car, shoulder to shoulder, watching the hush fall over suburbia, making its plain features lovely and strange.

They talked about how Greg was liking being a doctor in a small town—getting to know people, being relied on—how it tethered him, how maybe this was what he'd needed all along. They talked about how Patrick missed Africa a hundred times more than the sea, but how he still went hunting here in Montana, and fishing too. He had taken to fishing at night—fishing off the mirror, he called it—and it was as close to a religious experience as he had ever known: the fish mere implications in the fast-flowing water until suddenly the line was taut and they were in your hands, dripping and twisting and gilded in moonlight.

271

They talked about the cat in Cuba with a broken tail that had healed like a question mark, and how nothing would ever be as green as those fields in the spring.

At last, Patrick finished the last suds from his bottle and wiped his mouth. "We should strap this thing in properly before you go. I've got some more rope in this box over here . . ."

"The one with *rope* written on it?"

"That's the one."

"An orderly mind, something something."

"Mm-hm." Patrick started rooting around in the box, not looking up. "Speaking of which, how're you holding out?"

Greg understood. "Good. I've got it pretty much under control."

"That's great, Greg." His brother kept his eyes on the ropes he was unwinding. "I mean, sometimes I feel like Papa and I— like we didn't . . ."

"It's okay." Whatever it was, Greg didn't want to hear it. He was done with the past.

"I . . . I know I could've . . ."

"It's okay, Pat."

Patrick glanced at him, then walked toward the car. "I don't think it is." He pushed at the trunk with his shoulder, though it was as closed as it was ever going to be. After a second's grunting he gave up and started strapping the beast in place.

"I've been going through some of Papa's old papers, you know," he said. "It keeps me busy in winter."

"Yeah?" said Greg, glad of the change of subject.

"Some of this stuff—the stuff that never got published I mean—it's like he . . ."

"What?"

His brother only shook his head. "He got so mad at you about all that shit. So goddamn *angry*. Did you ever think— I mean, maybe that's why he could be so mad, but love you best at the same time?"

"He didn't love me best," said Greg, latching on to the only thing he could understand. "Not for long, anyway. I wish you wouldn't say shit like that."

"It's fine. My dad loved me, I know that, but not all love is equal." Patrick grinned. "It used to drive me crazy, but I got over it. I had Mom, I guess."

"Not a bad trade," said Greg with forced cheer, helping him pull the last knot tight. He didn't feel cheerful, but then, he couldn't have said precisely what he was feeling.

"I don't know about that, but she did pretty well for me."

"I just mean . . ." Greg shrugged, carefully casual, "she could be pretty cool with us, but at least it didn't matter what we did, you know? No amount of trophies or fuck-ups was going to change anything. But Papa . . ." He hesitated, swallowed. "You're walking this tightrope, and you do one thing wrong and . . . It's— it's a lot of pressure to put on a kid, you know? It was a lot."

"Greg . . . I, I'm sorry."

"I'm okay. I'm sorry I never let you win, Pat. I know I was a shit brother."

Patrick's beer tipped over as he set it down, but he ignored it, pulling Greg into an awkward hug. "Oh, forget about all that shit. I have. And anyway, I was never mad at you."

Greg said nothing. Patrick smelled like peppermint and tobacco and Patrick.

"Listen to me, Greg. He wanted you to be something that didn't exist, you know that, right? It never could have been enough, and even if . . . None of it was your fault, Gig."

Greg eased him back, passed a sleeve over his eyes. "Thanks, Pat, but . . . bringing up the dead doesn't do either of us any good. Can I use your bathroom? Long way to go."

"Sure. Second door on the right . . . Look, I—"

"—Don't worry about it. I haven't slept in forty-eight hours. I'm a bit loopy, that's all. Make sure you strap that thing in tight, okay? I don't want to lose it on the freeway."

Once he was in the bathroom he locked the door behind him and splashed cold water on his face, then sat on the floor, his arms around his legs, resting his forehead on his knees.

He was so tired. So bone fucking tired.

Just a little longer. Valerie and the kids would come. Winter would end and the job would get easier. He'd spend time with them and take them camping. Just a little longer.

At last he stood, washed his face properly for good measure, flushed the toilet, and headed out to give his brother one last back-cracking hug before driving out into the oncoming storm.

Jordan, Montana

1983

Greg woke in the swollen dark, his head throbbing fit to burst. The phone was squawking, each trill driving another shard of glass into his brain.

The digital clock on his bedside had run out of batteries long ago, but the clock on the wall, illuminated by a chink of streetlight, said 04:31.

The phone rang on and on. It could mean only one thing.

"Fuck." As much a retch as a curse.

He didn't bother with the bedside light—the bulb had popped the second time he'd turned it on and he'd never gotten around to replacing it—just swung his feet down onto the carpet of detritus blanketing the floor. One foot sent an empty bottle skimming away with a high clear whisper until it crashed into what sounded like a pile of pizza boxes, the other landed square in the patch of crusty melted carpet he'd been using as an ashtray. He could feel a cigarette butt pushing up between his toes.

"Fuck."

He staggered over to the phone that was still screaming. More debris went flying. Chinese takeaway cartons, pill bottles, empty beer cans, half-read books and untouched magazines.

When he finally reached the phone, he almost considered ripping the cord clean out of the wall. One good yank and there would be only silence. He could crawl back to bed like a bear to its cave and nurse his hangover in peace, maybe gather up all the half-empty pill bottles scattered around the room, make himself a chemical cocktail and finally sleep for good.

But it was only a fleeting impulse. A passing dream. He was needed.

"Hello."

"Good morning, Dr. Hemingway. I'm so sorry to wake you, but we've got an admission. Elderly female. A likely heart attack."

"All right, Miriam. I'll be there in five minutes. Try and keep her stable."

"Of course. Thank you."

Greg dropped the phone back onto the cradle and spent a few seconds leaning against the wall, piecing himself together, testing the bounds of his head.

Not good, but not terrible either. A not insignificant part of him still wanted to curl up in the dark, but these things were always relative, and for Greg after this last year the fact that it was only a part of him meant that he was doing pretty good.

He breathed in. He breathed out. Then he turned on the light and dressed in a crisp white shirt the dry cleaners had delivered the day before, some freshly pressed charcoal slacks, and a set of polished brogues.

Then he was sick, violently and without warning, and

had to change his shirt again. But that was okay, he had spares. The shoes were fine after a wipe.

He paused a moment at the door, his eyes roaming over the ruin of his grimy trailer that was always supposed to be a temporary stopgap until Val and the kids moved out to Jordan. He'd kept it in good shape for a while, until he'd been unable to keep lying to himself.

The journey back from the house in Bozeman last night had been another gruler. He would have gotten back after midnight even if he hadn't stopped off at a motel to relax himself on the way. Once he'd accepted that the need to make the drive wasn't going away any time soon, he'd hoped that it would at least get easier with time, that it would just become a part of life, but if anything it seemed to be the opposite. It was becoming more and more of a slog, more and more a thing he dreaded after a week of twelve-hour days and driving through blizzards or droughts to prescribe pills at the end of the world.

At least his day-to-day commute was short. His trailer sat in the northernmost corner of the hospital's land, so it was no more than a minute's walk into work when he wasn't making the rounds. He suspected it had been intended for a janitor or car park attendant, but it'd been empty when he'd arrived, and the rent was so cheap he had no doubt he spent more a month on booze.

He didn't bother to lock the door as he left.

Outside the main entrance, the ambulance was still parked askew, the driver's door open and the blue lights flashing with idiotic persistence.

When Greg passed through the doors a wave of warmth and clean antiseptic washed over him. He wanted to savor it and rest his aching brow against a hot radiator, but

Miriam was already running toward him, her red curls bouncing wildly around her troubled face, her sensible shoes slapping against the linoleum.

"We couldn't stabilize her. She's getting worse, Greg. Follow me."

There were only four beds in the whole hospital—she didn't need to guide him anywhere—but he followed obediently, the last of his hangover burning away in the sudden rush of adrenaline that always came in this moment.

Four patient rooms side by side, only one door open. Greg finally pushed ahead, already hearing the erratic beeping of the ECG.

Inside, Lillian—no doubt the only other nurse on duty—was leaning over the bed, checking vitals that Greg could tell from a glance were a train wreck.

He asked for the numbers anyway, as much to let Lillian know he was there as anything else.

She turned to him with visible relief, rattling off everything he needed to know.

As she moved aside, Greg saw the small figure in the bed, and cursed. Mrs. McKinley was barely recognizable as the woman from her last checkup only a few months before. She seemed trapped in her own personal hurricane, every part of her tensed to the point of snapping as the pain swept through her.

He moved to her bedside, took his flashlight from his pocket and shone it into her eyes. Barely a response. Not good.

"Marge?" He tapped her slack cheek. Her skin was hot beneath his fingertips, wrinkled and raw in a way that reminded him more of a newly hatched chick than a woman at the end of her life.

No, not yet.

"Marge, can you hear me?"

For a moment nothing, then, slowly, she focused on him, like a woman swimming up from deep water. She tried to smile. "Doghdah Hemngwah." But she was already sinking again, into some vast inner distance.

The ECG gave a low chirrup as her heartbeat became erratic. Greg didn't hesitate. "We're losing her. Get me the defibrillator."

Miriam was already waiting, offering out the paddles, the miracle machine ready beneath her arm.

"Stand back." Greg pressed the paddles into place, checked that no part of him was touching the bed, and nodded. "Clear."

Mrs. McKinley jolted. Her whole body warping in one almighty convulsion.

"Clear."

Again, like invisible fists slamming into every part of her.

"Clear."

Still the ECG gave only a broken, arrhythmic song, then all at once it cried out, that dreaded endless note.

"Clear," Greg whispered, looking down at her face screwed up in pain. He heard her teeth crack together.

"Clear."

Still the whine went on and on.

She had given him a bottle of Jim Beam for his birthday. He still didn't know how she'd found out when it was. And she'd sent him a card with a cartoon cat on it.

He dropped the paddles and started compressions.

"Come on, Marge," he muttered, "come on."

He could already see her lying on the cold table in the

morgue. Victim of a body that had betrayed her as she slept.

No.

"Miriam, take over." He moved to one side as she slid her hands onto Mrs. McKinley's delicate sternum, tilted back her head and blew into her slack mouth.

Miriam pumped, Greg blew, feeling her chest inflate like a balloon, desperately trying to get some air to her oxygen-starved brain.

"Doctor."

"Pump, Miriam, for fuck's sake."

"Greg." Lillian placed a hand on his arm.

"We're not letting her die!" He swung around, sending the tray in her other hand flying as he caught her arm, trying to make her listen. "We are not letting her die, do you hear me?" Scalpels sang over the tiled floor like bells.

The moment stretched. Greg could hear his own breathing, see Lillian cringing as if from a wild animal. The ECG howled on.

Greg let her go, suddenly tasting bile again. She stepped back, the movement lurching and instinctive.

"I'm sorry," he said. "I—"

Lillian swallowed. "It's okay, Greg, Dr. Hemingway. It's . . . it's okay."

It wasn't. It was about as far from okay as you could get, but there was no undoing it.

He turned back to Margery. Her face did not look peaceful in death. It was all scrunched up, almost fearful, as though she had known something awful was coming for her. Miriam moved forward and closed her cloudy eyes.

Greg breathed, blinked, fought to keep himself in

control. "Time of death," he checked his watch, "four forty-five a.m."

Miriam wrote it down on the chart at the end of the bed without a word.

Greg looked down at the ruin of Margery McKinley a moment longer. Minutes earlier it had been a woman, and now it was nothing but meat.

"We can finish up here, Doctor," Miriam said, her voice clipped, all professionalism.

Greg nodded, unable to meet his nurse's eyes, fearing the heat in his own would spill over if he did. He went out into the corridor.

Roger was seated in the reception, huddled in his winter coat. Greg must have completely missed him coming in, and no wonder. He seemed smaller, barely recognizable as the man Greg had first met that spring.

Roger lifted his head as he heard Greg's footsteps.

"Mr. McKinley . . ." Greg struggled for words. Looking into the old man's eyes felt like coming home to an empty house.

Roger said nothing, but two lines of tears ran down the weathered tracks of his face.

"I'm so sorry."

Roger only shook his head.

Greg had nothing else, no comfort to give. He sat down in the chair beside him. Outside, the wind was picking up, moaning as it ran over the hospital roof.

Greg remembered sitting in the corridor outside his brother's room, his father's gaze upon him. It was strange, the things that had survived the shocks.

His first kiss? Gone.

Those quietly accusing eyes? It could have been yesterday. It could be now.

Some moments were more than a tangle of neurons. Some of them were in you. In your blood and bone. In your soul.

"My father always used to say," Roger said suddenly, "that you should never go to bed angry. First rule of marriage."

Greg said nothing.

"But then, he never had to live with a woman as stubborn as her. My mother was a glass of sweet milk. And they were only married ten years before a horse kicked him in the head and cracked his skull open. Margery—" his voice caught. "We were married forty-three years, and we broke that rule more times than I can say."

"It was obvious how much you loved each other, Roger," Greg said, then immediately regretted it. Were platitudes the best he could do?

"Aye, maybe that's so. But still, my old pa wasn't wrong about much, 'cept horses maybe. Biggest argument we've had in a good long while, all over that bloody whiskey . . . Oh Lord, what a way to end forty years." He put his hands over his face.

Greg could only imagine what final words had been said, the petty grievances that had been unearthed.

There was nothing to say. He had no words to stop this man reliving that final night in every spare minute he had left.

Do you think—" Roger began, his voice still muffled by his rough hands. "Dr. Hemingway, do you think it caused it?"

Greg did not need to ask what. "No. Absolutely not. Heart attacks don't wait six hours to strike, believe me on that. Margery's heart, it was just worn out. There was nothing anyone could have done. She wouldn't have even felt a thing." Truths and lies mixed together.

Roger lowered his hands. "She was gasping."

"A reflex. That was only the body, the needle riding its groove. Your wife was already gone."

"I . . . I can't . . ."

"Do you think that when she went to bed, she didn't love you? Didn't know you loved her?"

He finally lowered his trembling hands. "No."

"So." Greg stretched out his legs in front of him. His right knee ached. "One bad night? A lifetime of love is no small thing, Roger. Do you know what some of us would give for that?"

For a moment there was no reaction. Then Roger nodded. "She was a good woman. A good damn-stubborn woman." He sniffed, wiped his eyes, and straightened.

It was like a tap turning off. Suddenly he was the same man who had stood in the corner of their bedroom, telling his wife not to lie to a doctor. "Thank you, Dr. Hemingway, for everything you've done. I know she wouldn't have had this much time without you. I appreciate it."

Greg nodded slowly, staring at him, stunned at the change. "Would you like to see her?"

Not a flicker. "No, thank you. I don't think that'd do me much good."

"Okay. I'll call you a taxi."

"No need for that. Nothing to stop me driving. Plus there's a storm coming, don't want to leave the truck here. I'll need it. Arrangements to be made."

"Okay." Greg hesitated. "Would you like to use our phone?"

"Naw, best I call the boys from home. It's not going to be an easy conversation. Junior's been trying to get us to move out to Florida for a while now. Always said Marge couldn't travel. Guess I'll need a new excuse."

They stood. Greg offered his hand, and the old man took it. His grip was surprisingly strong. "Take care, Roger. And again, I'm so sorry."

"Don't be, Doc. Won't do no good. Expect a fine hamper coming your way this Christmas." He tipped his hat, a smile creasing his still shining cheeks, and walked out into the new morning, into the remains of his life.

Greg began to feel himself slip in the weeks after Margery McKinley's death.

He supposed he should have expected it. There had been no shocks since he'd promised Valerie in Havana, despite a few ups and downs—nothing so far had stopped him getting out of bed or sent him howling through the streets. He'd even kept his problem in check except for the stop-offs on the way back from Bozeman. There hadn't been time for anything else.

Now, he could feel the familiar gears begin to turn, all those mechanisms in his head that had no breaks, no way to decelerate. He knew a big one was coming. A high. A manic phase. All different words for something that could not be explained, only experienced.

It was a relief, in a sense. The ups and the downs were dangerous in unique ways, and while it was true that the ups could ultimately be the more destructive, at least the pain was delayed. In the moment, every stupid thing he did would feel right.

He upped his marathon training. Every day, after a twelve-hour shift treating patients at the hospital or driving from farmhouse to farmhouse over an endless expanse of cropless dirt and snow-blasted trees, he would pull on his tattered old trainers and pound out into the snowy dark, running until his back ached and his legs felt like jelly and his stomach had twisted into a knot.

He'd been sick by the side of the road more than once, usually around the ten-mile mark, but he never let himself pause for longer than it took to spit the last of the bile out of his mouth before forcing his aching body back into motion. His feet were a mess of blisters, and his nipples bled no matter how many Band-Aids he used.

It helped. He was sure it helped. Don't give yourself time to think—that was key.

But soon, when he wasn't running, he was thinking about running. He had the route of the upcoming Boston marathon completely memorized. Every turn, notable feature, shift in terrain and elevation was neatly logged like a pile of index cards in his mind. He flicked through them constantly, finding himself muttering under his breath on his endless drives while the landscapes shuttled past unchanging like the backgrounds of cheap cartoons.

A part of him knew this growing obsession was a symptom, but it felt like a cure.

He still saw Valerie and the kids every weekend he could, finishing work at around nine and walking straight out of the hospital and into his car to start the 320-mile drive.

He'd given up asking her to move out to Jordan. She

still thought Bozeman was parochial, so what chance did Jordan stand, when the whole county's population was a staggering 1,500? With its one-screen cinema and its four-shelf library? She had a job in Bozeman. She was settled, in her own way. The kids had made friends at school.

No, it was over. This was the status quo now.

Of course, that didn't mean it was good for either of them. He could see the question in his wife's eyes every time he pulled his carcass out of the car in the early hours of Saturday morning. Was this it? The life for which he'd dragged her out of New York into this backwater flyover state?

He had no answers for her.

He was lying in Valerie's bed, the soft suburban streetlights spread like marmalade over the ceiling, the weight of her against his side. Neither of them had had the energy for sex—they rarely did these days—but it was still good to be there, still and for once not wanting to be in motion, listening to his wife breathe, wondering if she was asleep or awake.

It was almost like before. He'd been happy in New York, but he would have died if he'd stayed there. He knew that without hesitation, even if he could not have articulated it.

He'd lost his sense of purpose in that city, started to question things he had no place questioning.

But now here he was in the back end of nowhere, and those same questions were bubbling up again. Who was he, really? Would Valerie hate him if she knew?

She shifted beside him. "Are you asleep, Greg?"

He could smell her when she moved. That particular

scent that was not sweat or perfume but simply clean skin. "No. Just thinking."

Ironically, the more tired he became, the less he seemed to sleep, and when he did manage a few fitful hours he was running the same strip of sidewalk over and over, or pressing again and again on Margery McKinley's ribs, feeling her old bones slender as wicker beneath his palms, or back in his father's bedroom, all dressed up and knowing that the next moment the door would open and his father would look upon him, the dreadful anticipation somehow stretching out into infinity.

Valerie wriggled closer. Her lips touched his neck, not kissing, but resting there. He could feel them moving as she said, "Aren't you tired? It's such a long drive . . ."

"Yes." God, he was tired. His back and legs ached. His head, too. Not the pound of a hangover, but the dull thud of dehydration. "Taking a while to unwind, I suppose."

She was quiet for so long he thought she'd fallen back to sleep, but then he felt her lips move again, her breath warm and faintly tickling. "I know we've already talked about this, but I was having a drink with Tory the other day—"

"—who's Tory?"

"You know, Victoria. She's from my book club. I— I suppose you haven't met her." A moment's silence as the space between their lives somehow wormed its way between skin and skin. "Anyway. Her brother runs a practice over in the east of town. They're looking for someone to fill in spare hours. It wouldn't be much money, but you'd be here. And maybe it'd turn into something more permanent."

A car passed by, and the orange glow over the ceiling swelled into everything, then receded.

Greg thought of the four-bed hospital where Mary and Lillian would be waiting starched and professional come Monday morning. He thought of all the farmhouses where the descendants of those who had somehow been left behind as the nation spread West would have their doctor's visiting days crossed out on calendars that came free with their subscriptions to the *Jordan Chronicle*, ready to meet him on the day with a cup of coffee and a nod and a look of hard-won respect. He thought of Roger McKinley, who seemed to be getting thinner by the week, whose cough didn't seem to be going away.

"No."

"Greg," she sighed. "We can't do this forever."

That's true, he thought. *We can't. But we can do it a while longer.*

He loved her. He would always love her. And he knew how little that meant.

They lay in silence for a while, then Greg asked, "Do you talk about me often, with the girls?"

"Don't be like that. It's not like that."

"I don't mean it like anything. I only wonder what you all talk about. What do women talk about when there's no men around?"

"The same things we talk about when you're around."

"I don't believe that."

"I don't know, how many angels could stand on the head of a pin, mostly."

Greg could imagine them sitting in some coffee shop, their legs crossed, cups cradled between slender figures, sharing secrets only girls shared.

"Valerie. Do you think, if I was a woman, we'd be friends?"

"What?"

"If I was a woman, would we have been girlfriends, do you think?"

"I'd rather not imagine a world without my husband."

"But I'd still be me. You'd still be you."

"Stop joking, Greg." She finally rolled away from him. "Of course it would be different. You're my husband, not my girlfriend. Go to sleep. The kids will be up early."

Greg stared up at the ceiling. He listened to his wife breathe and felt his body ache. He tried to focus on it: this here and now. But then, inevitably, he began moving through the turns of the marathon in his head.

A week before the race, he broke his only iron-clad rule. He'd been so drunk that the next morning he couldn't remember anything but a few scattered snapshots. It was like someone had crept in and given him the shocks in the night.

He didn't remember getting dressed, but he remembered the feeling of the cold air on his shoulders as he walked through the dark. He didn't remember entering the bar, the eyes that must have swiveled in his direction, but he remembered running through the stock of tens in his purse as he ordered whiskey after whiskey, and finally hoisting up his dress to pull another roll out of lace panties. He didn't even remember why he'd done it, but he remembered how good it had felt.

And not all of that had been the drink, or his fucked-up brain. Maybe that was the worst thing. It had felt good. He'd felt happy, for the first time in months.

There had been no funny looks in the hospital the next day, no averted gazes while he was on his rounds. He could only hope that no one out in a dive bar as Tuesday ticked over into Wednesday was likely to be believed if they started spreading crazy stories about Jordan's beloved physician. Or at least that no one who'd seen him would have recognized the staggering, hairy-legged man in the red dress as the respected Dr. Hemingway who'd helped get their nana through the flu.

Perhaps being away for the marathon weekend would be a blessing. If people didn't see him, they'd be less likely to make the connection.

Greg felt a guilty bloom of relief as he left Jordan behind, driving up to Bozeman with only his running gear and his flight ticket piled up on the passenger seat of his car.

"It's not working, Greg."

Valerie had barely let him get through the door before she'd started speaking in a breathless rush, trying to make herself heard over the storm raging outside.

"I don't have a husband, I have a weekend arrangement. The kids hardly see you, and when they do, you're . . ."

She closed the door, and the sudden silence swallowed them.

Greg stood in the kitchen, his bundle of running clothes scrunched up in both hands. He was trying to listen, trying to focus long enough to take it in. He struggled for words.

"I told you, I can't— I have . . . people who depend on me."

"I don't want you to move to Bozeman." Her voice was stronger now, with some of her trademark steel in it. "It's not working. It hasn't been working for a long time."

It took him a moment to process this, then understanding blindsided him. It almost threw him off balance, but it wasn't enough to stop him. He had too much momentum, too much energy coursing through him. He couldn't have stopped if he'd wanted to. As if to prove the point, he realized he'd started walking circles as he listened.

"You've not been yourself. Half the time it's like you're a zombie, the rest I feel like you're going to bite my head off. And the mood swings, Greg. When you're manic I'm terrified you're going to get yourself killed, or kill someone else. When you're depressed . . . I can't go through it again. The despair. It seeps into me. And I'm sorry, I know it's harder for you than it is for me, I know it's a thousand times worse, but I can't do it any more. I can't . . ." Her voice finally cracked, and she covered her mouth with her hands. "For God's sake, Greg. Look at yourself."

He made himself stand still, but within a second he was rocking back and forth onto his heels. He could hear the tap dripping in the background, driving him crazy, but he made himself focus.

"And the kids?"

"You can't even look after yourself any more."

"They need a father."

"They're scared of you, Greg. Showing up at crazy hours. Phoning in the middle of the night, shouting nonsense. They love you, but they're scared of you. Of course you can see them, but not until you've sorted yourself out, seen a therapist. Something."

Phoning in the middle of the night? Had he been doing that? The surprise almost gave him purchase, almost let him see how far into mania he already was, how close to burning up . . . Then he was swept on.

"Scared of me? They're my children. What have you been saying to them, you bitch?" It felt good to get angry, to let anger fill him up so he couldn't feel anything else.

"Nothing."

"Liar."

"Greg, I . . ."

"Liar."

"I'm not the one who—"

"—Of course not!" He shouted now. "You're not the one who does *anything*. Zombie? I'd love to see you work twelve-hour shifts all week then tap dance your way down to Jordan every weekend. You think you're fucking tired? You don't know what tired is." He punched the kitchen cupboard, and his fist went clean through and smashed into the neatly stacked jars of marinara.

Valerie stepped forward, uncowed.

"You're the one who dragged us out here! I'm *sorry*, Greg, I'm *so sorry* I didn't drive the kids three hundred miles each way every weekend because you wanted to play doctor in hicksville. Sorry I didn't give up the last ragged shreds of my career you hadn't already taken to live in a trailer in Jordan fucking Montana."

She was angry, and that was good. Better than seeing that weary hurt in her eyes. It gave Greg something to focus on, so that he could avoid thinking about what was actually happening, that something was ending, breaking in a way that could never be made whole.

"You think this was easy for me?" she snarled. "Thinking you were cheating on me for months? Maybe that would have been better . . ." Greg flinched, and she pressed the advantage, grabbing his shame and squeezing. "Did you think I wouldn't find out? Showing up with nail-polish barely cleaned off. Stinking of cheap perfume. Stretched out tights in the fucking glove compartment."

He stepped back unsteadily, the floor dropping out from beneath him like a runaway elevator. The roaring engine inside him stalled a little, and the reality of what was happening flooded over him.

This can't be real.

"I . . . I—"

"—Go on. I'd love to hear it, Greg. I would *love* for you to make this make sense. For you to . . ." Her words dried up, and her eyes sought out his, but he couldn't meet them.

She knows. The shame, so familiar, burned incandescent, ate through him.

He spoke through clenched teeth. "I *need* it, Valerie." It was a plea. He heard the desperation in his own voice and felt nothing but contempt. "You don't . . . you don't understand."

"You're right. I don't." She said it softly. One hand started to lift toward him, but she brought it back down so hard it slapped against her thigh. "But I know I need a husband. Not whatever this is . . . I love you, Greg. But this is not working."

You can only fall for so long before you hit the ground.

He made himself breathe. He would fix this. Everything could be fixed if you just tried hard enough. "Valerie . . ."

"I'll start the shocks again, Val. I'll clean myself up, and cut out all this shit and—"

"—Greg!" It was a scream. She staggered, leaned against the wall. He moved forward to

293

catch her, all instinct, but she shook her head so fiercely her hair flew in all directions.

The music of a passing car drifted in. "Uptown Girl," incongruous against the storm inside and out. It grew and faded as someone else's life cruised by.

"Please. Just go." A few strands of hair were stuck to her lipstick. She'd always had such beautiful lips.

"I can fix this, Val," he tried again. "I can get better." He knew he was rocking in place, but he couldn't stop. The engine was revving back up.

"No, Greg, I don't think you can." She didn't sound angry now, only tired. "I wish you could, but I've heard it too many times. There's something broken in you and— I didn't mean that."

But she did.

"I'm not crazy." He needed to get out. Now. Right now. He went to the table and picked up his abandoned jogging gear.

"I'm not fucking crazy." He whispered it this time, clutching the old trainers and the stained T-shirt to his chest, and knew it was a lie. Outside the kitchen window, all the branches of the big oak tree at the end of the garden were convulsing, but there was no sound of wind, no ripple of grass. It was like the tree was moving itself, reaching out for something invisible, unreachable.

"I'm not crazy."

The rain came. He turned and almost ran through the kitchen. Valerie was still leaning against the wall, and he had to slink past her as though the slightest touch might burn both of them.

"I should have known this would happen," she whispered. "You're so like your father . . ."

He stopped on the doormat, his bundle of clothes falling from his hands. As he turned, he saw on her face that she realized what she had said, how deep it would cut him.

A second later he had crossed the length of the hall, and his hand closed around her throat.

The gears of the runaway engine inside him finally shattered. He was left holding his wife's neck, a shard of glass sunk deep between his knuckles, dripping tomato and blood.

He opened his hand slowly, then walked out, stepping over his jogging gear as he went.

Missoula, Montana

1983

A base to weather the storm, that was what he needed. Somewhere to sit this out until he could get some shocks. Once he had himself back under control he'd be able to go back to Jordan and look everyone in the eye.

He had to tell himself he was going back, that he was going to salvage something.

Right now he couldn't even look at his own reflection without shame welling up like sewage from a burst septic pipe. He'd had to take the mirror off the wall the same day he'd booked into the motel. There wasn't much he could do about the one in the bathroom, but he left the cabinet open for a while, angled over to the corner of the room. The problem with this solution was that he kept catching sight of himself coming out of the shower. An unwelcome gut-punch of reality.

He'd thought he was in great shape after all the running, but instead of trim he was gaunt. His hair was graying and getting thinner. And were those liver spots on his shoulders? He looked like a beached whale a few days into rotting, already well picked over by gulls.

In the end he asked for an extra towel and kept it hung

over the cabinet mirror. The cleaner had removed it the first two times, then given up the fight and accepted it as a new feature of room 102.

That was one thing Greg liked about this place already: they were used to weird. Used to haunted-looking solo travelers swerving off the main drag and into their rooms.

He'd spotted the motel when he was tearing westward out of Bozeman with no plan or destination, just his foot on the floor and his chin so close to the steering wheel he could smell the leather.

If he hadn't seen the sign he might not have stopped until he hit the ocean. But as the sky started to darken there was a flicker of neon to his right. He'd looked and turned in the same moment, reckless, nearly catching a semi coming in the opposite direction.

The blare of its horn and the crunch of Greg's tires on the gravel merged as he skid-spiraled to a stop outside the Thunderbird Motel, its name picked out in huge pink letters glowing twenty feet overhead. The building itself stretched out over the lot, its long walkway spaced with guest rooms lit up by a line of ice-diamond. And behind it all, the slinky curve of the Clark Fork meandered by, varnished by the sunset.

Something about the incongruity of it spoke to him. The whispering candy-fake glare of the neon sitting easy before the slow burn of the ancient river. The letters towering ecstatic over everything. A place that could only exist in America.

He had booked himself in with cash, intending to spend only the one night to lick his wounds. Yet here he was a week later, heading to the desk to pay the next week in advance.

The lobby was right next to his room, so the owner, Thelma, had heard his door open and was already looking up when he came in.

"Morning, Dr. Hemingway." She smiled. Friendly, but still cautious. Greg hadn't emerged from his room for the first five days of his stay, drinking water from the bathroom tap, eating nothing but pills from the bottle of Valium he'd found in his glove compartment.

When he'd finally let the cleaner into the room it stank of sweat and cigarette smoke and despair, though there wasn't much mess. He'd brought nothing with him, so the worst were the bed sheets crumpled into a soiled nest. Greg had sat in the shower for the half hour it had taken to make the room habitable again, letting the scalding-hot water wash over him.

Thelma had taken it all in her stride. For all her hard-learned caution, there had been no scorn or pity in her clear blue eyes. She'd seen this sort of thing before, would see it again, and wasn't in the business of judging.

Greg liked her for that, the same way he liked the quiet confidence she exuded seated there behind her neat desk. A fleet commander at the helm of a battleship.

"Morning, Dr. Hemingway," she said again. "Are you feeling better this morning?"

Greg realized he'd been standing there, slack-faced.

"Yes," he said, moving to the desk. "I'm sorry, Thelma, I'm still half asleep this morning."

"That's all right. What can I do for you? Checking out?"

"No. No, the opposite in fact." Greg found himself suddenly nervous, like he was imposing. "I was hoping to stay another week. I'd pay up front, would that be okay?"

"Oh, I think so, let me check."

She pulled out a thick logbook from its appointed place and started flicking through the pages.

Greg couldn't imagine a roadside motel was overrun with advanced bookings, but Thelma was a stickler for proper procedure in this and everything else. She took out her ruler from its appointed drawer and made a perfect long line with a red pen attached to the book by a length of string, topping it off with HEMINGWAY in her precise block capitals.

Stapled to the pasteboard behind her bowed head, haloing her like a saint, was a cheap sign picked out in scarlet letters: *Live well. Laugh Often. Love Much.*

Well, he'd managed two, at least. That wasn't so bad.

"You know, you really should be running a hospital." He spoke slowly, focusing on each word. "If half the wards I've been in had someone with your attention to detail in charge . . ."

She smiled at that as she returned the book to its den, and this time it wasn't just politeness. "Funny you should say that. Before I bought this place I was a surgical technician. I guess you could say that's where they beat being a stickler into me. I like things to be right. Helps keep my blood pressure down."

"Well, high blood pressure is no joke. Do whatever you have to. Doctor's orders."

She laughed, and Greg relaxed a little. He was used to having people like him at first, before they really got to know him, before they realized there was something wrong. Having it go the other way felt strange, but nice.

Still, he knew he didn't have much more talking left in him. He already felt exhausted. All he wanted was to go back to bed, swallow any Valium he had left and sleep a few days away.

He fought it, made himself listen as Thelma spoke. "Well, doctors don't need to be organized, they have long-suffering people to do that for them."

"True, otherwise I wouldn't have lasted a week. I wondered a lot, in med school, if I had what it takes . . ." He paused, remembering all the dropouts, all the disappointments. And then Valerie.

"But you got through in the end?"

"Yeah, just about."

"Well, that's all that matters. As long as you get there in the end."

He thanked her, and — still fighting the pull of bed and darkness and despair — went out and made himself jog up the hill to the 24/7 grocery store where the college kids could buy their junk food and beer. He went slow. Despite all the training and the fact that he was in the best shape he'd been in for about twenty years, his body still felt delicate somehow, like he was working some lingering poison from his veins.

He bought a sandwich and a Coke, hesitated before the long shelf of slyly gleaming quarts of whiskey, then added a Mars bar to the pile.

He walked back to the Thunderbird, taking small, careful steps and eating his chocolate with small, careful bites. He just had to take his time. He would get better. He always got better.

But then, he always got worse as well.

Key West

1938

"Careful, Gig." Les stared up at him, doggy-paddling to keep his head clear of the water.

Greg had climbed all the way to the top of the rocks, the peak of his own mountain island. It was probably only five times as tall as he was, but it felt enormous. He could see over Uncle Les all the way to the beach. John was stomping along the dark sand at the edge of the waves, finding crabs and smashing them to paste under his heel. Patrick and their mother were dozing under the same parasol, and under the next, Papa was reading a book for a few seconds at a time, putting it down and picking it up and glancing down the beach.

At last he saw Greg standing on his mountain outcrop and waved. Greg waved back with two hands at once. He couldn't make out Papa's face properly, but he was sure he was smiling.

"Watch this, Papa!" he called.

"Greg!" Les barked below. "Don't you—"

—Greg kicked off, his toes scraped raw by rough stone as the air became a rush and the beach a blur. The sea jumped up to meet him with a slap, knocking the sun's heat away in one cool pulse.

He felt something yank briefly on the back of his shorts, like when he caught his jacket on thorns. It took him a few seconds of sinking, silver bubbles slipping from his lips and tickling his cheeks, before he realized it must have been the rocks.

Then a hand closed around the back of his neck and yanked him upwards.

"Idiot!" Les shouted as Greg broke the surface. "You could have died!" He hauled Greg to the base of the rocks and lifted him clear of the water.

"Idiot," he muttered again, checking Greg over like someone looking for scratches on a dropped pair of sunglasses.

Greg tried to push him away, craning his neck toward the parasol on the beach. It was hard to tell from down here, but he was pretty sure Papa had already gone back to reading.

Uncle Les turned and followed Greg's line of sight, then looked back at him with a knowing smile that made Greg cringe.

"One last time, you're an idiot, Gigi. I'd guess there was half an inch between you and a four-foot grave."

Greg shrugged, feeling very small and very stupid and wondering why he'd even thought jumping was a good idea in the first place. As though Papa would care . . .

His uncle hauled himself up onto the rock next to him, water sluicing from his back.

"At some point you're going to have to learn to think before you act."

"I do think!" Greg burst out. "It just takes so long. It's

like, I have to do something, but by the time I know what I'm doing I've already done it . . ." He couldn't explain it, but Uncle Les was nodding.

"Ah, is that how it is?" He tilted his head and cleaned one ear with his pinky. "Like you have to do something, anything, right now or you'll explode? You're a Hemingway all right."

Greg looked up at him. Clouds drifted by but never covered the sun. Waves lapped around their legs.

Uncle Les shrugged. He shrugged like Papa: a brief jerk of bear-like shoulders. Greg suddenly wondered if that was how he shrugged . . .

"I've got no easy answers for you," he said, bringing Greg back into focus. "The only thing that helps me is to stop thinking about what might happen to me—that never bothered me—and start worrying about everyone else. The people I might hurt, leave behind, you know . . ."

Greg tried to look like he understood, but he must not have been very good at pretending, because Uncle Les laughed. "It doesn't matter. Next time just try and think about the people who love you. Your mom and Papa and me."

He stooped down and planted a wet kiss in the middle of Greg's forehead, the warmth of it like a flare after the cold water.

"Look after yourself for us."

Montana

1985

Greg woke to someone knocking at his door. The apartment was dark, the curtains pulled firmly closed with only one bar of queasy dawn light leaking over the floor.

His head felt thick, his tongue fat and dry in his mouth, misshapen as though someone had been chewing it like gum.

The knocking didn't stop. Greg groaned and pulled his pillow over his head, but it was no use. Sleep was drifting away, and a dull thud was taking its place behind his eyes.

Fuck it.

He rolled out of bed and made it halfway across the room in the dark before kicking an empty whiskey bottle and sending it spinning over the floor.

He ignored the stab of pain in his big toe and fumbled at the latch, but it was like he was wearing mittens. His head was pounding so bad he couldn't focus. He leaned it against the cold of the door, but then he felt the knocking running through his skull, shredding the swollen meat of his brain. "I'm coming."

Finally the latch slipped free and he forced the door wide open.

"What?"

"Dad?" A familiar voice. John. His son John. "What are you . . . Jesus."

Greg blinked. The light was pale and watery, but it was the fiercest he'd seen in days. It took him a few seconds to focus on his son's face.

He was so *old*. What had it been, five years? Was that enough for a boy to become a man?

"What're you doing here?" Greg asked. "You're in Italy."

John looked confused. "I told you I was coming, Dad. You wired me money for the plane, remember?"

Greg had only a vague recollection, and this time he couldn't blame the shocks. He'd probably had a few drinks.

"Are . . . are you okay, Dad?"

"Fine. Fine."

"I've been calling all night. I got off the bus seven hours ago. I had to walk here from town. It's . . . still okay that I'm here, right?"

He sounded nervous. The same blood flowed in their veins, but they were practically strangers. John had grown up in the years before Valerie—some of Greg's darkest—and he'd practically been raised by Greg's uncle Les. Maybe that was why he'd ended up so fully formed, so stable. Greg couldn't say. Since he'd stopped the shocks, the memories had come trickling back, of his childhood mostly, but he must have done some irreparable damage in those middle years when he was getting shocks every month or so. Those memories had been seared away.

"I . . ." Greg forced down a wave of nausea and tried to focus. "I was meant to pick you up."

One simple job to do in five years, and Greg had still

managed to fuck it up. But John didn't look angry. He looked sad.

Greg turned away, back into the darkness. "Come in, then. Make yourself at home. I'll—" His foot caught on something unseen in the dark, and he stumbled. John caught him easily, hoisted Greg back to his feet like he was made of cardboard. When had the chubby-cheeked boy playing with stick guns gotten so damn strong? But then, Greg had lost a lot of weight lately.

His mind wandered, and the next thing he knew he was being lowered back into his bed. The sheets were damp, from sweat or booze, he didn't know, but that was okay. The soft darkness was all he craved.

"Jesus, Dad," John whispered. "How much have you had to drink?"

Greg didn't reply. It was all wrong; a son shouldn't have to see his father like this.

"Ah, Dad . . ." John's voice was soft, muffled like he had something in his throat, and in the dark Greg felt him pull the covers up. The gentleness of it was more than he could bear, more than he deserved. He turned his face into his dirty pillow until the world faded.

A few days after he'd wired John the money to come visit, Greg drove out to Jordan. It was the first time he'd gone back since he'd fled.

His heels clicked cheerfully on the sidewalk. If he sped up a little, the sound was like the snipping of a seamstress's scissors. If he slowed his pace, it was like knuckles rapping on oak.

It was getting on for midsummer, and all the shopfronts were bronzed by the light, the cars blazing like coals fresh from the fire. The holidays were in full swing, and kids milled around the candy stores, the cinema, the arcade, weary parents dragged along like kites.

A few of them looked at him, a few of them pointed, but Greg had suffered worse. He didn't mind really.

One heavily freckled boy, at the corner to the park, had pulled on his mother's hand, pointed and said, "Look, Mommy, she's so big!"

The word had struck him unexpected, like a stone from a sling, pushing into him before he had the chance to deflect it.

She.

The woman, to her credit, had pulled the child into line and given Greg a pained smile. "I'm so sorry."

"Why? I am pretty big." Greg had smiled back without artifice and walked on.

And she—just for a moment, but no, he couldn't—had walked on through the park, not going anywhere except forward, watching the ducks send black ripples over the sun-bright pond.

But still, as he walked through the crowded streets, he found himself turning that one word over in his mind, how it had felt.

Good. That was the simple truth. Maybe he just didn't have any shame left, but that wasn't it. Here he was, in his extra-large crimson dress suit, his custom-ordered heels, his string of plain but tasteful pearls, feeling . . . happy. There was that damn word again.

Still, it was nerve-racking being out in public like this. Stone-cold sober, entirely in his right mind, on a bright summer day. This was new.

Greg wasn't sure what had brought him back to Jordan.

It had been his home for years, and he'd left pretty much without a word—maybe he only wanted to see it one last time, see some old faces. But if that was all, why come back like this?

He didn't know, but his feet seemed to. The click of his heels was unwavering.

The sun glowered. Perhaps the skirt suit had been a mistake, or the heavy red velvet. It had looked so bold in the shop, had felt so tactile beneath his fingers. He wished he'd had time to buy a silk scarf to go with it, to really set it off.

He turned a corner and paused, finally understanding where his feet had been taking him, why he had come back to Jordan.

Everyone knew the soda fountain on the main drag. Seemed like everyone in a ten-mile radius—Greg included when his calls allowed—went there for lunch in the summer to eat overly sweet pie and lumpy pancakes and drink the best ice-cold soda in the county.

The familiar bell tinkled as Greg slipped in. Same rickety tables. Same crappy radio droning the latest hits. Same faces lined up. It shouldn't have surprised him, he hadn't been away all that long, but it felt like a lifetime.

He slipped into a free seat at the counter, crossing his legs at the ankle.

Lanny the owner sauntered over, laughing with one of the regulars as he took his plate. Greg waited for him to say something as he turned, for any word of recognition, but Lanny let only the briefest widening of his eyes slip before he dropped his gaze and began furiously wiping the spotless countertop between them.

"What can I get you?" he asked, his voice rigid.

"I . . ." Greg hesitated, his friend's name on his lips. "A Coke, please."

One hard nod, and Lanny spun away to the soda fountain, his movements jerky as a puppet's.

Greg glanced along the line, waiting for someone to look up, catch his eye, for some smile, some nod or sign that they saw him. Fitz at least—how many jokes had they shared at this counter? Maybe he'd laugh, or get angry, or make it all okay. Fitz would say something and either way Greg would feel real.

The minutes swam by. The soda sank down his glass until there was just a pile of melting ice sitting at the bottom, and a row of men still frozen along the counter, all staring resolutely ahead.

Lanny stayed at the far end of the bar, polishing the same length of glossy counter over and over. No refill was offered.

He thought of saying something. He thought of shouting something . . . but what would have been the point?

Greg dropped a few dollars next to his glass, slid off his stool, and left.

In the safety of his car, he gripped the steering wheel and stared ahead at nothing. What had he wanted? A warm reception from his old friends? *Great to see you, Greg, what a beautiful dress!* Stupid.

He remembered the boy looking up at him with wide eyes. *She.* The word hummed through him, and there was no denying it any more. He knew what he wanted.

Soon he was back in his apartment and halfway through a bottle of whiskey, wearing his stained old polo shirt and slacks.

★

When Greg finally dragged himself out of bed it was nearly midday, and he only emerged then because the bottle of Scotch he'd left on his bedside table was gone.

He shuffled into the main apartment, holding up his baggy shorts with one hand and rubbing his aching head.

John was at the sink, wearing rubber gloves Greg didn't even know he had and working his way through a pile of plates that came up to his shoulder.

Greg tried to say something, but all that came out was a dry croak. God, he was thirsty. Where was that Scotch?

John finally noticed him standing there and turned around, a sud-laden plate in one hand. "Dad. How are you feeling?"

"Fine." Still a croak, but words at least. "I left a bottle by my bed . . ."

John's face fell, and Greg realized this probably wasn't the first thing he should have asked about with the son he hadn't seen for years.

"I poured it down the sink."

"Oh." Greg felt a brief flicker of anger, but it died like a match without air. He just didn't have the energy.

"Here." John filled up a glass with water and held it out. "Drink this. Are you sure you're okay?

"Fine." Greg sank onto the couch and took a sip. It soothed his raw throat, and he drained the rest in a few noisy gulps. The cold water hit his stomach like a bomb, and he was sure he was going to be sick.

John offered him another full glass, his face concerned. "You sure?"

"Yeah." Greg fought down nausea. "I've had a bad few days is all. You know how I get in one of those dark patches. You caught me at a bad time."

"Dad . . ." John gestured to the apartment. "This isn't a bad few days."

Greg made himself look around. Really look. The dirty plates John had piled beside the sink, the ones at the bottom covered in a fuzz of mold. The snowdrift of takeout cartons and pizza boxes he'd pushed up to the door. The coffee table covered in empty bottles. A huge pile of stained clothes festering at the back of the couch. The flotsam of a human shipwreck.

"I've been cleaning all morning, and I've barely made a dent."

"I didn't ask . . ."

"I know, but it made my skin crawl."

Greg tried not to show how much that stung.

"I think you need to see someone, Dad."

"I'm done dating."

"I don't mean . . . Dad, look at yourself. You look like a fucking ghost."

"No thank you, John. I've spent my whole life trying to cure myself, and it always did more damage than good. I'm done."

"It's not about curing . . . it's about talking to—"

"—No."

There was an awkward silence. Greg raised the glass to take a sip, but his stomach gave another warning lurch. He sighed.

"It's good to see you. Good of you to visit."

John sighed too, the perfect echo of Greg's, the perfect echo of Papa's and maybe all the way back to Adam. He dropped down onto the couch. "Yeah well, I'm glad I came to check on you. I wasn't sure if . . . but I was in the country anyway, and Les's birthday was coming up . . ."

311

"It's Les's birthday? How is he?"

"He's dead, Dad. He's been dead for . . . Jesus Christ." He ran a shaking hand through his hair. "He shot himself. Like Grandad."

"Oh. Oh yes." Greg took a slow breath. He did remember. "Sorry I . . . I'm still waking up. I know you two were close."

"Sure. He was like a . . ." Greg heard the unspoken words. They hurt, but he couldn't resent them. John had been pretty much raised by Les. "Yeah, he was a good man, but he was in a lot of pain toward the end. Diabetes. Amputations . . . He was never going to put up with that. That wasn't Les."

"True. Couldn't sit still for five minutes. I ever tell you how he sailed from Florida to Cuba in a full-blown hurricane?"

Greg was pretty sure he had, but John smiled and shook his head.

"The boat was so low in the water when he came in it would've sunk if he took a piss, but there he was: bailing away with an ice bucket you could barely get your fist in, grinning like a madman." For a second Greg could smell the salt, hear the waves, see Les's face all tanned and glowing. Then he came back to himself, an old man on a sagging couch.

"Sounds like him." John's smile was bittersweet.

"My dad thought he'd lost his mind. Chewed him out for weeks. Damn thing is, Les only did it to impress him."

"He didn't have to worry. Les could sail anything. He taught me."

"Pah," Greg waved a hand, "in that little bay. And where do you sail now? The Mediterranean? It's a pond. Try the

312

Gulf Stream, Bimini. Those waters aren't so forgiving."

"Well, I wasn't exactly spoiled for teachers."

Greg took the barb. "You learned from the best, in any case. I can't get out past the breakers without puking my guts out."

"Really? I didn't know that . . ."

"Yeah." Greg's stomach had settled; he took another more cautious sip of water. "Papa—your grandad—was mortified, of course, but not half as much as me. Used to drive me crazy. Like it was some unforgivable flaw. Kids are stupid."

Greg saw John nodding out of the corner of his eye. "I spent half my childhood on that sunfish you got me."

"Sunwhat?"

"Sunfish. The boat! You sent me the money. It was only tiny, but I loved that thing. The boat my dad bought me."

"Oh, yes. Shame I never got to see it myself."

John turned to look at him fully now. "You did, you came over in the summer. I guess it was after a round of . . . You weren't well."

"Right."

Greg heard a scuffling in the corner in the pause that followed. Maybe a mouse bedding down to sleep the day away.

John stood up so he could rummage in his pockets and pull a pack of cigarettes from his overly tight jeans. Kids.

He offered one to Greg, who shook his head. "Trying to cut down."

"Do you mind?"

"No, no." Nice of him to ask.

He opened the window over the sink and leaned against

313

the counter as he lit up. He took a long pull, looking very continental, then cursed when a sudden gust blew a fleck of ash into his eye.

Greg laughed. "See? Smoking's bad for you, the doctors all say."

John scowled at him for a second, then gave up and laughed along before taking another lazy, defiant drag. It was the first time they'd laughed together.

The silence after that didn't feel as awkward. John smoked, Greg sipped.

"You didn't look that bad."

They'd been quiet for so long that it took Greg a moment to connect his son's words to their previous conversation.

"Oh?"

"I mean, Les told me you hadn't been well. That I should be gentle with you, but . . . I didn't believe there could ever be anything wrong with you, so I guess I just ignored it. It wasn't stuff a kid would really recognize anyway, right?"

"Right."

"And maybe I was just happy you were there."

Greg could say nothing to that.

"Anyway, you came down and took a look at the boat. I wanted to show you how well I'd taken care of it, and you said it was swell. Les came and took a picture of us. He gave you the photo, and you stared at it, the two of us standing there with big cheesy grins on our faces, and you took a pen out of your pocket and wrote me a message, then you got in your car and drove away."

"I . . ."

"You wrote *fuck us*. Nothing but those two words on the back of the photo. Fuck. Us. I still have that picture, you know. I still have it." He flicked the stub of his cigarette into the suds and stared out the window. "Why'd you write that, Dad?"

Greg looked at his son's profile. Tall and straight-backed, but still a boy. "John . . . I'm sorry."

"Don't be. I got over it. Look, what I'm saying is, maybe Les was right. You need help, Dad. This . . . all of this, it's not right."

"I . . ."

"Please, Dad. You've got to look after yourself. For us."

And what could Greg say to that, except "I'll try."

Portsmouth, New Hampshire

1985

After a short flight, Greg stood in the arrivals hall of Pease Airport, staring at the main doors and the people flooding through them, his almost weightless suitcase clutched in one hand. Outside, a car would be waiting for him. It had all been arranged. All he had to do was walk, get into a car with soft leather seats and be driven to a quiet place with clean sheets where he could sleep a while, talk to some kind people. And maybe he really could get better . . .

He stood a while longer, swaying slightly, dreaming of the future he would build when he was better. He'd invite John back, and Patrick and Maria, have a proper get-together. He'd make it up to Valerie, and remember how to make her happy, how not to hurt her. He would see his parents again, and they'd sit round the big dining table with its silly porcelain figures and talk it all through.

As he turned away from the bright doors and walked back toward departures, he told himself that he didn't need help. He would get himself back on an even keel. He would apply himself, study doubly hard for the Florida boards, become a doctor again, settle down into a quiet respectable existence and . . .

No. It was time to be honest with himself for once. Whatever hope he'd had at that ordinary future was gone, and chasing it was killing him.

One more chance. He would give himself one more chance to find it on his own: a life that he could live.

PART V

Key West

1938

Greg dove into the pool, and the water closed around him like a dream.

He heard his mother shout as the splash speckled her book, but he didn't care. He held himself underwater, letting his momentum carry him forward.

After the morning sun, but before the midday blaze, the water felt neither warm nor cool. It felt like nothing, like he was flying, like the edges of his body had dissolved.

Maybe it should have felt scary, like drowning, but it didn't. It was the opposite of drowning.

He liked having no boundaries. No limits.

Just before he knew he would reach the end of the pool, he turned over in the water, and the surface was nothing but light.

MIAMI

1988

Greg paused in his daily wanderings outside a huge shop window. It was one of the big shiny-floored bookshops he avoided by habit, preferring to spend his ample free time haunting the secondhand stores, but it was hard to ignore his own name spelled out in giant letters. A sign blared through the meticulously clean glass, seeming to take up half the window display:

HEMINGWAY
NEW BOOK

And running along the very bottom in font barely a third of the size:

The Garden of Eden

Greg pressed against the glass, ignoring the smudges left by his grubby fingers, the clouding of his breath. In the middle of all this typographic vulgarity sat a small pile of books, a few with their covers facing coquettishly outwards to catch the gaze of whichever discerning reader might be drawn in by the name larger than their own head.

Sure enough, there was his father's name in manly block capitals, the title scrawled loosely beneath. Beneath that, a rough, perhaps cubism-inspired drawing—the sort Papa might have favored—of a woman holding a basket.

Greg moved to the edge of the window, ignoring the shop assistant looking out at him a little fearfully from behind the cash register. If he really pressed his cheek hard to the glass he could get enough of an angle to see Scribner's colophon on the spine.

Of course. Scribner wouldn't stop drawing blood merely because the patient was dead. Someone in the family must have approved, but Greg was well out of that inner loop by now.

No doubt this book wouldn't be the last. There would be an annotated collection of Hemingway shopping lists to follow, a leatherbound edition of every scrap of paper he'd ever scribbled on with worshipful scholarly annotations. If they could find a sheet of toilet paper his father had used, they'd publish it.

And the sign was so garish . . . Butter-yellow letters outlined in sea blue. A happy celebration of a new work by an old master, never even a hint that the master had never granted permission for it to see the light of day.

It reminded Greg of archaeologists scratching in the dirt and exhuming a lovingly buried corpse, placing it on display for tourists and schoolchildren to gawp at. After a certain passing of time the occupants of graves lost their right to rest in peace. Never trust the living to honor the dead.

He walked away with his hands deep in his pockets, the worn soles of his shoes slapping on the pavement with every step.

The work didn't even matter any more. That was the truth. It was the man that mattered, the legend, and none of them even *knew* him. How wonderful he had been. What a colossal pig-headed shit. The reading public knew a character that Ernest Hemingway himself had created. A character that had wormed its way into his blood and started speaking through his mouth, puffing his chest outwards for the cameras, until the real man forgot that he had ever been anything else but this story he was telling. Maybe that was the sign of a truly great writer, that they can tell a story so convincingly that even they believe it.

Hadn't he heard that before?

In an attempt to cleanse himself, Greg made a swift pilgrimage to his favorite bookstore: a signless pirate-grotto hidden beneath a well-to-do coffee shop on 1st street.

In truth it barely qualified as a store, being nothing fancier than a cellar-sized room with a few bare light bulbs and a hell of a lot of books—towers of books, drifting dunes of books, a landscape of books where daily avalanches and tectonic shifts would drag the new drop-offs down into darkness and belch ancient dust-choked tomes to the surface.

There was no pressure to buy. Greg could spend as much time as he wanted picking through the piles. The old lady who was always sitting in the corner, each lens of her glasses opaque in the gloom, seemed to spend half her time asleep, and the rest of it nose-deep in some obscure-looking monolith. Always in another world. In a way, Greg had probably spent more time in this musty cave than she had.

He had nothing else to do and nowhere else to go, so he took his time, selecting and discarding at his leisure:

A pocket edition of Shakespeare's sonnets with a tender birthday inscription on the flyleaf.

Gibbon's *Decline and Fall* Book II—which he was pretty sure was where the good shit happened—the first two hundred pages or so battered from someone's many failed attempts, the rest pristine.

An enormous copy of *Bartlett's Familiar Quotations*.

A surprisingly intact first edition of *The Great Gatsby*, bringing up sudden crisp memories of Frank, a man already well into the task of dismantling himself when the boy-Greg had briefly met him.

A field guide to the birds of Key West, lush with exquisite illustrations of talons and plumage and bright orange bills.

He was carrying quite a pile when he found Christine Jorgensen's autobiography at the bottom of a moldering stack of road maps for LA from 1962 to 1971. He picked it up and studied the face on the cover for a few seconds, the sultry eyes and blond hair.

She'd been in the papers maybe twenty years ago, and every now and then she still popped up. For a while the press had been obsessed with her, the GI who became a blond bombshell, complimentary if deeply condescending. But over the years the tone had soured, as Greg knew it would. A snarky headline about a canceled wedding here, a cutting comment about her "boxy" figure there, an interview where the questioner had treated her like a bearded lady in a cage.

He'd almost taken satisfaction in watching it happen. He felt ashamed of that now. Where had it ever gotten him? All the secrecy, all the denial. Say what you like about Jorgensen, she was living on her own terms. She wasn't afraid. Greg couldn't remember a time when he hadn't been afraid . . .

He put the book on top of his pile and headed for the counter.

He was carrying his fifty-cent-a-piece hoard home when he realized his path was taking him back past the sterilized bookstore again. He set his shoulders, determined to walk on by, but his feet seemed to have their own idea, slowing step by step until he stood staring again at his name picked out in glory. They'd already cleared his handprint from the glass.

The title was familiar, of course. Like a ghost come back from his childhood. His father had been working on that book for years, adding to it, cutting from it, revising and revising for over a decade. Papa had said more than once that everything in him was in it, and that it would never be published.

Greg sighed, and the bell jingled as he went in.

There was a concrete bench in Museum Park that was one of his favorites: a big austere thing he could stretch out on quite comfortably if and when he grew tired. It stood in the shade beneath a cluster of palms with a narrow strip of sea-canal cutting into the land behind, breathing a familiar scent of brine and rot that he found strangely comforting.

Sitting there, he could look out over the tough scraggly grass to the Museum of Science, watching the people come and go with his legs stretched out in front of him, trying to ignore the ache in his knees.

Parks were a good place to pass the time. Green places cloistered away from the smog and ruck of the streets, but with enough people passing by to keep his interest. Truth be told, he spent most of his time these days beached on one bench or another, a secondhand paperback or the day's paper on his lap, feeling time gather around him like the ink on his fingertips.

He usually bought a handful of different papers each day, queuing up for the morning's tabloids and broadsheets behind men in business suits stiff-backed with the important task of being an informed citizen.

Greg could never understand how seriously they scanned the headlines. How could the news be important when no one ever read a paper that was more than a day old? Everything important was forever, but within twenty-four hours the news was out of date, and within a week it was irrelevant.

When he had the energy, Greg read through the papers like a kid eating cotton candy, gobbling down handfuls of nothing.

Today, he'd brought a book from home and spent a dime on the *Miami Herald* from a newsstand on Biscayne Boulevard, but he didn't feel much like reading. Instead, he leaned back and watched the comings and goings of old men and gangly teenagers, couples with children, the occasional bird. A good way to pass the time.

The sun slowly shifted, pushing the shade away until it was beating down directly onto his shoulders, and that was good too. He let the warmth soak into him, closed his eyes.

He thought maybe he could spend forever like this, resting in the quiet places of this familiar city, watching,

327

reading, healing from some wound he had no name for and which no one had inflicted. Not hurting anyone.

He had tried too many times to put his life back together. He was done. It was better for everyone for him to live here, in the broken places. Make it a home.

On very good days he'd find the energy to rise early, get himself down to the flats in Biscayne Bay, and rent a ramshackle boat for a day's fishing. By the time he'd cast his line and settled himself down he always felt like a man who'd walked a thousand miles. Tired in his bones. But that was okay.

Fishing wasn't work, as long as you didn't strictly define it as battling leviathans like his father. Bonefish were placid creatures, and lethargic enough that you didn't exactly need to keep an eye on the line. It was fine to lean back, pull your cap low and let the rocking of the boat carry you away, the soft lapping of the water against the hull, the high mournful cries of ospreys or gulls. Sometimes their shadows would pass over his closed eyes, but he wouldn't open them to look up. It was enough to know that they were there.

Pleasant little sleeps, dreamless and all the sweeter for it. And then, the tug tug tug of the line he'd looped around his finger, he and the fish being pulled up together from the clean blue.

Those were the best days, but this morning it had taken him a long time to get out of bed, to convince himself that anything was worth doing. It had been nearly noon by the time he'd stopped at the newsstand, and he'd known when he bought the paper that he wouldn't read it. He didn't have to open its crisp leaves to know it would be like chasing the words through treacle.

So he just sat, eyes closed, letting his mind wander, aiming for blankness, but unable to stop his brain humming.

Yesterday, he'd finally finished reading the Jergensen book, and his thoughts kept drifting back to it. She'd revealed everything: her childhood, her time as a GI, the operation to make her a woman and everything that came after, but the thing that struck Greg more than anything had been her certainty. As a teenager in the Bronx and a soldier in the war she'd always known that she'd been born in the wrong body.

When he started reading, Greg was scared it was going to feel like looking in a mirror. But the more he read the more he'd realized that wasn't the case. He'd never had that unwavering certainty and still didn't. Hard to say if that was a relief or a disappointment.

She had written to her parents after the op: *Nature made a mistake which I have had corrected, and now I am your daughter.* You had to admire the sheer guts.

Greg had long given up pretending that it was only about the clothes. If it ever had been it wasn't any more. When those urges hit him, he didn't just want to dress like a woman, he wanted to *be* a woman—sometimes the woman he might have been, or sometimes a woman who'd come fresh into being, a woman with no history.

But did he want to be a woman always, every moment, unwavering? Could he really say that?

There were times when he hated feeling the blunt bulk of his shoulders as he tried to wriggle into a dress. But he couldn't pretend there hadn't been plenty of other times he'd loved having arms that stretched the sleeves of his shirt.

What did that mean? What was he?

He opened his eyes and looked down at the book on his lap. His father's newest, which he still didn't have the courage to open.

He'd been burned before. His father's collection of short stories had had more than a few gut punches smuggled in. In one, the son was a hell of an athlete, a hell of a writer, a golden child. But it had all turned out to be lies. The boy had copied a story he knew his father wouldn't have read, and it was only years later when stumbling upon the story in an old collection that the father had understood: his son was rotten, had always been rotten, all his skill and grace worth less than nothing because it was built on putrid foundations.

Tell me how you really feel, Papa.

Greg was a grown man. His father had been dead more than twenty years. It shouldn't have hurt, but if there was one thing he'd learned over the years it was that should and shouldn't didn't mean shit.

He stayed in the park, staring into nothing, his thoughts swirling and swirling and settling on nothing, until it was nearly dark and he was starting to get cold. Then he walked home in the twilight, cooked himself a microwave dinner that was bland and soft, and fell asleep in front of the TV, the volume turned way up.

On the boat, or on the benches, he dreamed of little. And when he did, it felt less like dreaming and more like the world slipping into him, passing through his porous membranes so that the wind was searching through his branches, the waves gliding over his sleek prow.

At night, the dreams were more potent. Perhaps it was

330

the darkness. There was nothing to feel, nothing to hear. Only his own heartbeat and the grinding of the traffic outside. Perhaps it was simply that he slept deeper, allowing memories he'd thought long vanished to rise up like ghosts.

One night he dreamed of Patrick as he had been: sat out on the porch in the evening, layered in shadow like a lion's heart mantled in fat, turning and turning a baseball in his hands as if one more twist might open it up like a puzzle box, as if everything would make sense if he could trace the whole world with his fingertips.

He dreamed of the ducks at the holiday resort his father had taken them to. Not the ones he'd shot, but the ones in the pool behind the canteen. Each day he would save some bread from his lunch and head back there, sometimes with bloody feathers still clinging to his shorts from the day's sport. He'd sprinkle crumbs into the bright water and watch them dip their vivid beaks and patter patter the food down their long throats. He named them—foolish childish names, but it had made them feel like friends. And every morning he would go out with his father and blast the wild ducks into fireworks, molten green and gray and splashes of blue he had no name for, constellations of ruined flight that drifted windward long after the corpse was safely tucked in his belt. Then back home for lunch, saving bread from the table to feed Hector and Brave and Napoleon, no contradiction in his heart.

He dreamed of that caustic hospital corridor, listening through the door to his brother's skull slowly filling up with blood. Dozing off there and waking up to find his father's hair pink. The strange comedy of it in that terrible moment. He'd forgotten that . . .

And he dreamed of his mother, turning slowly before the mirror, her arms held out, her head tilted just so for no one but herself.

He often woke in the middle of the night, and it would take him a while to remember where he was. Key West. Miami. Bimini. Los Angeles. Havana. Jordan. Tanzania. New York.

For a moment, he was in all of them at once. For a moment, he was nowhere. The Earth had spun away beneath him in the night.

He took his father's book with him wherever he went—tucked under his arm, placed beside him on the bench, under his head while he dozed over the gin-clear water of the Keys—but couldn't bring himself to read it.

Sometimes he would get up in the morning and, instead of putting on his old polo shirt and cargo shorts, he'd put on a stained old sundress. Then instead of going out he'd sit in the front room with the TV turned loud and maybe he'd watch for a few minutes before his attention drifted. That was all. It didn't feel special, or exciting, or even painful any more.

Days passed like clouds—an endless slow succession. He grew his beard.

One day a girl in the library asked her mother, why isn't that old man wearing shoes? And Greg didn't know why his feet were bare. Whether he'd left the house without them, or whether they'd fallen off, or whether he'd been barefoot for weeks.

There were only traces of the crushing darkness that had dogged him throughout his life. He could get up most mornings, could look at photos of his childhood without explosions of rage or despair, could drink a glass of whiskey without finishing the bottle. Instead of darkness, there was twilight. His days passed in a kind of persistent numbness, a cotton wool fuzziness in his head and beneath his skin as though someone had taken him apart for examination and fitted him back together from memory, a few crucial screws left over at the end.

He felt almost nothing, but cried often.

Maybe he'd just had too many shocks over the years. Maybe they had burned away something irreplaceable.

Well, it wasn't so bad, this half-life.

In the end, the thing that woke him up was a call from Patrick.

He got home late after a day fishing on the flats and was planning to go right to bed before dinner, but the phone started ringing the moment he walked through the door like it had been waiting. It took him a second to recognize the sound. No one had called him in so long.

He sat on the chair in the front room and coughed as a puff of dust rose around him. He picked up the receiver cautiously.

"Heya, Gig."

Patrick.

"Hello?"

Greg tried to speak, but his voice caught in his throat, raw and ragged. How long had it been since he'd spoken to anyone?"

"Is this the right number? Hello?"

"No, it's me." Greg's voice came a bit easier. He squeezed the handset tight. "It's Gigi."

"Oh, hello, Greg. Are you okay? You sound rough." Patrick sounded exactly the same. Exactly.

"Only a cold."

"Oh, well I wanted to, you know, check in. I know I haven't called in a while, and I . . ."

He trailed off. Greg knew he should fill this silence, say something witty, but he was out of practice.

"And anyway," Patrick forged on, "it was Papa's birthday the other day. Not sure why I always think about you on his birthday, but I do. So, thought I'd check in."

"That's good of you, Pat. I didn't know."

"Well, why would you? Doesn't make much sense."

"No, that it was his birthday. Guess I lost track." He looked around the barren room. There was just the TV, the phone, and the couch, nothing to say he even lived here. He tapped at the arm of the couch and watched a fresh bloom of dust rise.

"Easily done . . . I've got to be honest. I don't really have anything to talk about. I guess I wanted to hear my little brother's voice."

Greg took a deep breath. "One sec, Pat. There's someone at the door."

"All right."

Greg put the handset down and covered his face with his hands. He didn't cry. Just stayed there a moment, letting the emotions run through him like electricity. He wasn't used to feeling like this; his defenses had rotted away in his isolation.

When he'd mastered himself, he picked up the receiver. "Sorry, I'm back. Delivery. Wrong house."

"No problem. So what are you up to, Gig?"

He thought about that for a second. "Not a lot. Been doing some thinking, I guess."

334

"I get that. I always get nostalgic around this time of year. Maybe it's the heat."

"I didn't think you were the nostalgic type."

"Maybe the years are catching up with me. Can't help but remember the good old days. Sitting by the pool together, drinking stolen rum, smoking stolen cigarettes."

"We had a pretty good childhood, when you put it like that."

"Yeah I guess so. It's the damnedest thing. Sometimes all that feels like it happened a thousand years ago, or to another person, but sometimes I swear it happened yesterday, and I can't figure out why my hands are all shaky and my back aches, because I was *just there*, you know?"

"Yeah, I know."

"And that's the thing, I suppose. I've been thinking about back then a lot and . . . what we talked about . . . Sometimes I worry it was me."

"I . . ." Greg tried to follow. Tried to remember. "What?"

"That it was me, I mean . . . that I wasn't always the best brother."

Greg shook his head, confused. "What are you talking about? You were great, Pat, I'd have gone crazy without you."

"Well . . ." He hesitated with a soft wheeze, and it was the first time he sounded his age. "I just worry there were times I wasn't as in your corner as I should have been."

"But—"

"—Thing is, it was all I had over you." The words started to come out all in a tumble, a pebble tumbling into an avalanche. "I know I said I was never mad

335

at you, but . . . I always told myself I was fine, you know, being struck out and outshot and outrun every single time, and mostly I was, but looking back . . . I guess maybe I just wanted you to hurt a bit. And I thought: it's Greg, he'll be fine, he's indestructible. But . . . but no one's indestructible. No one. And now I worry, he really needed me, that skinny little kid needed his brother, and I just made it worse because I was a jealous shit."

"I . . ." there was a long silence. Greg tried to get his thoughts in line. He wasn't used to thinking this much, this clearly. It was like waking up from a coma. "Don't beat yourself up, Pat. I don't think it would have made a difference. The moment Papa caught me wearing Martha's dress, it was a done deal."

"That's kind of you, Greg. I'm not sure I deserve it, but . . ." A long shaky breath as he gathered himself. Then his voice turned gruff. "Martha's dress? I didn't know that's how it happened. What did she say?"

"Honestly, I can't remember. I still haven't got it all back from the shocks. She probably wasn't thrilled."

"I don't know. I bet she'd seen stranger things."

"Oh, no doubt." Talking about it openly like this with his brother, he'd always imagined it'd be torture. But it was a relief, like finally putting down a heavy load.

"Do you still . . . ?"

"Dress like a woman?"

"Yeah."

"Sometimes. Depends how I feel."

"Guess it wasn't just a phase."

"No."

"I'm sorry, Gig."

Greg thought of a thousand things he could say, and

336

he settled on, "Well, I did smash your brains against a car dashboard, so maybe we're even."

"Ha. That? Nothing. I've had worse hangovers."

"Oh, that I can believe. You could never handle your drink."

"And your drink could never handle you."

"I'm not sure what that means."

"Me neither, but it sounded good in my head."

"Ah, probably damage from the concussion then."

Patrick chuckled, and Greg thought he heard him slap what was probably a sensibly chinoed knee. "Do you remember Papa's pink hair back then? Messed around with Martha's hair dye and fucked it up."

"Oh, Jesus, yeah I do. I was thinking about that the other day." Greg found himself grinning. "He looked like a cupcake at a girl's birthday party."

The chuckle turned into a guffaw. "It was damn strange waking up and having that be the first thing I saw. Thought I'd gone mad and I . . . Oh shit, that's my doorbell. Must be the grandkids. It was good to talk, Greg. I really am sorry I didn't call sooner. Time just got away from me."

"That's okay. There's numbers on my phone too."

"Yeah, well. Okay. Look after yourself."

"I'll do my best."

"Love you, Gig."

"I love you too, Pat."

Greg put the phone down then stared at it for a few seconds.

Look after yourself. Why did everyone keep telling him that?

★

337

A storm was rolling over Miami from the sea. After long months of baking heat, the city was almost salivating as it approached. The cracked earth in the parks, the car windshields and sidewalks covered in dust, the scabbed-over drains and slow-roasted trash, all waiting for the coming deluge.

Greg hurried back, clutching his groceries with one arm and holding down his skirt against stray squalls with the other. He got to the corner of his shabby suburban street when he smelled the bruise in the air and knew the rain was coming any second. It was hard running in high heels, even modest ones—he didn't have the practice—but he wobbled along as fast as he could without turning an ankle and made it onto his porch right as the storm broke.

He stood and watched it unspool in one heavy sheet, picking up the yellow dust and foaming like champagne in the gutters, then he dropped the groceries by the door and stepped out into it. The deluge enveloped him eagerly, soaked his dress in seconds so that it clung to him. Then there was only skin and water, the rain retracing him anew every second.

Greg smiled, imagining his neighbors looking out their windows and seeing the wild-eyed hermit they worked so hard to ignore standing on his lawn in a dress in the pouring rain. They'd shake their heads at each other, pull the curtains tightly closed, and go back to *The Cosby Show*. He chuckled.

It had been hard work getting out of bed on time this morning—he'd felt like a snail pulling itself out of its shell—but he managed it, and he was glad.

One day at a time.

A gust of wind slapped at him, and he suppressed a shiver

before giving up on his foolishness and heading inside. He dripped on the kitchen floor as he set a pot of coffee to heat on the stove and wrung out the socks he used to stuff his bra over the sink. They were poor imitations of the real thing, but it was amazing the difference they made in how he felt walking out the door.

If he was lucky, and he didn't chase after it, and the stars aligned, then sometimes, briefly, he could forget himself and all the bruises and the scars and inhabit *she*. No fireworks, no trumpet, only a change in the tide of his soul to hers.

It was that easy, not an action so much as a release, as easy as forgetting what she was supposed to be. It was funny how it only happened on the days she dressed as a woman, but that when it happened the clothes didn't seem to matter at all. Maybe it was less about the clothes, and more about what made her want to wear them. In those moments she didn't care. She just knew it felt right.

But they never lasted long. Times had changed, and as long as she kept her head down and minded her own business the worst she'd gotten was stares and frowns. But that was all it took to bring it all crashing down. A group of kids scoffing as they passed by, a young mother crossing the street with her stroller, a moment of wide-eyed surprise from a bartender and *she* flinched back into *he* so suddenly it left him reeling.

He was still thinking a lot about the book he'd read. Jorgensen's sense of self had never been this fragile. She hadn't cared how people had looked at her, what they'd said or printed about her. She knew who she was in her bones.

What if Greg was only pretending? Playing some stupid tragic game?

The coffee pot started whistling, and Greg jumped. He'd been standing at the sink in a pool of rainwater, a crumpled sock in one hand. He quickly took the coffee off, then went to his room to pull off the dress and wrap himself in a bathrobe.

The coffee smelled good as he poured. He popped in a sugar cube, but didn't stir, then stood for a while with his hands wrapped around the mug, letting the warmth soak into his knuckles which he was starting to suspect were developing arthritis. Too many punches thrown.

Maybe he was being too hard on himself. Okay, so he wasn't Christine Jorgensen.

He'd spent his whole life denying this part of himself. Ignoring it and hoping it would die from neglect. And now he was just going to throw on a sundress and be a confident woman?

Did he even need the clothes at all? He closed his eyes and made himself relax. There was no one else there, it was okay. Relax.

She stared into her coffee, cleared her throat. "Hello, I'm . . . Gloria. Nice to meet you."

Stupid. But she smiled anyway.

She sipped the coffee, gave a gentle hum of pleasure, and went to her room. She sat on the bed as the rain beat against the window and looked around for something to occupy her mind, but there wasn't much. Somehow she never seemed to keep hold of anything for long. It all got given away, or lost, or left behind when she inevitably uprooted herself.

There was a newspaper from two days ago, her father's

last book lightly covered in dust on the bedside table, her worn-out tennis shoes by the bed, a few magazines. Not much to show for fifty-seven years on the planet, but at least it was clean, tidy.

Gloria—she took a moment to let the name settle around her—picked up the book on a whim, wiped it clean with the flat of her hand. Why was she keeping it around if she wasn't going to read it?

The only sound was water on glass. She felt tucked away in here. Concealed.

She opened the book on a random page, surprising herself. The text was small and densely packed, like the publishers were trying to concentrate as much Papa per page as they could manage. And that was what this was, wasn't it? Papa.

If anything of her father could be said to remain, it was on the page more than in any photograph or grave. Maybe even more than in his children. Children were a biological legacy, but a novel was the imprint of a soul.

She rubbed her thumb over the paper. A little rough. Not the best quality. A way of making a few more pennies per book, she supposed.

And almost before she knew it, she was reading, skimming through at random.

The prose was perfect, of course—sparse and understated, but somehow tense with power. Skimming her eyes over the carefully laid out sentences was like watching a swell of water rippling over the face of the sea, knowing anything could be beneath. A marlin, a dolphin, a shark.

There were two main characters. A man and a woman. Their names came up again and again as she flicked along.

Outside, a flash. Gloria looked up to see the sky vivid white, all the buildings crudely sketched in charcoal and gouache. Then darkness, only an echo of the gone-away world stinging in her eyes as she returned to the book.

The man was no doubt her father. Most of Papa's male characters fit neatly into one of two molds. Himself—the stoic hero. Or the enemy—some effeminate critic or conniving Jew. In some ways her father, for all his labyrinthine complexity, had been a simple man.

Thunder smashed through the house. She jumped, then smiled at herself. There it was again, an unforced smile. It felt good. She turned on the lamp and leaned back against the stained headboard.

As for the woman in the book, who knew? It could be anyone. That was the unspoken fear of all those who had known Papa: of opening some lauded masterpiece and finding your flaws, your failings, your unreflexive narcissisms—discovering that none of it had gone unnoticed. And how could you complain? It wasn't you, after all. It was only a character.

But you knew. And he knew.

Maybe Hadley, the first wife whom Greg barely remembered, would walk the streets of some European city. A vague blur of demure submissiveness, one hand on some not-John's young shoulder.

Or Martha, figure of eternal hatred because she'd refused to be another Hadley, refused to bow her head and gratefully take her place in the background? Would she take the stage as an incarnation of hysterical womanhood?

Or maybe even Gloria's own mother, Pauline. Despised as much as Martha—though for the opposite reason. Where Martha had left, her mother had planted her feet.

Even when she'd lost the war and been cast aside, she'd never quite given up hope that one day Ernest Hemingway might love her again.

Did she live anew in these cheap pages? The tilt of her head when she was thinking carefully? The way she drank her first ice-cold martini in the evening? The natty neckerchief she wore when she wanted to look down to earth . . .

The rain outside looked thick enough to drown in. Gloria didn't know how long she'd been lost in thought.

She turned to the first page. The lightning spoke again, but this time she was ready for it. Her coffee cooled untouched by her elbow as she read. She didn't skim this time, but turned the pages quickly.

It didn't take long before Gloria was more than a little sick of the obligatory salt of the earth but artistic but straight-shooting but sensitive but masculine hero and his underwritten wife.

She read on anyway.

"He lay there and felt something and then her hand holding him and searching lower and he helped with his hands and then lay back in the dark and did not think at all and only felt the weight and the strangeness inside and she said, "Now you can't tell who is who can you?"

"No."

"You are changing," she said. "Oh you are. You are. Yes you are and you're my girl Catherine. Will you change and be my girl and let me take you?"

"You're Catherine."

"No. I'm Peter. You're my wonderful Catherine. You're my beautiful lovely Catherine. You were so good to change. Oh

343

thank you, Catherine, so much. Please understand. Please know and understand. I'm going to make love to you forever."

The storm was fading, or perhaps passing on to saturate another city. Outside, the city was shaking itself off like a bathed dog, sparkling and new for a few precious hours.

Gloria sat on the bed, not moving, just piecing through her frayed memories.

You take after me in that. In a lot of ways . . .

Her father dozing outside her unconscious brother's room, hair roughly cropped and pastel pink.

He got so mad at you about all that shit. So goddamn angry. Did you ever think— I mean, maybe that's why he could be so mad, but love you best at the same time?

Her father cutting her mother's hair boyishly short, saying he should grow his own hair a little longer to match her.

He hid more from you than anyone else. Probably because you're so similar.

Her father holding her close, his voice slurry with drink. *I remember a girl in Paris and wanting to go over and kiss her just because she had so much damn red lipstick caked on. I wanted to get that lipstick smeared all over my lips.*

I should have known this would happen. You're so like your father . . .

You have a rotten apple on the branch, and you look at the tree.

She thought about that passage that had driven her crazy over the years. The one about the boy built like a pocket battleship, full of a darkness only his father could understand.

She'd always thought he was talking about the depressions

they'd both suffered through, what she thought of as the troughs, but her father had called the black ass. Their quick temper. Their competitiveness. Their talent for violence. Could it really have run deeper than that?

The book was still open on her lap, inviting her to seek out further clues, but she closed it.

Maybe Papa had understood, maybe he hadn't.

Maybe the people on the street were laughing at her, maybe they weren't.

It didn't matter. This was her life. Her story.

And again, Gloria smiled

Missoula

1995

The neon headland of the Thunderbird Motel came surging into view as Greg pulled the bulk of his rental car free from the hard shoulder. He grimaced, digging one fist into his lower stomach and pushing down—it was the only thing that seemed to dull the throb that lingered there.

Was the pain supposed to run this deep? He hoped he hadn't burst a stitch.

He winced in the glare of an oncoming truck, then let go of the steering wheel to shift down a gear with his free hand. There was the blast of a horn, and he grabbed at the wheel again, hauling the car back into his lane.

The pink and blue glow of the motel bloomed like a video game sunset, rising, flaring, and splitting into the lovely lettering he'd been looking out for the whole last hundred miles.

He breathed through his teeth, longing for another painkiller, and shifted the car down a gear again. Now he was crawling along the highway, ignoring the angry flash of lights in his rearview mirror, his eyes only on that giant capital T dead ahead.

It must have been later than he'd thought; Thelma was

locking up the front entrance as he nosed his car clumsily into the parking lot.

She turned, holding a hand up against the glare of Greg's headlights as he rummaged through the glove compartment and wolfed down a Valium, followed by one of his new heart pills for good measure. God knew the thing must be under some strain tonight.

He finally noticed Thelma standing blinded and shut off the engine.

She lowered her hand and peered into the dark, her night vision shot as Greg opened the door and eased himself out of the car. For a moment the only sounds were the ticking of the cooling engine and Greg's shoes crunching in the gravel. She said nothing even as he moved forward with small, cautious steps, and he realized she had no idea who the shadow lumbering toward her was.

He leaned against the railing at the bottom of the steps, hoping to hide how much it hurt to stand up straight. "Hey, Thelma, how's your blood pressure?"

"Greg?"

"Thelma."

"Are you okay?"

He thought about this quite seriously. "Hoping to be."

"What does that mean?"

"I had to have some surgery. Nothing major, I just . . . needed to come back. Needed somewhere safe to lie low, heal up."

"Surgery? Greg, is something wrong with you?"

"Well . . ." he hesitated. "No, nothing wrong, only a . . . a gesture of commitment, or something like that."

She frowned at him. She'd seen Greg dressed as a woman often enough over the years and had never seen fit

347

to pass judgment, but maybe this would be the final straw, the limit of her stout midwestern heart.

She pulled her coat tighter around herself. The wind ran invisible overhead, tearing itself to shreds against the stars. "Well, you don't look too good. Maybe you should go back to hospital."

"No." Greg leaned a little more heavily, fighting the urge to press his fist into the flesh below his gut. "I've spent enough of my life in hospitals. They only let me out because I had a trained nurse who was willing to look after me." He smiled to himself, knowing it would be invisible. "Guess I—"

"—Goddamn it, Greg. I'm not your private nurse."

"I know that. Can't a man lie to fly the coop? That hospital was like a prison."

That mollified her for a moment. Then, "Did you drive all the way here? You can't— You're shivering . . . Come inside a minute."

He wasn't shivering, he was trembling. Then again, Thelma probably knew that.

Greg hauled himself up the steps as she clicked on the light in the reception. Everything was still in its proper place: the keys glinting on their hooks, the stationery neatly lined up on the desk, the sign telling him to live, laugh, and love.

He rested his shoulder on the doorway, savoring the sight. He felt better already.

"Well," Thelma muttered, "I still think you should be in hospital, but it's your life I suppose." She moved round to sit at her desk and pulled out the ever-reliable red book. No doubt it was a distant descendant of the tome she had opened on Greg's first stay, but functionally, spiritually, it was identical. "You better believe I'll charge you for new sheets if you bleed in the bed."

"That's fine," said Greg softly. He felt very tired now, closed in the warmth of the Thunderbird's belly.

"A week?"

He fought to keep his eyes open. "Maybe a bit longer . . ."

She looked up at him and snorted. "I'll have to juggle some bookings around . . ." but she drew a long red line through the month, overriding any previous scratchings, and wrote in her clear block capitals: HEMINGWAY.

"Why do you keep coming back here, Greg?" She kept her head down as she worked but raised her free hand and made an odd twirling gesture, as though invoking something, everything. "Driving all this way. I know you don't have to. You could stay in the best hotel in New York for the rest of the year. But you keep coming back . . ."

It was a reasonable question. Greg could have obfuscated with a few select truths. That the Thunderbird was closer to the highly specialized center he'd attended, or that a backwater motel in Missoula was a better place to hide from the world than the country's foremost metropolis.

But none of that would have been the real truth. He watched the red pen being recapped and returned to the pot, the red book sliding back into its appointed space on the shelf. "I guess I wanted to be somewhere where I know someone cares."

Thelma closed her eyes for a moment, then took the key to room 102 from its hook. "Come on, Greg. You need some sleep."

This time, instead of handing him the key, she stood and

349

walked him the few short steps to his room, letting him rest one hand on her shoulder, letting him lean on her. When she opened the door, it felt just like the first time.

He moved past her into the room, each step carefully placed, cradling the stabbing pain that radiated up from his groin like reverse lightning bolts of agony.

As he eased himself into the bed and Thelma clicked off the light, the thought came to him that maybe this pain was too much. Maybe the surgeon had fucked up and even now blood was silently flooding the unlit chambers of his body.

He would die like his mother, drowning in himself.

Ah well, too late for regrets. Time would tell.

He rolled onto his side and fell asleep.

Greg did not die in the night. Slowly but surely his relentless body began to heal.

Two days later, when he was feeling strong enough, he walked out to his car in the cool morning sunshine. He was feeling delicate, unsure. He'd expected that after the operation he would wake up every morning a comfortable and unwavering she, would be accepted by the world and in return he'd be granted one stable self at last.

Of course, it wouldn't be that easy.

He leaned against the car for a moment and slipped one hand under his jeans to carefully feel the place where his genitals used to be, exquisitely painful to the touch. He hadn't had the courage to look yet—strange how squeamish you could be when it was *your* body that needed your medical attention—but everything seemed okay. As long as he rested and took his antibiotics, he was on the road to recovery.

So where did that leave him? Exactly where he'd been before, sans penis and testicles, and with no idea how successful the vaginoplasty had been. He'd tried to find one of the few doctors in America who actually had experience at the operation, but there were no seasoned professionals for this sort of thing. He could have gone to Europe, sought out Jorgensen's doctor if he was even still practicing, but he was worried his courage would have failed him if he took that long.

He should be panicking, surely? This had been his big commitment, the culmination of years of coming to terms with his true self, and he was still . . . him.

But he couldn't find any panic, or even regret. He felt strangely calm. At peace. There had always been days when he felt entirely and unambiguously Greg. Why should that change now?

The road climbed toward the college on his right, receded to infinity to his left. Wildflowers frothed along the verge in both directions, reckless blooms a thousand shades of blue. He could see the blue of a marlin high in the water, and the patch on a mallard's wing, and Thelma's eyes. Thelma behind her tidy desk, a little older every time he saw her but her eyes always the same, bright and hard as mussel shells. He remembered that long drive home after the shooting competition, half asleep in the passenger seat, the Cuban sky flashing outside the window. That sky was there too, moving through the flowers with the wind.

He opened the trunk and pulled out the ratty old backpack he'd taken from the hospital. He wasn't quite sure what he'd brought. A few spare changes of clothes, more heart tablets, maybe some Valium if he was lucky. There was less pain now, but less than a bullet in the crotch could still keep you up at night.

He took his care package back to his room and rooted through it. Found, to his pleasure, the hoped-for drugs. Less to his pleasure a convenience store sandwich so decomposed it seemed on the verge of sentience. A change of shorts, pants, a polo shirt, a few crumpled dresses. A blond wig.

He thought of his mother, undressing after a dinner with Papa, laughing, her pale skin luminous against the vast blackness held at bay by the window. Her gray dress low over her back. The hush of her silk scarf pulled from her throat and thrown in Papa's direction, so light it had lingered in the air.

He lay back on the bed. Strange, how close to the surface these fragments seemed these days, pulled so easily into life by a touch or a smell. Already it was fading. Her face unclear, the pout of her smile obscured. Only a sense that it had been lovely.

His mother now was just an echo in his mind, an impression left in mist. But that was okay. He wasn't chasing her any more. Maybe he never had been.

He went to the bathroom and splashed cold water on his face.

The past was no good to him now. He was here. Still here.

He slipped his hand beneath his pants again. And despite everything he felt a surge of excitement. No going back now.

He didn't want to imagine what his father would have said if he'd lived to see this, but his father wasn't there. No one was. Not Papa. Not his mother. Not Patrick, nor Les. Not Valerie. Not John.

"Just me," he said.

And who was that?

He sat on the bed and closed his eyes, and stayed that way for a long time.

And then, at last, she opened them.

She made herself breathe slowly—in through the nose, out through the mouth—and left the safety of her room behind, moving barefoot down the hall.

She had dressed as a woman at the Thunderbird before of course, but not like this. She couldn't say what the difference was, but she felt it.

It wasn't Thelma behind the desk any more, but the girl who had started covering the slow hours. She wasn't sure if she felt relief or disappointment at that.

The girl's cheerful ponytail bobbed as she glanced up, then returned to whatever she was reading beneath the counter. A few seconds, and she bolted up again, her back suddenly military straight.

"Mr., ah, Hemingway?"

Just a nod in reply.

"Are you . . . okay?"

"Fine, thank you. Thought I'd soak up some sun while I can. Fall's coming early this year."

The girl's gaze swept over the knee-length orange summer dress she was wearing. Modest but eye-catching. "But . . . you don't have any shoes."

"I'm not planning on going far. Maybe down to feed the ducks."

"Mr. Hemingway—"

                              "—please, call me Gloria."

To her credit, there was only the slightest hesitation.

353

"Gloria." The name on her lips was divine. "Thelma said you're still recovering from surgery. Are you sure you're up to it?"

"It's nice to know Thelma still worries about me, all the trouble I give her."

"I'll be totally honest. She told me to make sure you didn't do anything stupid."

"If that's not love I don't know what is."

They smiled at each other.

"Gloria. Please. Go back into your room, get a few more days' rest. Soak up some sun on the balcony. I'll bring you in some coffee, how about that?"

Gloria considered. "I'd prefer a glass of iced rum."

The girl pursed her lips. "Coffee. You're still recovering."

"I'm a doctor. Trust me that—"

"—*Coffee*. Keep this up and all you'll get is ice water."

Gloria grinned. She liked this girl. "Coffee sounds lovely, thank you."

"All right . . . I'll see you in a few minutes, ma'am."

"Okay."

And it was. It was okay.

His son Patrick came to visit with no fanfare, no call or letter in advance. Maybe that was the point, to catch him off guard, see how he was living day to day.

Well, if that was the plan, he was fresh out of luck. The cleaner had been in an hour before, spiriting away any telltale pill bottles, changing the sheets, bringing order to the universe. And Greg had felt very much Greg for a few days now.

Admittedly he was dressed in an expensive dirty-blond

wig and a blue dress with matching high-heeled pumps, but he'd only been trying the outfit on. The clothes didn't define him any more, but he'd swapped into shorts and a clean blue polo shirt for Patrick's sake.

He looked pretty respectable, in his opinion. Just another dad. No demons in the cupboard, no devils in the basement, nothing but the slight hesitation in his motions when he stood up or sat down to tell that anything was out of place.

The only real surprise was that Patrick had brought his girlfriend, a smiley, quiet woman called Danielle who mostly just sat on the chair in the corner and observed. She had the air of Jane Goodall staying motionless so as not to startle chimps in the wild.

Still, Patrick must have heard what was going on from Ida, Greg's latest ex-wife—the woman couldn't keep a secret to save her life. Not that this was a secret. If it was he might have still been married to her.

He'd had a good few years with Ida, even if it had never exactly been a passionate love affair. They were two old divorcees in need of a little more comfort in life, and she'd looked after him as well as she could, made sure he ate, and took his heart pills, and kept an eye on him through the peaks and troughs with only a bit of grousing. And he'd looked after her as well as he could, which mostly meant letting her share the safety net of his inheritance.

Patrick sat himself on the side of the bed and cleared his throat, and Greg realized his mind had been wandering. "I was just in Italy. I saw John."

"Is he okay? Still with that girl?"

"Yeah. We talked about you."

Straight into it then. "I can imagine."

355

"Nothing bad. He said he still thinks about you a lot."

"Well, that will have to do, I suppose," Greg said, but without bitterness. John had tried, and Greg had to admit he wasn't in a position to complain about absent sons, with his record of fatherhood stretching behind him like an abandoned freeway.

"Well, he sends his love."

"He could send me a letter as well, every now and again."

"How are we supposed to know where you are, Dad? You never stay in one place more than six months."

Greg had meant it as a joke, but at Patrick's defense a spark of the old anger rekindled. "He always manages to get in touch when he needs a couple hundred to tide him over."

"Ah, Dad. He hasn't asked you for any money in years."

"Is that what he tells you?"

Patrick had no counter for that, though he was right. Greg hadn't had much more than a Christmas card from John in half a decade. If anything, it was Patrick who was always ready to pick up the phone or pen a quick note when the coffers were running low.

Greg let the anger go. He didn't mind. It was a dance he was familiar with, from both sides. How many times had his father fished him out of trouble, despite all the bad blood and spiteful words that had passed between them? What else was family, if not a freshly signed check from someone you wouldn't want to spend half an hour in a bar with?

The truth was the silence hurt worse than the out-stretched hand, but he was proud of John for making the break so cleanly, for realizing no amount of money was worth the heartache.

Easy for Greg to say. Even now, his share of the residuals came every six months. Checks from beyond the grave. It wasn't really his money he was passing on to the kids, it was his father's.

Patrick let Greg think for a minute, then came straight out with it. "So, you're going by Gloria now?"

"You've been talking to the staff?"

"Of course. It's not that I don't trust you, Dad, but it's good to get a second opinion."

"You make me sound like a tumor."

"Come on, Dad . . ."

"Well yes, I use a few names but that's my favorite."

"Do you want me to call you Gloria?"

Something in the way he said it . . . Was it mockery, anger? Or some other emotion Greg was less used to.

"No. Not you, Pat. I'll always just be Dad to you. Maybe *my old man* if you're feeling sore at me."

"But to everyone else?"

"Sometimes." He took a breath. "I live as a woman about seventy percent of the time now. I don't keep track, but that feels about right."

"So . . . you just decide which person you're going to be? Greg or Gloria?"

"It's all Greg," he tried to explain. "And it's all Gloria. Because it's all me, you see? The names help, that's all. I'm not two people."

"Right." Patrick nodded slowly like his father had made an insightful comment about the weather. He clearly had no idea what Greg was talking about, but he was trying. "So how does everyone know what to call you?"

"The dress is normally a pretty good giveaway."

Patrick nodded again. "I . . ." He glanced at his girl-friend. She gave a half nod back. "I suppose I wanted to say . . . I don't think— I mean, it's—"

"—I don't need you to tell me it's okay, son," Greg said. Gently, but firmly. He felt calm, his heart steady in his chest.

Patrick blinked. "You don't want to hear it?"

"Well, this went beyond what I *want* a long time ago. It's about who I need to be. I wish I'd realized that sooner."

"Right . . . Dad?"

"Yeah?"

"What happened?"

Greg sighed. "I guess I just got tired of being ashamed."

"All right."

And that, surprisingly, was that. They all went out for steaks.

They talked about nothing much; what Greg saw in Miami, a city Patrick hated; Michael Jordan ending his retirement; Patrick's hunch that John and his beautiful Italian wife might be hitting a rough patch; what happened to Margaux's glittering career. Patrick made a big show of telling Greg what a good thing it was that he and Ida had split. That she was a human mosquito draining his bank account. That the only thing Patrick couldn't understand was what Greg had ever seen in her to begin with.

Greg didn't bother to explain to his young, naive son how the things you look for in a woman can change. Soul-mates were hard to come by, and after sixty passion in bed seemed less important than a good firm mattress.

They'd had a good thing going, he and Ida. She'd been

good for him, and he for her, but nothing was forever. The op had been her limit, and that was okay.

Greg didn't say much. He ate his steak and watched his son talk and hold the hand of the pretty girl beside him. He drank his first beer in three weeks and declined a second. He watched them both climb into their car and head off into the evening, leaving Greg behind so they could get back to living their lives. Lives that were realer and more intense than anyone else's in the world.

He envied them, for their youth, their beauty, their certainty, but he wouldn't have traded places with them. His victories might have been small by most measures, but they were hard won and they were his.

A month later, with the sun beating down on the gravel outside the glass doors, Thelma took the key from her hand and placed it neatly on its designated hook. Gloria watched her carefully, trying to commit every detail to memory, not knowing when or if she'd be back.

Everything about Thelma was precise. The motion of her hands, the lines in her book, the arc of her frown as she turned. She was so utterly herself.

"What?"

"Nothing. Just thinking I'll miss you."

"You're not going to ask me to marry you again, are you?"

"Not if you say it like that, I'm not. Well, goodbye, I guess. I'll try and give you a good long break before I show up again."

"Oh, come on. You're welcome any time, Greg. Oh, sorry, should I—"

Gloria laughed. "You can call me whatever you want

and I'll answer. Sure, any time. Maybe not too often. I couldn't do it to you."

Thelma looked out the window for a moment, sighed, then back to her. "Ninety percent of the time you're just fine. You're great. Don't be so hard on yourself."

Gloria nodded. "Sure, but that last ten percent . . . that's a doozy. I know that."

Thelma pulled a face, but Gloria held out a palm, looking not at her but out into the furnace of the day, all the cars outside brought to a scalpel's brightness.

"I know it's not always been easy and . . . I guess I want to say it, you know? That I'm grateful to you—that's all—for putting up with me." She could hear the finality in her own voice and realized the truth. This was the last time. The Thunderbird had been a safe place to hide from the world, but maybe that wasn't what she needed any more.

Maybe Thelma heard it too. "What'll you do now?"

Gloria considered. "Live, I think. It's a full-time occupation."

One last smile for them to share, and then she picked up her bags. "Keep an eye on that blood pressure, Thelma," she said, and headed out into the light, determined.

Miami

2001

The beach was crowded, choked with happy families, joggers, dog walkers, elderly couples hand in hand. Gloria sat on the sand and watched them go by, content to feel the sun on her back and be alone with her thoughts.

Miami had changed so much over the years. It had become a city of malls, and superstores, coffee shops and over-priced boutiques, of roads choked with traffic. On her way to the beach, Gloria had walked through Brickell, once a neighborhood of shady mansions where a lifetime ago she had lingered on the way back from school just to smell the air, its scent of private gardens and sunbaked car polish and orange groves. Now it was a labyrinth of glass canyons, full of suited men and women rushing from building to building with the urgency of generals preparing for war.

Only here, where the glass and concrete gave way to this pale strip of shore, did she feel like she'd come home. She stood, and walked down into the water, let the waves nose blindly around her callused feet.

She felt completely relaxed, even though she had plenty to worry about. Most urgently, she was almost out of money. If Ida didn't release the accounts soon, she wasn't sure what she was going to do. She'd already resorted to panhandling for bus fare a few times when she'd run out of cash before remembering she couldn't just get more from the bank.

In any case, she'd rather starve than ask Patrick, or God forbid, one of her kids, to send a check. And the rest of the family wouldn't have flipped her a quarter for a gumball machine. Most of them had probably forgotten she existed. She learned most of the family news through the papers these days. Marriages. Movie deals. Margot's tragic suicide, another link in that long chain.

Urgent problems, by any measure, but it was hard to feel worried. If Gloria's life had given her one thing, it was a sense of perspective. And standing here, at the ragged edge of the sea, her problems seemed even smaller than normal. She'd survive somehow, same as she always had before.

She listened to the waves, the gulls. She took a slow breath.

She and Ida would patch things up, or Gloria would swallow her pride and apologize and beg her for a ticket home. They'd already gone through a full-blown divorce after the operation, then gotten back together when Gloria had remembered how hard it was looking after herself all alone, and Ida remembered how much she hated not having money in her account, and maybe even started to miss Miss Gloria a little bit too. They could get past a tiff about Gloria's investing strategies.

From the corner of her eye, and through the haze of the greater distance, she could see the Cape Florida Lighthouse rising defiant against the sky. A hint of a smile crooked one corner of her mouth as a wave of nostalgia washed over her. She remembered all the times she and Patrick and Papa had climbed the Key West Lighthouse so long ago. The older she got, the brighter and clearer those memories seemed to become.

Her parents had still loved each other then, and neither of them would ever have dreamed there was anything abnormal about their youngest child. Les was still sailing wild and reckless as a pirate in the Gulf, Rodolfo still playing in the distant streets of San Francisco de Paula, Margot still waiting for her brief life in whatever quiet place was set aside for the unborn. Another world, swept away with the orange trees and the shady sidewalks, long gone.

Once, she would have given anything to go back, but now? It had been such a long and winding road to bring her here, whole and alive, and not much of it had been easy. So much struggle, so much heartbreak. Had it been worth it? She was still making up her mind, but she couldn't wish it all away.

Her past was who she was. She couldn't shed it any more than a tree could shed its rings.

Still, a small dose of nostalgia never hurt anyone. The lighthouse shimmered invitingly, but Gloria had errands to run, and a party to get ready for. She turned and walked slowly back into the maw of the city, back toward her rental in Coconut Grove.

"I can't believe she did that to you, Glory. How could she be so heartless?"

Gloria didn't correct her on the name. The music was loud enough that the girl had certainly just misheard. In any case, Gloria was her first, her favorite, and perhaps her truest name, but not her only one. Tomorrow she might be Greg again, or she might be Vanessa or Thelma, but tonight she was Gloria. She felt completely Gloria, head to toe, inside and out.

"Well . . ." She tried to think of something diplomatic to say, swaying to the music. "My sons would say the woman is essentially a huge tick that somehow managed to get hold of a driver's license and a Porsche." She smiled. "Well, I can tell you how she got the Porsche: my money. The driver's license matter we'd have to bring up with the state of California . . . The thing is, she's also a terrific good time when she's in the mood, and she has a hell of a left hook, which I feel is a very underrated quality in a woman."

The girl—woman really, though she seemed so young—Louise, laughed despite herself. She'd shown only a brief shock when their host Rebecca had introduced them earlier in the evening, and Gloria liked her for that. "If she's sucking your blood, why not divorce her?"

"Now why would I do that? It's not all one way. That was the deal we made when we got hitched: she sticks around and acts as my secretary, minder, and nurse. And sometimes she gets the cans from the top shelf for me—she's a tall woman. In exchange I provide her with fine cars, holidays, Michelin-star cuisine, and anything else she asks for. And we try to be kind to each other."

"Oh, Glory, you deserve better than that. It sounds like a business deal, not love."

Gloria took a sip of gin and adjusted the strap of her dress. It was low-slung, and the feeling of the hem against her sternum was delicious. Across the room, a man she vaguely recognized from college—the second attempt probably—glanced up at her, then looked sharply away.

She didn't care. "Well, there's different types of love,

and anyway, you're too young to understand, or maybe too good, but there's a lot to be said for being married to someone you like rather than love."

Louise frowned. "Like what?"

"How can I explain . . ." She took a moment to think.

The party hummed around them. All different types from all over the city mingled beneath the soft light of the chandelier. Alicia Keys warbled in the background, only half discernible over the chatter, the laughter, the sound of glasses meeting.

"Louise, what do you most regret in your life?"

"Me? I don't know . . ." The girl looked genuinely puzzled. Gloria supposed pretty girls were rarely asked questions more probing than what do you want to drink. "Not going to med school in England when I had the chance? Not sneaking out and having more fun when I was a kid—I was such a goody two-shoes. I don't know . . ."

"You see, I've noticed that people's regrets are usually of a kind. They tell a lot about a person. It seems like you only regret things you haven't done; not mistakes you've made. As for me, I have a lot of regrets, but the ones that keep me up at night are the people I've hurt. Does that explain it?"

Louise cocked her head and scrunched up her pretty nose. "I guess. It still seems a bit sad though."

"Don't worry about me. I'm happy enough." It was strange to say, but it was true.

"But I still don't understand why she cut off your money. How does that even work if it's *your* money?"

Gloria laughed. "Oh Lord. I haven't had control of my own money for years. I suffer from certain . . . let's say ups and downs of personality that make me an unpredictable spender. Normally I wouldn't mind—it doesn't get in the way of day-to-day life—but the problem arises when I'm in sound mind but want to make a large expenditure. Unfortunately, my concerned wife has no ambition. I came here to make money. Heaps of it, I'd imagine—which would be good for her, she could upgrade to a Ferrari—but she panicked when she got wind of it. Pulled the plug before I could buy a single stock."

"You came here to invest?"

"To speak to my accountants in person. For obvious reasons, stocks in airlines have never been lower than they are right now. Gutless people pulling out their money the moment some line on a screen ticks down. But at some point people are going to realize that people still need to travel. Businessmen still want to go back and forth between New York and London. Producers still want to go back and forth between London and LA. People still want to see their family or sit on a beach without numbing their asses on a shitty train seat for two days. This is America, and convenience is king, terrorists or no terrorists."

Louise tilted her head to the other side, twisting one long lock of red hair between her fingers. God, if Gloria was twenty years younger, or—be honest—if this woman showed the slightest sign of interest . . .

"So you were going to invest in airline companies? Buy now, and when people realize that we aren't going back to the Oregon trail any time soon . . . Well, it makes sense, but it's still a big risk. I couldn't imagine flying for a good while."

Gloria gestured with her drink. "Well, I plan to keep enough in the bank to ride out a good while. The thing about Americans is that we like winners—no, we like being winners. And if we don't fly, we're giving in to those bastards. Excuse the crudity, but it's what a lot of people will think. And no red-blooded American will stand for that. Flying is winning—or at least, it's not letting them win. It's a matter of time.

"So, if my devoted wife will let me, I plan to make a fortune. Looks like she won't though. Ah well."

"You don't sound too upset."

She shrugged. "There are worse fates than not being able to make more money. What will be will be. I just wish she'd loosen the stranglehold a bit, maybe let me buy myself a beer."

"That's awful."

"No, it's inconvenient. I've survived worse." Gloria glanced over Louise's shoulder, to where a small host of young men were eyeing the girl from across the room. "But I've monopolized your company enough. I think there are more than a few people wishing I'd get out of the way. Sorry—show any interest and I start to ramble."

She glanced over her shoulder. "Hmm. There'll be guys like them at every party from now until rapture. I think I prefer your company."

Gloria looked at her, the curiosity in her eyes . . . Gloria fascinated her, but the feeling wasn't mutual. "It was good meeting you, Louise. Hope to bump into you again."

After the party, she crossed the street to be away from the scrum of people hustling for taxis. Back in her day, you drove home after a party no matter how much you'd drunk, and if a cop caught you then you slept it off in a cell and they gave you coffee and breakfast before sending you on your way in the morning. It was probably a change for the best, she knew that, but everyone was so damn uptight these days.

A little way down the street she found a small playground for the local kids, the metal frames of the swings and climbing frame glinting in the darkness. It seemed as good a place as any to wait for things to die down.

She squeezed herself into one of the swings, high heels dangling from one hand, and rocked herself gently back and forth. The moon was fishhook-thin overhead, but the stars were brighter for it. It would have been perfect if not for the blue-red flash of a plane zipping its way through heaven. You couldn't look up without seeing a plane these days.

She leaned her head against the chain of the swing with a smile. When had she gotten so old and curmudgeonly?

She'd have to give Patrick a call before too long. They could reminisce about old times and grumble about kids these days and Gloria could get it all out of her system. It would be easier on Patrick to wait for a day when she felt like Greg, but sometimes she forgot—it was all her, after all—and Patrick always did his best anyway, God bless him.

"Hey."

Gloria tensed. The voice had come from behind her, and when she turned she saw two broad-shouldered young men silhouetted in the streetlight. They stood by the gate, blocking the only way in or out.

"You okay?"

The speaker stepped to the side, and she got a glimpse of his face. Asian, hair close-shaven, a tattoo crawling up his neck. His eyes didn't have the glint in them Gloria had learned to recognize, that flash of something halfway between anger and fear, but you never could tell.

Sometimes they didn't want to hurt you because they hated you, but because they knew they'd get away with it. Gloria had a missing back tooth to attest to that. She never even saw who hit her.

"Fine, thank you." Her hands tightened around the chain of the swing. Every muscle tense as she waited.

"You sure? We saw you wander off alone and we were worried. Thought someone upset you."

She let herself relax a little. "No. Just wanted to clear my head."

"Okay well." He looked to his friend still swamped in shadow, who shrugged. "You be careful out here all alone. Do you know the hosts? Maybe they can call a taxi for you."

"Oh, I will, don't worry about me. I'll wait until things have quieted down, then I'll have them call a carriage."

"All right. Well, if you're sure. You have a good night, ma'am."

"You too."

The two men trooped off back in the direction of the house, and Gloria sat gently twisting on the swing, watching another plane skate across the stars.

She had to wipe her eyes. Ridiculous, the effect a little kindness had on her.

She woke to grit in her mouth and a dull throb in her temples.

The sun was on her cheek, and she lay with her eyes closed for a moment. She could hear the grumble of traffic, the distant cry of gulls, and the sea.

How had she gotten here? She vaguely remembered leaving the party in the early hours of the morning, one or

369

two martinis past good judgment. Sitting on the swings for a while. And perhaps getting into a taxi . . . Ah, now she remembered. She'd been flapping her big mouth about how her wife had cut off all her money, and the taxi driver had kindly advised her that people with no money did not get to use his taxi as a public service before kicking her to the curb. How chivalrous. She finally made herself sit up, spit out her mouthful of sand, and take stock of herself.

Not too bad. Hangover mild, so it probably had only been one drink that had pushed her over the edge. Still, she felt a bit worn out, bruised and breathless as though she'd been rolled all the way here from the party. Her head ached. Her feet ached. Even her chest ached.

She'd changed her mind; she wanted to go back to being young, when she could drink a bottle of whiskey, get in two fistfights, win them both, and still get up bright and early for work.

But such was life. She'd had a good time last night, and now she had to pay for it. No pleasure without an equal dose of pain—maybe plus interest—was surely hard-coded into the laws of the universe.

And anyway, the pain seemed a distant thing. Her body might have been battered and bruised, but *she* felt great, like the whole world was waiting for her to step forth and conquer it.

It wasn't hard to recognize the early symptoms of a manic episode. Once, that would have terrified her. Now, she noted it as another woman might have taken note of the weather. It would be what it would be.

That was the beauty of her life as she'd arranged it. There was only so much damage she could do.

Things would work out. Look at this: dumped out of a taxi in the middle of the night, and waking up on what she was pretty sure was the Bear Cut sandbar on the north of Key Biscayne. Probably the most beautiful spot for a hundred miles.

She didn't want to get up, to break this moment and sully the sand with her footsteps. She couldn't even see any sunrise joggers or early morning yoga practitioners. If time stopped right now, with her washed up at the end of the world, that'd be just fine.

But nothing lasts forever, and when the sun had grown hot on her shoulders and the first dog walkers and fitness fanatics had started marching past, she stood. It was only then that she realized she was naked. She'd been using her lovely red dress, which had not been cheap, as a blanket. Whether the wind or a particularly fashion-forward seagull had taken it she didn't know, but it was long gone. She'd even lost her wig, but at least her handbag was still nearby, with her underwear scrunched up inside it.

No idea why she'd taken that off. Drunk Gloria was a bit of an exhibitionist.

So was drunk Greg of course. Some things didn't change. A soul was a soul, she supposed.

She wondered when she'd next feel like Greg. She still did often enough, if less and less. Maybe if she'd figured all this out earlier . . . but there was no sense worrying about that. One ticket, one ride. So make the most of it.

She looked down at herself, the sun tracing the shape of her with warm, unflinching fingertips, casting the scalpel scars around her chest and genitals into vivid relief.

She knew that there were not many people who would have called her beautiful, that some would see only a body hacked into a rough semblance of a shape. But sitting there in that west coast piña colada sunrise, she felt beautiful anyway. She felt goddamn magnificent.

She laughed, one rough bark, then shook the sand from her underwear and pulled it on before walking down to stand in the waves. The water felt wonderful sluicing over her toes, so she waded in a little deeper and dunked herself into the bay.

She held herself there as long as she could, fighting the breakers until her lungs burned and the back of her head ached with the cold. When she emerged, breathless and shivering, every nerve felt cut raw, and her hangover was cringing in the corner.

Then she just stood there, waist-deep in the Atlantic, trying to decide what to do with her day. She knew she should go home, but after this—this morning, this place—going back to her dark apartment felt like a full stop.

And so she gave an audible sigh of relief when she saw it: a falling star frozen and set out on the distant curve of the headland. The Cape Florida Lighthouse.

Without another moment's hesitation she waded back into the shallows and set off along the waterline, letting the lacy hem of the ocean play over her every step.

She didn't make it very far before the cops showed up.

That wasn't surprising. To make it to the lighthouse, she'd had to walk Crandon Boulevard through the main residential area of Key Biscayne with its gated houses and its watered lawns. Floral undies might have been passable on the beach, but were most certainly not acceptable when walking past the homes of Miami's high society.

The cops cruised alongside her for a while, not even

getting out of their car. She did her best to ignore them, trying to walk like she had somewhere to be and hoping they'd decide she wasn't worth the trouble. She had her underwear on. Was the sight of her scarred old body really so appalling as to warrant a crime?

The cops seemed to think so. They flashed their lights once, the sirens giving a single blip like an over-excited dog, and mounted the sidewalk.

A touch dramatic, but okay.

Gloria turned as the passenger door opened and the bald head of a cop pushed its way up, the dome of his forehead shining brighter than the twin mirrors of the aviators that covered half his face.

"Sir? Are you all right?"

"Peachy." She smiled and carried on walking. "Out for a stroll. Good for the heart."

"Sir, I'm going to have to ask you to stand where you are."

"Okay, go right ahead."

"Excuse me?"

She sighed, kids these days didn't even understand the words that were coming out of their mouths.

"Sir? Stand where you are."

She heard the other car door open and let her steps slow. "Can't I just finish my walk? Am I hurting anyone?"

A new cop was walking forward, lean and sinewy like there was nothing but coat hangers holding up his uniform. No aviators on this one. His tiny eyes were scrunched into raisins as he caught up with her.

"Sir, please don't make this hard." He tried to reach around her for her bag.

That was too much. Gloria turned, placed a shoulder in the middle of his chest, and gave him a firm but gentle shove backward.

He staggered, looking more shocked than angry.

She smiled. She wasn't as strong as she used to be, but she still had what it took to surprise a beanpole who spent his life riding around in an air-conditioned cruiser.

"Look, sir. We need you to put something on, then we'll let you be on your way."

"I don't have anything. I think some gulls stole my dress. Can I report that as a crime? Oh, and ma'am."

"Excuse me?"

"Miss would do, but I think ma'am is more respectful."

The cops face hardened. "Listen, buddy, cut the shit. I'm not joking around here. I will bust you."

The world could only change so much, Gloria supposed. She sighed and turned to take one last look at the distant lighthouse, imagining how it would have felt to climb those cool dark steps and look out over the freshly minted sea.

It would have been nice. Ah well.

"Why don't you fucking try?"

It didn't go particularly well.

She'd had the element of surprise, to be sure, and even ten years ago she would have made a good show of it. But she wasn't late fifties Greg, she was sixty-nine-year-old Gloria, and when the cops each grabbed one of her arms she found there was pretty much nothing she could do to stop them forcing her down onto the baking-hot sidewalk.

Her underwear came off in the scuffle, but she didn't care. At least after that they started calling her ma'am. The

374

only thing that was embarrassing was going down without a proper fight.

They had her cuffed in thirty seconds, a humiliating record, and even so she was breathless when they sat her in the shade of the cop car and dropped her handbag over her crotch, her chest aching more than ever.

The cops had called for backup. She might have told them not to bother, that she'd decided her resisting arrest days were behind her, but she was too busy trying to breathe.

The second car didn't take long. The door opened, and a young Latina woman with long black hair squinted at Gloria through the shimmer rising from the pavement, then nodded to her fellow cops.

She walked over with slow, considered steps, her thumbs through her belt like a gunslinger from an old Western, but when she spoke her voice was quiet, respectful.

"Hello, I'm Officer Ramos. You can call me Sophia if you like."

Gloria squinted up at her.

"My colleagues thought it would be best if a female officer took you in."

"Well, that was thoughtful of them."

"Can I have your name?"

"I suspect you're asking for my legal name, for your records."

The cop nodded. "Yes, but it'd be nice to have something to call you, ma'am."

Gloria, let her gathered breath huff out. "Legally, Gregory Hemingway, but you can call me Gloria."

"Hi, Gloria, nice to meet you. I hear you've been resisting arrest."

She was oddly charming. Was this the cop equivalent of a bedside manner? "Not very successfully, I'm afraid, but yes. I've always had a bit of a problem with authority."

"Are you going to cause me trouble?"

"I wouldn't dream of it. I can tell from a glance that you're not a woman to be trifled with."

Her lips twitched. "You promise?"

"I'll come quietly. It's a paradox: I don't like authority, but I do have something of a soft spot for a strong woman. And a strong beautiful woman, well, I'll be putty in your hands. I'd swear on scouts' honor, if I'd ever been a scout."

That twitch again. Gloria hoped it was a smile she was suppressing, rather than disgust at being flirted with by an old and naked woman who probably smelled of booze and exhaust fumes. "I'm going to have to place you under arrest, I'm afraid."

"I'd assumed as much."

"You have the right to remain silent. Anything you say can and will be used against you in a court of law. You have the right to an attorney. If you cannot afford an attorney, one will be provided for you. Do you understand, Gloria?"

"I suppose so."

"All right then, shall we get you out of this heat and into my nice air-conditioned car?"

"That sounds lovely. Can I put on my underwear?"

"By all means."

"Then I'm all yours, Officer Ramos."

Ramos unlocked her cuffs, but didn't lay a finger on her as Gloria stood and got dressed, only opened the car door and placed her hand over the metal of the roof as Gloria slumped into the back seat.

376

"You okay back there?" she asked as she dropped behind the wheel.

"Just fine."

"Okay. Let's get you down to the station and see if we can clear this up."

"If only it were that simple. You make it sound like a trip to the principal's office."

"Biggest principal in the world." The engine growled into life.

"Hmm, I doubt I'll be finishing my walk any time soon."

"You never know. Where were you going, anyway?"

"Thought I'd climb the lighthouse."

"Any reason?"

"They always make me feel nostalgic."

Gloria's last day came calm and sunny through the window of her cell.

She woke on her thin mattress feeling surprisingly well rested. Her chest, which had been giving her trouble throughout her internment, seemed finally to have settled down. She breathed easy.

Even so, she didn't get up. There wasn't much to do in a ten-foot-by-ten-foot room.

She knew what today was, of course. She didn't try to keep track of these things—if anything she tried not to—but somehow, she always knew in her bones when it had come around. October 1st. The day her mother had died.

Fifty years ago, now.

Fifty years.

Had it really been that long? She could see her face clearly as if she was standing in front of her. Not a beautiful woman, she could finally admit, or at least not as beautiful as the ghost that had haunted her mind for so long. But what flesh-and-blood person could ever compete with an idea?

And that was what her mother had been. Flesh and blood. Confident, but sometimes a little cold. Studiously well dressed, but sometimes conscious of her boyish body when they had parties by the pool. A devoted wife, but not always the best mother. She'd tried, though. Looking back, Gloria could see that. In her own New England emotionally repressed way, she had tried. And she had loved her children.

She remembered her in LA, standing in that stinking prison cell in a building full of rough men she didn't know. Gloria had read the autopsy. She knew now how tired her mother must have been, how often she must have felt light-headed. But she came to walk her child out of that place herself.

"Mama," she said, her voice raspy from disuse, swallowed easily in the small silence of the cell. "It's me. It's Gigi."

She tried to find words to gather up all the years that had gone by, the mistakes and regrets, and the feeling that was flowing through her that was not forgiveness, because there was nothing to forgive.

But there didn't seem much point. Her mother wasn't listening. She was gone, vanished into dreamless atoms.

Only memories remained, precious memories, more and more of them every day. They rose up now like green shoots after rain, swelling, tumbling over each other.

Her brother turning handstands in the pool, his lean body cut from gemstones in the midday sun.

Valerie chewing away at her bottom lip as she read, both legs curled over the side of the overstuffed armchair they kept in the corner.

Broken bottles at the bottom of a harbor, their jagged edges worn smooth by the sea's endless handling.

Lorian, not as that lonely girl forced to spend the day with a broken father, but as the baby she had been, looking all around with her big rockpool eyes like she wanted to eat the whole world raw.

Papa and her mother dancing in the living room, his big-bear shuffle uncharacteristically gentle as he let himself be led by her slender arms. Frank Sinatra crooning from the radio. The cat trying to rub itself against their legs without getting stepped on.

The bad memories had haunted her for so long. She had almost forgotten how many good ones there had been.

A knock at the door. She sat up.

"Hello?"

The lock clunked, and the heavy steel swung inwards, revealing Officer Ramos, surprisingly small and delicate beside the slab of the door. Gloria hadn't noticed that about her the first time, and it was obvious why when she took a half step forward and leaned in the doorway. She moved with the confidence of someone twice her size, someone ready to take the universe by the throat.

"Heya. Just dropping someone off and thought I'd check in, see how you're getting on, Greg . . . Gloria! Sorry, it's on the paperwork."

"Officer Ramos." Gloria grinned, and it wasn't pretense. "What an unexpected pleasure. And don't beat yourself up. I am Greg sometimes.

379

"Okay." She inspected the corner of the cell. "Do you choose, or . . . how does it work?"

"Ah." Gloria rubbed a hand through her increasingly wispy hair. "Even I'm not sure how it works. And to be honest, I don't much care. I'm always me, and right now I'm Gloria. That's enough."

Ramos nodded, but her eyes didn't move. "Do you ever regret it?"

Gloria hesitated, unsure of the question, then remembered this woman had seen her naked.

"I'm sorry," Ramos finally looked up, embarrassed. "I shouldn't—"

"—It's fine. I'll be honest with you. I've never regretted it for a second, even when I'm Greg." She grinned, feeling the truth of it. So many mistakes, so much bitterness, but she'd drunk his way down to the sweetness at last. "It's the best thing I ever did, aside from, you know, having kids and all that sentimental stuff."

Ramos smiled back. "Fair enough. I'm sorry, that was rude."

"No harm done, really. But by all means, be rude if you feel like it. You're my first visitor, that means you get special dispensation."

"Your first— oh . . . well, glad to be it. I always like to be special."

"No need to worry there. And you don't have to feel sorry for me. I haven't told anyone I'm here besides my wife, Ida, and she's pretty pissed with me right now."

"Why not?"

"It'd only worry the kids, and they've got their own lives to get on with. They've put up with enough. Besides, it's hard to find time in my busy schedule of staring at the ceiling. It's very relaxing here. Very calming. They could make a packet if they gave the place a coat of paint and sold it as a Zen retreat. Besides, Ida will come around. She probably thinks I'm better off in here for a while. Maybe she's right."

Ramos was staring at her with a funny look on her face. Gloria raised an eyebrow. "Are you surprised I'm married?"

"I've been a cop for five years, nothing surprises me any more."

There was something so compelling about her, with her tilted head and her cocksure attitude. Did she have any idea how young she was, how fresh to the world? "I believe that."

"You did come pretty close on that sidewalk, I'll admit."

"If you think that was bad, you should have seen me thirty years ago. I know it doesn't look like much, but this is the work of a lifetime."

"I meant talking to you. You weren't what I expected from the call."

"Well, aren't you kind. At least, I assume you're being kind. Hard to tell when I don't know what you were expecting."

The twitch again. Definitely stopping a smile. "What did you mean, 'work of a lifetime'?"

"It's hard to explain."

"Try me."

"Yeah?"

"Yeah."

"Well . . . you've heard of my father?"

"Ernest Hemingway? Sure, he's a writer, isn't he?"

"Was."

She hesitated. "Oh right, of course. A plane crash or something?"

"If only. He killed himself."

"Oh. Yeah, I did read about that. I'm sorry."

"It's okay. It was a long time ago. You ever read any of his books?"

"No. Why?"

"It doesn't matter. He was just a certain type of guy . . ." Gloria struggled, trying to find the right words. "And maybe we weren't always the best fit. I guess I was pretty sore at him for a while, but the older I get the harder it is to stay angry . . . we're all just doing our best, you know? He did his best, and he had his own black ass to fight."

"Black ass? Who was that, his mortal enemy?"

"Yeah, I suppose so. It's sort of a . . . family feud." Gloria looked out her thin bar of window, half blue sky, half the dull underbelly of the freeway that passed by the prison. "Everyone knows Papa killed himself—well, nearly everyone—but most people don't know that my grandfather killed himself too. And my uncle, and my aunt, and my niece."

"God . . ."

"Papa used to call it the black ass. I don't really know what it is, I only know that it is, and that it's powerful." She shook her head and turned back to Ramos still leaning in the doorway, her face unreadable. "It nearly got me, more than once, but I'm still here, you understand? I've fucked up a lot of things, but I'm here."

Ramos stared at her a moment, then blew out a long shaky breath.

"Sorry," Gloria laughed, suddenly embarrassed. "Never let an old fool start rambling."

"No," she said, "I understand."

They shared a gaze.

"Anyway." She pushed free of the doorway, brushing her hands on her trousers and suddenly dispelling the heavy atmosphere in the room. "I only wanted to check on you, make sure you were doing all right."

"I'm doing fine. If you really want to help me out, you could ask them to give me my heart pills. The staff here have the medical sensitivity of a pot of clam chowder. Ida would kick up a stink if she knew. She's militant about me taking my pills."

She frowned. "That's not right. I'll talk to someone on the way out."

"My hero."

"Well, take care, Gloria."

"Same to you . . . Look after yourself out there."

Once she left Gloria sat in silence again, adding the young officer to her growing wellspring of memories. The easy way she leaned, the rough swagger in her walk, the thick black mane of her hair. Young and cocky and alive. Godspeed to her.

Well, she supposed she should get dressed. The day had to start sometime.

She'd bent down to pull on fresh underwear when the pain in her chest returned, a pulse that seemed to travel over her ribs and down into her belly in one rush. She paused to catch her breath, waiting for it to pass as it always had before.

When the next pulse came it felt like a grenade had gone off inside her, a pulverizing roar of agony. She barely noticed when her cheekbone cracked against the tile floor.

She managed to roll onto her back, staring up once

again at the mold-stained ceiling as the pain rose and rose and then—miraculously—receded.

But no, it was Gloria that was receding, falling away.

The awful rasp of her lungs faded, and she could feel her body growing distant, her control of each group of muscles being severed like spider's silk in the breeze, until she had left it behind altogether. She was surprised how much affection she felt for it, here at the end, how sad she was to see it go.

Then the memories returned, even stronger than before. A thousand fireworks all at once.

Light running through sugar cane like water.

Her father's broad shoulders as he bent over his desk.

A sparrow falling through the sky.

His mother, kissing his fevered brow.

Dark eyes with the whole world inside them.

Her first taste of Cuban rum.

Rodolfo's slender back, vanishing into the night.

Patrick's sleeping breaths, one bed over.

Papa lifting him above the cheering crowd, his face full of pride.

The smell of Miami after the rain.

Valerie.

And, one last time, the lighthouse.

And still she was falling, into them, through a storm of moments that moved faster and faster until at last they broke apart, not torn but dissolving, into each other, into everything that had once been Gregory Hemingway.

Gigi.

Greg.

Gloria.

Me.

"Nearly there. Come on. No? All right, here."

Papa pulls him up onto his broad back, hooking an arm under each of his legs, and resumes climbing. Patrick's already running ahead, just a pair of grubby soles flickering on the curving stairs above, always lost behind the turn.

They rise step after tireless step until, all at once, they walk out into the sky.

"There you go, Gig," his father says, but makes no move to put him down. From the balcony collaring the lighthouse, Key West is spread out beneath the dusty twilight, a model village of amber and gold.

He shifts on his father's back, the beauty waking him from half-sleep. The ocean gleams to the horizon, gemmed with the dark specks of boats coming and going, tiny red sparks living and dying on their hulls and masts. Gulls trail behind on stiff and lazy wings, or ride the last of the thermals over the town, drifting up with stately grace until they're lost in the haze.

Patrick has dashed round to the far side of the balcony. Only his back is visible as he looks out to sea, both hands gripping the rails as though ready to vault over and join the birds in flight. The last of the setting sun is behind him, gilding him in fire.

The three of them watch the world turn as the first stars catch and flicker in the west.

Until the silence is broken by a low, bone-aching hum, and a beam of burning gold splits the early night above their heads. It hurts him even to look at it, so bright it seems like a lance of the vanishing sun hanging over them. Then the sound deepens, and the light swings away; slow above, yet with impossible speed in the greater dark beyond.

He stretches up and lets the blaze of it wash over the very tips of his fingers. For a moment he can almost feel it, then his grip fails and he settles back onto his father's shoulders.

"Papa?"

"What is it, Gig-man?"

"What are lighthouses for?"

"Partly to be beautiful, because they are that."

"Yeah."

"But mostly, they're to guide ships home when they get lost. In the fog or the dark. They bring them home safe."

He sighs, tightens his arms around his father's neck. "That's a nice thing to do."

"Yes. Not much nicer."

They say no more, but look out together into the deepening night, over and into the world below, curving away beneath their feet. Infinite, and waiting.

Thanks to

My Mom and Dad, Jody and Jim, Estée, Grace, Audrey, and Stephen, for everything.

And to Reg, for keeping me company in the long hours of editing.

Michelle, for years of advice and support.

Amy, for patient reading and feedback.

John Ash, for excellent agenting. This book would never have found a publisher without his support and insightful feedback.

Francesca Main and everyone at Phoenix, especially Lucinda McNeile and Frankie Banks. If you've enjoyed this book, thank Francesca. Every page is better for her editorial touch. If you heard about this book or saw its lovely cover in a bookshop, thank the Phoenix team, whose work to give the book its best life has been invaluable.

Charlie Castelletti and Erick Jackaman, for deeply appreciated sensitivity feedback.

Claire and everyone in my London Library Emerging Writers cohort, for helping me take myself seriously as a writer.

Paul Hendrickson, whose book *Hemingway's Boat: Everything He Loved in Life, and Lost* is the original well-spring and authority on the real Greg's life. The idea that Greg was heading towards a distant but resonant light-house on that last walk is a direct nod to Paul's vision of Greg's final day, and an acknowledgement that this book would not exist if Paul hadn't first bucked the trend of all previous historians and given Greg the love and dignity they deserved. If you have any interest in the subject of this book, I urge you to pick up a copy of *Hemingway's Boat*. It's thoroughly researched, beautifully written, and deeply compassionate.

And last of all, thanks to you, reader. I'll probably never meet you, but I wrote this for you.

Further Reading

Carlos Baker, *Ernest Hemingway: A Life Story* (Collier Books, 1988)

Richard Bradford, *The Man Who Wasn't There: A Life of Ernest Hemingway* (I.B.Tauris, 2019)

Amanda Fortini, *The Importance of Not Being Ernest* (*New York Times*, 2013)

Ernest Hemingway, *A Movable Feast* (Arrow, 1964)

Ernest Hemingway, *Death in the Afternoon* (Arrow, 1932)

Ernest Hemingway, *The Garden of Eden* (Pharos Books, 1986)

Ernest Hemingway, *The Complete Short Stories of Ernest Hemingway* (Scribner, 1987)

Gregory H. Hemingway MD, *Papa* (Simon & Schuster, 1976)

John Hemingway, *Strange Tribe* (Lyons Press, 2007)

Lorian Hemingway, *Walk on Water: A Memoir* (Simon & Schuster, 1998)

Mary Hemingway, *How It Was* (Weidenfeld & Nicolson, 1976)

Valerie Hemingway, *Running with the Bulls: My Years with the Hemingways* (Ballantine Books, 2004)

Paul Hendrickson, *Hemingway's Boat: Everything He Loved in Life, and Lost* (Bodley Head, 2011)

Paul Hendrickson, *Papa's Boys* (*Washington Post*, 1987)

Jeffrey Meyers, *Hemingway: A Biography* (DaCapo Press, 1985)